D0464478

Books by Harry Crews

The Gospel Singer

Naked in Garden Hills

This Thing Don't Lead to Heaven

Karate Is a Thing of the Spirit

Car

The Hawk Is Dying

The Gypsy's Curse

A Feast of Snakes

A Childhood: The Biography of a Place

Blood and Grits

The Enthusiast

Florida Frenzy

Two

All We Need of Hell

The Knockout Artist

Body

Harry Crews

Scar Lover

Poseidon Press New York
London Toronto Sydney
Tokyo Singapore

POSEIDON PRESS
Simon & Schuster Building
Rockefeller Center
1230 Avenue of the Americas
New York, New York 10020

This book is a work of fiction. Names, characters, places and incidents are either products of the author's imagination or are used fictitiously. Any resemblance to actual events or locales or persons, living or dead, is entirely coincidental.

Designed by Karolina Harris
Manufactured in the United States of America

1 3 5 7 9 10 8 6 4 2

Library of Congress Cataloging-in-Publication Data
Crews, Harry, date.
Scar lover / Harry Crews.
p. cm.
I. Title.
PS3553.R46S33 1992 91-37810
813'.54—dc20 CIP
ISBN: 0-671-74489-5

This book is dedicated to my main most man,
Sean Penn

''Guilt is magic.''

James Dickey

Book One

1

Pete Butcher had not meant to speak to her. And he probably would not have if she had not stared at him so directly as she stepped out of the shade of the oak tree in front of her house to stand in the sun on the sidewalk. The only place he had seen her before was in the yard, close to the trunk of the tree, dim as a ghost in the deep shade. But this morning he had to pass within a foot or two of her because she had come out to stand on the sidewalk. He could, of course, cross the street, but that wouldn't do now that she had her eyes locked directly on his.

He felt a little chill on the back of his neck, and with the chill came the thought that she wanted to tell him something. Something he did not want to hear. Something personal. And in his experience, something personal was always something bad.

People were forever telling him something he did not want to hear. Something bad. The only time he had ever been in San Francisco, he had been standing on a corner with a terrible hangover—sour stomach, splitting headache—standing on a corner waiting for the light to change, when a dirty little man walked up and said: "I'm passing blood."

The hangover pounded in his head. He reached out his hand to take hold of the light pole for support "What?" he said.

"Blood."

"O.K. All right." He turned his head.

"Look at this."

When he looked back, the little man was bending over. There was a spot of blood on the seat of his trousers. Staying like that, bent over nearly double, the little man said: "Four days now, I'm passing blood. My stool is full of blood."

His stool. God. The light wouldn't change. The traffic was too heavy to cross the street against it. He was stuck there on the corner with the filthy little man bent over, a spot of crusty blood big as a tomato staring up at him. He could, of course, have walked away without crossing the street. But he couldn't leave the old man bent over proposing the bloody seat of his trousers to the world, leave him with nobody to look at it.

"Hi," she said.

He didn't want to answer her but he did; to do otherwise would be bad manners.

"Hello," he said.

She had stopped right in the middle of the sidewalk and he was surprised by how tall she was. He himself was an even six feet and her eyes, deep-socketed under a pale wide brow, were bird-bright and very black and looked directly into his own and had about them something he could not put a name to, but whatever the name was, trouble was at its source. She looked as if she had just received bad news or else she had some bad news that she felt it was her obligation to give him.

"I see you ever morning," she said.

"See *me?*"

"Through the window in the front room there." She turned slightly to point to a window looking out over the wide porch.

He felt like he was taking root where he was standing and that the longer he stood there the harder it would be to move.

He tried to think of something to say. Then: "I saw you once or twice out there . . ." He held up his arm and pointed. "Out there by the oak tree."

She shifted on her feet and said: "I come out for a breath of good fresh air sometimes in the morning."

She was getting him just a tad pissed off. She didn't have bad news or good news or apparently any news at all. But she was going to make him late for work standing here talking about nothing.

He concentrated on looking at her, *really* looking at her. He thought that might embarrass her into getting the hell out of his way.

But she only stood very still and let him look his fill. She looked him directly in the eyes and didn't move a muscle, not a twitch.

Her face was a thin triangle, with a sharp chin and a high long nose whose bridge was perhaps too thick. And her cheekbones were high and flat as an Indian's. Her skin seemed almost translucent, with tiny blue veins tracing a faint pattern at her temples, the veins disappearing right into her straight flaxen hair, which was fine and long and pulled behind ears that were beautifully shaped wtih full lobes, pierced and holding rings of heavy dull gold. Two things struck him simultaneously: Her face was strangely odd, quite unlike any face he had ever seen, and at the same time, she was beautiful. He realized perfectly well that her face was not the sort that people called beautiful or the world thought of as beautiful. But nonetheless he thought her beautiful all the same. Strange. It unnerved him. Maybe what he thought was beautiful came from her bright, deep-set eyes, troubled and pained even though she was smiling a tentative smile, a thin smile that seemed to want to tremble but did not.

Her breasts were full and high, unnaturally full because her body was as thin as her face. The light cotton dress she wore fell straight from her wide shoulders with no break at all at her stomach and hips and yet her calves were full and muscled, reminding him of a runner's. She wore thong sandals and her toenails were painted dark purple. It was only when he raised his eyes from the dark nails on her high-arched, finely shaped feet to her face that he realized she was utterly without makeup. Maybe that was what unnerved him. Her face could have been that of a freshly prepared corpse waiting for the finishing touches of the undertaker's brushes to put the blush back into her cheeks and color onto her tremulous mouth.

She made no move to get out of his way but only stood regarding him, her head slightly canted to the left on her long neck, in which a clearly visible pulse beat just above her collarbones, bones insistent and thin as a bird's. He thought she would move to touch him. Without thought, not meaning to do it, he took a step back.

"Not many mornings nice as this," she said.

"What?" Her voice had been low, nearly a whisper.

"This time of year anyway," she said in a voice a little louder. "Not many mornings nice as this."

He looked at the sky, brightening in the east. "I've not really give it much notice. Other things on my mind."

"Lordy mercy, I guess we all got that."

"What?"

"Other things on our minds."

He recognized her voice as the voice of his people, flat, nasal, with hard *r*'s, a voice that had drifted down into Jacksonville, Florida, out of the pine flats of south Georgia. It made him inclined to like her. But she had trouble—he could feel her full of it—and he did not like trouble. And certainly not other people's. His own blood carried as much trouble as he thought he could deal with because the trouble in his blood reached back through his dead mother's and father's and crippled brother's, who was not dead but ought to be. He ought to kill his brother. The thought would come to him sometimes in the dark of a sleepless night. He ought to kill him. He would have done it for a dog. But the release he would have given to a dog he would not, could not, give to his brother. No wonder his hatred for the world made it so hard, so very nearly impossible to live in it.

"For some anyhow," she said.

"How's that?" He had again lost the drift of their conversation, of what they were talking about—if, in fact, they were talking about anything.

"For some," she said, "this is one of them specially nice mornings."

His gaze had drifted across the street to the shadowed fronts of houses that looked as though nobody had ever lived in them.

"Yes," he said, "I guess so."

What he wanted to do was step around her and leave. He didn't know quite how to do it without being unseemly. His mother had gone to great lengths to impress upon him the importance of seemly behavior, before a fiery Sunoco truck had taken the pickup she was riding in with his father on the way to town to sell a load of hogs for money they needed for doctors worse than they needed the hogs for food. His crippled brother was expensive.

"But for others, this won't be a day at all," she said, she too now looking at the houses across the street. "For some, what kind of day it is is the last thing on their minds."

He did not answer. He was not going on with this. Trouble that was not just trouble but pain as well had leaked out of her into the tone of her voice and he was not going on with this.

"You haven't been living there long," she said, pointing toward the rooming house next door.

"No," he said, "not long."

"I know how long," she said, "cause they taken Ma to the hospital four days after you moved in."

"Oh," he said, not sure of what to say next. And then finally: "I'm sorry."

"Ma's got the cancer," said the girl.

God, God. She was going to do it, tell him all of it, if he did not get away, but he did not know how to manage it without being unseemly. Her mentioning her mother had brought his own mother's voice bell-clear into his ear, admonishing him against unseemly behavior and how generally sorry and no-good people were who did not avoid unseemly behavior. He stretched his neck to breathe. His lungs felt constricted. A drop of sweat turned loose in his left armpit and plunged down his ribs. The sweat was icy cold.

"First they took one off," she said, pointing briefly at her left breast.

"I . . . I . . ." He started around her. Without seeming to move, she glided in front of him on her heavily muscled runner's calves, her thonged feet sliding on the sidewalk without a sound.

"They weren't through with her then though," the girl said.

He found that rather than look into her eyes suddenly gone flat and lightless, he had dropped his head back and was staring up into the sky. There were no clouds, no sun.

"I wish it was something . . ." he began.

"But it's not," she said. "The other one had to come off too. But it seems like she's gone be all right. Live anyhow. We won't know for five years, they say, if it'll come back or not."

"I've got to go." He glanced at his wrist as though at a watch. But he didn't own a watch. His wrist was naked. Maybe she didn't notice.

"First the left one," she said, "and then the right one." She looked off toward the place where the rising sun was finally breaking clear of the houses across the street and said bitterly: "God only knows what's next."

It sounded to him as though death was next. "I have to go." But he did not move.

"That's where Daddy is now," she said. "He's over there at the hospital. Waiting to see how it all comes out. She might come home anytime now. They say she's strong enough."

He had seen her father every day since he moved into the boardinghouse. Her father sold firewood for a living, and worked tirelessly over the woodyard at the side of the house under the arching limbs of the oak tree. Everything he did was done with muscle and sweat. No electric saw, no gasoline. One-man bow saws instead. A lot of mallet, ax, and wedge. He had often wondered how a man could support his wife and daughter with such work.

"I guess I better get going," he said.

She leaned toward him and spoke rapidly. "You like to come and eat supper with me tonight?"

"I don't think I'll be able to tonight," he said.

"Thought you might be tired of that boardinghouse cooking."

"That's thoughtful of you," he said. "And don't think I don't appreciate it." He edged past her.

Just as he was about to take the first long stride away, she said: "I was lying. Wasn't even thinking about the boardinghouse or the cooking. Wasn't even thinking about you. I was thinking about me."

He had his back to her. All he had to do was keep going. But his dead mother's voice was loud in his ear. This girl was talking to him. He couldn't just walk away when she was still talking, so he was frozen, one foot stopped half in the air, like a rabbit caught in the lights of a car at night.

"I'm just so lonesome," she said. "I'm scared. Ma gitting sick and them cutting the whole front of her off. Daddy at the hospital all the time. And me here by myself in—"

Whirling around, he cried: "I'll *come.* I'll *come.*" He did not want her to tell him about her mother's disease, her father's pain, her own loneliness in the enormous, dark, unpainted and rotted two-story house. He could not bear such details. He did not know what he would do if she started on it all again that night, but for the moment he had stopped her. Maybe even changed her a little. She was smiling.

"My name is Sarah," she said before he could turn from her.

"Pete, my name is Pete." His voice was too quick, too loud.

"I know," she said, as he was about to hurry away from her.

"You know?"

She made a vague gesture toward the boardinghouse. "Mr. Winekoff."

He turned and fled down the sidewalk, knowing that what he had come to think was true. Max Winekoff was trouble. Anybody who was ancient, retired, and had nothing to do but walk over the entire town every day gossiping, taking care of everybody else's business but his own—mainly because he had no business to take care of—*had* to be trouble. Pete, walking fast because he was late, couldn't tear his thoughts away from old man Winekoff, and he wondered seriously if the bastard ought to be killed. Pete knew he was capable of doing the job. As twisted as his world had become, he thought he might be capable of anything.

2

The Jacksonville, Florida, Bay Street Paper Company was separated from the St. Johns River only by dozens of railroad tracks. Pete had decided the St. Johns River must be the dirtiest river in the country. The thick hot wind blowing off it smelled of garbage, gasoline, and raw human waste. A ditch full of shit that would, he was convinced, burst into flame if you set a match to it.

The stink of it and the explosive colliding of boxcars ramming into each other filled the warehouse—big as a blimp hangar—through which he had to pass to get to the boxcar where he and George worked. Nobody referred to George as George. They called him the Burnt Nigger, but never to his face. To his face, they used no name at all. Except for Pete. From the very beginning, if Pete had to talk to him he used the man's name. He was not going to call the man a burnt nigger just because he had been branded across his back from shoulder to shoulder. Pete tried to avoid talking to him altogether, but that, of course, was impossible. After all, the two men did spend the entire day in a boxcar together.

And George was Pete's worst dream come true. He had the habit of talking for what seemed like hours about nothing but things personal and horrible, full of death and threats of death and not just blood but also demons.

But Pete had to hang on to the job because he had no options. When he discovered in less than a week that he was not going to be able to take going to school at the University of Florida under the GI Bill, he had come back to Jacksonville and finally found this job in a boxcar with George just before he got down to his last twenty dollars. Pete had no skills except for a strong back. And that was all the boxcar demanded.

He was lucky to have any job at all. Jacksonville was filled to overflowing with south Georgia dirt farmers looking for work, looking to sell their sweat and callused hands, because that was all they had to sell. There had been very little rain for the last three years running and the drought had forced thousands of desperate men and their desperate gaunt women and children to flood into Jacksonville. So enduring George was just one more thing he had to do. He simply had no choice.

"You late again, goddammit!" screamed the foreman to Pete as he came through the metal doors at the front of the warehouse. Pete was not, in fact, late. The huge clock on the wall showed that he'd managed to make it with two minutes to spare. But the foreman said that to everybody who came in even if they were thirty or even forty minutes early, which nearly everybody was. Some men were as much as an hour early. This was not the time or the place to be out of a job. So the men did whatever they had to do to please the foreman. Pete thought the foreman was probably crazy from too many years of breathing gasoline fumes and the odor of unflushed toilets coming off the river.

The foreman talked with a dead cigar stub caught in his black teeth—Pete had never seen him without it—sitting behind the thick mesh wire that caged him in where the metal doors opened into the warehouse. Pete had never seen him except from the waist up, because he was always sitting on a stool in the wire cage, which he apparently never left. The rumor was that the foreman sat on a chemical shitter the entire working day so that he would never have to stop screaming at the people who worked for him. Pete couldn't vouch for that one way or another. He saw him only when he came into work headed for the boxcar that was always waiting for him, and then again when he left at quitting time. He did see him the few times he and the Burnt Nigger came into the warehouse to eat lunch. The warehouse was very nearly as hot and airless as the boxcar but its shadowy dimness somehow made it seem cooler.

A whole squadron of forklifts raced dangerously between the aisles of high-stacked paper products, headed toward the huge trucks backed up at a wide wooden dock that fronted on Bay Street. The foreman controlled it all from his wire cage with a battery-operated bullhorn. For so small a man, the bullhorn sounded like a trumpeting elephant when the foreman demanded to know where a forklift was or why it had not finished loading a truck. Despite the oil-belching forklift engines, the foreman's voice always carried above the roar, angry, demanding, and unreasonable.

He was fascinating to Pete, who could have watched him all day, the blood always high in his tobacco-colored skin, the veins at his temples looking as though they would burst. It was rumored he'd been in that wire cage for forty years screaming at the forklifts, which were known only by numbers, never by the names of the drivers.

The foreman snatched up his bullhorn now, his neck swelling with rage, and screamed, "Seventeen, have you passed out, or died, or what the fuck ails you? Your truck should be loaded and gone." No matter how early a driver had come to work, the warehouse had not been open long enough to load a truck, but that didn't matter to the foreman as far as Pete could tell.

There was a telephone with an open line to the loading dock so that the truck drivers could communicate with the foreman, tell him how slow, how fast, or how sloppy a forklift driver was, and then the foreman could scream at the forklift drivers, bellowing at them by their numbers and generally ragging their asses. The forklift drivers had no way of communicating with anybody. They could only take the abuse and go faster, which made them dangerous. Daily there were calamitous accidents among the dim, dusty aisles of the warehouse, which resulted on some days in one, or two, or—on really frantic days—as many as three drivers leaving the warehouse on stretchers.

Fascinated as he was with the madness of the foreman, Pete didn't realize he had stood rooted to the spot where the foreman had first asked him why he was late. The bullhorn turned on him now full blast from two feet away inside the wire cage. "You waiting for directions, you fucking asshole? That Burnt Nigger caint last in the car forever by hisself."

Pete jumped and fell into a little trot and was almost run down by a forklift racing out of one aisle to turn and race down another. He trotted through the warehouse and out onto the concrete ramp and into the boxcar.

As hot and airless as it was in the warehouse, going into the boxcar was like stepping into an oven. He smelled George before he saw him. But the smell didn't bother Pete because he knew he would smell much the same way in less than an hour, much the same—rank enough, sure as hell—but not *really* the same. Pete had never met another man, black or white, who carried the odor George did when he was sweated down. In a way, it was not even offensive. It was a sweet stink that had about it the tinge of crushed almonds. But then nothing about George was like any other man Pete had ever met.

From the door of the boxcar, Pete turned and saw George, wearing the brightly colored clothes he always seemed to favor, there in the dim recesses, working as steadily and tirelessly as the pendulum of a grandfather clock swinging. He was a massive black man—so black that when the light struck him just right, there was a rich undertone of heavy blue about his skin—with massive arms and a huge head—a head that was made to seem even bigger than it was by the twisting, coiling ropes of hair that fell to his shoulders.

Pete had come to learn that these coils of hair were called dreadlocks. But it was not only that he knew what the snakelike hair was called, Pete knew entirely too much about George, more than he wanted to know about anybody. But they were stuck in the same boxcar and George was twice as big as Pete, and George's body was strung from head to heel with thick ropy muscle. Not just the sort of man that anybody would want to tell to shut the fuck up. But Pete had long since stopped even thinking about saying such a thing. They had been working together for almost three months and got along well enough.

In a kind of warped way, it seemed to Pete, they had even become friends of a sort. On good days when Pete was lucky, he could tune George out and not even hear what he was saying. But because the girl, who herself had something twisted and strange about her, had stopped him on the sidewalk and talked of cancer and death, Pete knew that this was not going to be one of those days when he could tune out anything. He would have to suffer it all.

Pete stood in the door where there was a hint of a breeze now and then, avoiding going deeper into the boxcar just as long as he possibly could. At the far end of the car in the bad light, George was bent at the hips and swinging first to the left to take up a bound stack of cellophane—which was surprisingly, incredibly heavy to be nothing but packaged clear cellophane—and then to the right to put the cellophane onto a conveyer belt covered with little round wheels. Gravity, rather than any kind of motor, caused the bundles of cellophane to roll out of the car into the warehouse, where two other men stacked them on pallets. The conveyer belt could be easily moved about the car, wherever it was needed.

George glanced up and saw Pete standing in the door, and a great smile flashed in the dusky light and George's matted, thick eyebrows shot up as though in great surprise. George had the widest, longest, and whitest teeth Pete had ever seen. But even as he looked at Pete, George never stopped the rapid, swinging movement, a movement he held tirelessly all day long. On their worst days with the heaviest loads to deal with, Pete had never seen the slightest sign of tiredness in George. Never once had he even heard George breathe heavily, while Pete himself, for long periods of time on bad days, gasped and choked for air like a wind-bustled dog.

"Whoaaaa, Pete-Pete, mon," called George, still holding the smile. "Ya take de break ta watch George break de back, hey, Pete-Pete, mon?"

Pete did not answer but walked down to take up his position on the other side of the conveyer belt from George, and began his own swinging motion with the cellophane that he would have to lift all day.

"Ya ass hangin raw meat, Pete-Pete?" said George. "I hear de fockin mon wit de fockin horn all de way here in de car yellin ya ass." George was still smiling as though at a great joke, his massive but agile body never missing a beat with the cellophane.

Pete only looked up and acknowledged George's words with a nod of his head. George spoke in a high, lilting voice that had a British sound to it, the kind of British sound Pete had heard only in the movies. It had taken about three weeks of working with George before he could understand all of what he said. Since then he had learned all manner of other things about George despite his best efforts to tune him out, simply not listen, or think of something else while he was talking.

He knew that George had brought that voice from the island of Jamaica, wherever the fuck that was. Somewhere out there in the Atlantic off Florida, but Pete didn't know where or how far, nor did he give a damn. George happened to be here in Florida because he had a wife named Linga (what kind of fucking name was that?), whom he feared as a believing Christian might fear the devil. George had never told him straight out, but it had come through clear enough over the weeks George had talked about her. She had come to Florida and she had *made* George come with her. They were Rastafarians. That was what the head of twisted hair—the dreadlocks—was all about.

Entirely by chance, Pete knew a little patchwork pile of what were probably lies about the Rastafarians. He had learned whatever he knew from a black guy from Georgia that he had racked with in the same squad bay in the Marine Corps. The guy was nuts about everything Jamaican, and especially Jamaican music, which he played constantly. He also greatly admired Rastafarians. He even had a picture of a Rastafarian in his locker, a bony-faced, big-eyed man with the same kind of twisted and matted shoulder-length hair that George had. From being with the black guy for six months before he was transferred to another outfit, Pete only knew that Rastafarians were a kind of cross between witches and devils and conjurers of evil or good. Hell, he knew about conjure women from growing up in south Georgia, and while blacks feared conjure women, whites thought them harmless bullshit artists. Rastafarians also smoked an incredible amount of weed, which they called ganja and seemed to worship. Pete had tried smoking marijuana with his black buddy and found he preferred Jack Daniel's sour mash. But he did like Jamaican music, he did like that. As far as the ganja and the magic or spirits it brought when you smoked it, that was just dumb nigger bullshit. And Pete meant the word *nigger* when he used it or thought it. He had to make his own peace with all that when he came out of Georgia and went into the Corps. All blacks weren't niggers. And a lot of whites—even Orientals, for that matter—*were* niggers. Being a nigger just meant being sorry and low-down in the most bullshit, worthless kind of way; it had nothing to do with color, even if someone was as black as George, who Pete had decided was not a nigger. Fuck it—all the fight and fuss about the word *nigger*—it was not something Pete talked about. He figured the only head he had to get straight was his own. And about that, his head was straight, that if damn little else.

The ends of Pete's fingers were already bleeding from forcing them between the sixty-pound stacks of cellophane (he had tried gloves when he first came on the job but no matter what kind of gloves he bought, they were torn from his hands within three days, so bleeding fingers were just part of the job), and he, his clothes, even his socks, were soaked through with his own sweat. And for the last ten minutes or so he had been aware of George's great flashing smile falling on him as he turned to the conveyer belt and faced him. But Pete would die and go to hell before he asked what the fuck he was smiling about.

The work did not seem to bother George at all. He was as wet with sweat as Pete but his fingers never bled. They seemed to be hard as stone, with yellow pads of callus thick as leather. George talked shit and thought shit but he never seemed very far from a laugh no matter what dreadful stuff he might be talking his way through. The wild, swinging dreadlocks threw sweat across the boxcar, and his incredibly white teeth flashed in the bad light every time he turned his head.

"Pete-Pete haf ta eat de mon's shit," said George. "De mon wit de horn give de shit an Pete-Pete haf ta eat de shit an it make him head bad, him heart bad. Remember ya inside de inside, eat de man's shit ain shit."

George threw back his head and didn't so much laugh as bray, loud choking haws that always reminded Pete of a goddam mule. It usually made Pete smile in spite of himself, but it didn't today. Not this fucking day with that fucking girl and the fucking talk of cancer.

"I don't eat anybody's shit, George. Just do your fucking job." Pete shouldn't have said anything and regretted it as soon as he spoke.

George brayed again before saying: "I and I do me work an haf ya work, too."

Well, that was true. On days when Pete was faint with heat and exhaustion, George took up the slack and never said anything about it. Strange fucker. Like that Pete-Pete shit. And the "I and I" shit. Sometimes he only used one "I" when referring to himself but often he used two. But he always referred to Pete as Pete-Pete, had from very nearly the start, and there had been nothing Pete could do or say to stop him.

George suddenly stopped and his thick, stone-hard fingers—nimble as any safecracker's—unbuttoned his shirt and had it off without missing a single stack of cellophane. Pete stopped dead still and simply stared. It was the scars. Jesus, the fucking *scars.* They were all U-shaped and the same size. Big as horseshoes. One burned into his right shoulder, eight more in a straight line across his thickly muscled back, and one on his left shoulder.

Pete knew they were the work of Linga, George's wife. He did not want to know it, but he did.

She had branded him. One for each year he had been with her. The branded flesh was raised and bumpy and spotted in places with bright red tissue. Pete went back to work, feeling his throat contract and his stomach turn over, as though he might puke. And he might. He had before. But it was not because of the sight of the scars or the thought of being branded. *It was because Pete loved the scars, and he knew he did. He wanted to touch them. It was the knowledge that if they had been on a woman, he could have—would have—licked them that made him want to puke.* The knowledge dumbfounded him and set his nerves afire with self-loathing. He never could keep himself from staring at them when they were revealed to him the first time every day. And George knew he stared. Sometimes George remarked on it. Sometimes he did not. Today he did.

He smiled and touched his right shoulder briefly. "Linga," he said, and hefted another stack of cellophane onto the belt. "Life," he said, and did another stack. "An deaaatthh." He drew the word out over another bundle. He kept the stacks coming as he talked, always smiling as though what he was talking about was just the funniest thing in the world. "Aaaaahhhh, but Pete-Pete, mon, nuh worry ya head. Ya heart. Deese." He indicated the scars he carried. "Deese all life, yeah! Don bran no dead mon corpse, yeh?" And then when Pete did not answer: "Up o down? Right o wrong? Yeh o no?"

That was enough to move Pete off the mark and set him back working, saying as he did, but without looking at George: "None of that shit, George. Got it? Fucking pack it back in your sack and take it with you when you go. You let your wife burn you the fuck up? That's your business." He made himself raise his head and meet George's eyes. "I . . . don't . . . give . . . one . . . shit. We've been through all this. Drop it."

"Mebbe Linga let de focking mon wit de fockin horn die. Ya like?"

Pete refused to answer and kept his pace with the belt.

"Mebbe Linga let one ya people ya don like, got de eye on ya, mebbe Linga let *dem* fockin die. Ya like?" He was chuckling now, a sound like a dog growling.

Pete didn't look up when he said: "Do it. Tell her to fucking do it and leave me alone here, George." Then he did look up, anger having totally replaced the sickness in his guts. "*That* I like."

They worked on for some long time now, silent except for the occasional growling chuckle coming from the throat of George who—as always—showed no signs of the effect of the intensifying heat of the boxcar. But Pete was meeting the first wall of the day. That's the way he thought of it—*first wall of the day*. He was choking and every muscle in him hurt. He had thought he would get used to it after a week or two, but coming up on the time to break for thirty minutes to eat lunch, he always felt—even after three months of working in the car—he always felt that he might not make it.

So he did now what he did every day at this time, he fixed his mind on something outside the work he was doing and let his body get by as best he could. Today, because of what George had said, it was Linga. It was killing. He let the last thing George said play in his mind, repeating itself like a stuck record. He didn't have to listen to hear it, and it played over and over in George's own voice: *Mebbe Linga let one ya people ya don like, got de eye on ya, mebbe Linga let dem fockin die. Ya like?*

You damn right he liked. He thought first of his older brother, who had returned his letters unopened since the death of their parents in the blazing wreck with the Sunoco truck. Pete didn't even know where he was now because his brother had stayed in the Army, a fucking lifer, and since his brother's last letter was one line, "I'll never speak to you again," Pete had lost track of where he might be. Well, at least the Army was three meals a day and a bed; it was good enough for the dumb fuck. And there had been many times of loneliness and grief and guilt—guilt for irreparably damaging his kid brother—when Pete could have killed his brother, killed anybody for that matter, so crazy had he become over what he had done. An utter fucking accident but it had still nearly driven him over the edge. But that was then and this was now. He thought of the caged beast of a foreman he had to pass every morning.

"Tell'er to kill the fucking foreman."

There was the slightest hitch in George's swing with the stack of cellophane he was lifting. "Say agin, mon?"

"I said tell Linga to kill the asshole in the cage." There were little gasps of heavy breathing between the words as he spoke them.

George's tangled eyebrows shot up; his wide teeth flashed. "Kill? Who now, mon, ya hear talk bout kill? It some more bigger difference ta *kill* and *let die*. Linga ain got kill in her. She Obeah woman. Obeah very strong. *Strongest.* Ya nuh *never* fock wit Obeah woman."

"Don't worry," said Pete.

He was through the wall, still breathing heavy but making it on through. It wasn't long till he could get out of the car and eat the two fried egg and bologna sandwiches his landlady made every morning for him to bring to work. *If* he could eat. Sometimes he couldn't.

"No, don't you worry, Brother George." It felt so good to know he had almost made it through the morning, through the wall one more time, that he could smile up into George's blue-black face. "I'm not fucking with your woman or anybody else's woman. I got enough shit to carry already."

"Ya talk crazy, nuh respec, cause ya nuh believe de magic." George briefly touched one of his scarred shoulders. "Magic. I and I branded wit de magic."

"What you branded with is bullshit, not magic."

"George be got nuh magic, ya say, mon? I tell ya life right now, mon. Look in an tell ya."

"I just as soon not hear it if it's all the same to you," Pete said.

"Ain up ta George, mon. Up ta de magic. When de magic speak, de magic speak. An mon, ya hip deep in de shit and goin on down. De magic know it. Ya know it."

Pete was genuinely pissed now and hurting for the lunch break. "I don't know any such goddam thing."

George said: "Try dis. I smell pussy on ya when ya walk in de car today, mon. Ya *heavy,* ya *ranking* wit pussy. Sign bad."

Pete laughed nervously and kept swinging the bundles of cellophane. "I wished to God I had been into some pussy. I could use me some, but I been as dry as a dying dog in the desert."

"Ya nuh listen. I ain say ya *got* pussy. What I say am de pussy got *ya.* Pussy on ya skin, it on ya clothes, it in ya hair, an I bet me las cup o blood ya taste de pussy in ya mouf, mon." On the last few words, George's huge head was back, his twisted dreadlocks flying, as he gave a great braying laugh.

It wasn't funny to Pete. The image of Sarah came to him, tall and oddly beautiful, standing on the sidewalk, balanced on her lovely high-arched feet, and Pete's mouth was flooded with something vaguely salty but not unpleasant, salty and wet as mist blowing off the sea might be. He wanted to say it was his goddam imagination but the taste of salt was real enough to make something in his chest seem to move in a strange way.

"Someday, mon, ya be beggin fo Obeah woman Linga magic, yeh, say *magic,* mon."

"I'd feel like a fool talking about magic, much less asking for it."

"Nuh true," said George, matter-of-factly now, not even smiling. And for the first time all morning, George stopped and very deliberately withdrew a pocket watch from the little pouch he had sewn into the band of his trousers. It was as big as a biscuit and gleamed dully of solid gold even here in the boxcar. He looked at the watch a long slow time before saying, "It time, ya dig? Eatin time. Where de fockin horn, mon? Where de crazy horn fockin, mon?"

On the last word, the foreman's hugely distorted voice exploded from inside the warehouse: "EAT IT IF YOU GOT IT AND GIT YOUR ASSES BACK ON THE JOB!" The voice had been booming all morning, but they heard it only when it said it was eating time. Otherwise it was just a kind of white noise that never bothered them.

"Les eat it," George said.

"Just don't talk no more about pussy and magic, all right?"

"Lock," said George. Then he did something he had never done before. "Ya wan ta . . ." He leaned toward Pete holding the shoulder with the most ragged and bitterly burned scar in it. "Ya kin touch dis if ya need de magic. Ain holdin nuttin but luck an ya kin touch it."

Maybe it was because it came out of nowhere, never having happened before, maybe it was Pete's exhausted, sweated, hurting body, but to his utter amazement, he raised his hand and with his index finger not only reached out and touched the scar but traced it through the whole looping curve of the horseshoe. As he did it, it seemed to Pete that he was far away and watching somebody else do this idiotic thing.

"Dat good," said George, his booming voice gone suddenly soft, almost crooning. "Ya safe today."

Pete snatched his hand back. "Fuck you and fuck that scar and fuck safe!"

George turned his head away and for the first time Pete heard something that sounded like grieving in it when he said: "Now ya on de wrong side. Make de magic mad."

He walked out of the car, Pete following, feeling as he did the sweat turn cold on his back.

Out in the sun, George turned and stared hard at Pete. The raised, branded horseshoe-shaped scars gleamed redder in George's black skin. The sweat on Pete's back went colder still.

"What?" said Pete.

"Magic gone member dis if ya come askin."

"For what?"

"You brudder."

"Not hardly," said Pete. "My brother doesn't even speak to me. I don't know where he is and don't give a shit."

"Not him," said George. "De udder one, one locked up in de sylum. One make ya heart rotten."

Pete was suddenly burning all along his nerves, and his icy spine had turned to fire. He felt his face flushing with blood. When he spoke, he did not recognize his own voice. "You don't know *him.* You couldn't know a thing about him."

George showed all his teeth and even strips of his purple gums in a bitter smile. "Jus wha Max Winekoff tell. He some more mon. Dat mon be some more, Linga say."

Pete stood in the stifling heat watching George wolf food out of a brown grocery bag and wondering if now he might actually kill Max Winekoff. He really did stand very still within himself—the oven-hot, shit-smelling wind off the turgid St. Johns River blowing steadily in his face—and consider the death of Winekoff and how it might be arranged. It amazed him how actions and coincidences, both large and small, some done willfully, some done without any thought at all, could so totally fuck up your life.

His first accident was hitting his four-year-old brother in the head with a hammer. The second was the blow not killing him but only turning him into a drooling idiot who had to wear a football helmet, specially constructed and strapped so he couldn't get it off, or else he would beat himself to death by constantly and mindlessly banging his head against any wall he could find. If the blow had killed him, maybe Pete could have buried the guilt with the corpse instead of carrying it like a permanent scar on his heart. And then there was the fiery Sunoco truck killing his parents, which his older brother was determined to blame Pete for. Hell, maybe he *was* guilty of that, too. If they hadn't needed money for his idiot brother, his father sure as hell would not have been hauling a brood sow and her litter to the market. And who had made the brother an idiot? He, Pete, had. And finally there was the bad luck—accident? coincidence—of walking into the first boardinghouse he passed after he got off the Greyhound bus—having lasted only four days at the University of Florida—already drunk from half a bottle of Jack Daniel's whiskey, and then out of a need he could not name, sitting down with old man Winekoff, the first person he met after he rented the room in the boarding-house, and babbling through the late afternoon and night about the curse and guilt laid on his life. But how was he to know Mr. Winekoff would tell every mother's son and daughter in the entire city—at least it was beginning to seem he had—tell everybody in the city everything Pete had told him in a drunken stupor? How was Pete to know that Winekoff had done nothing with his life for the last twenty years, since he retired at the age of sixty-five, but walk from daylight to dark talking to anybody who would listen about anything and everything he had heard or seen or knew or just thought he knew.

"Pete-Pete, mon," called George.

Pete looked away from the river toward which he had been staring lost in thought and back at George squatting on his heels in the narrow strip of burning shade cast by the warehouse.

"Ya got de grease in ya bucket," said George, "ya bes git it in ya stomach." He pulled out the biscuit-sized pocket watch and looked at it long and hard, as though trying to memorize something. "In fo minutes dat fockin bullhorn scream fo blood. Believe dat. What ya tinkin bout up dere?"

"Winekoff."

"Don."

"Why?"

"I ain de Burnt Nigger fo nuttin, mon."

"You *know* everybody calls you that?"

"Know what de magic say." George snapped his lunch bucket shut and stood. "Know dis. Horn just say time up."

Simultaneously with George's last word, the foreman's amplified voice trumpeted through the warehouse, across the tracks, and right on out over the turd-and-gasoline-smelling river: "OFF YOUR ASSES! INTO THEM CARS! UNLOAD'M LIKE YOU LIVE: HARD! WE AIN'T PAYING YOU TO JACK OFF OR FUCK THE DOG!"

George showed his mouthful of gold glittering teeth: "Fockin horn mon keep de fockin time."

3

He walked over to her house at quarter to eight that evening. The sun was already down behind the oak but there was still plenty of light. He had watched from his window for ten minutes before he decided it was time. There had been no movement in the yard or in the house. And no sound at all. There was a good chance, he thought, that nobody was home.

But before he could knock, the warped wooden door swung open and she stood there on the other side of the screen looking up at him. She had the tip of her tongue caught between her teeth.

"We didn't say what time," he said. "Is . . .?"

She drew in her tongue and opened the screen door. "It's all right," she said. "I got something easy."

What she had was fried chicken, collard greens, which she had canned herself, and hush puppies. He had never had hush puppies with chicken before.

"I've never had hush puppies with chicken before," he said.

She didn't say anything, just stared at him for a long strained moment. The chicken was all backs and wings. Cheaper, he supposed.

"I love a back or a wing," he said.

"I thought you would. I bet you from Georgia."

"I am. That's where I come from."

"I thought so but I couldn't tell for sure because you don't really sound like you do. Your voice, you know, the way you talk."

"People have told me that before. Don't know how it happened. Just one of those things, you know."

But he was lying. He knew exactly how he had come to lose his accent. He had spent literally hundreds of hours accomplishing it, working at it until he thought he now sounded like a goddam radio announcer. When he went down to Parris Island for Marine Corps boot camp, he'd had the bad luck of being thrown in with a bunch of guys from Brooklyn, and they teased him unmercifully about the way he talked, about his southern accent. And he had more fingers pointing at him already than he could bear: the finger of guilt over what he had done to his little brother, his brother's unforgiving finger over the death of his mother and father, and worst of all, his own finger blaming himself, filling him with self-loathing. So he went to the base library and got every book he could find on grammar and pronunciation, and even finally hired a tutor, until the day came when the most expert of linguists might have trouble knowing he was from the South. But he always pretended his way of speaking was an accident that had just happened and that he could not explain. And it was because he had managed to lose his accent that he got the idea of using the GI Bill to give college a try. Nobody else in his family had ever done it, but maybe he could work it.

Sarah stood in front of him without moving.

There was a terrible tension around her eyes. He found himself wondering vaguely if her mother had died. But he was afraid to ask. He didn't want to get her started about sickness and death. But the last thing they had talked about that morning *had* been her mother's illness, how her daddy was at the hospital waiting to see how it all came out. He couldn't just ignore it, just as he couldn't simply walk away from the little man with the bloody pants in San Francisco.

"I had a heck of a day today," he said.

She only nodded and quit chewing long enough to hunker her shoulders a little closer to her plate in a gesture he could not interpret. This was not the first time she had done it and he wondered if the mannerism was a symptom of her grief or just something she had always done.

"It was so hot," he said, "you could have cooked an egg in that boxcar."

This time she kept chewing and nodded her head. Which did not seem a normal response to him. He wanted to scream at her that it *had* been goddam hot in that goddam boxcar and that he didn't feel like sitting around eating chicken wings and watching abnormal responses. Why the hell didn't she ask him which boxcar? For God's sake, why should he be talking to her about being in a boxcar you could cook an egg in? But her mother was in the hospital, and her daddy had apparently not come home.

"You could, you could cook, well, anything and . . ." He dwindled off to silence. He didn't know how to finish the sentence. Finally he said: "I unload boxcars."

He waited for her to ask him what he unloaded, but she didn't.

"Cellophane," he said. "I unload cellophane at the Bay Street Paper Company. Another guy and I," he rushed on, feeling mindless and intimidated. "Two guys to a car. You couldn't guess how heavy a one-foot stack of cellophane is." He waited for her to guess. She didn't. "A one-foot stack of your normal, see-through cellophane, eighteen by eighteen inches square, weighs fifty-seven pounds. You throw those babies around all day when it's hot enough to cook an egg in a boxcar and . . ." Again he dwindled off to silence.

And while everything he was saying was true, he felt rotten about saying it, and rotten about having come here to start with, and even more rotten that he had not yet asked about her mother. The knowledge of her mother's condition lay like a weight on his heart. Worse, because he was avoiding saying anything about it, the subject so preoccupied him that it was as though the poor mutilated woman, her breasts sliced off like so much bologna, lay on the table between them. The smell of hospital corridors pinched his nostrils and he knew he was not going to be able to eat another bite of chicken. And so he held a greasy back in his fingers but never touched it with his mouth while he rushed on, telling her anything he could think of to tell her.

He talked at length about his experiences in the service and how he planned to start at the university in the fall on the GI Bill. He was eligible for the GI Bill even though the Korean War had ended while he was in boot camp. That was three years ago, when he'd gone into the Marine Corps. This job in the boxcar was only temporary. He had a brother who was in Korea when the fighting stopped. Just about everybody he knew back on the farm in south Georgia had joined the service. It was a hell of a thing, war was, although he himself didn't know anything about it except what he read in the papers, and reading was a favorite pastime of his. He'd always read a lot. Books were the most fascinating thing in the world. Then he noticed there were no books to be seen anywhere from where he was sitting, and he had to switch back and go into a whole thing about how books weren't everything though. And neither was the university, for that matter. After he had covered the general uselessness of schools, he started on movies, which he never went to, and followed movies with a discussion of politics, which discussion consisted entirely of the statement that he didn't know anything about politics. Nobody in south Georgia did.

He talked for a solid thirty minutes, during which he mashed all the grease out of the chicken back he was holding, and then all the bits of meat out of the bony little spine, until he could finally put it down. It looked eaten. But it had not been, of course, and he knew that she knew it. Her eyes had continually dropped to his fingers while he talked. Several times he had paused, hoping to make her say something. But she'd sat silent as a stone, and in the silence, he had wrung the little chicken back for all he was worth. The most he had been able to get out of her was two yesses and a single grunt that could have meant yes or no.

A hell of a listener, he thought bitterly and with a fury that shocked him. He realized for the first time that he would have liked nothing better than to beat the hell out of her for making him struggle over this lousy chicken while her mortally wounded mother lay between them on the table.

"Great little meal." He pushed his plate back. "But I can't eat another bite."

She pushed her own plate away from her and watched his greasy fingers.

"Look," he said, "I hate to eat and run, but I've had a heck of a day."

"Can't you stay and talk for a while?"

The sound of her voice made him jump. It was, he thought, the most she had said since he'd been there.

"I would," he said, "but I had a heck of a day unloading cellophane out of a boxcar. You couldn't guess how much a one-foot stack of—" He stopped short, realizing he was about to tell her what he had already told her.

She said: "We could watch the TV." He looked around for the set. "Except we don't have a TV now. We used to have a TV though."

He couldn't believe how much she was talking. Three consecutive sentences made it seem as though she were positively babbling. It was all too much. He stood up.

"At least wash your hands in the sink over here," she said, "so you don't get yourself greasy all over."

He walked numbly over to the sink against the far wall. She followed him and stood not more than inches away, watching as he washed his hands. "We'll have to do this again," he said, and then thought: My God, what am I saying? Have I gone crazy?

But what the hell, it didn't matter what he said. It wasn't going to happen. Ever. No matter what.

"Here's something to dry your hands on." She moved even closer to hand him a towel. Their fingers touched when he took the towel, and he was stuck by how soft hers were, soft as a baby's, though they appeared hardened, even scaly. She had him in a corner where the sink joined the wall and she was right behind him, blocking his path to the door, and he could only stand drying his hands long after they were dry, trying not to look down into her eyes, which were red and vague as though she had been crying. Strange that he had not noticed her eyes tonight, how sad and wide they were, how impossible it was to say what color they were. The full scent of her came to him for the first time. She had put on some kind of body powder or perhaps perfume. For reasons he could never have given, it broke his heart to think of her bathing while the chicken backs and wings simmered on the stove, and powdering her tall, lean body while the collards boiled. But whatever the reasons, they most certainly had something to do with her cancer-racked mother whom he distinctly felt still lying back there on the dining table among the chicken bones and half-eaten hush puppies.

"We think she's gone come home before long," she said.

"What?" he said.

"Daddy's still at the hospital waiting to see how it comes out. I got to call him again after supper. But he said the doctors thought she'd do just as good at home from now on."

From now on to what? he wondered. He stood there with the damp towel hanging from his hands, feeling himself sinking deeper into her life. There was nothing to say. Nothing to do. If her mother didn't come back home, where was she to go? Straight from the hospital to the ground? He felt his bowels loosen and he thought he would be sick. God, he did not want to hear this, did not want to talk about it.

"Doctors don't know everything," he said. He handed her the towel, and she took it. But she did not move for him to pass.

"They know more'n you'd think," she said.

Against his will he seemed to be encouraging this dreadful conversation. But why had he said that doctors didn't know everything? Where did that leave her mother? They had to know something. They had to know *a lot.*

"The good ones can do just about everything," he said.

"You should see what they've done to Mama."

"O.K.," he said, feeling more like a fool than ever. "Right."

She said: "When they taken off the first cancer, they—"

He kissed her. It was the only way, that or hit her, so he stopped her mouth and its talk of cancer with a kiss. She clung to him in a way he could never have imagined. Her tall, lean body was suddenly all curves and tension and heat. Her mouth chewed at his own. Her tongue struck like a snake and struck again and kept on striking until he was a little dizzy with it. Without thought of any kind, he put his hands on her hips and found them strangely mounded and soft and trembling. Where had all this flesh come from? She did not so much breathe through her nose as snort, the sound of it ragged and gaspy against his cheek.

He finally managed to tear her loose from him and to lean against the wall. She hunkered lower and leaned against him. His chin rested on the top of her head. The trembling of her body came right up through her skull and into his mouth. But when she spoke, her voice was curiously calm and flat even though her breath still rattled unevenly in her throat.

"You wouldn't think even doctors could take off the whole front . . ."

He kissed her again and his hands, with a seeming will of their own, took firm hold of the cheeks of her ass, and again he wondered where all this hot curving flesh had come from. This time when her body melded into his with that amazing strength and hunger, she half led, half dragged him away from the wall and away from the sink in a kind of frantic dance, right out into the dining room and past the dreadful table to a ragged beige-colored couch, where she set him down, collapsing beside him. This time he let her chew at his mouth as long as she wanted because he was afraid of what she might say as soon as she quit. And she did exactly what he knew in his heart she would do. Once somebody told him something personal, it never seemed to end, and as often as not was filled with the stink of rotting flesh.

"Mama may die," she said, holding him by the shoulders lightly but with surprising strength. He felt that if he bolted for the door she would tackle him about the ankles and continue without pause this deadly conversation on the bare wooden floor of the living room.

"You've got to think positive," he managed to say in his dry, croaking voice. "Medical science is advancing every day."

What were these insane things he was saying? He had known for a long time that madness was more contagious than the common cold. He had always felt you could catch it from somebody passing on the other side of the street. It had happened to him before. He supposed it would again. But that didn't take care of *now*. It didn't turn the conversation from where it seemed to be going, or for that matter even turn her reddened, vague eyes, which were locked on his mouth, waiting. He said: "We've all just got to take the wait-and-see attitude, be patient enough to wait for the miracles of—"

"They know enough to take'm off," she said, glancing briefly down at her own breasts. "They won't ever know enough to put'm back on."

He could not bear it. With a despairing groan he reached out and put one hand on her throat as though he would strangle her, but only pushed her onto her back on the couch. She held him firmly by the shoulders and drew him down with her. He felt her knees part beneath him.

"That's silly," he said, his tongue so dry and swollen in his mouth he doubted she understood him. "That was a silly thing to say."

Her knees spread wider and he was taken deeper into her amazing, soft saddle as the thin print dress rose magically. She was wearing peach-colored bikini panties. And she smelled even better now, the perfume of her bath powder mixed with something heavier, richer, saltier.

"I know what I know," she said. "They let me in before Mama ever woke up from the operation and when I raised her sheet, it—"

He stopped her with his mouth and at the same time put his hand through the band at the top of her panties. She was as slick and wet as a peeled plum.

After a long moment, he drew back from her and she said, her flat voice coming miraculously right through the breath that still rattled in her throat: "I don't act like this ever night."

He thought, God knows I don't either, but he said: "I know. I know you don't."

"I don't do this with just ever Tom, Dick, and Harry that comes along."

"I know," he said, thinking that along with everything else he had somehow caught her limited vocabulary.

"Actually, I've never done this."

"Done what?"

"It," she said. "Done *it.*"

He knew immediately she was telling the truth. The thought that followed was: *Then why are you doing it now?* It seemed a way out.

"We don't have to," he said.

"Have to what?"

"*It,*" he said. "You know, do *it.*"

Her eyes grew more opaque. "Don't you want to?"

"Of course." It seemed the only answer.

She relaxed a little. His breathing slowed. He felt her little racing heart become quieter under her breastbone.

"I know you respect me," she said.

"I do, I do."

Her reddened eyes narrowed. "You'll always respect me."

"Forever," he said. "If it's one thing I'll always do it's respect you." He eased his hand out of her damp panties.

"It's some that wouldn't," she said. "You have to be careful about respect in this world. It was one of the last things Mama talked to me about before they wheeled her out the first time to—"

He jammed his tongue into her mouth and frantically struggled to get his hand back down the top of her waistband. Her reaction was to moan and tear the top three buttons off his shirt.

With that enormous strength and vitality that she appeared to have none of at all she lifted his shoulders away from her, forcing their mouths apart, and said: "The buttons. The buttons."

At first he thought she was talking about the buttons she'd torn off him, which he really regretted because it was his best shirt, but then he saw she meant the buttons that closed the front of her thin print dress. She did not touch them herself but only pointed with a single finger to the place where they started at her throat, and moaned: "The buttons. The buttons."

He propped himself on his elbows and slipped the first button and then the second. As he struggled, sweating and moaning himself, trying to work up some semblance of a proper reaction, she made a quick sliding movement under him and he felt rather than saw her panties drop beside the couch where they lay. She had removed them with a grace and suppleness he would have thought impossible in a body so angular and lean. It was a movement he had seen in women before. When a woman really wanted to get out of her clothes, it became an act of pure magic. But God, what an ordeal a man could have trying to manipulate hooks and buttons and snaps and belts.

He was grinding his teeth now—forgetting all about making the proper sounds—in his effort to maneuver his hands under her back to unhook her bra. He looked down and saw her watching him carefully. She had raised her shoulders a bit to give him more room to work. But the damn bra simply wouldn't come apart back there. He struggled and sweated and ground his teeth, finally saying in desperation: "It won't come loose."

"Yes it will," she said.

"Can't you help me?"

Apparently she couldn't. "You can get it," she said. She had done the little trick with the bikini panties and he supposed she thought that was enough. Maybe making him take off her bra was her way of keeping a little romance in what they were doing. Maybe. He didn't know. He didn't know anything except that he wasn't going to let her tell him anything else personal, anything else that he would have to carry home on his back tonight. There was nothing to do but push on through.

And just as she said he would, he got it. Something gave where he was working back there and suddenly there was tittie everywhere. That's the way he thought of it: tittie everywhere. You wouldn't have imagined it in a million years looking at her all cinched up in the print dress, but naked, each of her breasts was as big as his brother's head. He felt better instantly. It wasn't going to be so bad after all. Maybe everything would work out.

"Oh, you honey," he said, telling himself that he was only trying to make her feel better, but knowing full well that it was he who felt better, and that was what made saying such a thing possible.

When she spoke, her voice was no longer flat but trembled right along with her breathing. "You think I look all right?"

"You look great."

"You think I look great and not just all right?"

For an answer he sent his cupped hand shooting between her legs and fell upon the breast, sucking like a baby before he got there. But he had hardly drawn her great dark nipple into his mouth before he knew something was wrong. Something bad. He lifted his head from her breast and found her watching him carefully through eyes that were not only narrowed but also filled with terror.

"What's wrong?"

"Nothing," he said.

"Why'd you stop?"

"I haven't stopped," he said. "Just relax. Be easy."

"All right," she said, her voice shaking worse than ever.

Maybe he'd been wrong. Maybe she was just too excited or he was too tense or . . . There was nothing he could see to do but try to bull on through. But when he took the same breast he'd had his mouth on into his hand, he gave a little cry and jerked his hand away as though he had put it on a hot stove. In the center of her breast was a knot bigger than a golf ball and as hard and solid as stone.

4

That night in his tiny room in the boardinghouse, Pete did not sleep very much or very well. The little he did sleep was shallow and filled with strange dreams. Not bad dreams, just strange—hardly dreams at all, filled as they were, not with people but with thick gliding shadows and empty rooms and unstoppered bottles that had nothing in them. For the most part he lay awake and watched his seabag where it sat in the corner beside the tiny dresser that had nothing on it but a comb. It had not been unpacked since he was discharged. Everything he owned, including all of his clothes, were still in the seabag. Why unpack it until he found a place to stop permanently? This was just a momentary stopping place, a pause in his life. Why in the hell had he lied to her about going to the university? There was no call for it. Four goddam days and he had had as much as he could stand of the University of Florida. It all reminded him too much of the Marine Corps. Somebody always telling you where to go and when to go and how long to stay when you got there. It was too much. But on top of that, to really make it something too heavy to carry, they put him in a dorm room with three goddam Jewish boys from Miami Beach, one of whom farted constantly. So he had left his seabag packed, and one morning, going out of the room to an English class, he picked up the bag and went to the Greyhound bus station instead. Everything, though, was temporary, momentary. Except death.

He groaned at the thought when it popped into his head. He wanted to slap himself for even thinking such a thing, not because it was death but because it was so silly. There he was, a grown man, just finished with a three-year tour of duty in the Marine Corps, lying in bed in the middle of the night, thinking that way about death. Still, so far as anybody could find out, death was the one permanent thing. A lot of horseshit had been written about heaven and hell and coming back after death as a dog or something. But all of it was horseshit guessing. You could line up all the holy men of history, including Jesus, and the lot of them would not do as much for you as a good cup of coffee. Or at least that was the way it was for him, the way it had been since he hit his brother in the head with a hammer. It was an accident. Anybody with two eyes could see that it was an accident. But accident or not, it had ruined his brother and left two permanent parallel scars on his brother's head just above his nose. And nobody ever forgave him for it. His mother and father went to their deaths believing him to be a malicious maimer of children. And his older brother wouldn't even speak to him now. Nor would any of his other blood kin. When he hit his brother in the head with the hammer, he had cut himself loose from all his blood. He might as well be dead and buried. He felt utterly alone in the world, and consequently, even though he knew it was an accident (he of all people ought to know what happened and how it happened), he still could not forgive himself. He permanently carried twin parallel scars like a weight in his heart. Never for an instant was he free of them.

When it was still a couple of hours before daylight, he got up to go to the all-night diner down on the corner for a pack of cigarettes, although he had quit smoking the day he was discharged from the service.

As he eased through the front door and out onto the sidewalk, he was startled to see a light in one of the windows next door. It was only when he saw the window that he realized how hard he had been trying not to think of her and what had happened on the couch. He had been making it too, making it right on through the night until he stepped out onto the sidewalk. And now the whole sorry evening came flooding back upon him. He stared at the window. Was it hers, that window? Was she in there now? And if she was, what was she doing? He had a quick flash of her standing half naked before a mirror looking at her right breast—the one that was turning to stone—maybe, despite her terror, even touching it.

It would be easy to find out who, if anyone, was in the room. All he'd have to do would be to step over there in the deep shadow under the arching limbs of the oak tree. No blind or shade covered the lighted window. She . . . He stopped the thought and tasted something bitter at the base of his tongue. Hadn't he done enough already? Was he now to become a Peeping Tom, catching night-time glimpses of a girl who had . . . had what?

Cancer, goddammit. Cancer.

There, a voice that was his but not quite his demanded, you've said it. Does that make you happy? Is that enough?

It didn't and it wasn't. He turned and went rapidly toward the diner to get the cigarettes he did not want. It was a short walk and he managed to hold an angry silence in his mind while he hurried along the street. There was one other customer in the diner: a puffy middle-aged drunk who snored with his head down on the counter. A waitress stood near the grill reading a movie magazine. She glanced up as Pete came in and then went right back to what she was reading. The teeth-filled faces of Rock Hudson and Doris Day looked out of the cover of the magazine. Pete got his cigarettes from a machine just inside the door and sat down on one of the stools. A short-order cook, who looked as if his feet hurt him, came down the counter and stopped in front of him.

"What'll it be?"

"Just coffee."

The cook got the coffee and brought it to him. "You want cream?"

"Black's fine."

The cook didn't leave but stood across the counter watching him. "This hot weather," he said, "we have to keep the cream in the cooler. Don't, it'll go bad in a minute."

Even though the man sounded like he was going to faint any minute from boredom and exhaustion, Pete was glad to have him there to talk to, to talk to about nothing, about everything in the world that was totally without consequence. He wanted to have a good long talk about little pitchers of cream spoiling in the summer heat.

"I never thought about it much," said Pete, "but I guess you would have a lot of cream go bad when it's hot like this."

"You wouldn't believe it," said the cook.

"Anything else besides cream?"

"What?" The word barely made its way through the man's yawn.

"Does anything else besides cream spoil?"

"You wouldn't believe it," the cook repeated. He looked down the counter toward the snoring drunk, a frown briefly drawing his tired greasy face tighter. The waitress still had not moved. "You just get off from work?"

"No," said Pete. "I don't go to work until seven."

The cook tried to smile but didn't quite make it. "You young bucks out having a good time, nothing to do but cat around town all night."

Pete's smile was no more successful than the cook's but he was truly enjoying this. This was just what he needed. "You know how it is," he said.

"I can almost remember how it *was,*" said the cook. "No more though. That kind of stuff is gone now. Me, I don't get off until eight this morning. By then, this place will be screaming. God, every morning it's like waiting for a battle to start. You ever do short order?"

"Never did," Pete said, wanting to get into a good heavy conversation about grits.

"Don't," said the cook.

A loud noise made them both jump. The drunk had jerked violently in his sleep and knocked the salt and pepper as well as the sugar off the counter. The waitress looked up but went right back to her magazine. The cook walked on his tender feet down to where the drunk was and cleaned up everything.

When he came back, he said: "That's my brother. His old lady won't let him come home drunk so he comes in here to sleep. And I tell you, if the boss ever finds him one more time with his head down on the counter like that it's the can for me." He paused and sucked his teeth and Pete saw them shift in his mouth. They were false. "Don't know where I'd git another job either. Can't move like I once could. Still, he's my brother and I can't put him out. Use to let him sleep in my car, but I don't have the car no more. The old lady was going to prayer meeting the other day and ran into a . . ."

Leaving a handful of change on the counter, Pete hurried away without hearing the rest. It was not so much what the cook said or seemed about to say that drove him into the street as it was that the drunken brother and the waitress with Rock Hudson and Doris Day resting on her slightly swollen paunch and the cook with his tender feet—all of it brought back Sarah and him on the beige couch and how terrible it had been, maybe would always be. Maybe he would never forget it or get over it. The thought of it made him suck frantically on the cigarettes as he rushed through the street toward the boardinghouse.

When he snatched his hand away from the thing growing in her breast, her eyes had swelled with terror, but she kept them steadily upon his. And he could not look away. But he could not go on with what they were doing either. Did she know she might have something growing in there? The same thing that was killing, perhaps had already killed, her mother, did she know that? Of course she knew. And now she knew that he knew. He was there on that couch, had been brought there, to confirm what she already at least suspected, or to help her deny it. And he had done what he would not have purposefully done for anything in the world. He tried to make himself put his mouth back on her breast, and when he could not do that, he tried to force himself to take her breast back in his hand. But he could not summon the courage. And worse, a thought occurred to him that made him abruptly take his hand away from the place between her legs.

Cancer was the crab. And where did the crab like to live? In the dark wet of some secret channel. He could imagine—no, plainly *see*—the voracious crab, the ugly meat-eating crab moving slowly in the deep channel of her, patiently waiting for him. They lay there for what seemed to him to be a very long time looking into one another's eyes.

Finally he said: "We can't do this."

"Why not?" she said.

"It's what I told you before," he said. "I do respect you. This is the first time I've seen you. It's not right."

Her eyes clearly showed that she knew he was lying and the lie only magnified her fear.

"I don't care," she said. "I don't care about that."

"I do." He averted his gaze and looked at the ashy-smelling fireplace across the room and the water-stained wallpaper above it, and a new lie occurred to him. "I respect this house."

"You respect the house?" she said incredulously.

When she spoke, she moved under him in an odd pained way, and he felt a coldness spreading in his stomach. "You'd understand if you'd just think about it. I came here when your mother . . . I came here at a bad time, and your daddy's out and this is his house." He stopped. He was only making it worse. "Where I come from a man doesn't . . ." He couldn't finish.

"Tell me why you stopped," she said.

"I told you."

"I don't understand."

"There's nothing to understand except what I said. I told you the best I could."

"I don't believe you," she said, surprising him with the hissing violence of her voice.

He pushed himself back from her and knelt between her ankles spread on the couch. "You've got to get up," he said. "Your daddy might come in."

Again he was surprised, even shocked, at the violence of her voice. "I don't *have* to do anything."

"You're being unfair," he told her.

"I don't know anything about fair or not fair," she said.

"Please." He pointed toward the open top of her dress and the bra that had been unhooked at the back and then pushed up under her chin. "Put your clothes on." He was careful not to look at her breasts.

She pointed to the same place he had and said in a voice not so violent now but sour and peevish, "I didn't do any of this and I'm not going to touch it." She looked toward the door. "Not even if Daddy comes in right this minute."

He stiffened where he sat. "Do you think he might?"

"He might," she said. "It depends on how everything came out."

He bent to her again and it was as difficult for him to get her bra hooked as it had been to unhook it. But he finally managed it. He got her buttoned and sitting up. Her panties lay like an accusation on the floor in front of them.

"I got to go," he said.

"Go then," she said. "You'll be back. Because you respect this house. You respect me."

He stopped at the door to look back at her briefly, but he didn't say anything.

When he got back from the diner, he sat on the porch and smoked and watched the window under the oak tree next door. God, if he could have gone on with it there on the couch, it would be all over now, or at least brought to some kind of conclusion. He didn't like to leave things ragged this way, up in the air, with her saying he would be back and all that stuff about respect. It would have been better if she had said it sarcastically or angrily, but that had not been the case. When she said he would be back, her voice had gone flat and final again.

He sat on the porch of the boardinghouse feeling tired and miserable. Once, he thought about calling in sick but he decided against it because he didn't know what he would do with the day. Maybe when he got in the boxcar with all those stacks of cellophane, sweating and breaking his back, things would be better.

The door slammed behind him and he turned to see Max Winekoff, vigorously waving his arms as if he meant to fly, and Pete felt something shift inside himself—something like the physical shifting of a load inside a truck, but it wasn't physical, this shifting, and he knew it. He knew precisely and murderously what it was. The grief that he carried—self-hatred—had moved from himself to this old bastard who had been talking his name around, and not only his name but his *life:* his wounded brother, God knows what all, everything, *everything* he had in a drunken stupor told the old man the afternoon he had staggered back from the university with his still-unpacked seabag and an intolerable load of despair.

Watching the old man stretching and windmilling his arms, Pete could barely remember the long rambling conversation (confession?) he'd had with him and certainly could not remember everything he had told him. But he could plainly remember the last words of his conversation with Sarah on the sidewalk.

Pete, my name is Pete.

I know.

You know?

Mr. Winekoff.

All right, the old bastard had told the girl next door his name. That was not so bad. In fact, that was not bad at all. Could happen to anybody, anywhere. But what about the Burnt Nigger?

Pete stared at the old man and felt lighter. The hard monstrous weight had slipped out of him and pressed itself on the person of Max Winekoff. Pete felt almost happy as his gaze burned into Winekoff, who wore clean khaki trousers and a khaki shirt. His hair was gray and close-cropped above a face that always wore an expression of almost demonic happiness. He was bending now, knees locked, hands flat on the floor.

"Is this something or is this something?" said Max Winekoff, his face upside down. He might have been anybody's slightly eccentric grandfather. But Pete did not have to listen to hear the Burnt Nigger.

De magic member dis if ya gone come askin.

For what?

Ya brudder.

Not hardly. We don't even talk.

Not him. De udder one, one locked in de sylum. One make ya heart rotten.

You don't know nothing about him.

Only wha Mr. Winekoff tell me.

"I was saying that for a man my age, this is really something."

Pete didn't answer him, and he knew the old man would not even notice. Max Winekoff loved to talk. In fact, he seemed to love everything: eating, walking, speculating about the world situation, on which he was well informed from constant newspaper and magazine reading in the evening.

He was still bent with his hands on the floor, not moving, looking up at Pete through incredible gray eyebrows. His eyebrows were as long as his hair. When Pete first moved into the boardinghouse, he had been startled by Mr. Winekoff's constant bending, but he had gradually gotten used to it. Pete would find him like that all over the house, sometimes in the little hall that led to the place where the boarders ate, sometimes just outside his bedroom door, now and then even on the stairs. When Pete passed him, he would remain in position, but he always spoke.

Coming out of his bend there on the porch, Mr. Winekoff said: "Bending and walking, walking and bending—it's been my whole life. You bend much?"

Pete heard himself say, thinking of the boxcar: "Not ordinarily but I've been bending a lot lately." But his heart was frozen with the fear of what he might do to the old man right out there on the front porch for anybody who might be looking to see.

"Keep at it," said Mr. Winekoff, "and you'll live forever. How old do you think I am?"

Pete didn't have to guess. The old man had told him several

times he was eighty-five. He told everybody in the house several times a day how old he was. He'd give his age and then flop into a bend with his hands flat on the floor.

A bell rang inside. Breakfast. The boardinghouse fed those who lived there two meals a day, breakfast and supper. And Mr. Winekoff ate incredible amounts at each meal, more than anybody else in the house. Fantastic. More even than the huge construction workers, many of them young men. Mr. Winekoff headed for the table where the meals were served family style, several tables loaded—groaning—with food brought on the long arms of a small army of sullen black girls: enormous bowls of scrambled eggs, severely undercooked, and plates of cool fat bacon, which was cut thick and hung limply from the boarders' forks, and stacks of pancakes, pale and spongy in the middle, and pitchers of light blue milk and then coffee.

Mr. Winekoff did not seem to care what kind of food was on the table. He had three mounded platefuls every morning and every evening, packing it in, because he was a great bender and talker and walker. He walked like a madman all day long, seven days a week.

And every day, without exception, he walked to the city zoo to see the yaks. He had always been a yak lover, or so he had told Pete, time out of mind. The walk to the fucking zoo alone was four fucking miles—two there and two back, all the way across the Trout River Bridge. But the old man always insisted in a calm voice with no bragging in it that he walked at least thirty miles every day, and Pete did not doubt it. The construction workers, who were scattered all over the city on different jobs, said they saw him everywhere, sometimes miles beyond the city limits.

And somewhere in his mad ramblings he had come across the Burnt Nigger and told him Pete's secret shame and guilt and cursed life. And if the Burnt Nigger had been told, how many others? Sowing stories of his maimed brother like wild oats.

Pete's cold heart was murderous watching the old man, and for the first time today he felt a measure of peace contemplating the amount and kinds of pain he might inflict on Mr. Winekoff. The old man was standing, looking down on Pete where Pete now sat in the rocking chair.

"You ought to take off one day and come to the zoo with me," said Mr. Winekoff, looking off toward the dining room, waiting for the tables to load up. "See them yaks."

"I don't think so," Pete said, listening to his own strange voice. "I don't think I like yaks. But if I ever do go with you we'll have to take a bus."

"A bus is one thing I don't need. Let me tell you something that'll help you through life. You listening?"

"I'm listening," said Pete.

"Ride and *grunt*. Walk and feel *good*."

"I get a lot of exercise unloading boxcars," Pete said.

"You've got to walk, nothing in the world like walking," said Mr. Winekoff. "Besides, you've got to see them yaks."

Pete wasn't even sure he knew what a yak looked like. But he thought maybe they looked something like a camel without a hump.

"I guess I'll take me one more bend before I get on in there to that table." The old man flopped double, hands flat on the floor.

Pete got up from the rocker and went to stand beside Mr. Winekoff. Mr. Winekoff wore a heavy, aged belt that was seamed with dry cracks. Right across his back where he was bending, the belt bowed up like a handle to a suitcase. With no volition of his own a wonderful satisfying notion was forming in Pete's mind.

"You ever fall down any steps?" he asked.

Mr. Winekoff cut his upside-down eyes to Pete. His happy face grinned. "Fall down any steps? I've never fell down—*once*. With my legs? My walking? Not hardly."

Pete reached over and hooked his hand under the old belt where it bowed up slightly over Mr. Winekoff's skinny back, and lifted him off the floor. He was incredibly light. Pete started around the side of the porch to the stairs leading up the back of the boardinghouse, carrying Mr. Winekoff—still bent double—like a suitcase.

"You carrying me just like a suitcase," Mr. Winekoff said.

"Yes, I am," said Pete, his heart lifting, "just like a suitcase."

Mr. Winekoff seemed to think that was wonderful. "You stronger than you look, son. And I can't imagine what you'd be like if I could get you into a walking program."

Pete started up the long straight flight of steps with Mr. Winekoff.

"Wonderful," said Mr. Winekoff.

"Yes, wonderful," Pete said. And it *was* wonderful. The first wonderful thing that Pete had felt in as long as he could remember.

He was at the top of the long flight of stairs with Mr. Winekoff. He stopped and turned and both of them looked down. "You did really good," said Mr. Winekoff, "carrying me up here. Got the old ticker pumping. You feel the old ticker pumping in your chest?"

"Yes, I do," Pete said. And he felt it not only pumping but singing with happiness. *Spread me and my story all over town like a cheap bag of cowshit,* he thought. *Now it's your turn to be spread.*

"That's a long way down them stairs," Mr. Winekoff pointed out, as though it was a thought that had just occurred to him.

"Yes, it is," said Pete. And opened his hand on Mr. Winekoff's belt and watched him go tumbling ass over elbow, his head banging the railings making a sound much like a kid running a stick along a picket fence, except that the sound was mixed with grunts and little yelps of pain. At the same time, though, Pete could not help but admire how smoothly the angular old man, his thin arms and legs bending and twisting at impossible angles, took the long fall.

There was a moment of silence and then Mr. Winekoff, after examining his arms and legs, his hard flat belly, cocked his head up at Pete and said: "You dropped me."

"Your handle broke," said Pete.

"Handle?"

"Suitcase."

Mr. Winekoff reached behind him and examined his old thick belt slowly and thoroughly. "Handle didn't break. You dropped me."

Pete said: "Yes, I did." And he was about to add: *And I'm going to tote you back up here and drop you again,* when he noticed that the old man was stretching his neck to look over the window frame into the living room, which had another window on the other side through which Sarah's house could be seen—he ought to know, he'd sat staring at the house through that window enough long and lonely hours to know—and he knew without even thinking that it was the house, maybe even Sarah herself, that Mr. Winekoff was looking at like a bird dog on point.

"What?" said Pete, because he could not see the house himself from where he was standing at the top of the back flight of stairs.

"God works in mysterious ways, His many wonders to perform," Mr. Winekoff said. That had been one of Pete's mother's favorite sayings before the accidental blow from a hammer had made her youngest son an idiot, at which time she had lost her religion entirely and her senses only partially—or at least that was what Pete's father had maintained several times a day: *Your ma ain't but partial lost her senses.*

"I know," said Pete, "but what you looking at?"

"Know what?" asked Mr. Winekoff, looking up at Pete.

"God working mysteriously, dammit."

"I never said nothing like that. Wouldn't want to put myself in danger of hellfire."

"How bout in danger of falling down these goddam steps again?"

"My handle didn't break. Couldn't unless it was malice involved."

Pete went tripping down the steps, having already forgotten about what the old man might be looking at, intent only upon dragging him back up to the top and letting him go down again, this time thrown with a certain force. But before he ever got to him, Pete heard his name being called faintly and when he looked through the window, he saw first the long white ambulance and then Mr. Leemer, his hands cupped around his mouth, calling—plaintively, beseechingly, it seemed to Pete—"Peeete! Oh, say, over there! Peeete!"

"The Lord has brought his wife home," said Mr. Winekoff, "and Mr. Leemer is calling you. I do believe it is your name, but then my hearing ain't what it used to be."

"He doesn't know my name," Pete said. "He's never spoken to me in my life."

Mr. Winekoff looked at Pete. "I can hear him out there now, and it's you he's calling. He knows enough to be calling your name."

"Goddammit," said Pete, "did you tell him that, too?"

"What?"

"Oh, fuck it."

"No *sir,*" said Mr. Winekoff. "No*sirree*bob, I never told him, nor nobody else, *Oh, fuck it.*" He popped up and fell into another bend with his hands flat on the floor. Without even trying to look at Pete, he said, "That ain't my way of talking, not today, not *ever.*"

Pete looked long and hard at the old man's belt bowed up on his back now that he was in his bend. It *did* look like a suitcase handle. Worked like one too. He glanced from the belt to the top of the stairs and back at the belt. It wouldn't take but a minute, but Mr. Leemer had really found the range now and he was calling for Pete's help like his feet were on fire. He had to go. He had to stop this. Every goddam body in the neighborhood had heard by now.

Pete went down the steps and around the house toward the sidewalk, which the slanting sun had thrown half in shadow. The ambulance was parked by the curb. He couldn't see whoever was sitting in the front seat but Mr. Leemer was standing at the end of the ambulance in front of the closed double doors. His arms had dropped to his sides now and he looked embarrassed and solemn at the same time.

He raised one of his long arms, palm out, and called in a strangely quiet voice, "Say, Pete."

As if on cue two young men dressed in white coats and pants popped out of the front of the ambulance, one on either side. From their expressions, which were very nearly no expressions at all, the two of them struck Pete as ice cream salesmen on a Good Humor truck, and he felt himself go slightly sick to his stomach considering what they had to be hauling in the long white limousine.

Pete walked across the lawn and, still on the sidewalk, stopped and looked at Mr. Leemer, who now had an ambulance attendant on either side of him. Both of them had toothpicks caught in the sides of their mouths, as though they might have made a quick stop at the burger place on the drive over. Their expressions had turned a little sullen, even angry.

Mr. Leemer looked slightly to the left of Pete's right ear and said, "I was wondering if you could maybe give us a hand here." He gestured vaguely at the ambulance. The old man was tall and lean, with long ropy muscles and veins big as pencils showing in his arms where they hung out of the sleeves of his shirt. His hands were thick and half closed as if about to take up an ax or mallet at any moment.

"Pete," he said, and then stopped as if wondering how to go on. Pete stared at him in amazement. Mr. Leemer had never spoken to him in his life. But then the man found his voice again. "The doctors say Sarah's mama is out of the woods. So I brought her on home. Nothing to do but try to look after her myself." His eyes, pinched from too many hours in the sun, turned briefly to the house. "Sarah told me all about you."

He looked back toward Pete and their gazes locked. The older man seemed about to smile but didn't, quite. What in the world had Sarah told him? Pete wondered. Surely not about the couch and the buttons and his hand fumbling at her legs, mouth at her breast. Did any girl tell her daddy such things?

One of the ambulance attendants, the one that looked more pissed off, said: "We don't need your help, feller. This ain't nothing but just a routine—"

Mr. Leemer turned on him. "It might be just a routine to you, mister, but it's my *wife*."

"We told you," said the other young attendant, "if your wife come home in our ambulance, she's got to go on a gurney, go all the way from the hospital to your bed in your house on the gurney. It's just policy. Insurance reasons for the company. Only policy, *goddammit*."

"Try to keep a civil tongue," Mr. Leemer said calmly. "I want Pete to help if he will. It ain't gone take but a minute."

"Let us do our job like we sposed to," said the young man,

blowing the toothpick out of his mouth, "be a hell of a lot quicker. If you'd let—"

"But I won't," Mr. Leemer said firmly. He looked back at Pete. "If Pete'll help us, that's what I want." He stared at Pete's right ear and waited.

"You going to help us, feller, or not? We don't need you, but if you want to git in on the act, then it's all right with us. But we got to *move*. We can't stay here bullshitting the rest of the day."

"Keep a civil tongue," said Mr. Leemer, still staring at Pete's ear.

"Sure I will," Pete said. It seemed the only thing he *could* say. "But I was on my way to—"

"Right," said the ambulance driver. "If it's got to be done the way the old man here wants it, my pard and me'll take the front and back. You and him take the sides. Nothing needed here but my pard on one end and me on the other but if he won't have it any other way, let's, by God, git it done." He was unlocking the double doors on the back of the ambulance as he talked.

"Keep a civil tongue," said Mr. Leemer. "This is family."

"This is *bullshit,*" said the other young man, blowing out his toothpick.

When the attendant pulled the narrow wheeled cot out of the back of the ambulance, Gertrude Leemer was strapped down on it, one strap buckled across her stomach and another across her ankles. She was not a small woman, but there was something very strange about her and Pete suddenly realized it was the curious sinking of her chest. He looked up from her caving chest to her face and saw how flushed and twisted with anger it was. Her hair was thin and wispy as smoke floating about her skull, but her sunken, black-lidded eyes were damp and burning with such fury that it caused Pete to move back half a step.

"Git these goddam straps off me," said Mrs. Leemer in a thick, phlegm-filled voice. "I can walk into my house! I ain't a cripple! They didn't cut off my son-of-a-bitchin legs!"

"Now Mother," said Mr. Leemer.

Her eyes turned to blaze upon her husband and he visibly paled. "Henry, you git these straps off me and let me walk! You'll pay for this!"

The attendants had her out of the ambulance now, one on either end of the gurney. "Mrs. Leemer, we've explained it's just policy and—"

"And I've explained your daddy licked his balls settin in the middle of the road, you bastard!"

The attendant smiled for the first time. "Damn, you got a fine mouth." He looked at Pete. "Grab one side of this thing. Leemer, you git the other and let's see if we can do this before dark."

As they moved across the yard, Pete looked up and there was Sarah on the porch, holding the screen door open. She watched them grimly, seeming as angry as her mother.

When they got halfway through the door, she said: "You've come back."

"I have, daughter," said Mrs. Leemer, "and a damn sight quicker too if they'd let me walk."

But Sarah had been looking at Pete, not at her mother.

They moved through the living room, down a short hallway, to a long high-ceilinged bedroom. There were only two windows and they were covered by faded yellow shades. When they stopped by a big four-poster bed, Pete said: "I'll just step out into the other room now if that's all right."

"Sure." The ambulance driver looked at Mr. Leemer. "That is, if it's all right with the old man."

"Thank you, Pete," said Mr. Leemer. "We can git'er now."

Pete didn't want to watch as they tried to move her onto the bed. He was particularly afraid somebody would lift the sheet off her before he could get away. He had no intention of stopping before he was safely in the street but just before he got to the front door, he felt rather than heard someone at his shoulder. He knew before he even looked back that it was Sarah. When he turned, she was not more than a foot away from him.

He felt a quick flush of anger. "Shouldn't you be in there with your mama?"

"Yes," she said. "I'll have to talk to Mama."

"Listen," he said, but then stopped while the two men came by with the cot. He thought one of them would speak to him. Neither of them did. "About last night."

"What about last night?"

"Your daddy knew my name out there." He pointed through the open door to where the ambulance was pulling away from the curb. "He knew it and I don't—"

"I told him."

"You *told* him?"

Her daddy walked into the living room. "Sarah, your mother wants to talk to you."

"You wait right here," she told Pete.

"I have to go to work," he said. "I'm late for work." But she disappeared through the door leading to the hallway.

"That Sarah," the old man chuckled. He came across the room with his hand out. "I'm Henry Leemer. But I guess she told you that." They shook hands. Her daddy's palm was hard, with thick pads of callus. He did not release Pete's hand but held it while he talked. "She sure did tell me all about you. I'm going to make a little coffee. Sit down, I'll get you a cup." He still had Pete by the hand and drew him over to the couch in front of the fireplace. "Sit down right there."

"I guess I could have one quick cup, Mr. Leemer."

Mr. Leemer didn't turn his hand loose until Pete sat on the couch. "You call me Henry. Everbody does. Now let me git that coffee."

The old man was back almost immediately, saying, "It's just instant. Hope that's all right."

"It's fine," Pete said. It was terrible. Made, Pete thought, with water from the faucet. He didn't drink it but only raised the cup to his mouth several times to dip his tongue in it.

"It's been hard," Mr. Leemer said.

"It *is* hard sometimes," said Pete.

"You're just going along minding your own business and then one day they come and haul your wife off to the hospital. But I think we out of the woods now. The thing is to hold on and sooner or later you're out of the woods."

"It's none of my business, but maybe she could've used a few more days in the hospital."

Mr. Leemer cut his eyes away and looked out of the window. "Wouldn't let us stay. Had to go."

Pete knew something of hospitals and doctors from his little brother's injury. "Run out of insurance, did you?"

"Never had none."

Pete set his coffee down carefully on the little table in front of him. No insurance? Everybody had insurance. Hell, even he had insurance. Kept his service insurance when he left the Marine Corps. A person was at the mercy of humiliation and slaughter in this country without insurance. "You didn't have none at all?" He was instantly sorry for what he'd said. It was none of his goddam business, and besides, he had to get to work, he had to get away from Sarah, and the sickness and death that seemed to be in the very air he breathed.

"Oh, I got life insurance. Ever penny I can rake together goes into life insurance. Been buying it since I was a young man. You want some more of this coffee? No? Anyhow, that don't pay off until you die. Got it all on myself. And they tell me my heart should of quit beating a year ago. Big as a watermelon, they say. My people all died of hearts big as watermelons. Don't know how I've lasted this long. Thank God for that heart anyhow. Leave the family in pretty good shape."

Pete could only stare. His brain felt numb. Cold and numb.

"Lots of things I don't understand, myself," said Mr. Leemer. "Hospital insurance or not, they got to let you in." He took the last swallow of his coffee. "But they ain't got to keep you."

Some of his mother's feeling and compassion Pete had thought long dead stirred in him and he could not help himself. "But Mr. Leemer—Henry—you don't mind me saying so, I know for a fact that there's agencies that . . ."

The blood ran high in Mr. Leemer's already sun-darkened face and he turned entirely away from Pete to speak. "I ain't never been on the dole. Welfare wouldn't fit me just right." He turned back to Pete now, a forced smile on his face. "We'll make it. We out of the woods."

Sarah came in and stood beside the fireplace. "Mama wants to talk to you." Mr. Leemer started to get up. "Not you. She wants to talk to Pete."

Pete said, "I don't think we ought to—"

"Just for a minute. To say hello."

To say hello? He didn't know the damn woman. But he could not find it in himself to resist when Sarah took his hand, and he allowed himself to be led into the little darkened room at the back of the house.

"Is this him?" asked the old lady in her phlegm-filled voice.

"This is him, Mama," Sarah said.

Pete could only glare at Sarah. This was him? Him who? What had Sarah told her about him?

Mrs. Leemer went into a coughing fit that sounded terminal. Sarah lit a Kool cigarette out of the package by the bed. The first deep hit the old woman took stopped the coughing and she only wheezed.

"You him?" she demanded through the wheeze.

"My name is Pete Butcher, mam," he said.

"You him then," she said, and fell back onto the pillow she had been straining to lift her head from.

She lifted a hand, thin as paper, and pointed a bony, trembling finger at him. It was, to Pete, like looking down the barrel of a loaded gun. "I've heard everything about you from Sarah."

"Yes mam," he said. He supposed she was smiling now, but he couldn't tell for sure. The strange twitch about her mouth could be from pain. He bent and touched her hand briefly. "I know it feels good to be home."

"I reckon your little brother'd feel good to be home too," she said bitterly, her eyes glittering black under her blue lids.

Pete caught his head in his hands. "Oh, Jesus, Jesus."

Mrs. Leemer said, again in her old bitter voice, "Jesus ain't gone bring him nowhere. It's you—"

Sarah stepped between them and stopped her mother. "I told Mama the thing I wanted most was to go for a walk, get out of this house." She cut her eyes to Pete. "I thought we would go for a walk. It's been such a long time since I been anywhere."

The old lady turned her head away. "Go then."

Pete made himself say what his mother would have had him say: "It was nice meeting you, mam. I hope your recovery is quick." Truly, he didn't care if she died before he got out of the room. Or at least he thought he didn't.

5

In the hallway, Pete stopped and took Sarah roughly by the shoulder. She leaned heavily against him. "Stop that, dammit!" he said. "What the hell are you trying to do? This has all got to *stop*."

"I don't understand," she said.

"Where did your mother find out about my little brother? Answer me, goddam you!"

"We all of us know about him, Pete. We've known it from the start. Poor thing."

"Never mind the *poor thing*. Who is the *we* you talking about and from which *start?*" He knew he wasn't making the best sense in the world but he felt himself angry enough to kill.

"Daddy and Mama and me is who I'm talking about. It ain't no shame in it. You ain't going to the university. You already went and come. Right after you rented that room over there, Mr. Winekoff was over here talking and he told us all about it. And it ain't no shame in finding out the university wasn't for you."

"Oh, goddam," said Pete taking his head in both hands. "Is it anything everybody doesn't know about?"

"I wish you wouldn't cuss at me like that. I don't deserve it. I ain't done a thing to you."

It was all he could do to keep from slapping her. He jammed both his hands into his pockets just to make sure he didn't. Because she was right. She had not done anything to him.

"Mama says she's gone find him."

For a moment Pete was too startled to speak. Then finally: "Don't you think I would have found him if he could be found? My goddam people put him somewhere they said I'd never find him. And by God, they were right."

"She says just as soon as she gets the money, she knows she can find him. She thinks blood ought to be together. She ain't herself right now, the hospital and all—if you knew her before you'd know how kind and good she is."

He almost wanted to laugh. As soon as she got the money! Well, let her say what she wanted to. She was fucking crazy is what she was. Or if she wasn't crazy she was so close to it the difference didn't matter.

"That Max Winekoff," he said, "I'll deal with that son of a bitch later."

"Try not to cuss, Pete. It's a beautiful day and Mama's back home and you taking me for a walk—which I haven't been on any kind of walk in a month of Sundays—so it's no need to keep on cussing. I can't understand why you keep on doing it."

He cut his eyes back to hers and stared hard, making her go pale. "I'm the one who doesn't understand. Have you lost your mind? Why did you tell your mama I was going to take you for a walk? Besides, I've got a goddam job. Why would I want to take you anywhere?"

"Because you care about me. Because you respect this house. And it won't hurt to take a day off from that old job."

"Are you crazy or just what?"

"Maybe I am," she said. "The only thing I know is I need to get out for a while."

He leaned down and hissed in her face: "The only thing I know is that I may break your neck if you keep on doing this to me."

"Doing what? What have I done to you?"

Mr. Leemer appeared at the end of the hall. "Is Mother resting all right?"

"She's doing O.K.," said Sarah. "Pete and me thought we'd just step out of the house for a while. Is that all right, Daddy?"

"I don't see why not. Mother and me'll be fine." He moved closer and put one of his enormous, stump-splitting hands on Pete's shoulder. "You take good care of this little girl, boy." He was not smiling.

"Oh, I will," Pete said. "I'll sure do that."

"Good," Mr. Leemer said, "good."

Pete, his jaw clamped tightly shut, went out of the house ahead of her, walking rapidly. She finally caught up with him on the blistering sidewalk.

"You don't have to go so fast."

"You said you wanted to go for a goddam walk, so let's walk."

"You shouldn't cuss."

"I can't help it when people are unreasonable. I haven't known you to do one reasonable thing."

"You haven't known me that long."

He kept walking fast and after about half a block she fell behind him, not much, just a step or two. He could hear her breathing and her feet slapping flat on the sidewalk. The heat was rising off the macadam street, off the curbstone, distorting everything.

"Where we going to?" she asked.

He did not look back. He didn't know where they were going, hadn't thought about it. But if she wanted to go for a walk he'd take her for one.

"To the zoo," he said.

"The zoo? What zoo?"

"The only one we got."

"I never been."

"You'll like it," he said. "They got yaks."

"What's a yak?"

"Kind a like a camel without a hump."

"I never seen a camel," she said.

He didn't answer but increased his pace. The thin slap of her feet fell farther behind him. When they turned onto Main Street, she called: "How far is it?"

For the first time, he turned to look at her. She was five yards behind him, her face flushed. He waited for her to catch up.

"It's only about two miles," he said.

"That's too far."

"The zoo is where we going, and that's how far it is."

She stepped off the sidewalk and ducked under a tiny pine tree that gave no shade. She sat down in some straw and looked up at him.

"I got to rest," she said.

"You might as well get up. We going for a walk."

She got up and then stepped out in the sun again. "I didn't mean for us to come out here and do like this. It's hot. I hurt."

"You hurt?"

To his horror, she reached up and gingerly took her breast, the one with something growing in it. "I don't feel good." She pressed her breast with the end of her fingers.

"Where do you hurt?"

She absently watched the cars going by in the street, leaving little rainbowed layers of oily combustion on the heavy air. "I hurt all over," she said finally.

He was relieved. He didn't mind her hurting *all over.* "You're not used to exercise," he said. "It'll be O.K. in a little while if we walk steady."

"I'm not able to walk steady. Not in this heat. If I could drink me a root beer I'd be a lot better. We might git the stroke out in this heat."

They were a littleway onto the bridge going over Trout River now. He stopped and took her arm and guided her hand to the railing.

"Hold on to this and we'll rest a minute," he told her.

"I need me a root beer."

"You see anywhere I could get you a root beer? Make it on to the zoo, and it'll be plenty to eat there."

"I need shade, too," she said.

"You see any shade around here? That's why we got to make it on to the zoo. Maybe it'd take your mind off root beers and heat if I told you a little something about myself."

She moved closer to him, pressing herself into his side. He turned abruptly and said: "I can tell you walking as easy as standing here, git you on in the shade with a root beer and let you watch a yak."

She locked her arm through his with a strength that startled him. "I got to hold on. I got the weak trembles. Besides, you can't walk too fast if I got ahold of you."

"We got to step lively if you want to sit in the shade with a cold root beer."

"I'm doing the best I can."

"That's what everybody says. But the best's not worth a shit sometimes."

"There you go, cussing again."

"Being a projectile puker'll make you cuss, make you do a lot of other things too." He hacked up a lunger as big as an oyster and spat it over the railing, and then turned and made her watch its long descent to the water.

"It's a long drop from here to the water," he said.

She stared at him, squinting from the sun. Her eyes cut first left and then right. There wasn't much traffic, and what little there was flew by in sunbursts of speed. Not another soul was walking on either side of the bridge. She held his arm tighter and squinted at him, but his face was dark in full shadow with the sun behind him. She could not see his eyes. "You hinting at something?"

He turned abruptly again and started walking, she holding his arm even more tightly than before. "I don't hint," he said. "Hinting is one thing I never do. What I'm doing is telling you a little something about myself."

"I wish you would. I don't hardly know a thing about you."

He took a deep breath and said: "When I was a baby, I was a projectile puker."

"A what?"

"A projectile puker."

"I don't believe I ever saw one." She had taken her hand away from her breast. She was smiling.

"There's nothing funny about it, not when something like that happens. It can cripple and maim."

"You ain't afflicted in any way," she said. "I can see that if I can't see nothing else. How long was you sick with . . . with . . . What was it you had?"

"I was a projectile puker and I don't know how long I had it. The thing about projectile puking is you don't remember it. My mother told me about it. Said nobody hugged me until I was four years old. They'd hold me as far away from them as they could even when they gave me the bottle."

"That don't seem right to me," she said.

"You or I would have done the same thing. We would if we had a baby that might send a solid stream of puke all the way across the room any minute of the day or night. It's just natural not to get too close to a thing like that." He was glad to see she had stopped touching her breast. "My mother told me all about how it was. She couldn't even hire anybody to take care of me. They were all afraid I'd shoot a stream of puke at them. Mom got so she couldn't stand me."

"Why, you poor thing," she said. She looked genuinely and deeply pained.

"Daddy couldn't stand me either," he said with some satisfaction.

"Wasn't there no medicine you could take?"

"They tried different things. None of it worked. Nothing to do but wait for me to wear it out. We've got to get a move on," he said.

Sarah followed him over the bridge. The steel gave off heat like a stove. He went just fast enough to keep her hanging behind his left shoulder. He thought she seemed stronger now that he had given her something to think about. Out in the middle of the bridge, he let her catch up with him. Her face was shining with sweat, and her thin dress stuck to the skin between her shoulder blades.

She said: "I'm feeling pretty terrible."

"Projectile puking is serious," he said. "In olden times, they would have left me out on a hill somewhere."

"Left you?"

"Sure," he said. "In the olden days, you started doing something like that they'd leave you out on a hill, let you starve to death."

"Oh, God." She had suddenly stopped there in the center of the bridge.

"Now what's wrong?"

"Don't holler at me. I got to go back. I got to see Ma."

"If that's what you want to do," he said.

But when he turned and started back across the bridge, she didn't move but leaned against the railing. "I can't make it. I'm sorry but I can't walk. You'll have to git me a cab."

"There's no way I can get a cab out here in the middle of the bridge. For God's sake, Sarah."

"You'll have to help me. I'm sick on my stomach."

He walked back to stand beside her and she put her arm around his shoulder. He took her hand and they started slowly off toward the end of the bridge, she sagging against him. Her face had been flushed red but now was leached to the color of salt. Her drooping eyelids had turned black. He tried to quicken the pace but she resisted. It scared Pete. What if she dropped dead out here on the bridge?

"You all right?"

She did not look at him as she whispered, "You nice to help me out like this."

He didn't feel nice. If he felt anything, he felt like throwing her over the railing. He was aware of the people flying by in cars staring at them, Sarah with her arm over his shoulder, still sagging against him. We the walking wounded, he thought. Jesus, and all the while he should have been at work. But he couldn't very well leave her on the bridge.

After they did finally get off the bridge, Pete called a taxi and they had to wait without shade on the grassy shoulder of the road because Sarah insisted she could not go any farther, not even to the little grocery store where he made the call, not even another fifty yards to the nearest tree. She was gasping and pouring sweat. And she had started with her breast again.

When the cab came at last, the cabby took one look at Sarah

and said, "The little lady get too much sun, did she?" Pete didn't answer. He saw that the cabby was watching Sarah massage and probe her breast. Some people had no shame.

The cabby persisted with his question until Pete said: "She'll be all right."

"Looks like she got too much sun to me."

"Yeah," Pete said, "I guess so." He hoped so, he desperately hoped that was what ailed her.

But when they got to her house, she wouldn't let the taxi leave. "Don't pay him. Make him wait, make him wait right here," she cried as she stumbled out of the cab and across the sidewalk to the porch. Pete waited by the cab for a few minutes and then followed her into the house. He found Mr. Leemer standing in front of the fireplace looking bewildered.

"Where's Sarah?" Pete asked.

"Back with her ma. She just went running on back there. Told me to stay out."

"She got too hot," said Pete.

"She seemed near bout crazy."

"I think she only got too hot."

"I hope that's it. I don't think I could stand nothing else."

"Daaaaddy!" It was Sarah, screaming from the back of the house.

Mr. Leemer knocked over a chair as he ran into the dining room. He was very pale and his eyes were wild. "Pete, you go on out there to the cab and don't let him leave. I've got to make a phone call to get Sarah in."

The whole house seemed to have gone crazy. "Into what? Where? Can you just tell me what's the matter?"

Mr. Leemer had the telephone book open and the phone out of the cradle. He was flipping pages madly. "Just git on out there and hold that cab. You'll be gone from here in a minute."

"But . . ."

"Go, son! We got a mergency here." By now Mr. Leemer was dialing.

Pete went back out to the cab and leaned on the window. "Hold it a minute, buddy. I don't know what's going on but it seems like we have to go somewheres else."

"I don't set in the goddam sun on a day like this for no goddam body," said the cabby.

"I know what you mean. It won't be long."

"Better, by God, not be."

Pete stood without moving by the front door of the cab for what seemed, because of the intense heat, a very long time. Finally Sarah came out of the house, seeming almost to stagger. "Come on," she said, opening the back door of the cab.

"Where we going?" Pete asked, sliding in beside her.

She made no answer but only stared grimly ahead.

The cabby looked at Pete. "Make up you mind, buddy. Y'all goin sommers or you stayin here? I'm bakin in this cab. I charge extry for settin in the sun."

"Git going," Sarah said to the cabby, her mouth still set grimly. "We don't have time to set and talk."

The taxi pulled away from the curb. "Where to?" asked the cabby. Pete looked at Sarah, who deliberately looked away from him. The cabby asked again, and when nobody answered, he said: "If nobody knows where we goin, pay me what you owe me, I'll let you out. I don't want nothin to do with nobody don't know where they goin on a day like this." They rode another half block in silence before the cabby said: "It's too goddam hot today to be messin with anybody crazy."

"Memorial Hospital. Emergency room," Sarah told him.

"That's better," said the cabby. "That's more like it."

"Why are we going to the hospital?" cried Pete. "Why the emergency room?"

"Anybody can see why, buddy," said the cabby. "I knew the little lady had too much sun."

"Daddy's calling the doctor," Sarah said. "He'll meet us there." She spoke calmly, looking straight ahead, but her color was really bad now. "Ma said it was the only way. It ain't a minute to lose."

"But you haven't said why we're going."

She looked at him for the first time since they got back from the walk. "You know why, you jackleg!"

In the front seat, the cabby chuckled and took a corner so fast it threw Pete heavily against Sarah. Their faces were nearly touching. They hadn't been so close since the night on the couch.

"No I don't," said Pete, and heard the lie in his own voice.

"It's why you quit."

"Quit?"

"On the couch."

"Couch?"

"Stop it!"

"Stop what?"

"Lying won't make it any better."

"Lying? Who the hell's lying?" And immediately he wished he had not said that.

"You'd rather climb a tree and tell a lie than stand on flat ground and tell the truth."

"I wish I knew what you were talking about." But he knew and he knew she knew.

"Respect Daddy's house, my foot!"

"I do respect it." He couldn't stop the lie. It was steamrolling on to God knows where.

"You ain't got the gumption of a blowfly. It's how come we didn't do it."

"Do what?" Jesus, Jesus, the fat was in the fire.

"*It!* You wouldn't even make love to me after you got me half naked! Now *that, that* right there is sorry."

The cab swerved when she screamed, narrowly missing a car in another lane. She was close enough to him now to take him by the collar and bite his nose off if she wanted to.

Her eyes were blazing. "And the same lump that kept you off me is the same lump that's taking us to the emergency room."

Pete slumped back against the seat and took a deep breath. "Jesus, Sarah, it's not done this way. Nobody goes to the emergency room with what you may or may not have. They go to a goddam doctor's office. There are tests to find out what's wrong. If *anything* is wrong. You don't go to the emergency room."

"Mama said it wasn't a minute to lose."

"Me backing off doesn't mean it's there, for Christ's sake."

"Mean *what's* there?"

Pete opened his mouth but couldn't speak.

"Cancer! You know well as me. Cancer!" she screamed.

In a voice barely audible, he said, "You said it, I didn't. But even if . . . if . . . if *it* was in there, you don't take the thing to an emergency room."

"Whose breast is it? Yours or mine?"

"Yours."

"Then shut up." She reached up and slapped the cabdriver on the side of his head. He'd been half turned in his seat, watching them, his mouth open, more than he was watching the road. "You paid to drive, not to listen to me."

The driver snapped around and ran the next two stoplights.

At the emergency room, the taxi stopped behind an ambulance while they got out and Pete paid the fare. They had to wait at the door for two men to wheel a bloody cot through. Whoever was on the cot groaned under the heavy gauze wrapping his face.

Once inside, Sarah sat in a chair by the wall. All the other chairs were filled with variously damaged people. The man next to Pete had his head wrapped in a bandage and his arm in a makeshift sling. At one end of the room, a nurse sat behind a desk filling out a form for a woman who held a screaming child.

"I think you have to go over there," Pete said, pointing to the nurse.

"I don't think I need to hear another word out of you."

The door opened and somebody was wheeled in on an ambulance dolly. The bandages made it impossible to tell whether it was a man or a woman. A panic was rising in Pete's stomach. He asked her again to go to the nurse behind the desk and she refused even to answer him.

He stretched his neck to breathe and said: "I wonder where the bathroom is."

He looked at her, and her eyes were not focused. Her thousand-yard stare went right through the other wounded and through the wall. He wondered if she knew he was there. "I have to go to the bathroom," he said. "I'll be right back."

She did not answer at all, and he went out the door and up the emergency drive and into the street, rushing through the thick, hot air like a swimmer flailing through water that might ultimately drown him.

6

That night Pete did not sleep at all. He tossed and turned in the sweated sheets of his bed and thought about everything he did not want to think about. Like a dog with a bone, he could not let it alone. He had deserted Sarah, terrified and alone. In the hot, steaming little room, he talked to himself constantly, but no excuse he could make relieved his scalding shame. What could he possibly have done if he had stayed? Nothing. Was he responsible for whatever she had (*cancer, cancer, cancer*)? Of course not. The answer to every question he posed absolved him of guilt, and yet it made no difference. He *felt* himself guilty, and nothing he could do would ever change it.

He could not bear the sight of the house next door, dark and decaying under the arching branches of the oak tree. But the house still impinged upon his senses. He thought he could hear it pop and creak, settling on its foundations. Toward dawn he made himself lie rigid and still in his twisted sheets. He seemed to feel Mr. Leemer and perhaps even the mortally ruined Mrs. Leemer watching him just on the other side of their dusty yellow window shades. Surely, sooner or later, Mr. Leemer would come looking for him. To say what? To accuse him of what? He didn't know. But lying utterly rigid and not moving even so much as a finger did not make it easier to bear.

In a kind of fugue state—he knew he was not asleep and yet it felt like sleep—he heard a banging at his door. When he opened it, Mr. Leemer hit him a frightful blow across the bridge of the nose. Lying on the floor watching the blood spread under his cheek, he felt an enormous sense of relief, wanted, in fact, for Mr. Leemer to kick him. But the kick never came and the blood slowly faded into the soiled sheets of his bed and he awoke not from sleep but from wherever he'd been, and his nose was not broken and he was not bleeding and he was alone in the room and he would have cried if he could. But the best he could do was lie in his bed rocking and groaning.

He got up and dressed quickly, and because he expected to see nothing of consequence, he turned and looked out of his window, and his whole world tilted. Surely he had stepped over the line all the way to crazy. Because there, on her front porch, looking calmly up at him, was Sarah, dressed exactly as she had been when he left her in the emergency room.

He went downstairs and out onto the boardinghouse porch, having no idea at all what he meant to do. Talk to Sarah? What in God's name might he say? There was nothing he could say, and yet he rushed out to the porch anyway.

And the problem was solved for him because Sarah was no longer there. All the shades were drawn in her house and it looked deserted. But then it always looked deserted. Maybe she had not been on her porch to start with. Maybe what he saw, or thought he saw, was only an extension of thinking Mr. Leemer had come to his room and punched him in the nose when, in fact, nothing of the sort had happened.

He ought to get his ass to work was what he ought to do. He'd already missed one day and the foreman would be in a rage, but just the thought of going down to the warehouse and standing in the boxcar made him feel like he was breaking out with hives and caused his stomach to pitch and roll. He knew he probably no longer had a job anyway. Missing one day's work could cost you your job at the Bay Street Paper Company. The foreman said at least ten times a day that he had not missed a day's work in forty years. He made it clear that sickness was not an excuse for missing work.

Pete had been so focused on Sarah's front porch, and on the fact that he was probably out of work now, that he did not hear Mr. Winekoff come out. But when he finally did hear a rhythmic breathing, punctuated with grunts and groans, he knew Mr. Winekoff was on the porch with him. Maybe Mr. Winekoff was the diversion he needed. Maybe he would drop him down the stairs another time or two.

He turned to see Mr. Winekoff windmill his arms and then suddenly drop into his habitual bend, knees locked, hands flat on the floor. The old man was watching Pete intently. "Breakfast's about over in there, son. Better git it while there's something left to git."

"My mind's not on eating," Pete said.

"It wouldn't be on doing your suitcase trick on the stairs, would it?"

"That wasn't a trick, it was an accident."

"When my handle broke, I guess you'd say."

"It felt like it broke."

"How can something feel like it broke when it didn't?"

"I don't want to talk about it."

"No, I don't imagine you would."

Pete took a step toward Mr. Winekoff, and the old man—without straightening out of his bend—scuttled crabwise another six feet away in a startingly rapid move.

"I'm not going to tote you up the stairs again. You don't have to worry."

"I ain't worried, because I'm not going to give you the chance." He scuttled even farther away as he spoke. Mr. Winekoff twisted his neck and stared up at Pete. "Things look better from down here. Blood rushes to the brain, massages the arteries. Look at me. I've got the arteries of a baby."

Pete only stared back at him.

"Well, then go inside and eat something, for God's sake," said Mr. Winekoff. "Don't just set there and wait to die. Death'll come soon enough."

"I'm not hungry. The thought of putting food in my mouth makes me want to throw up."

"Then it can't be but one thing. Proper exercise. How about taking that walk you been meaning to take out to the zoo and look at them yaks?"

Pete had never told him he meant to take a walk to the zoo and he sure as hell did not want to look at any yaks. But on the other hand, he knew he wasn't going to work, and he was afraid Sarah would appear again and he would not know what to say.

Pete said: "Seems as good a thing as any."

"What?"

"Go to the zoo."

"And see them yaks?"

"Might as well if we're out there," Pete said.

"That's more like it. You want to try to get something to eat before we go?"

"I already told you."

"You'll sure as hell eat when we get back."

"We'll have to try it before we know."

"Then let's do it." Mr. Winekoff straightened up and shook himself like some strange animal getting out of the water.

The old man was off the porch and into a hard-driving stride before Pete even moved from where he was standing. He had to break into a little jog to catch up. The old bastard could really walk too. Walking was a no-nonsense, focused, serious thing for him. They had covered a couple of blocks before Pete noticed that Mr. Winekoff's breathing was synchronized with his stride, synchronized to inhale every second time his right foot hit the sidewalk and exhale every second time his left foot hit. And his breathing was not only regular, it was noisy. Pete thought of pistons and drive wheels on steam engines. It was stupid and silly and enormously gratifying. It blew away the Burnt Nigger and the foreman and Sarah and her ruined mother and her father who had a heart big as a watermelon. Pete was beginning to enjoy the day and what he was doing with it, when the old man started talking about how intimate he had become with Chicago. Pete had never heard of Mr. Winekoff's intimacy with Chicago but he had heard similar stories. It wasn't really the story anyway, only that Pete would have preferred silence.

"I am very intimate—in the rigorous sense of that word—with Chicago." Mr. Winekoff read a great deal and would, from time to time, use a word like *rigorous*. They had stopped on the bridge going over to the zoo, stopped within twenty yards of where Sarah had collapsed. It was spooky and made Pete uneasy, seeming, as it did, prophetic.

"You and I are breathing Chicago," said Mr. Winekoff, holding on to the bridge railing and looking straight up.

"We are?"

"Look at that sky up there. Look at the air in front of your nose. We don't have enough industry here to cause that. No, that's coming from Chicago, all the way down here just to lie up there over our houses and sift down into our lungs. You could cut up this air and make cardboard boxes out of it. Yessir." He seemed now to be speaking with some satisfaction. "We're breathing Chicago, wearing it on our skins. Way down here on the Georgia-Florida border, we're more intimate with Chicago than lovers."

"I never thought about it," said Pete.

"Of course not. You nor nobody else, it seems like, or it wouldn't be like this. I wouldn't mind it if I was *in* Chicago, but I don't see why I have to be intimate with something a thousand miles away."

"It's something in what you say," Pete said. Maybe the old man was not a complete fool after all.

"From blue sky to blue air to blue lungs," Mr. Winekoff said happily, breathing deeply.

"I want to see the yaks," said Pete, although he did not, he only wanted to leave Chicago alone, because the way the old man had gotten him started thinking about it was rubbing him the wrong way.

"Ah, yes, the yaks." Mr. Winekoff started off down the bridge at a brisk pace.

He had told Pete a good deal about the yaks, starting up on them and never entirely leaving off. Turned out, though, they didn't look like camels at all. The old man straightened him out on that while they were still walking on the bridge.

"Like a camel?" said Mr. Winekoff. "Not hardly. More like an ox. In fact, a yak is the largest member of the ox family. What got you started thinking they might look like a camel?"

"Largest member of the ox family, you say?"

"Right. You got it *all* straight now."

But Pete had no idea what an ox family might look like. From what his brother had written him about Korea (this was before he put the twin indentations of a claw hammer between his little brother's eyes, lost his mother and father, and was slowly cut off from all of his blood kin), from his brother's letters, it put him in mind of a large bull pulling a plow through shallow water, out of which rose the effluvium of human shit, and followed by a very small, yellow Oriental.

Mr. Winekoff said yaks stood six feet high at the shoulder and they had long silky hair, beautiful hair unlike anything he'd ever seen. Oh, he was in for a treat, Pete was, besides the unspeakably wonderful benefits of a hike of two—four if you counted the return trip—miles over oven-hot streets that heat waves made undulate miragelike in the distance. Working a shift five days a week in a boxcar with George did not put you in shape for a walk like this.

"Is walking everything I said it was or what, you young puppy?" cackled Mr. Winekoff, dancing a little jig up ahead of Pete and never looking back.

He'd never called Pete a young puppy before. Nobody had that Pete recalled. He was a little startled that he did not take exception to it. Maybe it was the heat, but for whatever reason, he did not answer and kept plodding on slightly behind Mr. Winekoff. He did however, in that moment, realize that he was staggering along in the heat just behind the old man the way Sarah had staggered behind him. He kept his eyes fastened to Mr. Winekoff's back and said nothing.

"That's all right, you don't have to say a thing," Mr. Winekoff said. "I'm an old car with a lot of mileage but my carburetor is good. So I've been walking as hard and as fast as I can ever since I retired. You don't tell me a thing about walking day in and day out and I'll keep doing it till I get there."

Get where? Pete's benumbed brain struggled with the thought while Mr. Winekoff got back onto the subject of yaks. They came, he said, from the high desolate mountains of Tibet. That was the best thing, the old man thought, coming here all the way from Tibet. He thought that exotic, enough to make anybody wonder.

"What do you suppose they eat?" demanded Mr. Winekoff.

Pete had not thought about it. But now he did. It was something to do to try to keep his mind off the heat. The furnace blast of the sun seemed all the stronger now because they were off the bridge, and in the near distance he could distinctly see the green forest of trees that held the zoo.

"Hay, I guess." His tongue was thick with thirst and his lips felt wooden.

"What?" said Mr. Winekoff, still not looking back. "Speak up, boy. You sound like you got a mouthful of grits."

"I said I thought a yak might eat hay," Pete said, still having trouble with his thick tongue and unmanageable lips.

Mr. Winekoff did not miss a step, nor did he look at Pete. "Wrong. Your basic yak eats coarse, dry mountain grass."

"Oh," Pete said, his voice barely audible.

"You damn right," Mr. Winekoff said.

They were into the trees now, and the shade was almost unbearably wonderful and it revived Pete so much that he realized he had just been told a lie. Or maybe not a lie, but something was wrong. Jacksonville was a town full of itinerant sharecroppers and sons of sharecroppers who had drifted down out of Georgia when the crops failed, to sell their hands and backs to anybody or any business that had use for them. Consequently, everything about the sprawling place was poor. Pete knew he wasn't the only Georgia boy doing time in a suffocating boxcar with a Burnt Nigger. Coarse, dry mountain grass? Not in this lifetime. Not in this city.

He had read in the paper that the zoo had to sell its lion because it could not afford to buy horsemeat anymore, so Pete knew they weren't shipping in dry mountain grass from hundreds of miles away for something that looked like an ox.

As it turned out when they got it to the zoo—admission free if you were afoot or a dollar for a car, no matter how many were in it—the yaks did not look like oxen or even a member of the ox family, whatever that would look like (Pete found it impossible to even think about an ox *family*). Rather they looked like very tired milk cows without udders. There were three of them, so emaciated you could have hung your hat on their hipbones, and they were missing patches of hair—not long and certainly not silky—from their scabby hides and they were breathing heavily, their purplish tongues hanging from frothing mouths, as they leaned against one another in the sparse shade of a single tiny tree that was almost naked of leaves. They were enclosed in a wire fence about shoulder high, and in front of the fence was a sign that said all the things Mr. Winekoff had said, about how they were from the high, snowy country of Tibet, how their long hair could be woven into clothing, and all manner of other things that were obviously not true.

A number of small children stood about throwing stones at the yaks and eating cotton candy. The yaks did not move or seem to mind an occasional rock bouncing off their dusty hides, nor did the parents of the children object as they stood sweating in the oppressive heat. Pete leaned against the wire, his hands caught in it, stood there stunned, feeling little trails of sweat coursing down his body and an unhealthy anger building behind his eyes.

"Do these goddam things look any better in the wintertime?" he asked.

"They are fine animals and a long way from home," said Mr. Winekoff.

They are fine animals and a long way from home. So say we all, thought Pete, but it hardly answered the question he'd asked.

There was a number 3 washtub just inside the little enclosure.

There was something in the washtub. Pete leaned harder against the fence to get a better look. Corncobs. The fucking tub had corncobs in it. Old cobs naked of corn, and it was obvious to Pete there had not been any kernels of corn on the cobs in a very long time. They were desiccated and dusty and shriveled in the sun.

Pete was enraged. He wanted to bite the fence wire he was holding. "They're feeding these dying beasts corncobs."

And as if to prove what he had just said, the smallest of the three yaks staggered over to the tub, took up a cob, and chewed it. And chewed it. Slowly, regular as a clock ticking, its jaws worked over the cob. The animal's glazed eyes slowly closed and a small bubble of yellowish froth no bigger than the end of a man's little finger appeared at the corners of its mouth. And still it chewed.

Rage and hopelessness now building in him, Pete turned and walked away. Mr. Winekoff stood still as sleep, his hands in his pockets, nodding his old head in what seemed some satisfaction.

A short walk away—it could not have been more than fifty paces—Pete stood in front of an empty cage with a cement floor. It smelled strongly of piss. And a thought occurred to him that after the last red flash made the last dark mushroom cloud in the burning sky, it would still smell of piss. Lion piss. On a stake driven into the ground there was a sign—freshly painted, it seemed—that said LION. He stared at the empty lion's cage and at the track the lion had left in the cement pacing over the years, pacing and pissing and going quietly insane just there behind the bars, and he could feel the yaks over there behind him dreaming of Tibet and snow and long fine hair and useful yak lives.

How much lion piss would it take to saturate solid cement? How long could a yak stay alive on desiccated corncobs? How long could he, Pete, stand this? It would be a fine thing, he knew, to come out late some night and shoot the yaks, or maybe better, poison them. Shoot them for what? Poison them for what? There the thought got a little muddled in his head and he turned to see Mr. Winekoff still standing where he had left him, the two yaks still leaning against each other under the stunted tree, and the single small yak still chewing—doubtless on the same corncob, with froth at the corners of its mouth hanging in gummy strings, moving to the rhythm of its jaws. Mr. Winekoff's head, with its cap of clipped gray hair, moved almost imperceptibly too, nodding—Pete knew—keeping time with the yak chewing, and still chewing.

Pete started back over to Mr. Winekoff and saw for the first time, off to the left and not far away, another pen, with a wire fence not more than waist high. There were alligators in it. Huge alligators, lying totally motionless in the water as though they had been dead for years and were now preserved there under the shallow, slightly green water. They had come, no doubt, from the Okefenokee Swamp, along the borders of which Pete had been raised to manhood. He knew alligators. And he remembered them as great, black, shiny beasts, fast as cats in the cool, mossy water of the swamp. And faster still—over short distances—on dry land. Lying utterly quiet like some ugly monstrous plant rooted in the earth, an alligator could take a deer from twenty yards away. Did these here in the green water dream of cypress and moss and black water and bloody deer meat while a group of church school children pelted them with marshmallows? Pete hoped not. He hoped they thought and dreamed of nothing. And he realized in a flash of ugly recognition that such a state was what he hoped for—had hoped for since making an idiot of his kid brother—for himself. But that was impossible. No, not impossible. But possible only under the conditions of death.

He had moved up behind Mr. Winekoff. And quietly over Mr. Winekoff's shoulder, he said: "You worthless piece of walking shit, you brought me all the way out here to look at three dying animals."

Mr. Winekoff did not move or turn his head and his voice was dreamy. "High ranges of snow in the desolate mountains of Tibet. Plenty of mountain grass and long silky hair. Much beloved by the Tibetan people."

"We are not Tibetan people, you old fart."

Mr. Winekoff moved abruptly, as though yanked suddenly and rudely from deep sleep. He turned and looked at Pete. His eyes startled Pete. They were very red. His cheeks, a fine web of wrinkles, were wet. Could he have been crying? Pete could not remember ever having looked at Mr. Winekoff's eyes, and his cheeks were probably damp with sweat.

"And you come out here every day to do this?" said Pete.

"Every day. Every day for a long time now."

"How do you stand this goddam place?"

"Don't curse here. This is not a place for cursing."

"What is it a place for?"

"It's a place for . . . for . . . I don't know how to tell you."

"I don't have that problem myself," Pete said.

"Say what?" Mr. Winekoff cupped an ear with bent, arthritic fingers. "I don't hear well in the zoo. Sometimes I don't. Actually, most times I don't."

"Another problem I don't have. I hear good out here."

"That's why you ask dumb questions. That's why I can't tell you."

"What?"

Mr. Winekoff showed his deeply stained teeth in what might have been a smile. "Thought you heard good in the zoo."

"I do. My hearing's good everywhere."

"You say."

"Come over here. Little something I want to show you."

He took Mr. Winekoff by his thin shoulder and almost tenderly turned him, and Mr. Winekoff followed as Pete led him over to the enclosed alligators. He was not so tender with the church school children, who were still throwing marshmallows and screaming at the alligators. He jerked and pushed and actually kicked one of them, a pretty little girl with a mouthful of silver braces, incredibly thick and wired in every conceivable direction.

"You cocksucker," said the golden-haired girl he'd kicked. Her enunciation was clipped and perfect despite the braces.

When Pete had slammed his way through the children, making a little aisle for Mr. Winekoff to follow, he turned and said: "Them I know something about." He pointed to the alligators.

"Reptiles," said Mr. Winekoff.

"Reptiles your ass," said Pete. "What you're looking at is alligators."

"You ought to read more, son," said Mr. Winekoff. "They are *reptiles* and *alligators.* A mind is a terrible thing to waste."

Pete heard the pity in the old man's voice, but he was already so filled with the rage of the day that it had no effect on him. He just picked Mr. Winekoff up and threw him over the fence, where he landed in the scummy green water among the immobile alligators. Not a single alligator moved. But Mr. Winekoff never stopped moving. He was up. He was down. Then up again, his arms windmilling, but he could not keep his feet. Apparently the bottom of the pool was as thick with scum as the alligators themselves. The children screamed in delight. They stopped with the marshmallows and started searching the ground for pebbles with which to stone Mr. Winekoff, who was an easy target now because he lay very still in the shallow water. He had seen, as Pete had seen, an enormous bull alligator's tail move and his enormous head turn almost imperceptibly in the direction of the old man.

"Pete," said Mr. Winekoff, "this can only cause you trouble."

"Trouble? I've already got trouble," said Pete indifferently. A strange calm had settled on his heart. He was not happy. But for the first time that day, he was not unhappy. "Looks like you got the trouble now."

"There is much you do not understand," said Mr. Winekoff, lying very still, his head turned to regard the great green bull whose long saw-toothed jaws opened in what seemed to be a yawn, showing the deep mildewed pink of his throat.

The children were now utterly beside themselves. Several of them wet their pants as they danced and screamed and rained tiny pebbles down on Mr. Winekoff.

"Aren't you going to do something?" asked Mr. Winekoff, his voice as calm and steady as if he had been doing his bending and stretching on the front porch of the boardinghouse.

"Yes," said Pete.

"What?"

"Get out of this goddam heat."

Mr. Winekoff, with his curious calmness, eased to his feet, no longer paying the slightest attention to the great bull still exercising his jaws, and delicately walked out of the water, stepping over at least two alligators as he did. He came right up on the low wire fence where Pete was standing, dripping-wet green tendrils of scum covering his entire body, even hanging from his clipped and spiky gray hair. His eyes were flat and deadly as he stared at Pete, who felt something live and seemingly separate from himself lunge in his chest.

The beautiful, golden little girl kicked Pete viciously in the shins and screamed: "Do something, you shit!"

Pete slapped her hard enough to snap her head around, but she was quiet now and he saw for the first time a small group of men and women standing several yards apart from the children. They all wore little straw boater hats. Around each of the hats there was a paper band printed with the legend: FIRST BAPTIST'S SUMMER FOR CHRIST'S CHILDREN. As Pete watched, one of the men smiled and gave him a thumbs-up sign. When Pete turned back, the lovely little girl had a spot of blood in the corner of her mouth and the threat of killing in her eyes.

Mr. Winekoff still had not climbed the fence and stood on the other side of it, water and greenish scum slowly draining down his body. "I could have been killed and eaten," he said.

Pete was quiet a moment, his eyes locked with Mr. Winekoff's, before he said: "You can still be killed and eaten."

The old man climbed the fence and without a word to the screaming children, walked away. Pete watched him as he walked, much as a professional military man might walk, right past the yaks and right on out of the zoo, drawing no more than a curious glance or two from the few sweating couples ambling among the cages like sleepwalkers. Much later, when Pete had finally caught a bus, he passed Mr. Winekoff, his stride as strong and deliberate as ever, on the Trout River Bridge.

7

When Pete got back to the boardinghouse, he was not hungry despite having eaten nothing that day. But he was tired, very tired even though he knew there was no good reason for him to be. It would be easy enough to wait for supper, and he could—if he wanted to—load up then. He went straight to his room and drew his shades against the sight of Sarah's house next door. And then he did something that he had been doing with some regularity ever since that afternoon when he'd been nailing staples into fence posts putting up wire. He remembered.

He was on his knees, several staples caught in his mouth, one in his left hand, and the hammer in his right. His little brother was with him, though only four years old and too little to be of any help. But Pete loved his brother and liked to have him around and never minded the little boy asking endless questions that Pete could not answer. *Why is water wet? Why is fire hot? Why can you burn wood but not a brick?*

Pete placed a staple over a strand of wire, pressed the wire against the post, and drew his hammer back, swiftly and workmanlike, to drive the staple into the post. But as he drew it back, he felt the hammer strike something firm and meaty, as though he might have driven the claws into a side of beef.

It felt as if he had touched an electric wire, because in spite of there being no sound at all, he knew what he had done. He looked back and there was his little brother lying on his back, blood pouring out of twin indentations between his eyes—marks left by the claws of the hammer—blood a torrent now, running down into the bib of the boy's overalls. His eyes were rolled back into his head and still he had not made a sound, none at all. Pete had known his brother was behind him somewhere when he drew back the hammer to strike the staple, but had no notion he was right at his shoulder and close enough to be hit. For a long stunned moment he did nothing but watch the boy, whose left foot was twitching erratically, bleed. And his brother was never a little boy again, only something that shit itself and pissed itself and drooled and asked questions nobody could answer, because now he asked the questions in a voice and language no one had ever heard.

Since that time, Pete had been doing something he could not explain. Naked, he carefully examined his body in front of a mirror. And that was what he was doing in his room now. Maybe today it had been brought on by the savaged yaks or the empty lion's cage smelling of piss or the green, inert alligators lying in poisoned water too shallow to swim in, waiting only for death while suffering little children—and presumably anybody else who wanted to—to throw marshmallows and pebbles and God knows what else at them as they tried to sleep away a madness they could not understand, dreaming perhaps, as Pete thought the yaks must, of another, different time that was their home place, the place of their birth. Because whether the alligators had actually been born in the wild blackwater wilderness of the Okefenokee Swamp or the yaks in the high, snowy, nearly inaccessible fastness of the Tibetan mountains, Pete believed that both animals carried that knowledge somewhere in their blood and bone, scenes of their home places firing briefly and vividly now and again in their primitive brains.

of harmonicas, and the young man behind the counter said: "Thinking about buying something to blow, are you?"

"I was thinking I might."

"What did you have in mind?"

"Well, I don't actually play."

The young man said, "You'll want a Hohner's Blues Harp."

"Is that the best one for them that don't play?"

The young man smiled and his eyes seemed to sparkle. "The very best."

And so Pete bought the harp and walked home sawing it back and forth across his lips, seeming at times to hear in the noise he was making parts of tunes he had heard before, and mindless of people turning on the sidewalk to stare at him. If he had not been concentrating on his harp he would have thought to take the long way around and avoided walking past Sarah's house. But the longer he sucked and blew on the harp the more certain he became that he heard honest-to-God tunes. By the time he got to Sarah's, he was certain he could play "Taps" and the beginning of the "Marine Corps Hymn."

"That don't sound half bad, son." It was Henry Leemer standing slope-shouldered, his heavy hands half curled and one of his boots up on a chopping block in the shade of the oak tree at the side of the house. The voice itself startled Pete but what startled him more was the pleasant, almost cheerful note in the old man's voice. Pete stopped on the sidewalk, half turned, the harmonica still caught between his lips, and did not answer. "We've missed you, we have. Sarah's been asking after you."

Pete took the harmonica away from his mouth and asked, "How is she?"

"Fit as a fiddle. False alarm. Come right on back home. She's completely out of the woods, that Sarah is. Good a girl as a man could want."

"I've been real busy myself," said Pete. His lips had gone numb. The words seemed like angular bits of wood he was trying to spit out. They always did when he was lying.

"I know you have," cried Henry Leemer, suddenly becoming

Or it could have been started and sustained by the fact that the whole time he was growing up, his mother had constantly told him, "Take care of your heart and your heart will take care of you." She would, sometimes several times a day when he was shirtless in the summer, point to his bony chest and say: "Your uncles' hearts used to beat just like that." And he would look down and there between his ribs would be a tiny place where the skin pulsed. And she would point and say it again. She had four brothers, all of whom died with heart attacks before they were forty. Consequently, heart attacks were high on her list of favorite subjects to talk about, usually with a finger pointed at Pete's chest.

So today he stripped out of his clothes and stood before the warped mirror over his dresser and examined his pale body, watching particularly the place that still pulsed between his ribs. He had long since noticed that other people's chests often pulsed in the same way in the same place, but it made no difference. His mother had made him aware of the movement in his own and he would when he was young sometimes lie about on the bed or sit under a tree watching it for long periods of time. He could not have done otherwise.

Today after the sorry sight of the yaks, he examined himself from the nape of his neck to his heels, looking for blemishes or swellings or any sign of some difference from the last time he had examined himself, which had been the very day he deserted Sarah at the emergency room. But there was nothing. Nothing. And when there was nothing to find, he was vaguely disappointed, which made him wonder if he was some kind of pervert, because he realized how totally unnatural and irrational what he was doing was.

He went into the cramped little closet of his shower and scrubbed himself for a long time in the tepid water the boardinghouse provided. When he came out, he lay down on his bed, thinking not to sleep but only to wait for supper. But as soon as his head was on the pillow he was asleep, and when he awoke, he found he had missed not just supper but in fact the entire night—dreamless and dead to everything.

Instead of going down to breakfast (he did not want to see Mr. Winekoff), he dressed quickly and took a slightly longer way to work to keep from having to pass Sarah's house, which was still shut solidly behind the shade-drawn windows.

When Pete stepped through the door of the warehouse, he was met with the full blast of the bullhorn. "PICK UP YOUR PINK SLIP AT THE OFFICE, YOU WORTHLESS YOUNG DOG! AND DON'T EVER LET ME SEE YOUR FACE IN MY WAREHOUSE AGAIN! YOU DON'T COME TO WORK, YOU DON'T CALL! THE ONLY EXCUSE THAT WOULD SATISFY IS DEATH. AND GOD-DAMMIT, YOU AIN'T DEAD!"

Pete, surprising himself, walked right on past the foreman in his wire cage, not even looking at him, and back to the boxcar where George, sweat-shiny in the dimness of the car, was swinging blocks of cellophane onto the ramp that would roll them into the warehouse. He looked up and saw Pete.

"Oh, mon, ya feet in de street, Pete-Pete," he said. "I and I hear de horn."

"Jesus, that fucking little ape and his bullhorn does have a voice."

"Nuh horn, mon. Max, him tol me bout de shit."

"You heard about what happened while I was off from Max?"

"Mr. Winekoff. Him very old. Very good in de head, dat mon," George said. "Him by de house ta wash himself up some fo he go home. Ya do a bad ting ta him. Dat mon some dirty an stinkin him come ta de house. Very stinkin."

"I . . . I . . . couldn't help it."

"Ya on de bad side de magic now fo true, mon. Yeh."

"I ain't worried about the fucking magic."

"Ya talk lak dat, git back from me," George said, going back to swinging the cellophane.

"When did you see him?"

"Ya trouble in de ear lak ya trouble wit ya heart?"

Pete thought of his mother and the mirror and the pulse between his ribs. "I got no trouble with my heart."

"I tink mebbe ya do. Trow Max in de gators? I and I glad ya,

nuh me. An ya ear? Ya ask when I see him. I already tell. Max de mon wit de pride. A mon wit de power. He dent wan ta go up him house wit gator all on him."

"You don't know how it happened. The whole story."

"Linga show me no mon know de whole story. Magic know de story, mon." George reached up and pulled on two of his twisted dreadlocks for a long moment, staring at Pete as he did. Then he pulled a scrap of paper out of his pocket and handed it to Pete. "Ya ebber need, ya got, mon."

Pete looked at the paper, on which there was scrawled writin he could not read in the bad light. "What's this?"

"House. I and I wit Linga."

"Your house?"

"Ya need George o de Obeah woman Linga. Come."

"If I need?"

George went back to swinging bales of cellophane. "I got do d work now, mon. Ya don." He did not look at Pete. "Ya be in d care o God o Gods, Haile Selassie." Then George did somethin that surprised Pete about as much as if he had turned himself int a rabbit. George crossed himself.

"Yeah, I'll do that," Pete said, stuffing the scrap of paper in hi pocket.

Walking back home with absolutely no idea of what to do wit himself, nowhere to go, nobody to talk to, he passed a store th had a window full of harmonicas on display. To keep his mind o things (he did not want to be able to think about anything), h decided to buy a harmonica. His mother had always wanted hi to take up a musical instrument.

"You play a musical instrument and you can always pass th time of day," she would say. She herself played the banjo. (rather she played "Oh! Susanna" on the banjo. It was either th only tune she could play or else the only song his father cou sing. Pete was never interested enough to find out which, but was the only thing he could ever remember hearing them (together.

He went inside the store and stood in front of a glass case fu

very agitated. He threw his huge curled hands into the air. "We all have." What he said seemed a simple, if emphatic, statement of agreement. There was no accusation in it, or so it seemed to Pete, which for some reason deeply shamed him.

"I knew she was going to be all right," he said. He had absolutely no notion of what he was about to say until he heard himself say it. "I knew from the start it was nothing wrong."

"Well, women," Henry Leemer said, shrugging his shoulders. "Her mother and all, you know."

"I know," said Pete. "I know that." He not only did not know *that,* but he also was not really sure what they were talking about.

Pete raised the harmonica to his mouth and blew a few random notes, atonal and squeaking.

"I believe it's a split reed in that mouth harp."

Pete laughed and his laughter surprised him. "There may be a split reed in me. The harp's brand-new. Just bought it. But I don't know how to play it yet."

"You'll learn. If you just keep on sucking and blowing, it'll come to you. It's that way about most things in life."

"I guess," said Pete, looking at his harmonica.

The two men stood for a long moment regarding one another, until Pete could finally bring himself to say, "I got to meet this feller over at the boardinghouse, so I better be going."

Mr. Leemer said: "I guess you'll be dropping in from time to time."

"Dropping in?"

"Sarah and all, don't you know."

"Oh, yes sir, I'll be droppin in."

He went off down the sidewalk blowing his harmonica for all he was worth, not caring what it sounded like, only needing the sound as though to somehow distance himself from Mr. Leemer and what was in the dark, rotting house behind him. He, of course, did not have to meet anyone, but he wished he did, because he wished he had not lied. He wished it had not seemed necessary to lie. Lies helped nothing. He knew that, had known it for a long time, and known also that his whole life had become a finely wrought web of nothing but lies. Maybe that was not true, but that was what it felt like. Knowing all that, though, he also knew that if he had to go through the whole sorry exchange again he would have done exactly the same thing.

When he got to the boardinghouse, Max Winekoff was on the porch, leaning on the banister with both hands, examining the sky over the roofs of the houses across the street. He looked down at Pete, still on the sidewalk, and Pete stopped dead in his tracks holding tightly to the harmonica as though it were a lifeline.

"I saw you were talking to Henry," said Max Winekoff cheerfully.

Pete could think of nothing to say, and then he blurted: "His daughter's back from the hospital."

Mr. Winekoff regarded him, his bright pale blue eyes blinking rapidly. He was wearing clean and neatly pressed khaki trousers and a white short-sleeved shirt. *What about the goddam alligator pen?* Pete thought. *What about being a walking slimeball the last time I saw you?*

"I saw her come home in a taxi," said Max. He looked off again at the sky above the houses across the street. "Went over and talked awhile. Understand you went to the hospital with her."

What else did he understand? What else did he know? "Yes," said Pete.

"Yes? Yes what, son?"

"I went down to the hospital with her. Seemed the least I could do."

"She told me," said Mr. Winekoff, holding his maddeningly cheerful smile. "Indeed, indeed she did. Told me how you were the only one she wanted to go with her. Said you made her feel safe. Thank God, she got a clean bill of health, pretty young girl like that. Pain'll come soon enough. She's too young for that now though."

Pete would not go on with this. He refused. Why didn't the old man scream and curse and threaten? Pete could have taken that. But not this pleasant talk about how healthy Sarah was, without mentioning the shameful fact that he had abandoned her at the hospital. Winekoff must know, but he was not going to talk about it. That or the alligator pen either. Well, fuck it. Fuck whatever crazy notion he had in his head. Maybe he thought it hurt Pete more *not* to talk about it or get it out in the open, to pretend none of it happened. Well, if he thought that he was right.

Max Winekoff took a step back and sat in a rocker and threw his feet up on the banister. "Missed another day at work, did you?"

"I went," said Pete, "but they fired me."

Mr. Winekoff smiled, walked out on the sidewalk, and put his hand on Pete's shoulder. "Don't feel bad about it, son. A man's not worth a damn if he hasn't been fired. A really good man'll get fired more than some during his lifetime. Did myself. The thing to remember—and keep reminding yourself—is that we are fallible."

"Fallible?"

"Failed. We all got blind spots. Nothing you did at that warehouse made you less than the miserably failed human being you are."

Pete was not exactly sure what had been said to him. Was this the old man's way of talking about emergency rooms and alligators? If it was, Pete did not want any of that either.

"I got to get up to my room and take a piss," he said angrily.

"Never been a mother's son or daughter that didn't have to," Mr. Winekoff called after him as Pete bounded up the steps to the porch.

He went upstairs and lay on his bed and ran his already sore lips over his harmonica trying to find a tune. The notion that every single tune in the world was in there somewhere, caught in the reeds of the little harp, fascinated him. He would blow the thing, listening to the terrible noise he was making, and then take it away from his mouth and stare at it, thinking that it was all in there, knowing it was all in there if he could just find it. He thought that the harmonica was probably the best investment he had ever made in his life.

He didn't know how long he had been playing when the knock came at the door, but when it came, the dream of Mr. Leemer punching him in the nose rushed back upon him, along with the conviction that he *ought* to be punched in the nose, and he took his harmonica away from his mouth and lay very still on the bed. The knock came again.

"I know you're in there."

He got up immediately and went to the door because, thank God, it was only his landlady, Mrs. Jackson. She was a tall, bony, angular woman, a woman extremely fastidious about her person, although she did dip snuff, a fact that was only apparent when she spoke. She stood there in the doorway, her fists balled on her nonexistent hips—she was pencil-shaped—eyes mildly outraged behind her steel-rimmed glasses. With the exception of the old grandmothers and the old spinsters in south Georgia, Mrs. Jackson was the only woman Pete had ever known who wore her hair caught in a knot at the base of her skull.

"What is that dreadful sound?" asked Mrs. Jackson.

"Bought me a harp. Just learning to play it," said Pete.

"Don't you know there's sickness next door?"

"I don't think they can hear it."

"It don't matter whether they can hear it or not. You ought not to be in here blowing on that thing with sickness right over there next door." She licked her lips with her snuff-colored tongue. "Some people just don't have any feelings for the sick and shut-in. They're bad off over there. The three of them in that old house together and all of them sickly, one of 'm maybe dying. What ails you anyhow?"

The first thought that popped into Pete's head was: *I wish to hell I knew,* but he said, "Guess I just wasn't thinking."

"Well, I known that to start with, I spoke with Mr. Leemer just . . . He's as bad off as they are. Maybe worse."

"Jesus," Pete said. "What's he got?"

"Them."

Mrs. Jackson reached into his room and took the knob and slammed the door shut in Pete's face. Pete drew all the shades in his room and put his harmonica beside his shaving gear on the dresser and lay again on the bed. He could never have brought himself to say it, but Mrs. Jackson was right when she said that

Mr. Leemer was as bad off as the two women. He was an old man and getting ready to die himself with a heart as big as a watermelon, and his wife was wounded and his daughter was scared to death that she was going to end up with her mother's wounds. Well, there didn't seem to be any end to the number of bad things that could happen to you in this world. But he had always known that.

He started by peeping under his own window shade. Raising the shade just a little, the tiniest bit, he watched the house next door and, when it got dark, watched the lighted windows and wondered which one Mrs. Leemer might be behind, her new wounds healing. Or maybe not healing. That was the way it started but before two hours had passed, he had the shade up a foot, knowing full well that anyone looking back from the house could see him. It was the notion of his own guilt that made him look but it was also the notion of Mrs. Leemer's wounds and scarred and lacerated chest. The wound, what it might look like. Because as much as he had always—for as long as he could remember—hated and feared anything personal because anything personal always held something tragic, despite that hatred and fear, hurts and wounds, any bleeding or mutilation, always made him want to see, made him want to know. Know what? He didn't know. At the same time he knew this to be true, he felt it ran counter to his own nature. It was more than troublesome; it sometimes made him weep in the night. But there had never been a hell of a lot he could do about it, or so he was convinced. And so he had the shade up at first a few inches, then a foot, and then even that would not do and he pulled the shade back down and left his room.

Down on the front porch of the boardinghouse in the dark, Pete had no notion of what time it might be; he was again leaning against the banister looking at the house across the way. Without really knowing what he meant to do or wanted to do, he went out into the yard between the houses, which was nearly as bright as day under a heavy full moon. Drawn closer still to Sarah's house for reasons he could not have named, he finally found himself standing directly outside her window. The shade of the window was up a foot or so and he could see into the room, which was empty except for a single bed and a dresser and one ladder-back chair. A cover of *Life* magazine was tacked onto a far wall.

His face was only inches from the screen, when the door opened into the room and there was Sarah standing in the same simple print dress she had worn that night on the couch. And in stunned shock, Pete thought, My God, my God, now along with everything else I've become a Peeping Tom. Her color was pale but aside from that she did not appear much changed from the day he had abandoned her in the emergency room. He watched fascinated, not wanting to watch but watching anyway, wondering if she would take off her clothes, if she was about to go to bed. He knew he wanted to see the sick tittie, the one with the stone in it. In the fumbling and thrashing on the couch, he had not really seen it. He'd had it in his mouth but he had not had a good look at it.

He stared in spite of himself as she moved about the room with no apparent purpose, going first to the dresser to look into the mirror and briefly touch her hair with her hand and then to the bed, where she pulled at the corner of the spread and straightened again and looked directly toward the window where he stood. If he could have he would have bolted and run but he could not.

He stood looking straight through the screen wire into her face as she looked straight back at him, and he wondered if she could see him but he thought no, it was impossible. She was in the light and he was in the darkness and she could not see him. And then in a horror of fascination, he watched as she walked right across the room toward the screen and bent and, with her face only inches on the other side of the wire, looked directly into his eyes and said, "Hello there, Pete."

He could not at first speak but then finally managed to say, "Hi." The juvenile informal sound of the word when he said it to her broke his heart because against that word were all the images flooding his mind: the night on the couch, the walk to the zoo, her near collapse on the bridge, and the dreadful maimed people in the emergency room where he had finally abandoned her. But she only smiled. He wished that she would shout at him, curse him, revile him in some way that would relieve his sense of guilt and betrayal, but she did not. Instead she only held the steady smile as though they had somehow come across one another in a supermarket in front of the vegetable bin, as though it were the most normal thing in the world for him to be looking through her window in the middle of the night after she had come home from the hospital and he had not had the decency even to visit her.

"How you?" she said.

It was, of course, the very thing he should have said. If anybody should have been inquiring after the health of anybody he should have been inquiring after her health.

"Fine," he said. "I'm fine."

"I'm doing all right now too," she said.

"Listen, about that day in the emergency room, I . . ."

"Nobody likes a hospital," she said. "I didn't like it myself. I don't know anybody that ever has."

And in a moment of confession that he had not intended he said: "It was just a sorry damn thing I did. Look, I don't know what to say. I . . ."

"It ain't nothing to say," she said. "And it ain't nothing needs saying."

"Yes there is, Sarah. There's a lot needs saying and I wished I could say it. I wished I knew what it was to say, but I don't. But I know how I feel and I don't feel good. I . . ."

"Well," she said in the easiest conversational tone, "I'm feeling real good myself."

"That's not what I mean. You know that's not what I mean."

"Yes, I know."

"I wish I could tell you."

"You don't need to. I know." She paused and then: "They didn't have to take it off."

Oh, God, he thought, a little stab of exhilaration moving in his heart. If it had happened, if they had had to strap her down, put a cone over her nose, put her to sleep, and rip a breast off, she would be telling him all of it now. In excruciating and maddening detail, she would tell it.

There was a long sustained pause—a silence—in his mind and heart and then he realized he would have loved to hear it. This was personal in a way other things were not personal. This was not some bloody-seated little man in San Francisco whose name he did not know, whose life he did not know. This was Sarah. He had had his fingers on the wet peeled plum of her womanhood. He had had the dark hard jut of her nipple in his mouth.

So, he realized with a start, he was almost sorry that it did not happen, that she had walked out of the hospital whole. Otherwise he could have—*would have because she would have had it no other way*—heard it all.

He could have gone directly into the house and stripped her and examined the place where the knife had been. She would have let him. She would have wanted him to. She would have hated to let him see but *demanded* that he see in the same instant. And it would have been much the same with him. He could not bear the pain of it and he could not deny himself the pleasure of it. Well, pleasure. Maybe pleasure was the wrong word. Necessity. Maybe he could not have denied himself the necessity of it.

He did not understand. He was confused. It was as though something had come loose in his head, the thing that made thoughts cohere, the thing that made sense of his actions and the actions of the world.

She smiled and it seemed a pained smile. "They didn't have to take a bit of it. It was bad there for a while, not knowing and all, and being punched and probed and X-rayed and everything. But it wasn't all that bad. Them things can't be good. Not knowing can't be good, though, either."

"No," he said. I should have been with her. *I should have been with her.* Just knowing I was in the building, knowing I was somewhere out in the hall, would have been *something.* But I ran.

"But the way it was, well, it just wasn't as bad as it could've been," she told him.

And then there was another thought and he could almost see her thinking before she finally said, "But then almost nothing ever is as bad as it could be, is it?"

"No," he said. "I don't guess so."

But he felt the lie solid in his mouth as he spoke. Things could be every bit as bad as they could be. Or so he had always thought. He had never understood people who said that things could always get worse. Sometimes things could not get worse. They couldn't get worse because they took you right out to the limits of your strength, of your endurance, to the place where you had nothing left. He knew that. He had found it out with a hammer in his hand.

"Well," she said, "I thought to go to bed."

"I guess I ought to be doing the same thing."

"I'm feeling real strong," she said. "Like every minute, I feel stronger . . . and safer."

He thought: Everything can come back and get you. *Everything.*

She stood behind the screen obviously waiting for him to leave, but he did not move. "How's your mother?"

There was a long pause. "She's already up and around. But she . . . she pretty much stays in her room right now. But just like me, the worst is over for her. And she's getting better because she's so mad."

"Mad?" It jarred Pete, the word.

"As a hornet's nest," said Sarah. "Didn't you notice?"

He did, in fact, notice, but he said, "Not really."

"She stumbles around back there in her room saying, 'This just pisses the shit out of me!' " Sarah gave a gaspy little laugh and covered her mouth with her hand. "If you'll pardon my French?"

"I don't blame her for being pissed. I'd be pissed too."

"I don't guess it helps none though."

"It might."

"Yeah, it might. Anything *might.*"

Pete made no move to go. And then finally: "I guess I'll be seeing you then."

"Oh, yes," she said brightly, "I do hope you'll be seeing me." She stood very still and held his eyes with her own. "I *know* you're going to be seeing me."

The next day he did not go to see Sarah but he did not avoid her either. Twice before noon, although he had no job to go to, he passed in front of her house for no particular reason, each time slowing his pace a little, looking toward the house, and each time seeing no one, walking on a little way, and then finally coming back. The third time he passed the house in the late afternoon, her father was standing in the woodyard. The old man called to him and walked from the shade of the oak tree out to the sidewalk where Pete had stopped.

"Hey," said her father. "How you doing today, son?"

"Pretty good, sir," said Pete. "How about yourself?"

Mr. Leemer looked back toward the house and then to Pete again and said, "Oh, everything's coming along just fine."

Pete, thinking they had said all there was to say, started to move off down the sidewalk.

"She said to tell you your room was ready."

Pete stopped but did not turn to look at the old man. With his back to him he said, "My room?"

"Sarah fixed you a room. Up there."

Pete turned and saw him pointing to the second floor of the house.

Mr. Leemer said: "We ain't used that second floor in a long time. Some junk up there, I guess. Stuff you store you might need, you know. But it is three rooms up there and Sarah's done cleaned up one and fixed it for you."

"I'm sorry, Mr. Leemer, but I don't understand," said Pete. "I didn't say anything to Sarah about a room. I got a room over at the boardinghouse."

The old man stood for a moment and then looked down and lifted his left shoe as though he was going to examine the sole of it. Then he looked back up at Pete and said: "Well, we heard you lost your job and we thought to help you out maybe. Thought you could even help me on the woodyard out here. I could use a little help. We could all use a little help."

"How did you find out about me losing my job?"

"I didn't mean to pry. We don't pry. Mr. Winekoff, he come over to see the wife and we was talking and he told me how you lost your job down at the paper company where you was working, while Sarah was in the hospital." Henry Leemer coughed and looked off again toward his house and then back at Pete. "Jobs is hard to come by today. And I could use some help myself on the woodyard. Might not be able to pay you much, much as you was making at the paper company. But we known you was going off to college here at the end of the summer." He paused a moment to consider his shoe. "I'm all for an education. Didn't get one myself. But a man without an education ain't got much. Sarah just thought you could use the room up there. Ain't nobody else using it. Wouldn't cost you nothing till you got on your feet." He examined the sole of his shoe again and then in what was to Pete obvious embarrassment said: "We only meant to help out. We didn't mean to pry."

Pete said, "I didn't mean to say you were prying, Mr. Leemer. And that's an awful nice thing for you to offer to do for me, but I couldn't take your room for nothing that way."

"Oh, it wouldn't be for nothing," said Mr. Leemer. "I mean, I know nobody wants no charity. What I'm saying to you is that you'd *be* working. Most of the work I do in the woodyard is in the summertime getting ready for the people who burn wood in the winter—oil prices and stuff being what they are, you'd be surprised how much wood folks burn—and with the sickness in the house and everything I ain't cut the cords that I should've cut. To tell you the honest truth, you'd be doing me a favor to move in and help me out on the woodyard. I got a nearly brand-new crosscut saw, still brand-new cause I ain't had nobody to put on the other end of it."

Pete hesitated. "I do need a job. But it just seems too much for you folks to do for me."

"Sarah's done got the room fixed up. It wouldn't hurt nothing I guess to look at it, would it?"

"I guess it wouldn't," said Pete. The old man turned abruptly and went back to the woodyard and Pete walked toward the rooming house with his heart curiously lifted and feeling more optimistic than he had felt in days.

That night a little after dark, he walked next door to the Leemers' house and when he knocked, it was Sarah who answered.

"You come to see the room." She made it a statement and not

a question and, without waiting for him to answer, turned and walked back into the living room. He followed and it was as though it were the very first night he had been there, the night they had had the chicken backs and wings and he had discovered what he thought to be the secret of her breast. Mr. Leemer was nowhere about and there was not a sound to be heard anywhere in the house. He could not help but think of Mrs. Leemer lying in the back room, breathing shallowly, forever mutilated, waiting for the only thing she could possibly expect: death.

He was suddenly sorry he had come but Sarah walked on through the living room and turned left into a narrow little vestibule and started up some stairs. There seemed no alternative but to follow her. The only change in her he could see was that she was paler and somehow her walk was different. As though the center of balance in her body had shifted. It was a hesitant walk, tentative: it seemed to Pete to be the walk of someone who had just come from under the knife and who was recuperating from what could conceivably be a chronic and ultimately terminal illness. The very word *cancer* had the smell of death about it. Or at least it did to him, and he thought that probably everyone he knew always sensed death in the word. He knew without even having to think about it that just the notion that she might have—no, *did* have—cancer had changed her walk, her color, her very sense of herself. No doubt in the back of her mind somewhere she was afraid—maybe convinced that the examining doctors at the hospital were wrong and that she did carry the seeds of her death in her breast, just as her mother had. Doctors, after all, could be wrong. She carried with her now, and would perhaps forever, the acute knowledge of her own mortality. It was, for God's sake, a national campaign to associate cancer with death. It was enough to strike fear into the heart of anybody. Then why did he feel so lighthearted, optimistic?

At the top of the stairs there was a single bulb hanging from a black cord, rather a dim bulb but one giving enough light that Pete could see in a single instant that for years this place had been the storehouse for all manner of things. It could only be the debris and sloughed-off refuse of several lives going back over a long period of time.

Dark cobwebs hung where the ceiling met the walls, the walls themselves discolored, damply calcimine. And everywhere he looked all down the halls and in the large room giving off the top of the stairs—a room that looked as though it might have once been a kitchen for an upstairs apartment—everywhere he looked were enormous stacks of newspapers, most of them tied in bundles, and piles of old magazines and enormous balls of twine and things big as basketballs that looked as though they might be crushed aluminum. Old furniture—cracked ladder-back chairs, sofas with stuffing spilling out of them—tilted at odd angles, and in one place against the corner there appeared to be an enormous birdcage. He could not imagine himself living in this place.

8

Sarah never even stopped at the top of the stairs or looked behind her but went directly down the hall, and he followed her into a room where she touched a switch by the door; the light that came on was as dim as the one hanging in the hall but the room itself was immaculate. The floors had been scrubbed and waxed. The windows were clean and the furniture, though it was much like the furniture back at the boardinghouse—a dresser with a mirror, a chest of drawers, a single bed—was old and heavy and well made, and looked as though it had been wiped recently with some sort of polish that made it show the old good grain of the wood.

She looked at him and smiled. "What do you think?"

"It's great," he said. "It's a great room."

"You'll like it here."

"I told your daddy it was a fine thing for him to offer. But I don't think I can do this. I don't even know you folks and for you to give me a room like this . . ."

"Don't know us? Pete, I thought we knew each other."

"You know what I mean."

"No," Sarah said. "I don't think I do."

She went to sit on the edge of the bed and watched him through narrow serious eyes. "Tell me about the yaks," she said.

"Yaks?"

"The yaks we was going to see. Tell me about them. Mr. Winekoff said that you and him went out to look at them a couple days ago. That you went out there to look at'm while they was looking at me in the hospital."

"Mr. Winekoff talks a lot."

"Mr. Winekoff is a good old man. He doesn't mean anything. It's not anything for him to do all day but walk around and talk to his friends."

"Yeah," said Pete. "We went out there."

"And you saw the yaks?"

"There were three of them," Pete said.

"Why won't you tell me about them?" She touched the bed beside the place where she sat. "Come here and tell me all about how it was with the yaks."

Pete went reluctantly and sat next to her on the bed. "There's not much to tell. They were inside a big fenced-in pen."

Sarah said, "I don't know why it is but I thought about the yaks a lot when I was at the hospital. I guess it was because we was on the way out there to see them when I took down sick, or thought I did. I guess I just got the heat. It had been so long since I'd been out of the house and I was looking forward to seeing them yaks. But you can tell me about them and maybe sometime, well, when I'm feeling better—I somehow don't feel real good yet—we could even go see'm together."

Because Pete could not keep his eyes off her breasts, which looked exactly as they had the night he had been with her on the couch, because he could not keep from wondering what they looked like under the thin print dress—he couldn't get it out of his mind they'd somehow changed—and because the focus of his eyes and his mind shamed him, he started talking about the yaks, telling her all the lies that were on the sign and all the lies that

Mr. Winekoff had told him about how beautiful they were, Mr. Winekoff apparently believing everything he said despite the fact that the sorry animals inside the wire pen contradicted all of it. "Well, to start with," said Pete, "yaks come from Tibet and—"

"Whereabouts is that?" asked Sarah.

"Now listen, Sarah, you got to understand there's a lot about yaks I don't know. Including about Tibet. I don't know exactly where it is. I know it's way off yonder somewhere and it's real high country and full of snow and like that, and because it's full of snow, yaks have this long thick hair, really beautiful hair, hair just as shiny as you could ask for, and they say the people that live in Tibet make things out of the hair like clothing—"

"They make their clothes out of hair?"

"Yes," said Pete, "that's what I'm told. They make clothes out of yak hair. They do other things with yaks too."

"I don't think I'd like to wear nothing next to my skin made out of hair. It don't seem natural."

"Well anyhow, they're like oxes, yaks are, the biggest member of the ox family."

"Ox family?" Sarah said. "I don't believe I ever heard of a ox family."

Pete went on with it, all of it, feeling sillier and smaller and more fraudulent, and as he went on trying to explain, somehow sensibly, all that he knew to be a lie about ox families, doing it all to keep his eyes from that one right breast, although he knew it had not been altered—the very one he had had his mouth on, had felt the knot in (if the knot was not cancer, what was it?)—although he knew it was whole, unscarred, the same way he had left it that night on the couch, in his mind it *had* been altered forever, reshaped on a sterilized table under a knife. He tried desperately to keep from wondering what he did not want to wonder, and also to think of a way to get out of the room.

He talked for a long time and told even more lies than were on the sign in the yak pen. He was not very inventive in his storytelling but he did the best he could. He described the miserable animals—making them everything but miserable—shut up in the wire enclosure, elaborating at great length on how tall they were—they had now grown to eight feet at the shoulder—and how noble—they were noble animals—and how luminous their eyes were and how their fine great ears stood strangely from their marvelously sculpted heads and how mysterious it all was even in the midst of the tourists eating cotton candy and throwing peanut shells over the fence to the bemused, stunned yaks standing not in their mangy and damaged hides but in hides unlike any other in the world.

Sarah had grown progressively more excited. "Oh, I want to see them yaks. We have to go and do that."

"We could," Pete said, a little caught up now in the image of what he did not see at the zoo. "We'll go and see the yaks. It's plenty of time."

"I'm as strong as I ever was. Stronger really because I thought it was something wrong with me." She ducked her head before going on. "You know, Ma and all."

"I know."

"It's just that sometimes you think something's happened to you but then it didn't and sometimes it's a long time before you know for sure it didn't. It just kind of lives on . . . what *didn't* happen, in your head."

"I can certainly understand that," Pete said, although he did not think he understood any of it.

And then in a gentle, surprising move, a movement that was in a sort of slow motion, or at least felt that way, Sarah leaned toward him sitting there on the mattress and put her arms around his neck and pressed her mouth against his mouth, gently, in a kiss as soft as any mother's.

"I guess we might as well have it all out right now," she said.

Pete sat straighter on the bed. *It?* What, her breast? Out? Out of where? Her blouse? He wanted it; he didn't want it. And the whole thing unnerved him. A man ought to know what he wanted.

"I know you must be wondering," she said. And then when he did not answer, and he felt how blank his face must look: "You have to be wondering."

"I guess I am." He was not really sure what they were talking about. "If I understand you right, then I probably am wondering."

"Pete, you gentle and good man, you understand."

Well, if they were going to get it out in the open they might as well get it out in the open. "Understand about what, exactly?"

"My tittie."

He felt something grab at his heart and he felt light-headed. That word in her mouth. That nippled womanthing in *his* mouth. "Your tittie?"

"What you felt. What it was," she said.

"Felt?" he said.

"The hard place, not like a tittie at all."

God, he wished she'd quit saying that word; God, he wished she would say it the rest of the night.

"A tittie is supposed to be soft. I know a man wants it soft. And it must startle something awful if it's not."

"Not what?" The word repeatedly in her mouth had slowed his mind and he was not keeping everything very straight.

"Soft," said Sarah. "And it must startle if it's not soft."

He did not, could not, speak.

"The other one is soft."

"Yes," he said, not knowing at all what he was affirming, or that he had even spoken.

She reached over and took his wrist and placed his hand on her left breast. His fingers felt numb, and he was suddenly aware that his cock was hard.

"Squeeze it," she said, leaning toward him so closely that he could smell her breath. It did not smell sweet, but it smelled good. Thick with a musky saltiness and something else he could not put a name to, but he knew he must know what it was. He felt like he had been born knowing what it was.

He closed his hand on her breast. Gently. As though he thought it might be tender.

"You can do it harder," she said, and the smell on her breath that he knew and did not know was stronger. It was not only in her mouth, it was in the room. "Feel it as good as you want to."

Pete thought his cock would burst, and when he spoke, his voice sounded as if he had a bad cold and it trembled.

"You don't feel a thing but tittie in that one, do you?"

"No. Just . . . just you."

"Does it feel pretty?" Now her voice was as coarse as his.

"Yes."

She took his hand and moved it to her other breast and immediately he felt the hard place, the lump, distinct, isolated. But his cock grew harder and his balls actually hurt.

"See, I knew all along it was in there. It was in there before Ma ever discovered she had to have one taken off. But I was scared. I couldn't make myself tell anybody. And then she had the other one off and it just tore me all to pieces."

Pete was not really listening. Every sense he had was focused in his cock and the delicious ache that had started in his balls and the hard place in her breast that did not seem so hard now or so unusual or offensive at all. It only seemed part of her, and he wondered that it had ever shocked him or made him react the way he did. The very tips of his fingers closed over the solid place, but very tenderly. He was dumbfounded that he *wanted* to feel it. He did not think of her nipple, of taking her nipple between his thumb and forefinger, of taking her nipple in his mouth. He was fixated on what had only frightened him before.

He had been looking at his hand on her breast, and when he looked up, she was smiling. It seemed to him the most lovely and accepting and caring of smiles. It had been a long time since he had seen such a smile directed at him, and he knew exactly how long, could pinpoint the time exactly: since before the claws of his backswung hammer buried themselves in his brother's forehead.

"It's not sore," she said. "Or tender. And it's nothing to worry about. A lot of women have them. I just didn't know." The smile left her face. She looked on the edge of tears and her voice changed. "I just didn't know."

"But you know now," he said, "and it's all right." He did not take his hand away from her breast or the lovely knot his fingers touched, not so tenderly now.

"And I wouldn't have you," she said, smiling again, "have you here sitting on the bed with me. Touching me."

"I don't understand."

"Once I found it, I didn't let anybody see it or touch it or know about it. Then I met you. And I didn't know you. So you didn't matter. Don't look like that. I don't mean it that way. You were just somebody. I thought I could have you over and you could feel it and you would know because you weren't a boy but a man and you would know when you felt it and you would do whatever you did and then I would know. You were like . . . like a stranger. The way a doctor is a stranger. So you can let a doctor touch you anywhere. Because he doesn't matter." She covered his hand with her hand on her breast. "You matter now. Don't be afraid. It won't hurt me."

"I'm not afraid," he said, and he was not.

She took his hand away from her breast and put it back in his lap, and when she did, he felt her touch his cock, felt her press it, and then felt her trace the vein in the top of it all the way to where it ended against his body. She leaned forward and put her cheek beside his cheek and briefly touched the lobe of his ear with her tongue and whispered: "You sweet darling boy."

Without even meaning to, he moved her hand with his hand just slightly in his lap. Very gently she took her hand away.

"You go over to the boardinghouse and get your things now," she said.

"Jesus," he said. "Now?"

"Now," she said quietly but firmly. "There's a right time and a right place for everything. Last time was wrong. Next time will be right. Wasn't last time the wrong time?"

Pete knew his cock did not want to hear anything about right and wrong, but he said: "Yes, last time was the wrong time."

"And next time will be right."

"Next time?"

"Next time," she said. "Daddy lives by that. He says it's true but we just don't want to believe it. I'm sorry about it but even when you lost your parents . . ."

Pete suddenly forgot about his cock and everything else he'd been thinking. "Did that fucking Winekoff tell you that?"

"Don't curse when there's no call for it, Pete. There's even a right time and a wrong time for that. But no, darling, my daddy told me you lost your parents . . . and how you lost'm. Horrible. But they gone and we here. Now, go get your things and bring them over here."

"I could bring the stuff in the morning," he said. "It would probably be easier."

She put her arms loosely on his shoulders and balanced him in her steady gaze and said: "I think now is the time."

He was quiet a moment, then sighed and said: "O.K. I don't have much. It won't take long."

"It's all right. You take as long as you like. Now we got all the time in the world."

He left her sitting on the bed and walked to the door. Before he could open it, she said: "It's got a name."

He looked back at her. "What's got a name?"

"What you felt in my breast. What you felt that first night and what you felt just now."

"That don't matter to me."

"It does to me. I want you to know. I want you to know everything about me."

He paused and thought about that. Even now he sure as hell did not want her to know everything about him. And he was not at all sure that he wanted to know everything about her. He couldn't anyway. He knew that, if he knew nothing else. But she wanted to tell him and he remembered the smell of her breath and the touch of her tongue on his earlobe and her wonderful hand and he had no choice.

"What?" he said.

"The name?"

"Yes."

"A fibroid cyst. A lot of women have them. Maybe even most women. It's not something that will kill you. Some women have more than one. It doesn't matter a bit if it doesn't matter to the woman's man."

He smiled. "That makes it easy then. It doesn't mean any more to me than a freckle on your face."

He left her smiling, her beautiful high flat cheekbones dark under the overhead light, and walked out into the hall and between the huge stacks of old bound newspapers and magazines and balls of string and pressed aluminum and tilted furniture and down the stairs under the dim bulb and out into the street to the boarding-house, walking with a strange calmness now that it somehow felt as though he had finally come to the place he had been headed all his life.

Since he had never unpacked his seabag, it was only a matter of taking his shaving gear and brush off the dresser and putting them in the bag and shouldering it and walking back across to Sarah's. He did not even have to speak to his landlady because he paid by the week and it was still three days before he owed her anything again. A refund was out of the question, but being the kind of woman she was, there would be screaming about giving notice, and threats, and all kinds of noisy plans for how she would ruin him in the neighborhood. He left as quietly as possible.

Besides, around any corner in the house he was liable to run into Mr. Winekoff folded like a jackknife, from which position he was apt to have some alligator on his mind. Pete would not have blamed him. It was a shitty thing to have done—besides being dangerous—and Pete knew it, but after the shock of the yaks, after the blistering walk, he thought somehow what he had done was if not understandable at least forgivable. Although he could not forgive himself. The thought never even occurred to him.

When he got back to the room at the top of the house, he found Sarah sitting where he had left her, there on the bed, but now the bed had sheets on it and a pillow and a light blanket folded across the bottom of it.

"Put your things down right there by the door," she said, standing up. "Daddy told me you was going to work with him in the woodlot so I guess you better git on to bed. You probably won't need that blanket but I always like to sleep with something on my feet at night. Makes me sleep better." At the door, she stopped and there was a brief pause. She blushed and averted her eyes. "I'm going to tell you the truth. Always. And I hope you do the same with me. I want to hug you and kiss you but I know I wouldn't stop there. It's too soon, like I already told you, and I want it to be right."

Pete felt the sweetest little twinge in his cock. "I do too," he said, "and that's the truth."

He wanted to say something else, to say something—anything—to keep her there, but he could find nothing to say, so he stood under the bare hanging bulb watching as she smiled once over her shoulder and walked out of the door and down the hall. He listened to her footfall as light as a fox's on the stairwell, and finally it was quiet and he was alone in the room.

He went to bed and slept without dreaming and it seemed he had only just fallen asleep, when there was a knock at his door and Mr. Leemer's muffled voice saying, "Let's cut some wood, son."

Pete glanced at the window and saw that it was barely first light, but he was rested and ready, and hurriedly dressed and went downstairs, happily thinking of Sarah and last night. Nobody was up in the house and he found the old man sitting on the woodpile, smoking a hand-rolled cigarette. It didn't occur to him to ask what happened to breakfast because he never ate breakfast anyway.

The old man didn't say a word but got off the block of oak wood he was sitting on and picked up a Coca-Cola bottle that had pine straw stuffed in the neck of it. Mr. Leemer shook a few drops of liquid on both sides of a crosscut saw. Pete had seen the same thing done hundreds of times in south Georgia where he was raised. The Coca-Cola bottle held kerosene and it kept the crosscut from binding in the wood.

The sun was still not up when they pulled the saw the first time through the first oak log. Mr. Leemer worked with the saw like a man who has spent his life with one in his hand, unhurried but without pause, looking in those first few minutes for the rhythm he would hold all day. The old man's muscles were long and lean and apparently tireless, with high blue veins tracing through them. He would pour sweat and grunt but kept the rhythm of the pulling saw, and if Pete had not been in good shape from lifting all that cellophane out of all those boxcars, he could not have kept up his end of the saw. There was no talk at all, but at midmorning—about ten-thirty, Pete thought—the old man said, "Smoke," and turned loose the saw in midpull. His shirt and the top of his trousers were soaked with sweat. Pete himself was only damp across the shoulders and he wondered how an old man who was so lean could sweat so much.

Mr. Leemer took a can of Prince Albert tobacco out of his back pocket and with consummate skill rolled a cigarette and had it in his mouth and lit before Pete had even sat down. Pete heard the back door slam and then Sarah was coming toward them with a bucket of water, the handle of a dipper sticking out of the top of it. She took the bucket to her father first, who drank five quick dipperfuls, his hard Adam's apple bobbing in his thin, veined throat. He put the dipper back in the bucket and wiped his mouth with the back of his hand. He did not speak to his daughter, nor she to him. This was necessary business, not time for pleasantries, and when she brought the bucket to Pete, her only gesture was to smile and touch his hand briefly as she handed him the dipper. There was no ice in the water but it was cool, and Pete had not realized how thirsty he was until the first water touched his dry lips, which felt cracked though he knew they were not.

She was already walking back to the house when Mr. Leemer said: "Dinner, daughter?"

"It's on and cooking, Daddy," she said without looking back.

When she was gone, Mr. Leemer stared at the end of his cigarette, examining it carefully for a long moment. "Good woman, that Sarah."

"Yes sir," said Pete, "she is."

Henry Leemer never looked up but smoked his cigarette down to ash and rolled another in a few expert twists of his gnarled fingers. It looked easy but Pete knew it only took a lifetime of practice to be able to do it like that. His daddy had done it the same way; all his uncles still did. The uncles on his daddy's side of the family anyway, the ones who hadn't died of heart attacks. But they no longer talked to Pete. They made it their business not to see him and had made it clear he was not welcome in their houses since the accident ultimately sent his little brother to the state asylum after the Sunoco truck got his mama and daddy.

Mr. Leemer let the ash drop from his fingers. There was no butt to put out; he'd smoked it down to nothing. And since he didn't reach for his can of Prince Albert, Pete thought he was ready to go back to work, but he only looked over the pile of the woodlot and said: "I know this don't seem like much while you doing it, but it'll pay off come cold weather. This is good wood, good seasoned oak, and it'll bring a good price. You'd be surprised how many rich folk got central heat in their houses but like to keep a fire going in the fireplace all the same. Do it just to look at, I think. But I think I can understand that. Rich or poor, a man ain't nothing but a man, and a man just naturally likes to look at a fire when it's cold outside."

"I know what you mean," Pete said. "Back on the farm when I was growing up, I loved a fire. Still do to this day. A fireplace can be a lot of trouble, tending it and hauling ashes and all, but a fire is a lot of company, too. I'd rather have a fire for company than a lot of people I could name. I think it's because it's alive, moving, you know."

"Known it all my life." The old man paused and Pete thought he would reach for his can of tobacco again, but he didn't. "There's precious little comfort in this world for a man, rich or poor, seems like to me." He gestured toward the saw, which was lying across a thick block of oak, a double-bitted ax beside it. "I got to stay on the end of this saw, myself. The doctor bills has got me eat up. I don't guess I'll ever pay'm off till I die."

"Don't worry about them damn doctors," Pete said. "They make enough. They'll be all right without you."

"I guess." The briefest smile touched Mr. Leemer's thin mouth. "Tell you a little story my mama told me when I weren't nothing but a shirttail boy. She said if troubles was clothes and we could all take'm out and hang'm on a line, you'd look at everybody else's troubles and then you'd look at yours and you'd go right out there to the line and bring your own back with you. Everybody thinks what he's got's the worst, but that's only because a man caint know nothing but what he can see, and half the time he don't even know that."

Pete laughed and said nothing. He felt good, his muscles hot and the drying sweat cooling his shoulders there under the arching limbs of the oak tree where they worked.

"I still like to pay my debts though," Mr. Leemer said.

"Well, I do too. A debt is a thing I like to pay. If I don't, I don't seem to ever forget about it. Some people, it doesn't seem to matter much one way or the other. Daddy used to say that a man like that weren't worth his salt."

"I'm grateful to the doctors," Mr. Leemer said. "They done what they could. I think Ma may make it now. What they done might just work." He rose to take up the saw. "One thing we can be sure of, no man knows the day or the hour."

They went back to their work as silent as they came out of it and the next sound was Sarah calling from the back door that dinner was on the table. They went inside and Pete stood behind Mr. Leemer while he washed up and then he cleaned his own arms and face. They dried on the same towel, clean but old and stained with something that was not dirt. Sarah was wearing a little apron that broke Pete's heart. He did not know why. It was just because she was Sarah (he thought *his* Sarah—he couldn't help it) and it was a pretty little thing, the apron, and reminded him that there were houses where people lived out their whole lives instead of living like gypsies, and it made him think of them talking last night sitting on his (their?) bed and what they talked about.

She had set three places and had another plate in her hands with food on it. She nodded to the table. "Go on and git started. I'm just taking this back to Mama."

"Put my food on the table! What I lost was not my mind, it was something else!"

All their heads snapped around and there was Gertrude Leemer standing in the door to the narrow little hallway giving off the kitchen. Pete had not heard a sound—the door opening, her feet shuffling in her house slippers—but there she stood like death on a crutch. That was what Pete thought: Jesus, death on a crutch. Except she did not have a crutch. Nor did she hold to either side of the doorframe. The long gown she wore looked like it was filled with old coat hangers rather than a body, but Pete could clearly see the thick swathe of bandages across her chest.

Her eyes were deep in black sockets and blazed with something Pete thought must be the look that preceded murder. Sarah set the plate on the table and moved quickly toward her mother, saying: "I was bringing it, Ma. You ought—"

"Don't touch me," said Mrs. Leemer. "I can git there by myself!"

"I thought to feed you in your room," said Sarah.

Her mother only glared at her. Neither Pete nor Mr. Leemer had touched his food. In what seemed an interminable silence, Pete could hear a clock ticking somewhere.

Mrs. Leemer, walking slowly but with her back straight and her head up, moved to the place where Sarah had set her plate and said in a surprisingly loud—so loud that it made Pete jump—voice: "THIS JUST PISSES THE SHIT OUT OF ME."

"Now, Mother," said Mr. Leemer in a quiet voice.

"I ain't your mother and *this just pisses the shit out of me!*"

"There's no reason to cuss like—"

"It's ever goddam reason to cuss. And I'll tell you all again: *This just pisses the shit out of me!*" She stared across the table at her husband and lifted a thin trembling hand that became a thin trembling fist. "If they'd taken and cut your . . . well, you ain't got titties, have you?" Mr. Leemer's jaw had dropped open, and he seemed to want to speak but couldn't. "But you got balls. If they'd taken and cut your balls off, *both* your balls off, *wouldn't that just piss the shit out of you?*"

Nobody spoke and somewhere off in the silence the clock ticked on. Pete slammed his fist so hard on the table the dishes shook and the spoons in the bowls jumped. *"It would me, by God, it would piss the living shit out of me!"* His voice was unlike any he had ever heard come out of his mouth.

Mrs. Leemer beamed down upon him. "What did you say, young man?"

And Pete heard himself say in the same voice, and knew he

meant it, knew it wasn't just something he was making up, *"I said it would piss the shit out of me!"*

"I believe you said the *living* shit," said the old woman.

"I did," said Pete. "I said the *living* shit."

"Amen," said Mrs. Leemer, easing herself into her chair. "Let's eat."

And they did, they ate right through the meal in silence. Except for Mrs. Leemer's breathing. Her lungs whistled now and again. Pete did not know if this was something that had been with her a long time or if it was somehow connected with her operation. There was not much on Mrs. Leemer's plate to start with but she ate it all and then sopped the juice that was left with a bit of corn bread Sarah hadn't eaten. Everybody but the old lady seemed embarrassed.

Finally Mr. Leemer drained his glass of tea, pushed back from the table, and said: "Well, I don't guess it's anybody else is gon cut that wood."

"No sir," said Pete, and tried to smile.

"This just pisses the shit out of me!" said the old lady, and pushed against the table, but she was too weak to move herself, or at least she seemed to Pete to be.

"Yes mam," said Pete, and did not smile. He got up and went around to the other side of the table where she was sitting and eased her chair back. But when he touched her to help her up, she violently pushed his hands away: "I can get up by my goddam self." She stood up easily, glared once around the table, and moved silently back into her room.

Mr. Leemer said, "Pete, I guess you and me ought to go see if that saw'll still fit our hands."

"I guess we better." He looked at Sarah, who had her hands wrapped in her apron. "That was good, real good."

"Thank you," she said in a voice that was almost cheerful.

"Thank you, daughter. We got to git back to it." Mr. Leemer went out the back door and eased it shut.

Pete had not moved and Sarah came to him. "Thank you," she said.

"For what?"

"For taking Mama's part. For saying what you said."

"It was only the truth. And it was already said before I had time to think about it."

She touched his shoulder and smiled. "Don't you git too hot out there. Daddy's done that all his life. He'll work you to death."

Pete bent and kissed her lightly. Her lips parted. Their tongues touched briefly and she turned away and was at the stove by the time he had the back door open.

Out in the woodlot, Mr. Leemer watched Pete a long moment before he made a move to touch the saw, and when he did take the handle in his hand, he looked off at the far horizon and said in barely a whisper: "Thank you for what you did in there. I couldn't have myself, but it was only right, and I thank you."

"Sarah already thanked me."

The old man lifted the saw into the cut they'd been making before dinner and, still without looking at Pete, said: "She did?"

"Yessir."

"That Sarah!"

And they went at the saw and the wood in a way they hadn't earlier that morning. Mr. Leemer pulled like a wild man, obsessed, his breathing like bellows. Pete did not understand but he had no alternative but to stay with him on the other end of the crosscut saw. When Sarah brought water out, Pete drank but the old man did not and neither did he stop to roll a smoke. Even when the light began to fail, he never slackened his pace, and just as the sun was making its final quick slip behind the houses across the street, he dropped dead in the woodlot under the oak tree over the crosscut saw that had been singing all afternoon, Pete on one end of it, the old man on the other. Mr. Leemer never stopped pulling the saw, he only looked up in a slightly surprised way and, without saying anything, pitched forward across the saw and across the log, and when Pete touched him, he knew instantly that he was dead.

Book Two

9

Pete had no notion whatever what to do, whether to scream or to cry or simply to sit down beside the dead body and think. But he knew in a way that is given few men to know anything that he, Pete, was now in charge of this house, of this dead man lying across the oak log on the sawhorses, of the girl in the house, of the dying mother in the back room who seemed to believe that she could avoid death just by pretending that it was not going to happen. And this was something he would not run away from, could not abandon. Sarah was not just Sarah now, she was *his* Sarah, and her blood was his blood. She had brought him back to the place where blood is joined, to the place where the blood that beats in one heart beats in another heart.

Pete looked around to see if anybody had seen Mr. Leemer drop dead. He thought wildly that if somebody had been standing out in the street and seen it he could rush over and say something to him and he would know how to go into the house and tell Sarah that her father was lying dead out in the woodyard. But there was no one up the street or down the street or across the street or anywhere else he could see. He wondered how on earth he was going to go inside and say what he had to say, and in the moment he wondered that, he knew that there was no way to do it but to do it. He went in and Sarah was setting plates on the table for supper. She looked up at him and smiled. Pete took a deep breath and walked over near her and said: "Your daddy is dead."

Sarah didn't even blink. She kept smiling. "What?"

"Sarah, your father, he . . . We were out in the woodyard working with the crosscut saw and he dropped dead."

Her eyes glazed a little but the smile held, thinner now, but she still held it. "He did what?"

"Sarah, your father is dead. I wish it was some other way to say it."

It was then she screamed, which he had expected her to do when he first told her and was prepared for it. He put his arm around her shoulder and drew her close and literally stopped the scream with his other hand as gently as he could. "There was no other way to tell you but the way I told you. I wouldn't have wanted to do that for anything in the world, but now it's done and you've got to get hold of yourself so that your mother doesn't know. Not yet anyhow."

Pete took his hand away from her mouth and she stood, tears streaming from her eyes and her mouth still stretched in the shape of a scream, while he held her. When she could finally speak, she said: "I've got to go to Ma. I've got to go in there to her now."

"You can't tell your mother about this the way she is. Don't you see, it could kill her. She's too weak. We'll find a way, but it's no use rushing when we don't have to."

"She's stronger than you think. And she's got to know about Daddy."

At the mention of her daddy, her mouth stretched again and he caught the scream in his hand.

"I don't like to treat you like this," he said, "but you've got to get yourself together, goddammit."

"Don't cuss," she said in a tiny voice.

"As your mama would say, I think this might be a time for cussing. I know one thing—along with everything else that's happened, your daddy even dying pisses me off, and I know it's going to piss your mama off." He paused and looked back toward the door that led to the woodlot. "But the problem we got right now is I don't know what to do. We can't leave your father lying out there. It's not seemly."

She sniffed once and said: "No, we can't." She seemed to be steady and in control now.

Besides the terrible pain he felt for Sarah, the only feeling Pete had was one of intense helplessness. He had no experience with death, not directly anyway. He had gone to his grandparents' funerals and he had gone to his uncles', but that was back home in south Georgia when he was a boy. Back then it seemed that when someone died, the women simply all came in from the community and made everything go the way it had to go. They put out a cooling board and laid the corpse out on it and washed and shaved and dressed it, and people brought in food. Cakes and hams and beef and all manner of sweets would be spread around the house while the family and their friends sat up all night with the corpse dressed and ready for burial the next day.

But this wasn't south Georgia and he was no longer a boy and there was a man lying dead outside over an oak log and here he stood with this young girl without any idea at all of how to proceed. That was when he thought of Max Winekoff. Max would know what to do. A man that old had to know about things like this, had to have seen all of it before. Not for an instant now did he think of dropping the old man down a flight of stairs or throwing him over a fence into a pen of alligators.

"Listen," Pete said. "I'm going next door to get Mr. Winekoff."

Sarah said: "I've got to go out to Daddy. I've got to see . . ."

Pete took her by the shoulders and almost roughly set her on a chair. "You stay right there. Don't move. You understand? There's nothing you can do out there and there's nothing you can do until I get back. You stay right where you are. You promise?"

She did not answer but only looked up at him stunned, almost uncomprehending now that shock was setting in. He told her one last time not to move and raced out the front door and down the sidewalk to the boardinghouse. Since it was so late, Mr. Winekoff had just come back from the zoo and was sitting on the porch, his feet on the banister. Pete ran up the steps of the porch and took the old man by the arm.

"Come on," he said.

Max Winekoff seemed to be in some kind of fugue state, or perhaps only in some reverie of yaks wandering the mountains of Tibet. Wherever his mind was, Pete had startled him. He leapt to his feet shouting, "What? What?"

Pete said nothing and literally dragged him along behind him across the porch and down the steps, and it was only when they were going under the arching limbs of the enormous oak tree leading into the woodyard that he told Mr. Winekoff what had happened. Mr. Winekoff walked over to where Sarah's father lay across the log and touched his head not gingerly but firmly, giving it a little shake by the hair.

Then he looked at Pete: "He's dead, all right."

"Try not to be a goddam idiot." Pete's nerves were getting away from him. "I know he's fucking dead!"

"I thought you wanted my help."

"I do."

Mr. Winekoff took a step back and raised his liver-spotted hand and counted on his fingers. "You drop me down the stairs. You throw me to the alligators. And now you call me an idiot." He wagged his tangled eyebrows at Pete. "Don't sound like something you'd do to a man you wanted to get help from."

Pete raised his hands, palms up. "We'll talk about that later. Really, we will." He pointed to Mr. Leemer. "But right now we've got this to deal with."

"Not a very flattering way to talk about a dead man," Mr. Winekoff said.

"This is not a flattering time. I never had somebody drop dead on me before."

"Well, you have now."

"Can we get the fuck on with this?"

"Not if you keep cussing."

Pete held himself together with an effort of will. He wanted to scream, but it wouldn't help anything, and besides, he was worried about Sarah inside, worried that she had gone into the back room and told her mother what happened. Gritting his teeth, he said as calmly as he could: "Mr. Winekoff, I want you to help me. I want you to help me because I don't know what to do. There's two women inside, one of them sick to death, and I got this man lying out here dead over a crosscut saw."

"Of course I'll help you, son." The old man pointed to the body and said in a matter-of-fact voice, "This is a tragedy. But the only problem will be a problem of grief. There's no problem with the body. That's not the tragedy. There's a whole town full of people right here set up to deal with just this kind of thing. Dead bodies is their business."

"Jesus, what a thing to say."

"I think you're old enough to deal with the truth, and what I said was not a thing but the truth. Dead bodies—"

"O.K.! O.K.! Stop with that. Just tell me what we do."

"We'll make a phone call."

"A phone call," said Pete, unable for a moment to comprehend how something so simple as a phone call could have anything to do with solving the problem of a dead body draped across a log.

But it turned out to be just as Mr. Winekoff had said. He did make a phone call and an ambulance—or something that looked like an ambulance, just like the one that brought Mrs. Leemer home—took Mr. Leemer away with a sheet over his face.

And later over the phone, Pete was assured by a man with a deeply sympathetic voice that Mr. Leemer would be prepared during the night—they had something of a backlog just now, but it would be accomplished—and the deceased would almost surely be available for viewing by family and friends in the chapel tomorrow.

"Viewing?" said Pete.

"Viewing," said the man.

There would be, of course, the man said in a sadder and even more sympathetic voice, the matter of the selection of the casket, insurance policies or other arrangements for payment, and other details that were now coming from the man's mouth into Pete's ear like the buzz from a bee in a jar, but when he finally hung up the phone, he was able to go to Sarah, who was now in her room unable or unwilling to talk, weeping softly, rocking from side to side.

"Mr. Winekoff's taking care of everything," said Pete. He sat on the edge of the bed where Sarah was rocking and weeping and sniffling and he waited for her to stop.

When she did, she said, "Are you going to tell Mama?"

"I can't," Pete said.

"I can't either."

"Well, her husband's been hauled off dead, goddammit, somebody's got to do it."

"You don't have to snap at me."

"I didn't mean to snap. It doesn't seem like I mean any goddam thing I'm doing. The world seems about half unreal most of the time but this really takes the cake."

"Speaking of my father's death taking a cake is a terrible thing to say. It's not *normal.*"

"Have you seen, heard, or even smelled anything normal recently?"

"Are you talking crazy cause you're mad?"

"I don't know."

Pete went again to Mr. Winekoff, who said the obvious person to call would be the doctor.

"I think it's a little late for the doctor."

"You don't understand."

"A lot of people seem to be saying that to me lately."

"I can't help that. But that's what doctors do. One of the things anyway. And if the doctor can't come and tell her himself he could tell you if she ought to be told right now. I don't know how sick that lady is. I've been back there lately to talk with her about some things, and she seemed to me like she still had a lot of life in her."

"That's just the way she talks."

"Maybe, but the doctor's the best shot you've got."

Pete went back to the Leemers' house to find out who their doctor was and then looked the number up in the book and dialed it, waiting until a nurse finally answered and told him that the doctor was busy and could she have a number where he could be called back.

"This can't wait. I've got a dead man here."

"A dead man?"

"Right."

There was silence on the phone while the nurse seemed to be considering this. But finally she said in a disinterested voice: "Doctor will be right with you."

Pete waited for what seemed like half an hour but was probably only a minute or two until the doctor came on the line. He was no help at all. The dead man was obviously out of his hands and he told Pete that he had advised against taking Mrs. Leemer home to start with. "I told them she needed to be in the hospital where she could receive proper medical attention."

"I think it was a matter of running out of money," Pete said.

"That would have been the hospital bill. My bill is separate."

"Oh, well, that makes all the difference in the world."

"Sarcasm won't help."

"Right. No sarcasm. Just tell me this. Do you think she is well enough to hear that her husband has dropped dead?"

"That is a judgment not in my province to make," said the doctor. "I haven't seen her since she left the hospital. I can't help you and my patients are waiting."

"All of them alive with money in their pockets, no doubt."

The doctor hung up without saying goodbye. Pete went back to see Mr. Winekoff, and Mr. Winekoff could only say that he didn't see how they could rightly bury the woman's husband without telling her he was dead.

Pete was getting beside himself. "Did I ever say that? Give me credit for something."

"It's not a matter of credit. It's a matter of being dead."

Pete could only stare. "How old are you?"

"You know how old I am. Why do you ask?"

"I was wondering if it took that long to become absolutely fucked up in the head."

"Maybe you'd rather I'd go up to my room and read a book or something. I didn't git up this morning to be made sport of."

"I didn't mean it," said Pete, and he didn't. "I've just about played out my rope here. I was sawing wood with a man a little while ago and now he's on a slab in a funeral parlor waiting his turn to be fixed up for family viewing. It's more things to do than I can count and I don't know where to start. Why don't you do it, Mr. Winekoff? Go on in there and do it and let's get this show on the road."

"Show on the road."

"Just a manner of speaking. Will you tell her?"

Mr. Winekoff said he wasn't really that close to the Leemer family, he only knew them to speak to and to visit with once in a while. But Pete could see that he was lying. He simply did not want to face what none of them wanted to face and that was looking the dying woman in the eyes and telling her that her husband was at present being prepared at a funeral parlor. It just was not something a man would want to say to a woman, whether she was recently made breastless or not.

"Jesus, Jesus," said Pete.

Mr. Winekoff only said that if you walked a lot and ate plenty of food and took proper stretching exercises everything would be fine. Heart attacks would not be a problem in your life—or death. He promptly flopped into a bend that put his hands flat on the floor with his fleshless ass, bones clearly outlined through his trousers, in the air, and Pete left him there. Back at the house Sarah was still in her room, crying and rocking on her bed.

"You plan to stay in here all night?" he asked her.

"Please don't talk ugly to me."

"I'm sorry if it sounded ugly, but I was just wondering how long you could keep it up, this rocking and crying."

"You're talking ugly to me."

"O.K. No more ugly. But we've got to talk. Things are coming to a head whether we like it or not."

"I can't think. Nothing but that my poor daddy's dead."

"At least that's a start anyhow."

"A start?" She pressed a soiled handkerchief to her nose and seemed to straighten up just a little. "What do you mean, a start?"

"Death. That's a start. You said it out of your mouth. You've just been sitting up here trying to cry him back to life. I'm about out of patience."

"You don't know how it feels."

"I lost a mama and a daddy . . . and a little brother. I think that gives me a pretty good start."

"I didn't know that."

"Yes you did. You're just not thinking straight. But this is not the time to talk about that. This is the time to *do* something."

"I thought Mr. Winekoff was going to take care of it."

"Winekoff is an old man who has lost his brain."

Sarah looked up from her handkerchief, her eyes nearly dry now. "That is about the ugliest thing you've said yet."

"True though. He talks without the slightest notion of what he's saying."

"He still might take care of it."

"Take care of it, my ass."

"I wish you'd leave your ass out of it," she said with some heat.

"What?"

"You got a habit of putting your ass in everything you say."

"It's just something they say where I come from."

"You not where you come from now. Know what my mama says?"

He didn't answer.

"Well, do you? Or did you even hear me?"

"I heard you," he said. "And I don't want to know what your mama says." He had the fingers of his hands interlocked over the top of his head thinking that what he ought to do was walk away from this. Fuck his clothes. Leave'm upstairs. Just go. And keep on going until he could no longer remember any of it. But he had already made a vow with himself that running was the one thing he would not do. What the hell? What could happen? The old lady downstairs was nearly dead anyway. He was making too much of all this. He would go downstairs, tell her that Leemer blew a major gasket over his crosscut saw and was deader'n shit. If she fell over dead too they could bury'm at the same time, same fucking casket as far as he was concerned.

He took Sarah by the wrist and said: "Come on."

"Where we going?"

"Where the hell you think we going? To get this settled and done with. We've wasted too much time already."

She didn't say a word as he led her down the stairs. But at the landing he stopped. Mr. Winekoff was sitting on the bottom step.

"Git out of the way, old man."

He got off the step and looked up at Pete. "My name is Max Winekoff. Old *is* as old *does.*"

"Save me that shit." Pete came down the steps holding Sarah by the hand.

"Your mouth makes your grave six inches deeper every time you open it," Mr. Winekoff said.

Pete didn't answer him and headed toward the door leading into Mrs. Leemer's room.

"I wouldn't do that."

"Do what?"

"Mess with Mrs. Leemer."

"Somebody's got to take care of it."

"Somebody already has."

"You?"

"Not exactly."

"Then who?"

The door to the bedroom opened and there stood Gertrude Leemer, the heavy chest bandage insistent, as though it might have swelled, under the thin cloth of her gown. She did not look sick; she looked fierce, dressed for war. That was the image and line that formed in Pete's mind the instant he saw her. *Dressed for war.* It stopped him where he stood and because there was no light on in the room and all the shades were drawn, it was an instant before he saw, standing just behind her and at her shoulder, George and beside him a woman whose dreadlocks looked like living snakes, twisted and twisting. Her face was heavily marked with designs that at first he thought were tattoos, but then he realized the elaborate markings that covered her forehead and cheeks and nose and even went back into her ears had been made by a very sharp blade, perhaps a razor. He had seen such work before but only on men, never on a woman. He had even watched a boy in the Corps do it. A shallow cut was made and while the wound was still open, dye was put into it. The markings Pete had seen before were ugly and ragged and usually spelled out some woman's name or a slogan like DEATH BEFORE DISHONOR. But the designs on this woman's face were sharp and distinct, intricately curving and looping back upon themselves and dyed with every color Pete had ever seen. Whoever had made them had done it with consummate skill and the effect was startlingly beautiful if you didn't stop to think that it was on somebody's face. He instantly knew that this woman must be George's wife, Linga, and at first he thought she was white. Her nose was thin and finely shaped and her mouth unlike any he had ever seen on a black. But no, she was not white. She was a high yellow. A *very* high yellow. And she was every bit as big as George and the long dress—falling almost to her ankles—could not disguise the fact that she was as heavily muscled as a man. Pete could not take his eyes off her. Neither could he speak.

Mrs. Leemer glared at Pete. "Was it you that hauled my husband off?" She had to ask him twice before he could find his voice.

"I called the funeral parlor."

She had to ask him twice before he could find his voice because there was something that was horribly wrong about this, something terribly off-center and dead-solid crazy. The woman's husband had died and instead of grief and anguish, howling and grief, she was *angry,* dry-eyed and pissed to the end of the world, about where the body of her husband had been taken rather than the dreadful fact that she had lost him to death. If Pete had wondered before about her sanity, he didn't anymore. She was *nuts.*

With vicious sarcasm she said, "*You* called the funeral parlor?"

Sarah said: "He only did what he thought was right, Mama."

"Keep out of this," said Mrs. Leemer. "You've both done everything wrong."

"If we did, we didn't know we was," Sarah said.

"All you had to do was ask me. I knowed," her mother said.

"George, what the hell you doing here?" Pete asked.

"I called him," said Max Winekoff.

George shrugged his heavy shoulders. "I come ta de place death is struck, mon. Hep if I and I can."

Mrs. Leemer held up what looked like a thick envelope. It was easy to read the dark words across the front. "Last Will and Testament of Henry Sterns Leemer."

Pete was totally convinced now. Maybe in time her mind would be right again. Instead of tears or grief of any kind, she was waving a goddam piece of paper at him. And a fucking will at that. It scared him, but he could understand it. She'd lost both breasts in a hideous operation and then had her husband drop dead right behind that. It was enough to drive anybody off-center. Way off-center. He would just have to do the best he could with all of it. The main thing was to take care of and protect Sarah, and at the same time try to protect Gertrude from herself.

"Everything that needs to be done, that *will* be done, is right in here. He didn't hold with leaving nothing to chance," said Mrs. Leemer.

"Pete and every last one of us was only trying to protect you, Mama," Sarah said.

"Protect me from what?" demanded her mother.

"You've been sick and we—"

"Don't you think I know I've been sick, goddammit. I'm missing a little something up front here to remind me in case I forget."

"We was trying to do what was best for you," Pete said.

"That's true," said Mr. Winekoff. "They really were."

"Git me the number of where you took him at. We need to straighten this mess out."

Pete looked over at the telephone book but made no move to

pick it up. "He's where he needs to be. I sent him on to the funeral parlor."

"He ain't to be buried, he's to be burned."

Pete looked up from the phone book. "Burned?"

"Burned. Naked," Winekoff said.

"Naked?"

"Your hearing gone bad, son?"

"I'm a little confused is all. I thought you said naked."

"I did," Winekoff said.

"Burn him is what we're going to do," said Mrs. Leemer. "Without no clothes on. Henry liked straight talk. He always said to burn him. And that's what I'm here to do." She thumped the thick envelope she was holding. "It's all right here. He wanted to go out of this world the way he come in it. Naked."

"I don't know a thing about cremation," said Pete, "but that sounds somehow illegal to me. The government being what it is, it just seems that they'd insist on burning him up in a suit. With a tie on probably."

"Then we'll burn him our damn selves."

"You're talking crazy, Mama," said Sarah.

"I mean to do the job the way he wanted it done."

"You can't just burn up a body in the backyard. I know that's got to be illegal," Pete said.

"Nuh be in de mountains o Jamaica, mon," said George.

George's wife stepped from behind him to fill the door, fill the door with that body that looked to be entirely without fat and every bit as big and muscled as George's. Now Pete could see the designs in her face much better. Only an artist of great skill and patience and also great talent could have scarred her face into something arresting, compelling, and . . . *beautiful* was the word that came to Pete's mind.

She was holding Pete's eyes with her own, looking directly into his without, it seemed, even blinking. "You are staring at my face," she said in a lilting British accent.

"Lady," Pete growled, at the same time wondering why he had taken such an instant dislike to her, "anybody that didn't stare at a face like you got would have to be locked up where they keep crazy people. Just a fact, seems like to me. No offense intended."

"None taken," she said. "My face is scarred. Some say beautifully scarred, which seems something of a paradox, doesn't it? But never mind. There is something beautiful about all scars of whatever nature. A scar always means the hurt is over, the wound is closed and healed, done with. Did you ever think of that?"

Pete thought it was the rankest kind of bullshit he'd ever heard but he said: "No, as a matter of fact, I never thought of that."

"Pete—please forgive the familiarity of using your Christian name, but from all that George has told me, I feel as though I already know you—we simply need the body of Mrs. Leemer's husband." Linga paused a minute and smiled. Her teeth—all of them very white and very even—were inlaid with tendrils of gold that made her smile all the more brilliant. "Forgive me. I have not introduced myself. I am the Burnt One's wife. I am called Linga."

Pete closed his mouth when he realized that his jaw had dropped involuntarily at the sound of her voice. For some reason, the strangeness of it had not registered on him before. It was high and melodious and unmistakably English, the sort of voice he had never heard anywhere but in the movies, movies that were set in some place like London.

Linga glanced briefly toward George and said, "Not that it matters terribly much, but we are from the island of Jamaica but I was sent to convent schools in England and then educated further there by private tutors." Her smile grew even wider, as though she were about to give the punch line to a joke. "You see, I am the bastard daughter of a wealthy white man, one—and this is rare in the extreme—who had a conscience that drove him to behave properly by me, or at least properly as he understood it, or perhaps he was only afraid of his wife. I give you this information because I can see on your face that my voice has startled you. And I don't want that. I very much wish us to be friends." She signed once deeply and then continued. "But back to the subject at hand. Where did you take the deceased?"

"Pete-Pete, mon, she mean de dead body."

The smile dropped from Linga's face and she glanced briefly at

George. "I am talking, dickless one, and I should appreciate it if you would remain quiet unless spoken to."

She looked at Pete and waited for an answer.

Stunned as he was by what she said, it was a moment before Pete could say anything. "It's good to meet you, Linga." And instantly he hated himself for manners making the lie necessary, manners that lived in him still, taught him by his mother, years dead now.

"That hardly answers the question I asked you but it will do for the nonce."

She put out her hand, meaning, he thought, to shake his, but she took hold of it and drew him to her with surprising strength and speed. In the blink of an eye, her nose was nearly touching his. Shaking her hand was like shaking hands with a mattress. The ends of his fingers did not even curl at the edge of her palm. George's woman, this Linga, despite how pleasant she seemed, introducing herself and all, frightened Pete.

"Now," Linga said, "would you mind terribly telling us *precisely* where you have taken the body of Henry Leemer?"

Pete looked over his shoulder at the telephone. She still had him by the hand and the pressure was beginning to hurt. "I'll have to look it up in the telephone book." He heard the bones in his hand pop together and pain shot all the way to his elbow.

"That is not a good sign, Pete. It is not a thing that one should be proud to say, this business of having to look in the telephone book to find Henry," Linga said.

"You're hurting my hand, mam," said Pete. "And yeah, that's what I got to do. I don't even remember the name of the place, but I'll recognize it when I see it. And you really are hurting my fucking hand if you don't mind my saying so."

"I do, as it turns out, mind you saying so," said Linga. "And something you must always remember. I'll tell you this once and I'll not say it again. In many, many ways I may look and sound as a white person might look and sound, but my heart is a black's heart. Of my own volition, I turned my heart black indeed in order that I might be one with my people."

"Since we seem to be getting everything straight here, Linga, let me just tell you I don't give a damn what you might or might not be one with, or what you've had to do to get where you need to go. And you really are breaking my fucking hand!"

"Linga," George said in a soft whisper Pete had never heard before.

"What?" Her voice was suddenly defiant and fierce.

"It do nuh good ta break de mon's han." George spoke now with a deference that was total.

She looked down as though unaware she was even holding it. When she turned it loose, it was numb. Pete thought of something else immediately. *How curious is man.* Here I am caught in the middle of a death with the body, at least for the moment, lost, a hand numb to the elbow, and just finished—finished, I hope—talking to a breastless woman about the legality of burning up her husband naked or dressed in a suit and wearing a tie in the backyard—here I am caught in the middle of all this and what am I thinking about? Fucking. Just from the grip of her hand, Pete knew that she would be your basic *terror fuck.* He could not even imagine the strength of those thighs, but at the same time, he knew his cock was willing to risk being caught in them. Thank God for his brain, or his cock would have killed him a hundred times over by now.

"She some more strong, mon," said George to Pete. "Linga hab much mon in her."

Linga glanced briefly at George, her smile going ugly in a snarling kind of way, and then back to Pete, where she held his gaze with her eyes—eyes that were now clearly showing a kind of fierce anger. But she said nothing.

Has much man in her. Is that what George had said? Whatever, Pete was not going to ask, because he did not think he could stand the answer just now. He went directly to the telephone book and found the funeral home. It had a full-page advertisement with a listing of its services, an announcement that it also had various payment plans, and, in bold red print at the bottom, the exhortation not to skimp on a loved one this very last time it would be possible to show how you truly and deeply felt.

Pete didn't even dial the number. This was the place. He recognized the ad. He turned to look at Mrs. Leemer in order to disengage himself from Linga's glaring eyes. "He's at the Mortuary of Perpetual Care."

Linga said: "And what might they have done to him there?"

"I don't know, probably nothing," Pete said. "They said they were going to fix him up for viewing in the morning. But I remember they also said they had a backlog tonight."

"A backlog?" demanded Mrs. Leemer. "What kind of goddam backlog?"

"Of bodies, I reckon," said Pete. "I don't know what other kind of backlog you could have at a funeral parlor. Anyway, that's what the feller said."

"Jesus fucking Christ," said Mrs. Leemer.

Sarah, standing very quietly at Pete's shoulder, her face chalky white, said: "Mama, I never would have thought you could say a thing like that."

"It's a lot you don't know," said Mrs. Leemer.

Sarah, despite the fact that she was trembling and tears had once again begun to stream down her cheeks, said angrily, "Do you think Daddy would like you cussing like that? Both of us know he didn't hold with cussing."

Mrs. Leemer said, "It's not him that has to hold with anything. It's me that's got to do the holding now. Dial that number of the place wherever he is. I ain't got my glasses and I caint see to do it."

Pete read out the number and Linga dialed it. While she was dialing, she asked, "Are you quite sure you don't want me and the Burnt One to manage all of this for you?"

"He's my husband. I got a obligation," said Mrs. Leemer.

Linga handed the telephone to Mrs. Leemer. Pete felt Sarah press more heavily against him and heard her say something but could not make it out.

"What?" he said, bending to put his mouth near her ear.

In the same tiny voice, she said, "You smell good."

"You keep yourself together, you hear?"

"Yes, but I don't know how much more of this I can stand."

"Your father's dead. That was the bad part. This is all just bullshit. Don't worry about it."

"I've never seen Mama act like this before."

"You've never seen her with a dead husband before."

"You can be so kind," said Sarah, "and so sweet and then . . . then—"

"Tell the truth. You're telling me that I mess it up by telling the truth. You can't mess *anything* up by telling the truth."

"Every time you get in a tight spot, you *hide* behind the truth," she said.

"I do, do I?"

"I've noticed that about you."

From across the room where Max Winekoff had found a chair to sit at by the dining room table, he said: "She's right about that, Pete. And I've noticed the same thing myself. You let the truth get in your way all the time."

Without even looking at Max, Pete said: "I can take care of this without any help from you, Max."

"Whatever you say," said Max.

"Anything else I ought to know about?" Pete said to Sarah.

"Are you going to pick a fight right here, right now, in the middle—"

"No. Now be quiet. Your mama's talking."

That she was talking in a firm, steady, angry voice was not what amazed Pete, but that she was ramrod-straight, with the telephone in her hand, and still completely dry-eyed.

"Henry Leemer. *Leemer.* I already spelled it oncet and I ain't spelling it again."

There was a pause while she listened. "And you already said that, too. Twicet, if I can still count. But you bout to git on the wrong side of me and that's the side you don't want to be on. . . . You goddam what? . . . Got a tag on his toe and he's right there sommers. What's the funeral director already gone home got to do with it? . . . You ain't nothing but the mortician with a back-log? I'll tell you what you are. You in a world of shit, feller. I'm coming down there to git my husband and I'm coming right now." There was a longer pause. "The rules and regulations of the state say that, do they? Caint turn him over to nobody but another certified mortuary oncet you got'm. You got all that shit memorized and you caint even find my husband? You told me about the train wreck giving you a backlog already and I'm tired of hearing about it. Nobody on that goddam train was kin to me, but you got the father of my child down there that I put up with forty-three years of shit from and I'm coming to collect what's mine." She slammed down the phone and turned on all of them with blazing eyes.

"Did you ask him about the suit and tie?" asked Mr. Winekoff.

"Don't git me any crazier than I am. I could eat a pound of tacks right out of the sack like peanuts about now. And I wouldn't need nothing to drink behind them either."

She turned from the telephone and paced, first three steps one way and then three steps the other. Her stride was strong and quick. It was the stride of a crazy, over-the-edge woman whose grief had made her forget all about her sickness, her operation, forget everything but a single-minded obsession with finding her husband and doing what his will demanded that she do.

Hell, Pete thought, she'll probably outlive all of us. But she was definitely somebody that had to be watched, taken care of. And that job fell to him, Pete. She was, after all, the mother of the woman he loved and planned to spend his life with.

Linga opened a little sack that was on a drawstring around her neck. From the sack she withdrew a Sucrets tin and opened it. It was full of hand-rolled cigarettes. "It's time to burn one," she said. She took one out and George already had the match waiting when she put it to her lips.

Without puffing once herself, she held her hand out toward Mrs. Leemer. "I know we've been through this before, Gertrude, but if there was ever a time to smoke the holy ganja, it's now. It will heal your hurt and make you easy."

"Kools've near bout killed me," Gertrude said, "and you want me to add another ceegrette on top of them? Answer's still no."

"But you know this is not a cigarette," said Linga. "I've explained it all a dozen times—ganja, the good rich resin of the marijuana plant."

"And I already told you," said Gertrude, anger suddenly heavy in her voice. "If it looks like a ceegrette, and if you light it and puff it and smoke comes out of your mouth, then it's a ceegrette. And I don't care to talk about it no more."

"Good for you, Mama," said Sarah.

"You hush, Sarah," Gertrude said. "I think I can handle this without your help."

Linga looked at Mr. Winekoff. "Perhaps the time has come for you to see and know the healing powers of ganja. Will you smoke with us now?"

Mr. Winekoff leapt out of his chair, did one flat-handed bend to the floor, stood up, and said: "I've always liked you and George, but you know well as me, Max is my name and walking is my game. I ain't about to put smoke in my lungs, no matter what it's called. I thank you, but you know how I feel about it."

Linga gave a derisive little snort through her nose and passed the joint to George, who hit it three very hard times in rapid succession before he handed it back to Linga, who drew it down to a tiny fragment, which she flipped back onto her tongue and swallowed.

"Ganja make all tings bedder," said George in a voice so tranquil that it seemed holy to Pete, sounded as though he might have been praying.

"Is there any whiskey in the house?" asked Pete. "I'd like bourbon but I'll drink anything you got."

"Not now. Not ever," said Mrs. Leemer. "Lips that touch alcohol never touch mine."

"Or mine," said Sarah her voice louder now, sounding almost angry.

"I only asked," said Pete. "Pot doesn't do a damn thing for me, or at least it didn't the few times I smoked it."

"Ah," said George, "but ya nuh smoke de ganja like dis."

"The stick we just had was a bit thin, don't you think, George?" said Linga.

"I tink."

"Then why don't you roll up something very nice, very special," Linga said. "And Pete, in the absence of what you'd rather have—since at the moment you can't have it anyway—I suggest you try this with us. If you do not like it, don't smoke it again."

George reached and took a bag out of his back pocket, along with a book of rolling papers. His fingers acted as if on their own, with no conscious thought from George. In less time than it had taken Linga to get a joint out of her Sucrets box, he had one big as his thumb, twisted tightly and lit, and was passing it to Pete, who was sitting in a ladder-back chair near the dining table. Pete didn't have to be told anything about smoking it. He'd watched hundreds of guys in the Corps smoke. He took a very deep drag and held it and gradually an enormous pumpkin of pleasure exploded behind his eyes. He exhaled and then sat for what seemed to him a long time, regarding the joint he held in his fingers.

"I wish you wouldn't do that, Pete," said Sarah. "I've heard all about that stuff."

Pete did not answer but only studied the joint a moment more before taking another hit and holding the smoke longer than he had the first time. Every muscle in his body seemed to be in sweet harmony with every other muscle and the death of Henry Leemer no longer felt very important to him. When he exhaled the smoke, he again sat regarding the joint he held.

"What's wrong, Pete?" asked Sarah.

He looked up at her as if surprised to find her sitting there. "Wrong? There's nothing wrong." His voice was quiet and tranquil. After a pause, he said: "I think I'm where I need to be." He handed the joint to George. "I thank you," he said. And it was as though he were standing across the room listening to himself say the words.

"Ya go on wit it now, mon. We got de job ta do. I wan you in de good place fo dis ting we do, Pete-Pete."

All of them watched Pete in silence, a silence that seemed to Pete to stretch on for a very long time. And George and Linga were right. This was not like anything he had ever smoked before. He was deeply relaxed and all things seemed possible. He could feel himself smiling broadly and did not have the faintest notion why he was smiling. No whiskey he had ever drunk had brought him this quickly to the place he was now, to the feeling that not only was in his head and heart but seemed to have spread throughout his very blood.

Pete said: "I'm right now. I'm right in the place where I want to live."

"Dat de good an right ting, mon," said George.

Linga smiled and said in her wonderfully musical voice: "Perhaps George was right in all he told me of you. You may, in fact, be one of us."

"I am more than just right and we'll find out sooner or later what and who I am," said Pete. "That's just something we'll have to wait and see when it happens." His head was so light it did not seem joined to his body, but he felt strong and optimistic.

"I don't think I like this," said Sarah, "and I know I don't like you messing with that stuff, Pete."

"I only did what they did," said Pete, and laughed loudly.

"Why are you laughing?" asked Sarah.

"It am good ting ta laugh, little one," said George.

"It stinks in here," Sarah said.

"Only to the one who has not been to the mountain," Linga said.

Sarah's brow furrowed. "What mountain you talking about?"

"The one inside all of us, but only the few, the chosen, ever find it, ever climb it."

"Amen," said Mrs. Leemer. "But right now we got to go to . . . to . . . Where is it we got to go?"

"The Mortuary of Perpetual Care," said Pete.

"Ah, yes, the Mortuary of Perpetual Care," she said, laughing. "Don't sound so bad, does it, even if they do tie a tag on your toe and sometimes caint find you."

"I'm sure it's a fine place," said Pete.

"But not for Henry Leemer," she said.

"Midnight never comes where I live," said Linga, very slowly, very softly.

"Now she's gone to talking crazy," said Sarah.

"Not really," said Mr. Winekoff.

"Midnight comes everywhere." Sarah's face was puzzled and a little frightened.

Mr. Winekoff only said again: "Not really."

"Let's go git Henry," said Mrs. Leemer.

"And then what?" asked Sarah.

"Do what needs to be done, what he wanted done."

"We can't very well do this in a taxicab," said Pete. He was looking for a way out. He knew this was a job that had to be done, but he also knew he didn't want to be the one to do it.

"Me Hudson Hornet parked on de street, mon," said George. "We don need ta hire nuh cab."

"Hudson Hornet," said Pete. It sounded like a motorcycle.

"You too young to remember," said Mr. Winekoff. "A Hudson Hornet was a good car. Still is. At least George's is. Mint condition. How many coats of paint you got on her now?"

"I nuh keep de number," George said. "But all de time I paint dat Hornet I han rub till it shine lak de new piece o money."

"Let's don't talk about paint," said Mrs. Leemer. "How bout we see if we can git out of here."

"Max kin stay wit you. Me an Linga an Pete-Pete hab me mon, Henry, back home in some more little time."

"I ain't sending anybody else after my husband."

"I'll be glad to stay here and keep you company," said Max Winekoff.

Gertrude said, "I'm going, and that's that."

Linga rubbed her beautifully designed face, looked at George, then back at Mrs. Leemer. "I'll not countenance taking a wounded woman on such a piece of work as this. The three of us can handle all of it properly."

"I ain't wounded."

"You are indeed wounded," Linga said, "whether you wish to acknowledge it or not. You must listen to one who has been wounded many times, and I will, if I live, be wounded again. Wounds are something I understand well. In my case they started when I was born. But I don't have to tell you that, do I, unless of course you cannot remember the many talks we had about that very subject."

"I remember fine," said Mrs. Leemer. "It's nothing wrong with my memory. If you want me to stay I will."

"That would please me very much."

"Somehow I don't understand what the rest of you are doing," said Sarah. "I'm real confused. Everbody seems to know something I don't know."

"Try some smoke," said Linga. "You won't have to worry about confusion if you'll try a little smoke."

"I don't smoke."

Mr. Winekoff got off his chair and went to stand beside Sarah. He patted her shoulder affectionately and said, "Nor do I, my child." Then he chuckled long and softly as though at some private joke.

Linga's eyes had not left Mrs. Leemer's. "Then you truly understand, am I correct?"

"I understand," said Mrs. Leemer, touching her bandaged chest for the first time.

"Den it time ta do da ting," said George.

10

Outside under the streetlight, the sloping Hudson Hornet gleamed like an enormous shiny lump of gold. Pete could only stare. When he did look over at George, the big man's smile was as broad and gleaming as Pete had ever seen it. Linga looked as though she had just caught the scent of something rotten.

"Wha ya tink, mon?" said George.

"I've never seen anything like it. Really, I haven't. How many coats of paint did you say you had on it?"

"I and I nuh good wit dem figgers, but Linga say twenny-nine," said George. "Han rub ebber coat. Ebber bit I do by me an just by me."

Linga said in a soft and bitter voice: "You're thinking typical of a nigger, are you not, Pete? And, of course, you are right. The only way I could get him to agree to come to the States—agree without hurting him, that is—was to promise him a car. I bought this when it was a total ruin and George, with only the twenty dollars I give him out of his paycheck each week, restored it, turned it into what you're looking at. He kept not a penny of the money for himself but put it all into that . . . that *thing.*" She turned her head and sent a heavy glob of spit flying into the street. "So when you think this the typical work of a nigger, you are correct. Took him six months to do it, but he did it. As you know, the typical nigger is sick for a car and little else, except clothes perhaps, in some cases."

Pete had looked directly into her eyes as she spoke and now he raised both hands, palms up in a kind of resigned shrug. "George said you were a conjure woman, so I guess you can read goddam minds too," he said, "since you know what I think."

She looked at George, her hooded eyes going heavier. "Did you say I was a conjure woman?"

Before George could answer, Pete said, "Fuck what he said, forget it. Maybe he didn't. Maybe you're just pissing me off. And I don't even know you well enough for you to be pissing me off here in the middle of the night and the rest of the shit I'm in."

"Did this dickless one say anything to you about Obeah? Or that I was thought to be an Obeah woman?"

Pete looked from her to the car and back to her again, breathing deeply, trying to hold on to himself. Finally, with his eyes locked on hers, he said, "What the fuck we playing here, twenty questions?"

"I have no knowledge of what twenty questions may or may not be," she said. "But I would certainly like to know why you are so angry. What have I done to provoke you so?"

"Nothing. You haven't done a goddam thing. Just don't tell me anything else. I know too much about too many things already. Jesus, could we just get into the fucking car and go ahead and do what we've been sent to do?"

"Then there is absolutely nothing you want to know?" asked Linga in a hard, demanding voice.

Pete could feel himself going over the edge. He had to calm down. He turned away from them and leaned against the car, resting his forehead on the cool metal.

"Pete-Pete, mon," said George, "ya me fren?"

Pete did not move his forehead from the cool metal. He didn't want to look at them. Where in the fuck was all this coming from? he wondered. They were on a simple trip to steal a dead man out a fucking mortuary—which was a felony for all he knew—and here comes all this other shit right in the middle of it. Maybe he had slipped deeper than he could deal with. But then he thought of Sarah and his promise to himself that he would not run, which was his deepest, strongest impulse: *Run and keep on running.* But knowing that he was not going to run made him feel like he was in some last-ditch stand for survival. It really did feel like that.

"You know I'm your friend, George. You don't have to ask."

Pete took his head from the cool metal and turned to face Linga. "You want questions, do you?"

"You must have questions about all this," Linga said. "It must strike you as very strange."

"Nothing strikes me as strange, lady."

"I am not a lady," she said. "I am a Rasta. And if you do not have questions then I fear for your sanity. We, George and I, have to be the strangest thing you have ever encountered."

"You're wrong," said Pete. "You're not even close to being the strangest."

"Ask Linga questions, mon," said George. "She wan de questions."

"Keep your mouth out of this, George," said Linga.

"Good enough, goddammit," said Pete. "You want questions, you got questions. Sometimes when George is talking about himself, he says 'I,' uses only one 'I.' Other times he says 'I and I,' two 'I's. Why is that?"

Linga leaned closer to Pete, so close he could smell her. She smelled like something wild that had been shot in the woods. "When George uses only one 'I,' he is talking about only himself. When he uses two, the second 'I' is for his brethren."

"Brethren?"

"All other Rastas in the world," she said. "But more specifically the converts that I have made to my particular form of Rastafarianism here in this country."

Converts, for Christ's sake. Pete knew he didn't want to touch that, so he said, "Why does he call me Pete-Pete? I've told him a hundred times it's only Pete, but he keeps on with it anyway."

Linga smiled and said, "It is an affectionate way to say your name. It means he thinks of you as a brother, as one of us."

Pete paused a moment and looked long and hard at Linga. "The pet name you got for my buddy here—the dickless one, you call him—why is that?"

Linga's face hardened and she said: "That is a private matter and does not admit of a public answer."

"If you said what I think you just said, you either don't want to say or you can't say. Shit," said Pete, "I thought you was hungry for questions. And here I come with one you don't want to talk about. Strange, now that's strange."

"What is strange is that you would ask such a thing," Linga said, her face hardening still more.

"Not strange at all. Me and George are tight. We friends. Then I go and hear his wife call him something like that. My woman ever called me something like that, I'd beat her till she bled and then beat her for bleeding."

"And you might," said Linga, "might you not, wake up the next morning without a dick? You can take the dick off a man with a razor without his even feeling it."

Pete turned to look at George, who was staring down, seeming to examine the toe of his shoe.

"Jesus suffering Christ," said Pete. Then he looked at Linga. He was not going on with this. He could feel it taking him to a place that he could not bear or else to a place that would make him kill someone. Starting with Linga. She needed killing bad. He knew in his heart that she did. But it was not his place to do it. He knew that such a time might come, though, and when it did, he knew it would be an easy job of work.

"I think that about covers it, Linga," he said. "I think that's all the questions I got."

"You lie," said Linga, no longer smiling.

"There you go again, reading my mind. So if you can do that

you already know the other questions I have. Which is more than I know. Now can we get in the car and go get Henry Leemer?"

For an answer Linga walked around and opened the door and got in the front seat on the passenger side. Pete climbed into the back seat while George was getting behind the wheel and cranking up the Hudson. Pete dropped his head back and closed his eyes. But George left about four feet of rubber when he pulled away from the curb, which startled Pete, causing him to sit bolt upright and open his eyes. It was only then that he got a good look at the inside of the car and saw how meticulously detailed it was. Smooth leather seats. Dark velvet headliner. Mirrored chrome that looked like nothing so much as glass. Rubber on the floor that was not only unworn but unmarked. When George fired it up, Pete recognized the deep sound of Glaspak mufflers, as though the engine were running in a cave. The Hudson's shock absorbers smoothed the road like a silk sheet on a bed. So smoothly did it run that Pete was surprised when he glanced over George's shoulder and saw that they were running seventy miles an hour. It was late at night and there was almost no traffic and George ignored all stop signs and traffic lights. Pete had the feeling George always ignored them, no matter the time of night or how heavy the traffic.

Pete had not meant to say anything, but George's driving was so fast and erratic that he asked, "Get many tickets, do you, George?"

"Never," said Linga. "We are on the right side of the magic."

The fucking right side of the fucking magic, thought Pete. Maybe this bitch had simply gone crazy and taken George with her. But for the moment there was one thing Pete could do, and that was keep his mouth shut. He had written out the address of the mortuary on a piece of paper. He leaned forward, holding the paper next to Linga. "This is how you get to where we're going, Linga. This is the place. You're the educated one in the car. Tell George how to get there."

Linga did not turn her head but simply took the paper and held it close to the dash lights, squinting for a moment and then saying, "There is no problem. This place is nearby."

"Good," said Pete. "I knew you could handle it. And if you see an open liquor store, stop. I need to buy a quart of Jack Daniel's."

"We Rastafarians stay clear of alcohol, tobacco, all meat—especially pork—and all shellfish, snails, and scaleless fish, but I had to modify the diet to include scaleless fish. You can't convert a nigger in this country if you tell him he can't eat catfish."

"I only asked for a bottle, Linga, not a fucking lecture."

"We will not stop for alcohol. If you need something you may smoke ganja with us."

"I happen not to like it the way I do whiskey. True, I've never had any like you're smoking, but if it's all the same to you I'd rather buy a bottle. Is that a fucking crime?"

"It is not the same to me," said Linga, "and you heard Mrs. Leemer and Sarah. You heard what their views were on alcohol. So, for me, yes, it would be a crime."

"Forget it," said Pete. "I can live without it. At least for now."

Without turning her head, Linga said, "To be a Rasta is not just every black man's privilege, it is his right. But I am going to change that. I am going to proselytize—that only means to spread the word of Rasta as I understand it. That is why I am here in the States. Most of my converts will . . . Turn left, George, at the next light. Most of my converts will no doubt be black, but when I encounter special ones, I will embrace them gladly. That is how I know Henry and Gertrude Leemer and especially Max Winekoff, who brought me to them. He is, Max Winekoff, very special indeed."

"Max Winekoff is a fool," said Pete. "A very old fool, but a fool anyhow. He's good for nothing but running his mouth about other people's lives. If he's not careful, one of these days he's going to say the wrong thing about the wrong person and he's going to be a very old *dead* man."

"You speak out of ignorance. But then you are young. It is the ignorance of youth."

"All you need to know Max is a fool is to be able to see and hear."

"He is eighty-five years old and has the strength of a lion. And he serves a good and useful purpose in the world by getting the right people together with the right people. There is no chance that I would ever have known the Leemers if he had not brought me to them."

"You've got about as much business with the Leemer family as I do lying in a bed full of rattlesnakes."

Linga gave a short growling chuckle. "You are colorful, Pete, but that does not make you right. It is true that Henry never liked me, and I knew from the start I had no hope of converting him. Gertrude is another story. With her there is a chance of making her see the light of the Rastas."

"Gertrude could be made to see or believe or do anything," said Pete, "because she's right at the door of being crazy. Henry wouldn't have bought what you're selling in a million years. He was a hardworking and a good man who had the sense to—"

"To what?"

"It wasn't important. I'm tired of talking about this shit. I just want to get this job done."

"As I said before, you are only guilty of being ignorant. No great crime."

What had stopped Pete in midsentence was the thought of Henry's insurance money, money he had taken care to leave for his family. Pete didn't know how much it was but it must be a hell of a lot if he'd been buying it since he was a young man, and now on the very day of his death, this twisted creature with the illustrated face—this colorful buzzard—had swooped down as if by magic. But it wasn't magic. It was money. Pete remembered Linga reminding Gertrude of the long talks they'd had together. And in the same instant, he remembered Sarah saying that her mother had been trying to find his nearly destroyed, moronic brother and that as soon as *she got the money,* she was going to do it. He stared at the huge dreadlocked head of Linga in the front seat and felt himself caged with a lion. That bitch would eat them all alive—if Pete did not take care to protect the woman who was to be his mother-in-law, even if she was about two steps away from being completely around the bend.

Linga turned her head to look briefly at Pete in the back seat. "We are very nearly there, but permit me to tell you a bit more about being a Rasta. Perhaps it will cause some of your hostility toward me to abate. You have not asked but surely you must have wondered about our hair. I quote Leviticus 21:5: 'They shall not make baldness upon their head, neither shall they shave off the corner of their beard, nor make any cuttings in their flesh.' I could not convince Gertrude to leave off with the charlatan doctors but now she sees I was right and she was wrong. And as for smoking ganja, I quote you Psalms 104:14: 'He causeth the grass to grow for the cattle, and herb for the service of man: that he may bring forth food out of the earth.' There, George, at the steepled church, turn right."

Linga had been talking in a steady flat monotone, as though quoting something to a mentally deficient child. And Pete had no alternative but to listen. It made him want to lean forward in the seat and throttle Linga with his bare hands. But since he could not do that, he sat very still within himself and let her talk. "You, no doubt, find it strange that we quote the Bible, but, you see, we believe the Bible though not its charlatan preachers and blasphemous houses of worship. We believe Haile Selassie, king of kings and the emperor of Ethiopia. He will gather all Rastafarians someday back to our native land, the land from which we were dispersed, thrown like seed to all the winds that blow and scattered about the earth. But the day will come when we will gather again in Ethiopia under our great king and god, Haile Selassie. You can see from my face that I have been creased by the knife, but that is the least of the differences in me and other Rastas. In the next block, George, you'll see a building on the right. That is the place we are looking for. You would say, Pete, just as the other Rastas have said, that I am a renegade Rasta who is determined to make the religion embrace as many people as it can."

Pete spoke in spite of himself, having to unclench his teeth to do it. "No, you got it wrong, Linga. That's not what I'd say at all. What I would say is that you're one fucked-up woman that's about four slices short of a full loaf and not a goddam thing you said since we got in this car has made the least bit of sense to me, but that's all right because it doesn't have to make any fucking sense. It's all just so much spit in the wind as far as I'm concerned. But until all this is over, do you think we could just put a lid on it, you know, leave it the fuck alone?"

"Of course we can," said Linga.

George pulled into an enormous parking lot and stopped.

Pete would have killed for a pint of Jack Daniel's. He was very nervous. He knew this was all wrong. No doubt against the law too. "If I can't have any whiskey, you suppose we could smoke again before we go in? I think it'd make me feel better."

"That's not the question," said Linga. "The question is that Mrs. Leemer is waiting for her dead husband back at home, waiting to do his wish."

"Thinking the same thing myself," said Pete. "What brought my mind to smoke."

But she already had the Sucrets box out and was passing a lighted joint back to him. Pete had never in his life smoked any bud like this. But he still wished he had a bottle. He couldn't deny, though, that the fucking grass helped. It did not go to your lungs, it seemed to go instantly to every part of your body and light every cell up like a Christmas tree, and instantly everything you thought was of enormous consequence shrank to manageable proportions, and you could feel them shrinking—no, *see* them shrinking. He took two hits and passed the joint back to the front seat, holding the smoke and gesturing with his hands that he'd had enough. He wondered again idly if George grew this shit. And he thought that if he did he had every right to talk about magic, because he was a magician. The thought made him laugh as he exhaled, smoke catching in his throat.

"Better?" said Linga. She had taken none of the smoke and had already killed the joint and replaced it in the tin around her neck.

"Better," said Pete. "Much better. Let's do it."

They got out of the car and stood in what Pete judged to be a three-acre parking lot. The building was immaculate, white cinder block with iron gates across the entrance and lighted lamps on either side of the gates. The entire two-story building was surrounded with hedges so finely manicured they might have been tended with calipers. Four glittering black hearses stood side by side in an open-ended garage joining the building at right angles. At either end of the parking lot there were two very tall royal palms. Pete knew they had to be replaced every two or three months. Too far north for royal palms. But nothing was too good for the dead.

Linga led the way to the iron gates in long strides, looking neither left nor right. There was a small geometrically perfect garden inside the gates. And beyond the garden, great double doors with brass handles. The only lights burning were on the second floor, and in contrast to the rest of the muted, hushed, and well-tended grounds, those lights blazed brighter than a used car lot.

Linga raised her hand to a dimly lighted square doorbell.

"You better let me," said Pete.

She looked back over her massive shoulder. "Why?"

Because whoever answers will take one look at your face, scream, and call the fucking police, Pete thought, but he said: "You've been so goddam anxious to explain things to me, let me explain something to you. The world here happens to be white and you're black, or at least George is. But between your fucking hair and your decorated face, nobody in this building is going to open a door for you. Just let me handle it. Stand behind me until we get the doors open."

"You are wrong about what I can and cannot do. But I will defer to you in this instance." She smiled. "Does that make you feel better?"

"A lot better," said Pete.

He leaned on the bell and never got off it. Let the son of a bitch ring. Make them think it was another emergency. Another paying customer brought frantically by a grieving loved one. If this was going to work—and Pete was not at all sure it was—it had to be done with main force. It had to be war of a certain sort. But he felt very comfortable with George and Linga behind him. He also wished he had another hit of killer bud cooking in his veins, either that or several hard belts of straight whiskey. But since he could not have either, he stayed hard on the bell.

He heard a voice from somewhere inside that managed to be outraged, angered, and accommodating at the same time. Then a blazing light came on in the garden, and the double doors flew open. A prematurely balding young man stood backlit in the doorway. The light showed his fine round skull in perfect detail under his thinning hair. He was wearing a white apron that reached to the tops of his black shoes. It had flecks of blood on it. Behind him, two young black men stood on either side of a gurney. They looked bored and very tired. Another goddam corpse in a long night of corpses. In contrast, the balding boy who stood in the door in his blood-flecked apron had a face smooth of line and a professional heartfelt look that bespoke death as his life's work, work he took seriously. If you've got a dead one, his face seemed to say, everything I am or will ever be is at your service from before the first viewing to the last shovelful of dirt falling at graveside. Pete liked him immediately, and at the same time would have liked nothing better than to kill him. He reminded Pete of the sign in front of the yaks at the zoo, which described in great detail everything the yaks were not, had never been, and would never be.

In a voice that made Pete think of a radio announcer for a classical music station—lilting and soothing—the young man said: "Bring the loved one to the back. That is where we receive."

But you would receive here in a pinch, Pete thought. *Otherwise you wouldn't have the fellows behind you with the wheeled cot.*

"We didn't bring one," said Pete. "We come to git one."

Nothing changed in the man's face, as though he had not heard a word Pete said, and truly he had not, because he said: "There will be a young lady back there to help you with the paperwork."

Again Pete said: "We didn't come to bring one. We come to git one."

Now something changed in the young man's face. A slight twitching started at his left eye, and his mouth tilted in what wanted to be a smile, but there simply was not a smile in him tonight. The two black men had certainly heard. They may have been tired but they weren't deaf. With almost military precision they took their hands away from the gurney, on which they had been leaning, turned on their heels, and leaving the gurney where it stood, disappeared very fast around a far corner.

"I don't understand," said the young man, who still held his ground in the doorway, all manner of twitches having their way with his face now.

Pete lifted his hand to the iron gate and found it unlocked, which surprised him. But on second thought: busy night, much coming and going, unexpected train wrecks, men falling dead over their crosscut saws, no time for locked gates. Besides, it was all incoming. Until now. He pushed the door open and stepped through.

The young man said: "Only authorized—" but there his chin dropped and his fine radio announcer's voice stopped. Linga and George, who had been standing back in the shadows, stepped forward and came through the gate behind Pete.

Pete said with some satisfaction: "Pete, George, and Linga for Mr. Henry Leemer."

"I don't understand," said the young man.

Linga stepped around Pete, placed one of her massive hands on the man's shoulder, and said: "You have a dead man here and we want him."

"That's impossible."

"That is not impossible. Nothing is impossible. Look at my face."

But Linga had not had to tell him. His eyes, bulging as if with some kind of rare jungle sickness, held fast to her face, as though they would never move again.

He said: "This is against the rules."

"We didn't bring any rules with us," Linga said, "and you do not have any that we care about. Listen carefully, little man. His name is Henry Leemer. He is dead. We have come for him. We are taking him."

The balding young man was beaten and he knew it. He fell back on the only thing left: human decency. "I'm only the mortician. The funeral director has gone home. We've got a horrible . . ."

Pete said: "I know. Backlog."

". . . backlog. I can't be responsible. I could lose my job."

Linga still had not taken her hand from his shoulder and she must have given it some of her viselike grip because the young man did not so much wince as hunker. "There are other things that are of greater value than your job," she told him. "Your life, for instance. And responsibility? That's why we're here. We *are* responsibility."

Pete moved toward the undertaker, leaning very close to his frightened face. "Where do you keep the dead fuckers?"

"The loved ones are—"

"Never mind the loved ones," Linga said. "We are looking for the dead ones."

Pete could no longer stand the fear in the young man's face. He took Linga's wrist and removed her hand from his shoulder and stepped between them. "Look, man, you're in no danger here. We come to do a job. You got a job. We got a job. Let us do it and we'll get out of here. You can just pretend it never happened."

"But we've got'm logged."

Pete gave him what he hoped was a reassuring smile. "Then unlog him."

"Whatever you must do, do it," said Linga. "I am not interested in anything but getting the man we have come for."

The young man's voice suddenly became very firm. "Have you ever been in a slaughterhouse?"

Linga said: "I have been in many slaughterhouses."

And as suddenly as his voice had gone firm, it went weak, even helpful. "Right this way. It may take a minute. We've got—"

"You've already said."

"Yes, so I have," the young man said, leading them up a deeply carpeted circular staircase.

Pete smelled the place they were going to long before they got there, a mixture of chemicals, blood, and the dreadful offal of the disemboweled. It smelled to him like nothing so much as hog killing back on the farm when he was a boy. Except for the sharp acrid odor of chemicals. And that was what made Pete's stomach rise. He lifted his shirt and pulled it across his nose.

The undertaker saw him. "I told you," he said.

"Shut the fuck up," said Pete.

They were approaching a pair of swinging double doors that had glass panels in them.

A step away from them, Linga reached out and caught the young man by the collar, nearly lifting him off his feet as she jerked him back to look into her beautiful illustrated face. "When we go through that door, whatever you have in there, *whoever* you have in there working, just pretend that we belong here, that we have the *right* to be here."

"They've got to have security in a place like this," said Pete.

"Look at my face, white boy," said Linga, as though the young man could look anywhere else with his nose an inch away from hers. "Does this look like the face of one you would wish to upset?"

"No mam."

"Might you like one that resembles it?"

"No mam."

"You have a whole trainload in there. Please try not to be greedy. One more or less will not matter. Let us have the man we want and then forget the whole thing. Do you think you might do this for me?"

"Yes mam."

"You would not want, would you, for them to be preparing you for an early viewing tomorrow?"

"No mam."

"Let's get it done and quit talking," Pete said.

"Who's handling this, you or me?" asked Linga.

Pete said: "It looks like you are."

"How very perceptive of you," said Linga.

"Could I ask a question?" the young man asked.

Linga pushed him back a step and good-naturedly slapped him across the face. "Anything."

"What time did he come in?"

Linga looked at Pete.

"About dark," said Pete.

"Good, that's good," said the young man. "He'll probably be in the cooler. We had to get the train done and that's thrown us behind. They all *ought* to be in the cooler," he went on with some dissatisfaction, "but space . . ." He put his hand on his boyish chin and seemed to think for a moment. "Ah, could you . . . ah . . . sort of keep your heads down when we go inside, you know, look at the floor. The bereaved often do that. He might not even have been logged, the way things have been going around here tonight."

"Try not to think about it," said Linga. "This *will* work. We have the Rasta god and the Rasta spirits and we cannot be harmed."

The young man now looked truly alarmed. "Did you say God and spirits?"

Pete said: "Only a manner of speaking. She is a little strange, this one. I would try not to upset her if I were you."

The undertaker turned on his heels and resolutely marched through the door. All across the huge floor, men and women wearing gauze masks and rubber gloves worked over stainless steel tables with grooved tunnels for washing away the blood from the bodies they were working on. There was a great buzz of saws and a chipping of chisels and the unmistakable sounds of suction and great gobs of meat splashing into stainless steel buckets. Pete took his shirt away from his nose. It did not help anyway. A heavy humidity of tainted gore floated in layers, it seemed, over the entire room. It stank so bad it didn't even stink. Pete felt his nose rebel against the function of smelling anything: it just shut down. Not a head looked up from the tables where the men and women worked intently, some of them as bloody as the bodies they worked on. Hell, Pete thought, we could probably steal the whole goddam place and nobody would know it.

They followed the young man to a heavy steel door, something like the door of a bank, Pete thought. The man opened it and stepped inside, flipping a switch as he did. He pulled the door closed behind them. Pete's first thought was of Dachau. The corpses, men and women, were bedded down on shelves that were only about two feet apart. A neatly typed green tag was attached to each big toe. There was no smell now, none at all. Pete wondered if it was cold enough to freeze the dead. But no, that would not make any sense. They would only have to thaw them out again.

"Damn," said Pete.

"We're loaded," said the young man. "Capacity. We've had to borrow morticians from all over the city." He paused and held his chin reflectively. He avoided looking at Linga but turned to Pete. "I don't want to be presumptuous here, but what do you intend doing with the deceased?"

"Burn'm," said Pete.

"Burn'm?" asked the young man.

"You got trouble with your ears?"

"I'm sorry. I was only trying to save you trouble. We have already used the trocar on most of these in the cooler, but not all of them by any means."

"I don't really want to know, but I'll ask anyway," said Pete. "What the fuck's a trocar?"

"It is an instrument," said the young man, "that is inserted just at the bottom of the sternum and it effectively eviscerates the deceased."

"God of us all," said Linga, "you mean you've gutted these poor devils?"

"In a manner of speaking," said the young man. "Yes, we have effected evisceration without opening the stomach cavity. The trocar, through a rather small opening, effectively sucks out everything inside, but as I said before, all of them have not had the trocar."

Pete said: "No more details. Don't say another goddam thing."

In a peevish and wounded voice, the undertaker said, "If you had tried to burn one that had not been eviscerated he would have, in all likelihood, exploded on you."

Linga gave the man an almost shy and intimate smile and said: "I'm sure we would have thought to vent him nicely and avoid unsightly . . . *explosions.*"

Pete said: "Could everybody just quit talking and let's see if we can git on with the job we have to do?"

"Yeh," said George, hugging himself with his huge arms. "Quick. Be quick. I am some more cold here wit dese dat look now and see nuttin, look and see nuttin but all tings in dis wide world and de udder world, too. Yeh." His voice was steady but little more than a whisper. "We am be some more quick."

"You can start looking but there's a lot of them," said the young man.

"Beautiful," said Linga. "Very, very beautiful."

"He'll be hard to find." The undertaker was unable to keep the pleasure out of his voice for the task at hand.

"No he won't," said Pete. "He's got three toes missing from his left foot."

"Tree toes?" said George.

"Ax. The woodyard. Fuck looking at the tags," said Pete. "Look at the toes."

Naked feet stretched out of the bins all the way to the far wall. There were nine shelves reaching to the ceiling.

Linga said: "I'll take the top three. George, the middle three. Pete, you cover the bottom."

"Won't be necessary," said Pete.

They looked where Pete was pointing, and there, halfway down the aisle, were two long bony blue-white feet. Three toes were missing from the left foot. "Unless some other poor motherfucker's got three missing too."

"Never," said Linga, already headed toward the seven-toed cadaver. "We are on the right side of the magic. I would bet my face on it."

Pete turned to the young man. "Don't just stand there, asshole, get a gurney and a sheet. And be fast."

"Fast as I can. You don't want to be out of here any quicker than I want you to be." He sprinted down the aisle and through the heavy steel doors.

There were two sudden but brief noises just after the undertaker left the cooler.

"What the hell was that?" asked Pete, who had been a little jumpy anyway now that everything was so quiet. He thought he would have done better in the other room, where there was a lot going on. The sound out there was not so pleasant. He wouldn't want to pretend that. But it was *sound.* The quiet, along with all those slightly bluish feet sticking out from the shelves, made him jumpy. Christ, it was quiet as . . . well, death.

The two sounds came again. Briefer but louder. Pete jumped. "What the fuck *was* that?"

Linga only smiled and said: "The young man said most of these bodies had been eviscerated. What you hear comes from the ones who have not. Because what you just heard was clearly the sound of a corpse or two passing gas."

Pete was incredulous. "You mean one of'm farted?"

"Corpses do that more than one might think," said Linga.

Pete did not want to think about corpses farting, think about his life taking such a turn that he actually found himself in a refrigerated room full of farting dead people. He'd had other thoughts. Some he was not particularly proud of. He'd had, for instance, to make a conscious effort to keep from thinking of Linga naked on her back. No, not on her back. The only sexual possibility he saw with Linga was a buttfuck. With a buttfuck you wouldn't have to look at her decorated face. Beautiful though it was, it was not just the sort of thing a man wanted to be looking at when he got his nuts off.

A whole chorus of farts went off, like frogs going mad in a spring rain. And a wave of stink followed.

"Jesus, you smell that?"

"Shit," said Linga.

"*Dead* shit," said George, "long time dead shit."

"Enough about the shit," said Pete. "Where the fuck's the gurney?"

"Run out ob dem tings, I'm tinkin, mon."

Pete sniffed. "The shit smell's gone anyway."

"The cold has eaten it up," said Linga.

"Always something to be grateful for," said Pete. He was silent for a moment, staring down the rows of corpses, before he said: "Damned if I wouldn't kill for a drink."

"What a lugubrious thing to say in a place like this," said Linga.

"What a fucking what?" said Pete.

"Never mind," said Linga. "It looks as though we may have to leave here with Henry without a sheet. For all we know, that bloody little corpse worker may be calling the police."

"Keep yourself together," said Pete. "I think he's probably doing the best he can. And I know he's not calling the police. Your face makes a great argument, Linga."

Linga snorted through her nose. "He's making Linga wait. I do not wait for people. People wait for me. I may have to send you to look for him, dickless one."

George glanced at Pete. "Don call me dat here wit dese, Linga," he said, waving one of his heavy hands toward the shelved corpses.

"I shall call you anything I wish to call you, dickless one, and in the presence of whom I wish."

George flinched, examined the tile at his feet, and said nothing. Pete thought she probably could take him in a fair fight. He was also positive she would not fight fair.

The little man, panting, his breath fogging out in front of him, came racing through the door and down the aisle. A not very clean sheet was draped over his shoulder. The gurney he was pushing had crusted blood on it. When he got close enough, Linga slapped him on the side of the head, a blow that dropped him to one knee. He scrambled back to his feet, his left eye now shot with blood.

"You didn't have to do that," he said, holding his head.

Jesus, don't wimp, man, thought Pete, *or she'll fucking slap you down again.* He'd met Linga's kind before. She needed to be raped and then killed. But a long cheek-clapping fart made him snatch Mr. Leemer off the shelf by the ankles. It was as though Pete had been practicing the movement all his life. Henry, his mouth stretched open as far as it would go from the final grip of rigor mortis, slipped easily onto the gurney. He wasn't as toothless as Pete had thought. He had some pretty good ones there in the back.

"Cover him," barked Linga.

The little man draped him with the sheet.

"Now you push him," said Pete. "You look like you belong here, you know. White clothes and all."

"Right," said the attendant. "Anybody gets one look at the lady's face and it's all over." He had been settling the sheet over Leemer and had apparently forgotten himself. "Sorry. I didn't mean that the way it sounded. It is actually very good work."

"I have had men who would have killed for the privilege of touching this face."

"I'm sure you have," said the attendant over his shoulder as he started toward the heavy doors with Mr. Leemer.

Linga kicked him in the ass cheerfully. "You are not sure of anything, hairless one, or you would not be working here in the house of the dead."

Without incident, the gurney was pushed to an elevator and taken to the first floor, where Linga took Henry and the sheet up like so much laundry and threw him over her shoulder. Then she turned to the little man with the gurney. "You remember nothing of this."

"Nothing at all."

"Good," said George. "Dat be real good. Ya lib long an leaf plenny man chiles."

The night was very warm, with a hot, humid breeze blowing, and by the time they got Henry across the parking lot, Linga carrying him as easily as she would a child, he was limber as a wet dishcloth, which puzzled Pete. Once Linga got him onto the back seat, Pete took over and tried to make him sit upright, but he flopped around in an entirely unmanageable way.

Pete, sweat beading his forehead, fought with the flopping corpse to get it to stay straight. But what Henry seemed to want to do was curl up in an unseemly way on the floorboard.

"Fuck it," said Pete, "he doesn't care. Just let him lie down there. I don't imagine he much gives a shit how he rides." He saw the look on Linga's and George's faces and added, "I'll keep my feet off him. There's plenty of room."

"He is a man and your friend and you want to put him on the floor?" Linga said. "He is a man and he will ride as a man, sitting in the seat with his head up, for the final trip to his house."

Pete was in the back seat, again trying to arrange Henry, still wrapped in the sheet, but it was not going well. Henry flopped around as if deliberately trying to frustrate Pete's efforts.

"I thought he'd be stiff," said Pete. "Why the hell isn't he stiff?"

Linga said: "If you wish to know, I shall tell you. It takes about as long for the stiffness of death to go as it does for it to come. I have had much experience with this."

Pete momentarily quit with Mr. Leemer and looked briefly at Linga and thought: *I bet, by God, you have.* He had Henry sitting up nicely braced in a corner of the back seat now, but he was having trouble with his head. It kept flopping forward.

As Linga watched his efforts, she explained: "It takes the rigor of the dead as long to go away as it does for it to come. The bigger the man the longer it takes for him to set up hard. Mr. Leemer is tall but he did not carry much blood. The hardness starts in the hands and feet and works finally to the chest. The chest is the last to set up hard. As soon as everything is stiff, it starts to relax, the stiffness leaving the opposite way it came, from the chest out to the extremities."

Pete had heard entirely too much. "O.K. I've got it. I understand."

"You understand nothing."

"I understand as much as I want to." He had Henry wrapped like a mummy now. "I think we ready to go."

"It has to do with the blood," said Linga.

"Stop with the blood. This is bad enough as it is already, for Christ's sake."

"The more blood the body holds the longer everything takes. Mr. Leemer was a tall man but his blood was short."

"Get us out of here," said Pete. "Grave robbers go to jail. I read it in the papers before."

"The papers have nothing to do with me," Linga said. "We are robbing nothing. We are trying to do as the dead would have it done. This is not robbery, it is holy."

George said: "Git him chin off he chest, mon, wit him head up so dat him kin see."

"See?" Pete repeated.

"Pete-Pete, ya me fren? Do dat I say."

"And just how the hell am I supposed to get his head up?"

"Hold it," said Linga.

"Hold it?"

"By the hair. Get a handful at the back of his head and lift it."

Pete fell back against the seat, closed his eyes, and for the first time felt his gorge rise. "Roll one, George."

"At de house, mon," George said.

"Here. Now."

"I will get one from my tin," said Linga.

"Not a toothpick. A goddam joint. A big joint."

"George will roll it as we drive."

"Roll it now. *Now.* I want my head somewhere else for this ride."

"I unnerstan, Pete-Pete. Ya need ta go ta de holy place."

"If it's holy that'll do," Pete said. "That'll do fine."

"We need to move," Linga said. "The police have nothing to do this time of night but to fuck with parked cars with dead men in the back seat and niggers driving. There is no way to trust that little shit that got him out of the cooler for us."

"I really don't care," Pete said. "I've got way beyond caring." His eyes were still closed. He could feel the cold lump of Henry sitting beside him. "Are you rolling, George?"

George passed a joint as big as his thumb back to Pete. "Hit on dis, Pete-Pete. It take ya where ya need ta go."

Pete took down as much smoke as he could and held it as long as he could and then followed it with another hit. And before he exhaled again, he was as relaxed as Mr. Leemer and what had seemed absurd a moment ago seemed now not only right but absolutely normal. Pete had never *ever* smoked anything like this bud.

"How do you feel now?" asked Linga, pulling out of the parking lot.

"I don't. My brain's too shot down to feel anything."

"I don't understand this shot down you speak of."

"I don't either," said Pete. "And thank God for it." He was glad to see that Linga drove with more care and caution than George had.

"Mr. Leemer's head is not up," Linga said. "Hold his head up."

With no more thought than he would give to petting a dog, Pete took a handful of Henry's hair and snapped his head up.

"Better," Linga said, looking in the rearview mirror. "Now let him smoke."

"What?"

"Give him a bit of smoke."

Some little jolt of sense moved in Pete's brain. "The man's dead, Linga."

"His body is dead. That is of no consequence. His spirit is with us. Do as I say. How do you know his spirit does not need the holy smoke as much as you do?"

It seemed a perfectly sensible question to Pete, a question that did not admit of an answer. He jammed the joint between Henry's lifeless lips and left it hanging there.

"That better?" he said.

"Much better."

Pete laid his head back on the seat, still holding Mr. Leemer's head up, and found that he could think, and what he thought was that he did not want to smoke after a dead man. He'd liked Henry a lot. A good and decent man. But now a very dead one. And for the hundredth time in the last few days, he found himself marveling at what had happened to him. How he had managed to be in a restored Hudson Hornet with two black people from Jamaica with heads full of twisted dreadlocks, sitting in the back seat with a dead man who was wrapped only in a sheet with a joint half as big as a cigar sticking between his lips?

There was no reason to life. There was no reason to death. There was no reason.

"Do you think Mr. Leemer could pass the stick?" said Linga.

Pete, dreaming deeply now on the smoke, said: "I think with my help he could manage that. By the way, his head is cold and my fucking fingers are freezing."

"Never mind your fingers. It is not much farther. Pass the smoke to George. We all need the help of the smoke. There is much yet to be done. With four of us smoking, there will be more help."

"Yes," said Pete. He thought he had said, *Yes, we need all the help we can get and I, I especially, need help and Sarah needs help and Mrs. Leemer needs help and my drooling brother needs help and Mr. Winekoff needs help. At this moment I cannot think of a single soul in God's world that does not need help.* But all Pete had said was "Yes."

"I think I am lost," said Linga. "I never liked this city and I never liked this country and now I think I am lost."

"We are all lost," said Pete. "Believe me. We are all lost. And my fingers are numb."

"That is all right. This is to be expected," Linga said. "Mr. Leemer is still looking straight ahead and we will soon be there. Because now I know where we are."

"I'm glad somebody does." Pete put his head back on the seat and closed his eyes again. "I don't feel just right."

"You are fine," said Linga, "and we are not far from home now."

Pete repeated that he did not feel just right.

"After a stick of ganja, the spirits can come fast and hard," Linga said, wheeling the Hudson left at the light. "Relax and go. You may need to know something."

"There's nothing I need to know," said Pete, his eyes full of swirling colors behind his closed eyelids. He was aware that he was leaning now against Henry. Henry's cold shoulder felt good through the sheet against Pete's forehead, which seemed to have turned hot. That his head was pressed against Henry's dead shoulder did not bother him at all. He felt very close to Henry, and, in fact, although somewhere behind the swirling colors he knew Mr. Leemer was dead, another part of him refused to believe him dead. He was only bringing an old friend home. A friend he loved. Yes, he now understood that he loved Henry. He was the father of the daughter who had brought Pete home.

He heard George and Linga talking to one another in the front seat, but he could make no sense of the words. And it seemed to him they had been driving forever.

And then he was no longer in the car and he was no longer in the presence of Linga and George. He was walking through the sun-dappled shade of a wide, beautifully tended lawn toward a series of low brick buildings. And he was full of dread. He could barely feel his feet touching the ground. And he was cold. His head was so cold he could not think. But he did not need to think. And he did not want to think.

He opened one of the doors to one of the brick buildings and was met by a man wearing khaki trousers and a sweater with a red tie under it. His black shoes were brightly polished and he was smiling. He shook Pete's hand and his mouth moved, talking, but Pete could not understand him because he could not hear him. The man took Pete's elbow and led him through a series of long green corridors, passing many men and women. They all wore white and they all smiled pleasantly and spoke to Pete, who did not, could not, hear them.

The man took out a ring of keys and opened a door and Pete was met with a babble of talking he did not understand because it was in a language he had never heard. And shit. Not just his nostrils but his entire being was overpowered with the smell of shit. And it was young shit, the shit of children. He knew this and did not know how he knew it, except that he immediately seemed to remember that the shit of children had a sweet tinge to its stink that only made it more repulsive.

He and the man in the sweater were on a long ward with nothing but young children. None of them seemed to be more than eight or nine. Some sat motionless watching television sets suspended from the ceiling. Some rocked endlessly in chairs placed at tables where they endlessly passed square cards through their fingers. A surprising number of them seemed to be smiling, but their smiles were set and unmoving in their pales faces. And their eyes were dead. They might as well have been blind because they saw nothing. Pete did not know how he knew this but he knew it, or if they saw anything what they saw was not of this world but of some other. The floor over which they walked was tiled, and huge puddles of piss stood in pools, dull yellow, reflecting nothing. Young black men, white teeth showing in blinding smiles, pushed wheeled buckets and mopped endlessly at the yellow pools of piss. They all seemed happy, even the children who—Pete seemed to have been told but could not remember when or by whom—not only saw nothing but knew nothing and remembered nothing, not the past, not the present, and had in their beautiful skulls no notion of the future. Pete thought it was a condition much to be desired, even sought after at all cost. No price, he knew, could be too great to have what these befouled and piss-dripping children had.

And then he and the man in the sweater were standing in front of a boy who could have been four or could have been ten—or for that matter could have been eighty—because his face had been raped and pillaged and all that was human sucked out of it. He drooled endlessly, and his head was very large, the largest head Pete had ever seen, and it was covered with a football helmet. He sat on the floor and leaned against the wall, on which he beat his head and beat his head and beat his head with a sound like that of large nails being driven into oak or some other very hard wood. He was Pete's brother. And the only things Pete recognized about him were the twin indentations of the claws of the hammer Pete had driven into his skull.

The besweatered man walked away, still smiling, his heels smartly striking the tiled floor. Pete squatted in front of his brother, who he knew could not talk, and watched him drool. He did not so much want to cry as he wanted to die. Death was all that could release him, release Pete's lacerated heart. And release the child from his endless, mindless head banging, shut forever in a place that smelled of sweet shit and the burning acrid odor of piss. Nothing could ever be done about it. Nothing could ever forget it. Only death could find an end to it.

Pete squatted on his haunches and wondered how he had gotten to this place. What had brought him here? What did he hope to find?

"I forgive you," the child said, his mouth now free of drool, his eyes seeing now and full of the most awful knowledge.

"No," said Pete, not frightened or even astonished that his brother, who could not speak, had spoken.

"I forgave you before I was born," said the child.

"No," Pete said.

"I forgave you before you were born."

"No. You can't because I can't. It is beyond forgiveness and all hope."

"Touch me," said the child.

"What?"

"Touch the place."

"The place?"

"Touch the hammer place."

"No."

"You must."

"I can't."

"I am your brother."

"You are nothing. I made you nothing."

"You are a very grand person to have made nothing."

"No."

"No what, brother?"

"I am not what you said I was."

"Then touch the hammer place."

"I can't."

"If I can live with where you put it you can live with touching it."

"And what would that help? What would that matter?"

"Does it have to help? Does it have to matter?"

"Yes."

"You are grander than even I thought. You think you know what helps. You think you know what matters."

"I never said that."

"Then touch me. Touch us. The place between my eyes is yours. And it is mine. It is us. You can join us."

"I will join us."

"Do it. I have waited long."

Pete saw his hand reach for the child's face. And with two fingers he covered the indented scars. They were cold. Very cold.

"Better?" the child asked.

"Better," said Pete, closing his eyes, reducing the world to the two scars, and feeling his whole body go cold with the knowledge that he could not remove them, that they would live in him as long as he himself lived. And he knew that this was the way it would be forever and forever, perhaps even beyond death, death of himself and the death of the child.

Pete opened his eyes and found two of his fingers pressed firmly into Mr. Leemer's forehead just above the bridge of his nose. He did not move his hand. He could not remember where he was. And then gradually Linga's beautifully decorated face swam in front of him and then hardened into focus. And still Pete did not move his hand. And the coldness unlike any he had ever known, had ever imagined, moved out from the ends of his fingers and up his arms and through his chest and on down his legs until he could feel his feet freezing in his shoes. George and Linga were turned, their arms braced on the back of the front seat, staring at him. Nothing showed in their faces.

"You been gone a long time now, brudder," said George softly.

The voice seemed to come from far away.

"Brother?" said Pete.

"Brudder."

Linga said: "Did you know that a Rastafarian never shakes hands with one who is not a Rastafarian?"

"No."

She said: "Take your hand away and give it to me."

"But you've shaken my head already," said Pete. "I remember."

"Yes, I did, didn't I?"

Pete took his freezing hand away from Henry's forehead and put it into Linga's wide and thickly muscled hand. It was hot, hot enough to make his hand hurt, and all the cold, right down to his freezing feet, drained out of him.

"We are home," said Linga.

"Thank God for that," said Pete.

"Never mind God," said Linga. "We can live without God. We cannot live without the devil."

11

When they pulled into the driveway beside the house leading under the limbs of the oak tree to the woodpile, the lights of the Hudson Hornet briefly caught the gleaming crosscut saw still embedded in the log where Henry had fallen dead upon it. Mr. Winekoff was folded double, hands on the ground but head tilted upward, his eyes catching and reflecting the headlights. He stood up and approached the car.

He came to the driver's side and asked Linga, "Everything go about as you thought it would?"

"I did not think about it, Max," she said.

Max leaned farther into the car and looked at Pete in the back seat where he sat beside Henry, the sheet twisted tightly about the body.

"But you got him?"

"We brought back what we went to bring back," said Linga.

"Good," said Mr. Winekoff. "Wouldn't want to break a widow's heart. And we're ready for him. Everything is set up."

Pete leaned foward in his seat. "Set up?"

Mr. Winekoff said, "I took the sawhorses off the woodpile and put them in the dining room and got one of the doors off the closet. That's where she means to fix him."

Pete felt Henry's shoulder through the sheet, soft and pliable now as a baby's. "She doesn't need to do that, but she would do it anyway. Fix him. They always do."

"Fix him for the fire. She says she means to do it right. She has to—"

"Don't tell me," said Pete. "I don't need to hear it. I know."

"Do you want me to git the closet door?" Mr. Winekoff asked. "Be easier to tote'm that way."

"We have brought him this far without a door," said Linga. "We will manage the rest of the way."

"Whatever you say."

"That's what I say."

Linga got out and came around to the back door. "Let me have him."

Pete was glad to let her have him. He was still half caught in the dream or whatever he had had about his brother and he could still feel the indented scars on the ends of his fingers and his stomach growled and rolled, from sickness or from hunger he did not know, but his head was light and he did not feel well. He wanted to see Sarah. For some reason he could not have given a name to, that's what he wanted most. At that moment she seemed his only friend. The rest of these people seemed strangers, even the dead one to whom he had felt so close only moments before and with whom he had sweated and grunted through the day on the woodpile. He wanted no more to do with it.

Pete got out of the car and Linga reached in and took Henry as though he were no more than a child. The lights of the car were still on, the motor running, and as Linga carried the corpse over her shoulder toward the back door, the sheet fell away and Henry's old gray head bobbed against her back with each step she took.

Pete stayed with George, who killed the motor and turned off the lights as soon as Linga had disappeared through the back door.

Then on the way to the house, Pete asked, "What was that Linga said about God?"

"Rastas sometime beleeb an need God but if He here o if He nuh here make nuh matter. De debil it is dat walk de earth, lookin fo ya, him lookin an be always dere fo ya. Dat why de right side o de magic so portant."

"The right side of the magic?"

"Yeh."

"I always thought you were fucking joking, man. But you really believe that shit, don't you?"

"I and I nuh joke much ebber on dat. An magic? Pete-Pete, ya kin use dat word *magic* o ya kin use wha ya lak but a mon know when he right and he know when he wrong. Ya be wrong, ya put yasef wit de debil. Dat sound lak de joke ta ya?"

"No."

"No mon wit de brain tink dat a joke. But den dere be fo all time wit us de crazy. De tinkin wrong. De tinkin wrong all time walk wit de debil and fine demsef eatin dere breakfas in hell. Dat be clear ta ya now mon?"

"It is clear enough for tonight," said Pete, sorry he had asked.

"Dat, Pete-Pete, dat right dere de tinkin wrong. But ya young mon an mebbe it all come clear in ya head. But only mebbe. Long ya take de breath, dere hope."

Not really, thought Pete. He was thinking of his brother's hopeless breathing, banging his head against the wall, his drooling mouth having lost everything of any consequence. That he had life was of no consequence. But he said nothing and followed George up the steps into the house.

Every light appeared to be on and the dining room was ablaze with a high-intensity desk lamp that had been brought from somewhere. Perhaps it was Mr. Winekoff's, he being a voracious, non-stop reader late into the night. And there in the middle of the dining room, lying on the closet door supported at either end by the sawhorses, was Henry, completely naked, his thin bony legs slightly parted and his pubic hair thick and gray. His cock was uncircumcised and small and brown as a young boy's. His balls lay full in a distended and wrinkled sac. On either side of him on the closet door were boxes of cotton and alcohol and two safety razors and after-shave lotion. Jesus, after-shave lotion! There were other bottles and cans on the door that Pete did not recognize.

Pete stopped and felt the breath catch in his throat. Cotton was stuffed up Mr. Leemer's nose and a small piece of it hung out of the side of his mouth, and another piece showed from between the thin cheeks of his ass. Mrs. Leemer had a can of shaving cream and Henry's face was lathered from neck to nose. He had quarters over his eyes. Linga was at the foot of the table working on Mr. Leemer's thick yellow toenails with clippers so large they looked like wire pliers. Every time she managed to break through one of the nails, using both hands to do it, the nail clipping would fly off and strike a far wall with the sound of a twig breaking. A bit of black substance was beginning to come from one side of Mr. Leemer's mouth.

Linga pointed with her clippers and said in a quiet, conversational voice, "He is purging, Gertrude."

Mrs. Leemer, who was still vigorously lathering, said, "Thank you," and used the bit of cotton hanging from her husband's mouth to swab it clean and then daintily replaced the cotton in the corner of his mouth.

Mrs. Leemer reached for a razor and seemed to see the men for the first time. "Git," she said. "This is woman's work."

Pete, who was breathing again normally after nearly smothering in astonishment, said: "If you don't mind my asking, what is it you're doing?"

"I do mind."

"Preparing the corpse," said Linga.

"Satisfied?" Mrs. Leemer asked.

Pete was not. He'd always wondered why the women where he came from insisted on doing this. He wanted to know what Henry was being prepared for. Dead was as prepared as anybody could get. But he thought it best to leave it alone.

"Where's Sarah?" Pete said.

"I think she said she was going to her room," said Mr. Winekoff.

In a voice harder than a man's, Linga said, "We will not ask you again to be gone from here." She said it without looking up from Henry Leemer's feet, where she was having a particularly difficult time with one of his big toes.

George almost ran over Mr. Winekoff getting out of the room, with Pete following closely.

In the little hallway leading to the front door, Mr. Winekoff said, "I'll be on the front porch of the boardinghouse when you need me."

"I tink I rest in me Hudson fo some more while," said George. "Rest me in de Hudson and tink bout de straight razor Linga care in her shoe. Linga lak dat razor, lak ta care it in her shoe an dat make some more shit for me ta tink bout. Linga some more good wit dat straight razor."

"Razor?" said Pete.

"In de shoe."

"In her goddam shoe?"

"It de nigger in her. She tink it mus be some law dat all niggers got ta care de razor in dere shoe."

"Probably a useful thing to know," said Pete.

"Fo sho now, mon. Dat a sho an certain ting. But restin up in me Hudson gon take me down. I come loose dis way, me Hudson tighten me up. Come on, Pete-Pete, mon, an res up wit me and de ganja in de Hudson."

"I don't think so, George. I had the most god-awful dream—I guess it was a dream, but it didn't feel like it—I had it when we were on the way back with Henry. It was about . . . well, it wouldn't do any good to tell you about it. It's complicated and doesn't seem to make a lot of sense."

"Don tink on de sense, mon, an put de ear on de ganja. Wha de ganja say bring it true. It bring de spirits an de spirits dey don lie ta ya, mon. But ya kin nebber know ta hear les ya learn ta trus. Ya nuh trus anyting some much, I am tinkin."

"I trust you, George, you know I do."

"Don tink bout me, mon. Ya trus de spirits." He turned to go but Pete put a hand on his shoulder and stopped him.

"Do you know what they're doing back in there?" He pointed toward the dining room they had just left.

"Fixin up de dead mon. Ya know dat good as I know dat."

"I know that. Mrs. Leemer told me. Fixing him for what?"

"Fo de fire. Fo de burnin."

"Damn, George. Burning? Where in the hell do they think they can burn him?"

"Linga an me hab de camp—many Rastas an much land—way out dere in da Cedar Creek. Dey may be gon do it dere. Linga tell Henry's woman no need ta worry on it."

Pete knew right where he meant. Cedar Creek was just north of Jacksonville and the name Cedar Creek made it sound like a beautiful place. But there was not a creek, Cedar or otherwise, anywhere near it. Or if there was Pete had never seen it. It was a fucking swamp, was what it was.

"It's not enough dry wood out there for a wienie roast, George. I've been out that way more than once, and I know."

"I hab stack an stack o dry oak lef ober from when it be cold. But I be tinkin ta bring more dan some from de mon's own woodpile here fo him luck on de journey home."

It seemed to Pete that Mr. Leemer had run out of luck some time back. Seeing him lying naked on a shelf in a room filled with other dead people, a room cold enough to keep hamburger in, made Pete feel that the luck had pretty much run out.

"Well," said Pete, "I hope to hell they know what they are doing."

George became very serious. "Linga know all time wha she am doin. Eben when Linga don know wha she am doin, she know wha she am doin. I hab me whole life cause I know dis."

"I'm obliged to you for telling me." Pete did not doubt for a moment that what George had said was true.

"Linga say cause o de big mistake ya born who ya born, cause she tink ya a Rasta."

"I don't believe we had one in the whole state of Georgia," Pete said.

"Ya hab leas one till ya lef, I am tinkin. I go now ta join wit de smoke in me fine car. Dere is some more goin on now here in dis house I nuh lak."

"There is none of this that I like," Pete said.

George touched Pete's hand briefly before leaving, saying, "Ya wrong dere. But ya gone fine wha ya fine if ya look o ya don look."

Pete stood where he was for a moment, marveling at the truth of what George had said. He was now going in search of Sarah. And with all that had happened, would she be waiting for him? Wanting him? And he her? A miracle. And a tingling in his loins reminded him that the greatest miracle was yet to come.

He knew where her room was and also knew that she would not be in it. She would be in his room. He took the steps to the top of the house two at a time and when he reached the top landing, just as he had known it would, a thin line of light showed under his door. And his loins quieted but his heart pounded.

Pete opened the door. A dim lamp she had found somewhere was burning on a table in one corner of the small room. She was lying on his bed, long and lean, her beautiful hair fanned around her head and a folded washcloth over her eyes. He had opened the door very quietly and she did not move. Her mounded breasts rose and fell smoothly, regularly, and at first he thought she was asleep. But she was not.

"Pete?" she said, even though he would have thought she could not possibly have heard him enter.

"Yes," he said.

"Did you do what you said you were going to do?"

"Yes," he said.

"Sit on the bed," she said. He did. "Take my hand." Her hand was long and thin and chilled. She grasped his hand and closed on it with surprising strength.

"Is he downstairs now?"

"Yes. In the dining room."

She took the cloth from her eyes. She had been crying but her eyes were dry now and shot with a web of veins, with deep circles of a bruised color, not black but a light purple.

"The dining room?"

The only way to tell her was to tell her. "They brought his sawhorses in from the woodlot and took down a door to place on the sawhorses."

"And he's on . . ."

"The door."

"Who else is there now?"

"Your mother and Linga."

"What are they doing?"

"Preparing your father to be cremated." He had almost said burned but at the last moment realized what a brutal word *burned* was. "It was the way he wanted it. They are only doing what he asked to have done."

"You know where?"

"Where?"

"Where will they do it?"

"George and Linga have a place out at Cedar Creek. There's nothing there for miles around but marsh and swamp."

"I know the place. And it's dreadful. Ugly. They're going to burn up my daddy in the middle of the night in the ugliest place I can think of."

Pete thought: *One place is as good and as bad as another.* But he said: "I think your daddy would have wanted it that way. I don't mean it being ugly and a swamp. He was just a man that wanted a job done when he wanted it done. He didn't strike me as a man concerned with appearances."

"It doesn't have to be done this way."

"Maybe," said Pete. It was the only thing he could think of to say.

"Do you know how much life insurance he left?"

"No."

"A lot. There could be a preacher and music and flowers and a church. Nothing about what they're doing seems right."

That fucking insurance. He wondered if he ought to talk to her about it. About it and the illustrated buzzard circling over it. But this was the wrong time, the wrong place.

"Except that was the way he wanted it," he said.

"Hold me."

He bent over her and put his arms under her, felt her shoulder blades, as thin and delicate as a bird's, and felt her heart beating against his chest.

"Could we kiss?" she asked.

He put his lips softly on hers and felt a passion that was hot and desperate rise to meet him. Her mouth opened and their tongues touched and touched again. Her breath, the whole inside of her mouth, tasted sweet beyond saying. And her mouth was hotter still. And her breasts seemed to grow fuller under him and one of her hands, which had been buried in his hair, slipped out of it and slid down his spine to the small of his back and he stretched full beside her and her hand, long fingers splayed, pressed hard into his back before she slid it under his belt and he felt her fingers touch his flesh and they were no longer cold. They were hot and restless there on the muscles of his back under his shirt.

Her mouth was no longer frantic against his and her breasts no longer full and rising. Though she made no move, he could feel her open like a flower. With the hand that was not on his back she did something with her blouse and when it opened she was not wearing anything under it. Her hand moved from under his shirt to the back of his head and she moved his face between her breasts and he thought: If I have a home to come to, I am there.

"Tell me," she said, "what they are doing."

He knew she meant what they were doing with her father and he did not want to tell her, but he did. "He must be bathed."

"Bathed?"

"Yes. And his nails clipped and cleaned and his hair and eyebrows trimmed, and—"

"I ought to be down there,' she said.

"No. Daughters do not prepare their fathers."

"Never?"

"Never."

"Then I ought not to be down there?"

"No."

"I ought to be here?"

"Yes."

"Then I am in the right place?"

"Yes."

"I have passed from him to you."

"That is for you to say."

"I have passed from him to you."

Where had their clothes gone? There must have been much movement, hurried movement, but he remembered none of it. In the dim, shadowed light from the lamp on the table, they were naked on his bed and everywhere he moved she was there to receive him and everywhere she moved he was there to receive her.

"And this is the right time?" she said.

"This is the right time," he said on no authority but the language of his heart. His head had nothing to do with this.

She made a sound in her throat like a mourning dove and they were joined, and for a moment the whole world seemed to be very still and they were no longer kissing but their eyes were joined as their flesh was joined and he felt something hot and immediate start behind his eyelids and he knew they were tears. Both her hands came up and brushed his cheeks.

"I can't help it," he said.

"It's all right. It is a good thing. This is a good thing." And the tips of her fingers touched his cheeks again.

"And we are one blood now," he said.

"Yes," she said, smiling widely and happily and holding him to her, "we are one blood."

He wanted to tell her how he had lost all blood in the world but had now found it again when he had given up all hope of ever doing so. But he did not know how to say it, and the world that had gone very still was moving again, great rhythmic waves of movement that he did not even know had started until it was beyond stopping and with wonder, awe, surprise, and love he suddenly understood that it was her, his Sarah, and it was him, and they were not separate in the moving but together as water is together as it washes in upon the shore and back out again and in again, and finally in the mingling salty water pulsing in and out upon the shore—a pulsing that had become an image in his head—he heard the mourning dove cry again, more urgent now, and she was quiet under him, her mouth on his, and her own cheeks wet with tears.

12

The funeral pyre was only about five feet high, but it was made entirely of lightwood, the wood from the bottom of pine trees where the turpentine drained as the tree grew older. Nobody used only lightwood to burn in a fireplace. It burned too hot and too fast. Lightwood was used to start fires. A few sticks of it placed under oak logs would have a fire roaring in a matter of minutes. The funeral pyre was all lightwood from Henry Leemer's own woodlot.

When Gertrude was told they meant to use George's cured oak to do the job, she'd only shaken her head and said, "Burns too slow. We'd be out there the rest of the night and all day tomorrow burning him up. We'll use lightwood and we'll use his. It's only right."

"We can't haul enough lightwood to do the job in George's Hudson," Pete said, "even if he'd let us. Which I don't imagine he would, the Hudson being in the cherry condition it's in."

George said: "Ma fren got de flatbed truck. We go borry and do de job in dat. We kin use de same truck to haul Henry and de door on."

"I hope you don't mean to burn up a perfectly good door," said Pete. "From the short time I knew Henry, I don't believe he'd want the door burned and that isn't necessary anyway."

Mrs. Leemer turned and looked at Pete a full minute before she spoke. "I don't recall asking you what you thought."

"Mama, Pete's only trying to help. And God knows he's done everything he could. Please don't be mean with him and us tonight."

They were all sitting at the kitchen table drinking coffee. Henry Leemer was in the dining room on the closet door covered with a sheet. His eyebrows had been trimmed neatly into a shape they had never been before, and the hair in his nostrils and ears trimmed, which had never been done before, and he had been dusted with a powder he had never used before after a good bath, which he took from time to time but always resented, and his short gray hair combed down with Vaseline, which he had never used on his hair because he never combed it. Now and again Mrs. Leemer glanced in his direction. Nobody else did. Everybody else concentrated on the coffee cups in front of them. Gertrude Leemer had seemed to get stronger as the night went on, and she was dry-eyed and very businesslike and anxious to get on with the job at hand. And it was her very strength and dry-eyed, businesslike behavior that convinced Pete he had been right in thinking that all of this had made Gertrude about as crazy as she was ever likely to get. It unnerved him even to watch her.

"I'm not being mean now and I'm not going to be mean. We're going to do what Henry wanted done and I'm going to see that it's done his way. George, I'd take it as a kindness if you'd go and get that truck, you and Pete. It's gone take one of you to drive the car and one to drive the truck. Sarah and me'll get the wood together while you're gone."

"I'll be pleased to help too," said Linga. "I have always been strong and handled a lot that was heavy in my lifetime."

"I ain't exactly weak, goddammit," said Mrs. Leemer. "They cut my tits off, not my arms and legs. I've always been strong when it was any need for me to be strong. This is the last thing I can do for Henry and I mean to do it right. He could be a son of a bitch at times—who can't?—and he rubbed me the wrong way more than he had to. . . ." She stopped for a moment and stared back to where Henry lay covered with the sheet on the door, her brow drawn in upon itself, and she seemed to be in deep thought. "By God, now that he is lying over there dead and I think about it real hard, that Henry Leemer was a self-made son of a bitch. Yes, that is what I would say if I had to say. If he's gone on to his just reward he's gone have a long hard time of it." Her head jerked and a shudder passed through her. "It's not a damn thing I can do about that now. I did what I could do while he was still here. And it's one thing for sure—on a hot night like this, he won't keep very long before he starts to go bad." She looked at George. "Now git the goddam truck."

"Do you want me to go next door and get Max?" Pete asked. "He said he'd be on the porch if we needed him."

"Leave him on his goddam porch," said Gertrude. "I know the way Linga feels about him, but I'm running this thing we're doing right now and we'll do it my way."

Linga, nothing showing in her carved and brightly colored face, said: "He is your husband and this is your house, Gertrude. I am here only to help, not to tell you what should or should not be done."

"Well, that's the way it's gone be. I got nothing agin him. Hell, most of the time I even like him, because he's done a lot for us. Wasn't for him I wouldn't know Linga and George." She stopped talking and for just a moment seemed to lapse back into deep thought, silent, her wide brow knitted. Her eyes drifted down to stare at the table briefly but when she looked up again, the old savage fierceness was back in her face. "But all that old man has to do with his life is walk and talk. Mostly talk. And it ain't a hell of a lot that's good that ever comes out of his mouth," she said to Pete. "If he talks on and on, telling me all the mud and crud that's stuck to you, I know what he must say to you about me when I'm not there. No, leave him. Henry tolerated him but he never trusted him. I don't either, so leave him out of the rest of this."

George and Pete went north of Jacksonville out into the swamp over narrow roads covered with oystershell under a bright full moon that made the knee-high saw grass of the swamp wave like water under a strong wind. Finally they got to an Airstream trailer, where a pack of dogs had been sleeping in the front yard until George and Pete pulled up.

"Stay in de Hudson, mon, an wait fo me," said George.

But he didn't have to say anything because Pete was not about to get out among the dogs—tall, lean hunting dogs, going mad with barking and growling, long teeth glittering in their huge mouths, which did not seem to have any lips. But George stepped right out among them as though they were not there. The dogs quieted almost instantly, a few of them circling and sniffing him before they wandered back close to the trailer and dropped down to sleep again. A light came on in one of the windows.

After George was gone, it was a minute or two before Pete saw that hides of animals—possum, coon, squirrel, rabbit, and tiny Florida deer that grew hardly bigger than a good-sized shepherd dog—were stretched over nearly the entire surface of the outside of the trailer. Pete knew they were tacked down to dry. They would be tanned then with the tannic acid of oak bark. What would be done with them after that, Pete could not imagine.

George was back out of the trailer almost as soon as he went in, and he came to the rolled-down window of the Hudson and said, "I drive de truck. Ya take me car . . ." He paused and looked hard at Pete. "An ya be more dan some careful wit dis Hudson. Eberting I got in de world I got in dis car. I let ya dribe de truck and I take de car ma own sef, but den ta do dat ya hab ta get out here wit de dogs." He smiled a friendly and vicious smile. "Dese dogs, dey don't care nuttin fo Rasta meat. But dey do lak ta hab dem some white mon. Dey eat ya up, mon, right quicker dan de biscuit." George leaned into the car, putting his elbows on the window, leaned so far in that his face nearly touched Pete's. His odor was strong, blending sweat and ganja. "Now, Pete-Pete, ya me bes fren but dis is ma Hudson so ya be fockin careful. Ya *will* be careful, right, Pete-Pete?"

"*Fucking* careful, right," said Pete.

"Dat damn fine," said George, "jus so us got de unnerstandin."

"I do understand. Believe me." And he did. He drove the car back to town as though it were loaded with nitroglycerin.

Back at the house, they loaded the truck with lightwood and Mr. Leemer, the sheet bound and tied tightly about him. Gertrude worked like a trooper, going after the wood like the end of the world, and nothing they could say could stop her. Sarah was soundlessly crying but her mother's eyes were dry and a little wild.

"Gertrude, we can get the rest of this done by ourselves," said Linga. "It really isn't necessary for you to help."

"I've got an obligation you could never understand."

Linga said quietly: "I would understand. I understand more than you think I do, more even than *you* could imagine. I am only saying it is not necessary."

"I will decide what is necessary. And as far as what I know about you, I think you sell me short. I didn't get this old by being a fool."

"Mama always was strong-willed," Sarah said, smiling against the tears shining on her cheeks, "and a little hardheaded."

"Watch your mouth, Sarah."

"Yes mam."

After they finished loading, Pete and George got in the truck and led the way with the women following in the Hudson.

When they got out into the swamp, traveling on the same kinds of cracked oystershell roads that Pete and George had driven over to get the truck, going much deeper into the swamp than they had gone before, they finally pulled up to a purple double-wide trailer.

"Wha ya tink bout de home, Pete-Pete?" George asked.

"It's damn fine, George," said Pete. "It's better than fine. I wish I had something like this way the hell and gone out here in the swamp so that I wouldn't have to deal with people. So that I wouldn't have to deal with the fucking world."

George gave a great braying laugh as they were getting out of the truck.

Gertrude was already out of the car supervising the unloading and stacking of the wood. Every piece of it had to be laid to her satisfaction. It didn't take long, and when they were done with the wood, they placed the door with the tightly bound sheet still around the body of Henry Leemer on top of the pile they had made. Linga went into the trailer and brought back blankets for them to sit on, placing the blankets with an almost geometrical precision around the stacked wood holding Henry's body.

"You got any gasoline, George?" said Gertrude. "I don't mean to fuck this up."

It was the first time in her life that Sarah had ever heard her mother say "fuck" but she held tightly to Pete's arm and said nothing. George went into his trailer. It was covered with the same kinds of hides as had been on the Airstream, but there were more of them, nearly hiding the double-wide in hair. A freshly dressed buck, his antlers still on his head, was nailed to the front door. George was back quickly with a five-gallon can of gasoline.

"Pour it," said Gertrude. "But not on Henry. Don't git none on him."

George carefully poured the gasoline, threw the can off into the saw grass, and looked at Gertrude.

"Make a torch," she said.

"Don't you think a few words ought to be said?" asked Sarah.

Pete had been about to say the same thing and he turned to look at Sarah's mother. They were all looking at her.

"You know how you daddy felt about churches and preachers."

"We're not in church, Mama."

"It's all in his will. He said if you didn't have anything to say to him while he was alive, not to say anything to him when he was dead. Said he didn't reckon as how he'd hear whatever you had to say anyhow."

George wrapped a heavy piece of burlap, which he'd already soaked with gasoline, around a stick of lightwood and took a cigarette lighter from his pocket.

"Give it to me," said Gertrude.

George handed her the burlap-wrapped piece of wood.

"Light it."

George touched the lighter to the burlap and it flashed instantly into a huge fire.

The lightwood and the door and Henry Leemer did not so much burn as explode when Gertrude touched the burning torch to the pyre. The force from the flame blew her backward a step and when she stopped, she had no eyebrows or lashes and the front of her thin hair was singed above her face, which was now beet red. When Sarah tried to touch her, she brushed her hand away.

"But you been burnt," said Sarah. "We need to find something to dab on your forehead, if it's not anything but Vaseline. You can't see it because it's on your face, but you did get blistered some."

Gertrude pointed with the burning stick she was still holding and said with what seemed to be more than a little satisfaction: "Not as much as him."

Pete, whose arm Sarah still held, thought, *But you ain't dead as him either.* He said nothing, though, because since the pyre exploded, a mad aspect had come upon Mrs. Leemer. Nothing that Pete could see had changed, but her eyes were wider and wilder, her hair stood from her head like fine filaments of wire, and the tendons in her neck, which were always hard and exposed, now quivered like struck bowstrings.

The air was heavy with the smell of burning flesh, but it was like nothing Pete had ever smelled before. He had thought a lot about it on the long drive out. He had known it was going to smell. That much meat could not help but carry an odor. For some reason, he had thought it might smell like frying bacon under which the flame was perhaps too hot. But frying bacon would not cover what was coming into his nose. It was very sweet. If he had not known it was human flesh he could have liked it. The thought did not make him feel very good about himself. A little voice in the back of his head said, *Maybe you'd like to eat a little bit too, you son of a bitch.*

And with the sweet, repulsive smell of the burning flesh guilt and self-hatred, sharp and sudden as an electrical charge, caught his blood and held it in a memory of his ruined little brother, leaning somewhere now against a wall banging his head, drooling and talking in a language nobody had ever heard. And Pete had put him there. He felt himself cursed before man and God. He would somehow have to live with it, and someday he would have to die with it.

Pete shook his head hard and stared away from the fire toward the far horizon where the moon hung, full and nearly as bright as the sun over the waving saw grass—shook his head not to clear his mind of the image of his ruined brother, which he could not do—it would be there forever—but to clear the sweet burning flesh from his nostrils because he suddenly and without warning had associated the smell with the curse he felt he had placed upon his own life.

Henry Leemer, melting now into the glowing coals of the high hot fire, had known he was a walking dead man, had known that it was not *if* but *when*—his heart as big as a watermelon: Pete could not help smiling fondly even now at the old man's phrase—he would die of a massive coronary, so he had taken every penny he had and put it into term life insurance to keep his family safe with a roof over their heads and something to eat when he was gone. He had left nothing to chance, nothing to acccident.

A man like Henry Leemer would never have struck a child with a hammer because he would have made sure he knew precisely where the child was standing before he swung the hammer. With each and every staple fixing the wire to the fence post, he would have checked on the little boy, perhaps said something to him, perhaps let him think he was helping with the job ("Now you hold this staple—be careful of the points—in your hand until I drive this one and then you can hand another one to me"), and the little boy, wearing his gallused overalls just like the grown man and the same kind of straw hat on his head against the sun, would have held the staple and watched and waited and stood in full sight of the hammer, and he would never have been struck.

There would have been no chance. No accident. And today there would be no drooling idiot banging his head against institutional walls, cared for by people who were not his blood, people who knew nothing of him but his name. And the child, had he been in Henry Leemer's keeping, would have gone home and eaten his supper with his mama and daddy because they would never have met the Sunoco truck on the road to the stock market to sell the last brood sow they owned. That terrible, brutal, sweet, stinking smell in the air was the smell of a man with a man's care and concern and knowledge of what *might* happen in an unpredictable world. And he had made his fight against that world of chance and accident which could never be seen or even imagined.

But Pete was convinced, had been convinced for a long time before he met Henry Leemer, that he himself was not such a man and would never be. Henry Leemer's blood kin stood around him now sending him on his way the best they could, sending him the way he wanted to be sent. Pete would have no blood to send him on his way.

Sarah, who had been with her mother, came to him and took his arm and squeezed herself into him and buried her face in his shoulder and said in a voice that was a whisper: "Thank God, it's nearly over."

And Pete, whose mind twisted with tortured memories he lived with night and day, turned and put his hand behind her head, felt the fine shape of her skull, buried his fingers in her soft flaxen hair, and pressed her still harder against him. "Not over," he said. "Nothing ever ends."

She pulled back and looked at him, "What?"

He smiled down into her face and said, "It was nothing. Just talking to myself about all this."

"I know," she said. "But you said something about nothing ever ending. I don't understand."

"I think we all try to understand too much."

"Yes," she said.

"I've got a question for you," he said, still smiling down into her face.

For the briefest moment she looked puzzled and then pulled him closer. "Ask me," she said. "Ask me anything."

"Are you going to give me a baby?"

She drew back so that her eyes met his. "I am going to give you babies." Her voice was quiet and serious and sad with the weight of what she was saying. "A houseful of little ones. I feel it in my bones. It will happen."

"Thank you," he said.

Her eyes still on his, she said, "You have made this horrible day at least bearable. I will live the rest of my life for you."

"And the babies," he said.

She smiled. "Yes, the babies."

"I believe you," he said.

"Believe that if you believe nothing else."

And truthfully there was not much else he did believe, but he believed that. In an uncertain world, he believed that would happen.

There was much snapping and cracking from the fire, which was only a bed of red coals now. Pete and Sarah had their backs to it and neither of them turned to look. From where they stood, the heat was intense enough to be uncomfortable, even painful, but neither cared.

The fine little lines at the corners of her eyes deepened as her smile deepened. "I want a basketball team," she said.

"You want a what?"

Behind them, Sarah's mother said quietly, "He's going. By God, is he ever going now."

"A basketball team," said Sarah.

"You're going to have to be clearer than that with me, girl." And without his thinking about it at all, Pete's hand moved to the top of her rump, there where the crease started that would not end until it passed between the fine smooth flesh of her legs, to the place where he was now centered in spite of himself.

"Five boys," she said. "I've always wanted my own basketball team around the table."

"What if there's a girl?"

"Women babies are acceptable. We need a referee to keep the peace."

And for an instant, but only for an instant, Pete saw himself with Sarah at his table with his children, his blood, in a quiet house that was home. But then the image was shattered with the cracking and breaking of Henry Leemer's bones, and sparks and ash exploded upward into the night sky, flying across the perfectly round moon starting its descent into the tree line on the far horizon.

Pete and Sarah turned from each other and toward the brilliant red coals covered now with a fine white ash. In the middle of it was the form of a man—not a form really but a kind of dim outline of what had been Henry Leemer. None of his bones seemed to have survived the red bed of coals, but his skull had. The fire had not even cracked it and the deep sockets of its eyes were, Pete thought, looking directly at him. Pete knew it had to be his imagination, or perhaps his terror, or maybe only his most profound hope for the future, but he felt the skull knew and approved what had passed between Sarah and him even while its flesh was making the final passage to the place where all flesh must end. There was a curious pleasure and elation rising in his chest. He did not for an instant question that the dead knew what the living did not know, could not know.

This impossibility was not new to him. Before his little brother had been placed in an asylum where he could be cared for, before the fiery deaths of his mother and father, Pete had often looked into the eyes of the child, a child who could not talk, who befouled himself and drooled constantly, and he believed with all his heart that the little mutilated boy knew something that none of the rest of them knew. Whatever mysterious place he lived, whatever mysterious images he saw were reserved for him and the privilege of his kind. Pete never said anything about this to anybody else in the family. The world called such thinking crazy. Pete thought of it as love and called it love. He knew he loved the child in a way that was different from the way his mother or father or brother or any of the rest of his kin loved the child. The hurt made it so. None of them could know what Pete knew because Pete had been the instrument of his brother's ruined life.

Linga came out of the trailer with a gourd-shaped bottle. "I want to shake these over the fire," she said.

"What is it?" Gertrude asked.

"I can't tell you," said Linga, "because it takes a whole lifetime to know what is in this bottle."

"Then you best keep it in the bottle," said Gertrude. "Henry don't need it."

"It can't hurt," said Sarah.

"No," Gertrude said. "Nothing can hurt now."

Linga said: "It will make the passage easier."

"Do it."

Linga swirled the bottle and the fine powder flew out over the hot coals and hung in a layered mist, held there by the rising heat, before finally settling into them.

When the mist of powder had settled, Sarah said: "What now?"

"Nothing now," said her mother. "It's over."

"It's not over." Sarah pointed to the deep-socketed skull. "What about . . . about . . ." She could not bring herself to say what she was pointing at. "What about the rest, the part that did not burn?"

"He left no instructions about that," Gertrude said.

"It would be easy enough to bury," Pete said.

"If he'd wanted anything buried, he'd have said so," Gertrude said. "We'll bury nothing."

George waved vaguely to his double-wide nearly covered with hides. "It more dan some live tings in dis swamp, mon. More dan ya tink. Fore de sun go down, all dis dat is lef be scatter ta de far place."

Gertrude said: "He didn't say anything about that either."

"He probably never thought much about it, I wouldn't imagine," Pete said. "Nearly everybody thinks it all burns up. But it never does."

"You people are talking about my *father,*" said Sarah. She was in tears again.

"Yes," said her mother, "we are talking about your father. The final talk at the final place, so this is not the time to get sentimental over it."

"If I can't be sentimental now," said Sarah, "when can I be sentimental?"

Her mother stared at her hard across the cooling fire. "He's gone now and you can talk any way you want to and be any way you want to and it won't change a thing."

"He was good to you," Sarah said. "There's no need to talk like that."

Gertrude smiled a thin, hard smile. "And what would you know about how good he was to me?"

"I know. I just know I know."

Pete said: "I do wish I had a bottle. If I could ever use a drink I could use one now."

"I wish you did not drink hard liquor, my friend," said Linga. "Rastas do not drink spirits because it is something we do not need. Maybe the time will come when you will not need them either. Maybe you will come to find that my way is the only way, in which case many things in your life will change."

"Save me the sermon," said Pete. "It didn't help a thing. I still need a drink."

"I'm beginning to hurt some," said Gertrude. "Stiffened up, I guess, being in one place so long. It's been a long night."

George pointed to the skull, so white now it seemed to glow in the smoking black ash around it. "We kin do nuttin till it cools. It nuh be cool enough yet."

Linga said, "We could have some smoke and talk."

"Talk about what?" asked Sarah, holding tightly to Pete now, her eyes dry again.

"Him." Linga raised her hand toward the skull.

Sarah said: "I don't know what we'd say now that it's gone this far."

Linga pointed toward the pipe that George was packing. "The smoke will tell us what to talk about."

They watched until George had finished with the pipe. He lit it and passed it to his wife for the first hit. She drew deeply and held the smoke and passed it to Pete. Slowly the pipe made the circle around the fire without Gertrude ever touching it, nobody saying a word over the cooling ashes. When it got back to George, he cleaned it, packed it again, and passed it. Even Sarah smoked because Pete handed her the pipe and told her with his eyes to do it. She coughed a little but by the time the pipe got back to George a second time and he set it in the grass beside him, the circle sat silent as the final lip of the moon disappeared behind the dark wall of trees on the horizon. The light in the east was coming up.

"I nuh know Mista Henry good," said George finally.

"Nor I," said Linga.

"I knew him *very* well," Gertrude said.

"He seemed like a good man," Pete said. "Seemed like he had a good heart."

Gertrude giggled. "Even if it was as big as a watermelon. Yes, he had a big heart and I knew him very well."

"Why talk like that now, Mama? I wish I . . ." Sarah could not finish.

"Because this is the time for the truth."

"I felt when I was near him that he was a good man," Linga said in her slow stoned way.

Gertrude said, staring hard at the skull: "He would have been a better man if he'd had somebody to horsewhip the fear out of him every day of his life. He lived every day of his life rotten with fear."

"If you are going to talk like that I'm going to leave," Sarah said, but she held tight to Pete.

"Leave then," her mother told her. "Pain lets you know who you are. He lived scared all his life. And now it's come to this anyway." She waved her hand at the skull. "It always does."

"Some of us have lived scared. There's no shame in it," said Pete.

"All he knew was that woodlot and worry. And it was not necessary."

"Maybe God knows what is necessary," Pete said, "but He never tells."

"I would not worry about God if I were you. I'd worry about the devil," Linga said in the same slow sleepy voice.

"I've never heard anybody say such a thing," Sarah said.

"God," said Linga, "has never done anything to me or for me. But the devil, now the devil has been with me all my life."

"I don't know anything about either," Pete said. "Fire up the pipe. By the time it passes around once more, it will be time to do something. We will have to decide on something even if we don't like it. If I smoke enough of this, maybe I'll quit thinking about whiskey." He stared off at the dark tree line on the horizon for a moment. "But somehow I doubt it."

Linga started filling the pipe. "If you knew how Rastafarians are treated where we come from, the jobs we are given, how we live out our whole lives in shacks, how we are thought of as the lowest of the low, you would know something of the devil. I don't think you would spend much time thinking of God."

She passed the pipe. The ashes cooled. The moon was down.

Pete was lowering his head to the pipe, opening his mouth to receive, when he saw them. Men and women—all of them young and dressed in clothes of all the colors of the rainbow—stood quiet and completely still; they had the fire, the little encampment, entirely encircled. Their faces—grave, the eyes ganja dead—loomed out of the fading darkness. Many of them were white, but most of them were black, and there was one who was unmistakably an American Indian. All of them seemed to be in their twenties, gaunt, and in various stages of filling their heads with dreadlocks. Some of them had locks as long as George's, others had only short, twisted, spiky beginnings. Only the boy who was clearly an Indian had his hair braided, and each of his cheeks was marked with three thin blue scars running from just under his eyes to the corners of his mouth.

Pete, the pipe forgotten, looked from face to face without making eye contact. Their eyes seemed focused on nothing. Nor did they seem to be breathing.

"Pete." It was Linga's voice and he turned toward her. "My converts. Good Americans all. But now good Rastas, too. Their compound is deeper in the swamp, and made entirely by themselves. And they belong to me. Linga Rastas."

Pete picked up the pipe. "You got some fire?"

"But of course," said Linga, passing him her lighter.

13

It was long after daylight—the sun up and the day already hot and thick with humidity—when Gertrude invited them into her room for the viewing. George was not there: Linga had taken him to his job at the boxcars. But Max Winekoff was. He had still been sitting on the front porch of the boardinghouse when they got back from burning Henry and was very upset that he had not been included when they all left for Cedar Creek. But he had been easily mollified when they explained that in the midst of grieving and having to find a flatbed truck to haul the corpse, they had simply overlooked calling him and they were sorry and apologized for it. His old face, mottled with hurt and anger, had calmed down immediately.

"It could've happened in any family," Mr. Winekoff said. "It was so many of us it's a wonder somebody else wasn't forgot and left behind."

Pete thought Mr. Winekoff a little nuts or just trying to save face by saying such a thing. Even counting the corpse, there were only six of them. Not exactly a crowd, not even close. Maybe he knew he simply wasn't wanted at the Cedar Creek burning and was just trying to put the best face on it he could.

But he was invited to the viewing and he considered that an honor. As soon as they got back home, the mason jar of ashes, which might or might not have contained some of Henry Leemer, was put on display in the middle of the mantelshelf, and Gertrude had disappeared into her bedroom with her husband's surprisingly bright skull, having announced that there would be a viewing shortly to which she would call them when she was ready.

None of them knew what to make of it, although perhaps they should have from the way she had treated the skull from the very beginning when it was plucked from the ashes of the lightwood fire, back at George and Linga's double-wide at Cedar Creek.

"Dat ting cool now. We kin git him out," George had said, gesturing toward the skull from where he was reclining, propped up on one elbow, on his blanket. His wife was beside him, nodding out occasionally from the ganja she had smoked, her beautifully illustrated face changing colors and designs from the light of the dying fire.

"Yes, I was thinking the same thing," Gertrude said. "Henry's cooled down by this time."

"I'll go in the trailer and get a sack," said Linga.

"I'll carry him the way he is," Gertrude said, getting stiffly to her feet from the blanket she had been sitting on for some time.

"The skull is not all that's there," said Pete. "There will be enough left in the ashes to nearly fill a burlap sack."

"The rest can stay," Gertrude said. "But the skull goes with me. You could git me a jar of some kind, though, Linga, if you have one."

"I have plenty." She went into the trailer and came back with one. "I'm sorry I can't do better. This is one of the mason jars my Rastas use for canning fruit, but you are welcome to it if you think it will do. The rubber seal will make it airtight."

"Don't worry about the seal. Henry, I think, will rest comfortably wherever we put him now." Gertrude gave a little chuckle.

"Mother!" cried Sarah. "That's a dreadful thing to put him in. We'll get a proper urn later. We should have thought to bring one."

"But we didn't," her mother said, "and we won't be getting another one, proper or not. It's right in the will. It says, 'Keep me if you want to but in nothing special. The first thing that comes to hand will do.' " Gertrude took the canning jar. "Well, as it turns out, this is the first thing to come to hand." She held out the jar in Pete's direction. "Dip," she said.

"Dip?" repeated Pete, whose dick was hard from lying close to Sarah on the blanket they shared.

"Ashes," she said. "Dip this full from somewhere right there in the middle. Try not to git any wood splinters or pieces of bone."

"Mother, for God's sake, we can't do that, it's not civilized."

"I'm only following instructions, young lady," said her mother hotly. "If Pete caint do it I think George will probably help me out."

"But you don't even know what you're dipping into that jar," Sarah said.

"Does it matter? Your father thought it did not. Tell me how it matters what is in the jar."

Sarah could only stare unbelievingly at her mother through white wisps of smoke still rising though the fire had long since gone out.

"I can do it," said Pete, getting up from the blanket, his hard-on killed from all the talk of bones and ashes.

He took the jar from Mrs. Leemer's hand. She had taken the lid and the little rubber gasket off and kept them. Pete looked into the blackened pool of ash and then into the neck of the jar he held in his hand, and then finally at Mrs. Leemer.

"Any special place you want me to get'm from?" he asked.

"One place is as good as another. Just dip."

Sarah put her hands over her face. "I can't watch this. I would never have believed . . ."

"Don't watch it then," said her mother. "The night's been too long for me to care what you watch. Spare me that, too."

Pete had had about enough. This had all been bullshit from the start anyhow. It had pretty much ruined the memory of Henry for him. Every time he thought of him now, he would remember him lying naked on a door with a piece of cotton sticking out of his asshole. Pete had no doubt that it was just such indignities as lying naked to the world, his asshole violated by a wad of cotton, that Henry had hoped to avoid by being cremated. But somehow he had not reckoned on his loving wife's skillful hands.

He bent and scooped the jar full from the center of where the fire had been. The ashes were cool enough not to be uncomfortable. Maybe he'd gotten a bit of the old man in the jar and maybe he hadn't. He really did not give a shit one way or the other. He was hungry, tired, and he wanted to fuck Sarah. While the fire leapt around her father, she had put her head in his lap, pretending to sleep, unzipped his fly, and damn nearly gotten him off less than an hour ago. He had whispered to her that she really ought not do that while her father was burning up. But she had whispered back that it took her mind off how ugly everything was that was going on. Since he had been lying through his teeth anyway, Pete didn't whisper any more. He had wanted her mouth right where it was. But the sooner they could get out of this swamp and back to his bed the better. He handed the jar to Mrs. Leemer, who was standing now, and she screwed the metal cap back on the top. She didn't bother with the rubber gasket but only tossed it into the blackened ashes.

She held the jar up to the rising sun and looked at it. "That ought to keep you, Henry."

Sarah, who had taken her hands away from her face, said in a strained, distraught voice: "That may not even be him. It may not even be a little of him in there."

"You were his daughter, so you can worry about that if you want to. Me? I don't think I'll lose much sleep over it."

"If you *must* think about this," said Linga, "just think that it is only a ceremony, a ceremony he wanted."

"I can't imagine he was thinking of anything like this," Sarah said.

"Maybe he was only trying to avoid something else. Anyway, it's over," Pete said.

"Maybe, maybe not," said Gertrude. On legs that were a little wobbly from sitting too long, she walked out into the round blackened place where the fire had been and picked up her husband's skull like a bowling ball. She hooked the two middle fingers of her right hand in his eye sockets and put her thumb in what had been his nose. She actually raised his skull up to her shoulder in the classic bowler's stance, and the thought flashed on Pete that that was what she intended to do: bowl him. But she did not. She only looked around at all of them and said: "I think the job is done." She nodded at the skull. "This is all I'll be taking. George's animals can have the rest. I suspect that his bones will make some pretty good gnawing. They might as well serve some purpose: they're no good to him anymore."

"I think you've lost your mind, Mama," Sarah said in a soft and deadly serious voice.

Gertrude actually smiled when she looked at her daughter. "No, child, I've not lost my mind, only Henry. And I'm taking this." She held her husband's skull hooked in her fingers in a kind of triumphant gesture toward Linga, as though toasting her with it. "I'm taking this home with me because of something Linga taught me. Hadn't a been for her it never would have come to me." She held the utterly white skull high over her head, where the rising sun caught it and made it gleam and seem to glitter. "Here is the final scar. The final wound has healed forever into the final scar. Henry's scar I'm holding protects him from all the hurt and grief of the world. When you think about it like that, it's goddam beautiful. I want to keep it with me for as long as I live so that when things go bad, I can have it to remind me that someday the last wound will come and leave a scar that will never hurt or bleed or give me any dreadful miseries that will make me scream and cry and beg for mercy against the pain. The final scar makes all of us safe from the world." Her voice had grown quieter as she spoke. And the final words she spoke were almost a whisper and while she spoke them, she slowly lowered Henry's skull and hugged it to her breastless chest and let her head fall forward over it. Nobody moved or made a single sound. Somewhere far away a crow gave a long raucous call. And as if the crow's call had been some kind of signal to move, Gertrude lifted her head and her cheeks were wet with tears for the first time, but her back went suddenly ramrod straight and she said in what sounded like a deliberately harsh, growling voice: "We done all we can do here. It's over. The animals can clean up the rest. I think it's time to get started back home now."

George looked at Pete. "I know one ting. De fockin horn mon, him nuh die." He pointed one of his long, callused fingers at his own chest. "An dis Rastamon got ta lib an die by de fockin horn mon. Right o wrong, Pete-Pete?"

"Nothing but the truth," said Pete. "Sad, George, but the horn still calls the tune you dance to." But he was not looking at George when he said it. He still had his eyes locked on the skull hanging from Mrs. Leemer's finger. As did everybody else. Sarah was openly weeping, weeping harder than Pete had seen her weep since her daddy fell dead on the woodpile. It was as though something profoundly vital had broken in her and turned loose a torrent of grief unlike any Pete had ever seen before. He took her by the shoulders and turned her to him and held her tightly against him until she calmed. He pushed her back a little way and looked into her face. Her eyes were completely shot with blood and a thin dribble of snot was draining from her nose and Pete thought her as beautiful as he had ever seen her.

"What is this?" he said softly to her.

"It just come on me when Mama said what she said. It takes some of the terribleness away from the night. It was such a beautiful way to think about it all, and we owe it to Linga. Ain't no other way to say it—we owe her."

"You don't owe Linga a goddam thing," said Pete.

"I never liked her, if you want to know the truth," Sarah said between sniffles. "Or trusted her either for that matter. But it was a beautiful way she taught Mama to think about all of it."

"Yeah," said Pete, "it *was* pretty, wasn't it? Just the kind of thing that'd nip a widow's guts out but"—and here his voice turned hard and cold—"on the other hand, what we still got is a man whose heart busted and he's deader'n hell and gone to ashes to boot."

The color drained from Sarah's face and she appeared for a moment to stop breathing. "You can say the worst things I ever heard. I don't know if I even know you or not."

"Maybe you don't, but I know Linga and this whole fucking scam she's running out here. She smells your daddy's insurance money and that's what this is all about. You were right not to like her or trust her. Linga is bad news, the worst news you ever come across in your life. This is the wrong time and the wrong place to talk about it. But I will tell you this—as long as I'm breathing and I'm on my feet, she'll have to come over me to get to you or your mama."

Sarah was about to say something back to Pete when George stepped up and put one of his huge hands on Pete's shoulder. "Listen, Pete-Pete, a job nuh de worse ting dat kin happen ta a mon," he said. "Nuh job at all be de worse ting dat kin happen. I got ta git me back ta town o de fockin horn mon be take me job."

Pete said: "I've got to go out and find something to put my back to first thing tomorrow. Somehow I've got in the habit of eating and I'd hate to have to give it up."

"You've got a job," Gertrude said curtly. "We'll talk about it later. Right now what I'm wanting to do is to git Henry on home and myself in bed. This has about wore me out."

"What are we going to do about the truck?" Pete asked. "If we take it out there where we got it, how the hell we getting home?"

"We leeb de truck where am now. Nuh like to move by himsef, de truck. Ma fren know. Ma fren know him git de truck. Him nuh work de job fo nuh mon. Run de trap an grow de hemp. I work it dis day tonight." He looked over at Linga. "O mebbe sometime Linga . . . Nuh, bad tought. Nuh tinkin good. I mesef make it good." He raised a hand and tugged gently at a dreadlock. He looked from the truck to Linga and back again. "Linga need be home de house."

"I'll go over there if I want to," Linga said.

George only stared at her and shook his massive head.

Gertrude, cradling the skull in the crook of her arm, said: "This has certainly been a glorious time we've had out here. A lovely time. Don't go and ruin it with no argument. We'll all go back in the car. There's plenty of room. I ain't big as a bird." She looked down the front of herself. "I lost a little flesh when I was in the hospital."

So the two men got in the front seat, George driving, and the women in the back seat. Linga lit a stick of ganja out of her Sucrets box, took a hit, and passed it. It never got back to her. She lit a second. But when that one was smoked, she never lit another.

Gertrude had been gently stroking the top of her husband's skull, as though it were some strange and exotic pet riding in her lap. Sarah looked at her once, and then looked away. Nobody else seemed to care one way or another. Until she started singing. Then everybody looked at her; even George twisted his neck to look into the back seat every chance he got.

Gertrude kept gently stroking the skull while she sang, "Hush-a-bye, don't you cry, go to sleep, my little baby. When you wake, you shall have, all the pretty little horses . . ."

"I think he's gone to sleep for the last time, Mrs. Leemer—he's not likely to wake up," Pete said.

Gertrude sang the lullaby on to the end before saying: "And exactly what would you know about it?"

"I will answer for him, Gertrude," said Linga. "He knows nothing. Nothing at all is what he knows."

Then she sang another lullaby and kept on singing and stroking the skull all the way back into town.

They passed the boardinghouse and there was Max Winekoff with his feet propped up on the banister. He looked pissed off and hurt, as though he might blow a gasket any minute. But that was before Gertrude held the grinning skull up to the window. He did not so much get up from his chair as very nearly fall out of it to race down the steps and into the drive leading up to the woodyard, where George stopped the car and they all got out.

Max said, pointing at Henry: "Sainted Mother of Jesus, is that Henry you're holding there?"

"Yes, it is," she said. "I've brought him home." She turned the grinning face of the skull toward the woodpile. The saw was still in the wood where he'd dropped dead. "At least you won't have to be on a woodpile anymore, Henry."

"Jesus, woman," said Max. "What do you intend doing with that . . . that . . . *thing?*"

"Not a thing at all," she corrected him. "It's Mr. Leemer, or what's left of him. And as far as what I intend doing . . . I am going to prepare a viewing. And you are invited."

That was the first time Max had taken his eyes off Henry's skull.

"Why invite me now," he said, falling into a pout, "when you didn't invite me before?"

"An oversight, Max. On my dead husband's eyes, I promise you we plain and simple forgot." She held out the skull to Max. "Would you like to hold him a minute? His head's as smooth as a baby's."

"Maybe later," said Max as he fell back a step. "Just now I'd think it best if the two of you were together. I'm glad you forgot me and didn't just leave me," he said.

"Never," said Gertrude. She turned to Pete. "Would you put his ashes on the mantel over the fireplace?"

Sarah said: "Mama, you don't know there's a thing in there but burnt lightwood and dirt."

"Never you mind, dear," she said. "It's the thought that counts. Why don't you go in and make some coffee for everyone while I prepare for the viewing."

"You keep saying that," Sarah said. "What're you talking about?"

"A little surprise."

"What kind of surprise?"

"Oh, but if I told you it wouldn't be a surprise, would it?"

"I don't like surprises."

"I do," said Gertrude, "and I'm going to love this one."

"I'll make the coffee," said Sarah, striding angrily toward the house.

"I'll run George on to work," Linga told them. "Don't start without me. I love a ceremony."

"She said a *viewing*," said Pete. "That's what she called it."

"A name is only a name. It will be a ceremony. I'll make it one."

Linga got into the Hudson and George got in beside her. George and Pete shook hands through the window and Pete said: "Don't be a stranger, and thanks for the help. Couldn't have been done without you."

"Nuh stranger me, mon. Ya come see yo fren, fo true."

"Your mama," Pete said, truly sorry to see his friend leave.

"If we don't hurry up it will all be over before I get back," Linga said.

She roared out of the driveway, spinning up a rooster tail of dust.

"Little fast, ain't she?" said Mr. Winekoff.

"Try driving with George sometime," Pete said.

"I don't plan driving with anybody. Walking's my game. Walking—"

"You've told me before. I've heard that, Max. I can smell Sarah's coffee from here. Let's go get a cup." He raised the dark mason jar up toward the sun. "And let me put this fucking thing on the mantelshelf for her."

"Pete, show a little respect. That's Henry Leemer, as good a friend as a man could have, you've got in there."

"Maybe, maybe not," said Pete.

"I don't understand."

Pete said: "I don't either. But the best part of it is that I don't give a flying fuck what may be in it."

"Your grave got deeper, it just got deeper."

Pete handed the jar to Max, who took it reluctantly. "You care so much about him put'm on the mantelshelf yourself. I'm going for coffee."

"Pour me a cup too," said Mr. Winekoff. "I need a cup. This won't take but a minute. I've been up all night wondering why I was left out the way I was."

Pete didn't answer but went on into the house, where he found Sarah sitting at the dining room table, her head in her hands. She looked up when he came in.

"What in God's name can she be doing in there?" she asked.

Pete poured himself a coffee and sat down. "Thought you might tell me. She's *your* mother."

"I sometimes wonder if I ever knew the slightest thing about her."

"Truth is, nobody ever knows much about anybody else. Try not to let it worry you."

Linga came sliding into the driveway and was out of the car almost before the engine was off. When she saw them sitting at the dining table, she let out a heavy sigh of relief and said, "It has not happened yet. I can see it in your faces."

"What else can you see in my motherfucking face?" snapped Pete. He was exhausted and should have been upstairs in his bed with Sarah. And besides, Linga's comic-book face was beginning to piss him off.

"That you are a man of many bad words," said Linga.

"Get yourself a cup of coffee, Linga," Sarah said. "I don't know how long this is going to be."

"Or *what* it's going to be," Pete said.

Max came in from the living room. "Hard to think of Henry being in that jar."

"I wouldn't worry about it," Pete said, "because he probably isn't."

Max pointed to the hallway leading to Gertrude's room. "How long she gon be in there?"

"Why don't you knock on the door and ask her?"

Linga said: "I would not do that."

"All this has made her a little sick, I think," said Sarah.

"She was already sick from the knife she was under," Max said.

Pete tapped his temple with his forefinger. "She means in the head."

"I do not!" Sarah said with some heat.

"Well," said Pete, "it wouldn't be any shame in it if she was, after what went on out at George's place."

"What *did* you go out there for?" asked Max.

"You don't want to hear about it," Pete said.

"Of course I do."

"Then just say I don't want to talk about it."

"Can't blame you there," said Max. "Woman coming back home with her husband's head under her arm."

"Shut up, Max," said Sarah.

From somewhere back in the hall, they heard Gertrude's lilting voice not so much calling as singing: "It's tiiiime. Peeete, it's time."

Max Winekoff looked up from his coffee. "Was that her? By God, I believe it was."

The rest of them sitting at the table turned their heads and looked at the little hall to Gertrude's bedroom. Pete's name came again, long and pleading, like the bleating of a goat.

Max said: "It's her and she's calling you."

"I can tell who she's calling, goddammit." Pete raised his cup of coffee and took another long sip. The bleating call came again. He looked up from his cup to Linga across the table. "You think we could burn one before this goes any farther?"

"You think we should?"

"If there was whiskey in the house I'd say no. But since we dry here and since I don't know why she's calling me, I think we should. A fast one. She don't sound like she'll stay back there long. She'll be out here all over us."

Linga had the joint out of the box and lit before he even stopped talking. He drew deeply and held the smoke while he heard his name called long and loud again.

"Why the hell you suppose she's calling me?"

"You are her friend," said Max.

"You're her friend too. Why doesn't she call you?" He turned to look at Sarah. "Her daughter's sitting right here at the table. Seems like she'd want to see her. Linga's a friend and a woman besides. Hell, I'm just a male boarder in this house." The calling was louder and came at shorter intervals.

"I'll go," said Sarah.

Pete pushed away from the table and stood up. "No, she's calling for me and I'll go. But there's nothing to say the rest of you can't be right behind me."

"Good," said Max, "that's the ticket. You lead the way and the rest of us will follow."

Pete looked over at Max, hard-eyed, his voice distant. "Max?"

Max was instantly out of his chair. "What do you want me to do? Just name it and you got it."

"I want you to shut the fuck up."

Max dropped back to his chair. "I didn't deserve that."

"It's not what you deserve in this world, Max. It's what you get." Pete looked toward the hall. "I don't know as how I deserved to have my name being called by a breastless woman in a room with her husband's skull. But that's what I got."

"Go, Pete," said Linga. "Go now. Whatever this is, we must get it over with, or you'll have a madwoman back there. I don't like the sound of her voice. She is on the wrong side of the magic, I can tell you that."

Sarah stood up and took Pete's arm. "We'll go together. The others can come or not—whatever pleases them."

Pete looked down at her and touched her hair. "Maybe I ought to go alone. And then when I see everything's all right, you can come."

"I'm *coming,* Pete. She's my mother, you know."

"I know."

"It is only right," said Linga. "Sarah belongs with you. It is blood going to blood. It will calm Gertrude. Take her with you, Pete. But let her through the door first. Don't look at me that way. I know what I'm talking about. I know much of death. Back in Jamaica, I have led many death ceremonies."

"Linga," said Sarah, "please stop with the death thing. We know what has happened. All of us know that much."

"I don't know what happened," Max said. "I wasn't there."

"Keep quiet, old one," Linga commanded. "This is not a game." Then to Pete and Sarah: "Go now. We will follow right behind you."

Pete said nothing else. He took Sarah by the elbow and eased her into the hallway to her mother's bedroom. Still holding her arm, he guided her slightly in front of him, right up to the bedroom door, which was warped with damp and showing green mildew along the side where the hinges were.

"Open it. I'm right with you," said Pete. "And the others are right behind me. You have nothing to be worried about." He could smell Max's breath coming over his right shoulder.

Sarah pushed the door open and stepped inside. The others gathered behind her in the doorway. Nobody made a sound. Pete could hear his own breathing. Mrs. Leemer was lying in a four-poster bed dressed in her wedding gown, yellow now with age, the lace around the hem a little ragged. At the foot of the bed, atop one of the posters, was her husband's skull. It had been positioned so that it looked directly down upon Mrs. Leemer, whose smile was calm and contented.

Pete felt Sarah's shoulder go stiff in his hand and a little shudder run through her.

Her voice was ragged when she spoke. "Mother, what have you done, for God's sake?"

"Put Henry where he can see."

"See what?"

"Me."

"*See* you?"

"Right. He can see me but he can't do a damn thing about it. He can't do anything ever again." Her voice was quiet, conversational. She ran her hands down the front of her dress, over her hips. "Don't you think it's just a miracle that my wedding dress fits me so good after all these years?"

Sarah, who had been standing utterly still, her mouth slightly open, said in a strangled voice: "Mother, what on earth are you doing?"

"Lying in bed in my wedding dress, which, by the way, was your grandmother's dress too. Someday it will be yours."

"I don't know," said Max in an offhanded way. "It'll take some doing to get that yeller out."

"Oh, I can handle that," said Gertrude.

"I would never doubt it," chuckled Max Winekoff.

Gertrude said, "Linga, you look like you got something on your mind."

"It is never a good thing to separate a man's bones. I didn't say anything back in Cedar Creek—I thought it was none of my business—but I never expected"—she pointed to the skull atop the bedpost—"anything like this."

"He doesn't have to sleep up there," said Gertrude. "I wouldn't do that to him."

"Sleep?" said Sarah, trying to keep the horror out of her voice and not succeeding. "Sleep? Is that what you said?"

"Linga," said Gertrude, "pitch Henry over here to me. I'll show Sarah what I mean."

"I do not make sport with the bones of the dead," Linga said.

"Sport?" said Gertrude. "Well, the Good Lord knows I don't either. Will anybody pitch him over here?"

"How about handing him to you?" said Max. "I think I could manage that."

"You always were a gentleman," said Gertrude. "Just lift him off the post and bring him over here to me."

Max stretched and took the skull off the post. He hefted it in his hand, as a farmer might do to judge the weight of a cantaloupe. He looked at Gertrude and then at the rest of them. "I'd a thought a skull would've been heavier. This thing don't weigh hardly nothing."

"It's not what a skull weighs," said Gertrude. "It's what's inside that counts."

"But this one's empty," said Max, peering into an eye socket.

"Exactly," said Gertrude. "Now are you going to hand him to me or not?"

Linga had fired up a stick and was taking deep drags and holding them down until her eyes watered.

"Could you share a little of that, Linga?" asked Pete, momentarily taking his eyes off the skull.

Linga did not answer until she held the smoke in her lungs as long as she could. "I cannot do that. I cannot share smoke where the bones of the dead are not treated with honor. I have told Gertrude many times that after a stick of ganja is smoked, the spirits come fast and hard. So with this . . . I protect myself. But the smoke cannot, *will not,* protect you when you treat the bones of one already in the other world the way you are doing."

"Keep the shit. But I think you ought to know: I'm onto you, bitch."

"You should never speak to me that way. You want no contest with me. I am starting to think that George was wrong about you."

Pete said: "There's every chance he was."

Gertrude said: "Max, hand Henry over here to me."

Max held the skull against his chest and cut his eyes to Pete.

"Do it," Pete said.

He had seen people off-the-wall, his mother for one after her youngest son had been turned into a drooling idiot. And Mrs. Leemer was no longer playing with a full deck. She might come back from it or she might not. He liked her well enough but he really didn't give a damn if she managed to pull herself out or not. A thought came to him that came to him often: I've got a big enough bag of shit to carry as it is. The person he wished he could help was Sarah, who was gripping his arm so tightly and pressing herself into him so hard that he had to brace his feet to keep her from pushing him across the room. He was going to be as good as his word to himself. He was not going to run. He was going to gut it out if for no other reason than Sarah. She was nearly as deep in shit as her mother. Her breathing, face pressed against his shoulder, was as shallow and rapid as a Chihuahua dog's.

Max had given Mrs. Leemer the skull and she held it at arm's length in the air above her face, turning it in her hands slowly as though she might be looking for something. Finally she placed the skull close beside her head. With the two of them on the pillow, almost literally cheek to cheek, Pete thought that there was not a hell of a lot of difference in Henry's bony grin and the thin-lipped smile of Mrs. Leemer.

"On good nights he can sleep right here," she said. "What do you think?"

"I think no good can come of it," Linga said.

"It's worse than that," said Sarah in the smallest of voices. "It's horrible, too horrible to even think about."

"Then don't think," said Gertrude. "This is my house and my husband, and you might as well get used to doing things my way."

"I don't have to get used to something ugly," Sarah said, a blush of anger rising out of her throat to turn her face very red. "And I sure don't have to get used to this."

"Max?" said Gertrude. "Would you do something for me?"

"Anything."

"Come here and get Henry and stick him back on the bedpost."

Max got the skull and did the best he could to put it back where he got it. It was not a good fit and he had to struggle for several minutes before he had it placed to Mrs. Leemer's satisfaction.

"To tell the truth, I don't feel like sleeping with him," Gertrude said, "and for the first time in better than forty years, I can by God do something about it." She stretched long under the sheet. "Now that *does* feel good. You do get my point, don't you?"

When nobody would answer, Pete said, "I get your point. Believe it or not, I *do* get your point. But I guess we all ought to get out of here and try to get some sleep."

Pete herded everyone out of the room and was reaching for the light switch when Mrs. Leemer said: "Leave it on. I want to look at him for a while." She paused and gave her thin-lipped smile. "What I actually want is for him to look at me."

At the door, Pete turned and asked, "Did you *ever* love him, Mrs. Leemer?" He was sorry for the question the moment it was out of his mouth.

But Mrs. Leemer pursed her lips and then almost as if she was speaking to herself, which she was, she said: "Love? Love?" She was not looking at Pete anymore but at the skull. "I don't think Henry believed in love. Or if he did he didn't know how to show it. But I loved him. I know I desperately loved him. Maybe that's what made our marriage a living hell." She sighed deeply. "I loved him like nobody else *could* have loved him." She smiled up at the skull and gave a little wave with her thin bony hand. "And now it's over. It's come to the final scar."

Pete could think of nothing to say back to her, so he opened the door quietly, stepped through it, and eased it shut behind him. Through the closed door, he could hear Mrs. Leemer's voice talking on.

14

Pete lay down beside Sarah as tired as he ever remembered being, and he slept right through the day. They were both sound asleep by the time their heads were down. When Pete awoke, he was disoriented and confused but rested. But then he remembered. The room, the death, the roaring fire, and all the rest of the whole sordid thing. And Sarah. Where the hell was she? He remembered curling into her, and thinking how lucky he was in spite of it all. But now she was gone and he intended to find out where.

He got out of bed and went down the narrow hall to the closet-sized shower Henry had managed to install before he fell dead over his crosscut saw. There he scrubbed himself down good and even though he had to go through something of a contortionist's act to do it, he scraped his face clean using bar soap for lather and a razor that he should have thrown away a week ago. It was while he was shaving, looking into a broken fragment of warped mirror, that he smelled food. Somebody was doing some heavyweight cooking downstairs. He raised his head and breathed deeply. His nose told him what he smelled was beef. His brain told him that was impossible. The Leemer household went strong to fatback and occasionally to pork chops. And who was cooking anyway? Sarah surely. He certainly hoped it was not Mrs. Leemer.

When he walked out of the old lady's room earlier that morning, he had thought of her as just another huge problem. Nuttiness was a problem he had seen enough of in his mother after his little brother was turned into a vegetable to know that he wanted nothing to do with it. But—and his guts gripped and twisted at the thought—he, Pete Butcher, was the head of this house, at least for the moment, and he would have to deal with it whether he wanted to or not. He sure as hell was not going to put it all on Sarah and walk away.

He was through with that. No more walking or running or trying to sidestep whatever was in front of him. For one thing, he knew now, that simply does not work. You can run as far and as fast as you like but wherever you end up, you still have your head, and the sum of every moment of your life is locked right inside that bony little box holding your brain. So he had decided without it ever being a conscious decision—although he knew his feeling for Sarah was the source of it—to bite on the bullet and face whatever there was to face.

Hell, he had thought over and over again, I'm not Superman. I can only do what I can do. And if that's not good enough, then fuck it. If the only way he could have Sarah was to take everything that came with her, then so be it. He found it strange beyond saying that thinking like that, discovering that decision, had brought him great peace. And strength. That too. He was no longer the Pete who had moved into this wretched house. Somehow, when he wasn't even paying attention, something had changed him into a man he had never been before, or even hoped to be, because he had convinced himself it was impossible.

Back in his room, pulling on fresh jeans and a T-shirt, he realized for the first time since he had drawn back the hammer to hit the staple and nailed his little brother right between the eyes instead, he was not afraid. Being Pete Butcher was more than all right, it was pretty damn fine. He was worth something after all.

When he turned to the door of the little room, Sarah was standing there smiling the shy, secretive smile that sometimes came out of nowhere, and it had been a long time before Pete realized that it was only the smile of love and deep caring. And once again he felt himself the luckiest man alive.

"I thought I heard you in the shower."

"And I thought," Pete said, "I smelled steak cooking downstairs."

"That's what you smelled," Sarah said, "a huge London broil."

"A London broil?" He couldn't keep the astonishment out of his voice.

"A London broil. I didn't sleep very good—do you know you snore? Well, you do—so I was up by noon and went to the grocery store. I didn't go right away, actually. It was probably three-thirty before Mama got back."

"Got back? Where the hell from?"

"It's a long story, but like I say, it was near about four o'clock when she got back and give me the money."

"What money would you be talking about?"

"The money to go to the store. She said we deserved a good supper. And it's ready to eat and she's sitting down there waiting for us right now. She's even invited Max Winekoff over."

"Sarah, you know all this is confusing, don't you?"

"If it didn't confuse you, you wouldn't be right in the head."

He almost said, *Speaking of being right in the head, how's your mother?* But he caught himself in time. "Your mother seem all right?"

"How do you mean, all right?"

He sighed deeply and said: "Let's don't dance about this, Sarah. I don't like to dance. We both saw her talking to your father's skull this morning."

Sarah's pretty mouth went grim and thin as a knife blade. "Our supper is getting cold, Pete." She half turned in the door and looked back at him. "And I'd appreciate it if you'd try to always remember that whatever else that lady downstairs is, she's my mother." She took a deep breath and rushed on. "I don't know the ins and outs about it all, but that poor skull downstairs was my daddy's and her husband's. She done for him what he asked her to do. It's not many that would, but she did. Everything he asked for he got. Try to remember that, too."

Pete went to her in the doorway and turned her toward him and cupped her face with his hands. For a long moment he simply stared quietly into her eyes. "You know what I think?"

"What do you think?"

"You're never going to get that basketball team from me if we get into the habit of talking to each other this way."

That strange little smile came on her face as she pressed herself into him and said against his shoulder: "The only thing I know for sure is, the fire is still on under that Dutch oven and the finest beef you ever laid eyes on is going to be ruined if we stand here much longer."

Still, he held her face cupped in his hands so that she had to look at him. "You haven't gone and done something like change your mind about your own personal basketball team, have you?"

"Not hardly." Now her face brightened and her shy, tentative smile turned into something else. "Truth is, I been thinking about two basketball teams. If we had ten boys they could play each other."

He kissed her on the nose and took his hands away. "Fuck it," he said. "If five boys, why not ten? I'll just take up bank robbing as a hobby."

She was suddenly serious, the joking gone from her voice. "Daddies don't cuss like that. My own daddy didn't hold with it, and I don't either."

Pete said: "You're right. It's just a habit I picked up in the Marine Corps. A bad habit. I didn't know it really bothered you."

"Well, it does, but it'd bother me a lot more if I was a mama. I never heard my daddy cuss in my life."

"Then I'll just have to quit."

"Good."

"It won't be overnight but I'll do it."

"Nothing has to be overnight," she said. "Now for God's sake, let's get down to the supper table."

"Let's do it and say we did."

She went ahead of him and he followed down the narrow hall full of junk and on down the narrow stairs to the kitchen. The room was brightly lit by the naked hundred-watt bulb hanging from the ceiling on a black wire and by six tall red candles, each one of them held by what looked to be cut crystal. Something about the candles struck Pete as very wrong. It looked like a fucking birthday party, not the kitchen of a man who had died and been burned naked in the swamp the day before.

Max Winekoff sat on one side of the table and Mrs. Leemer on the other side, facing him. Max had a napkin tucked into his collar, a knife in one hand and fork in the other. His face was flushed and his eyes were bright and a heavy sweat covered his upper lip. Pete had seen the look before. It always came upon Max Winekoff when he was in the presence of food. But it was Sarah's mother who stopped Pete just as he stepped into the kitchen. What in God's name had happened to her? She wore a bright red dress that looked brand-new. Some sort of flower was pinned to the front of it. She had on too much makeup, and somebody had spent a lot of time trying to make her thin, fire-singed hair set in curls that twisted about her ears. They had not succeeded.

Max Winekoff looked up from his empty plate and said: "I was counting to a hundred before I went ahead and started without you, Pete. And I was already to sixty-three. You can't keep a man like me in front of food like this very long and expect him to wait."

"Try to remember where you are, Max," Gertrude said. "You would have waited all night if I'd told you to."

Along with everything else, her voice had changed too. It was imperious, full of authority, and carried an edge of hostility, or so it seemed to Pete. She did not look at Pete or Sarah when they came in but stared straight across the table, looking neither to the left nor to the right.

Sarah took Pete's arm and led him to the head of the table. "You sit here while I dish up the meat."

Pete said: "Can I help you or—"

Mrs. Leemer's cold voice cut him off in midsentence. "Sit. That was Henry's place and now it's yours. Sarah can manage well enough alone."

Pete wanted to object about taking Henry's old place, but he did not want to talk any more to Mrs. Leemer than he had to. He supposed Sarah could manage, but the heavy cast-iron pot on top of the stove was the largest Dutch oven he had ever seen. And he had never seen a table so covered—loaded down—with food. It looked as though every vegetable in season was on the table: squash, corn on the cob, peas, a huge bowl of greens with ham hocks on top, and other bowls filled with steaming food Pete could not identify. A sideboard held fresh-baked bread and three pies.

A place in the center of the table had been left for the London broil and as Sarah was setting it there—the meat topped over with carrots and Irish potatoes and whole onions floating in thick brown gravy—she said: "This was Daddy's favorite, a London broil cooked like a pot roast. Mama insisted we have it in his honor."

"That's not quite right, Sarah," her mother said. "I insisted that we have it. Period."

"Still, I thought . . ."

"Never mind what you thought. Pour the tea and let's get on with this. It's been a long day." For the first time, she cut her eyes at Pete and then at Sarah. "I didn't lie in the bed like some I could name. There's some changes going to be made around here, so I've been up and doing and by God, I'm tired."

Sarah began pouring iced tea into glasses set around the table. "Mama, if it was anybody in this house that needed rest it was you." She glanced up from the glass she was pouring to look at her mother, who stared straight ahead and did not seem tired at all. She only appeared harder, fiercer and angrier, or maybe it was just determination—Pete couldn't tell. But he had heard Sarah say often enough that her mother was a strong-willed woman who had always been able to do whatever she had to do.

"It wasn't a thing in the whole world," Sarah said, "that couldn't wait until you rested up, Mama, from . . . from a long hard night without a wink of sleep."

From across the table Pete knew she could not bring herself to speak of burning her father.

"You're wrong there, sister woman." Sarah was filling her mother's glass now, and her mother's bony hand closed tightly—tightly enough to turn the ends of her fingers white—over the hand that was not holding the pitcher. "Time is passing. The goddam clock is ticking. I can hear it if you can't." She held on to her daughter and glanced over to Max Winekoff. "Dammit, Max, cut that meat and start dishing up the vegetables. Let's *do it.*"

Before she'd finished speaking, Max Winekoff was on his feet, leaning over the table hacking at the London broil, his face red, and his upper lip heavier with sweat than ever. Pete took a dipper of peas and a wedge of corn bread and then passed both, the peas in his left hand, the corn bread in his right, to Mrs. Leemer, forcing her to turn Sarah loose. He could see how badly shaken Sarah was and he did not blame her. Mrs. Leemer looked and sounded angry enough to kill. She was so intense, wound so tightly, that the very air around her seemed to jell. Pete wondered if she might have a stroke, but then he wondered about so many things it occurred to him that maybe a goddam stroke would be a blessing. And he recognized the moment for what it was, a time either to get a handle on whatever was happening or to let the whole thing get so far beyond him that he would never be able to do anything about it. Sarah, white-faced and trembling, had gone quickly to her own chair and not so much sat as collapsed onto it. Pete's first obligation, maybe only obligation, was to her. If he, Pete, was there for any reason at all, it was to protect Sarah. Max Winekoff, he could see, was oblivious to everything but the food in front of him. He had managed to get a ragged chunk of London broil onto every plate and was tearing into his own food, his breathing making little sounds that could have come from the throat of a dog, and Mrs. Leemer was focused on him now. She had not touched anything on her own plate but only sat rigid, a slight tremor shaking her bony hands on either side of her plate.

"Max!" she very nearly shouted.

Max stopped dead still, startled, a forkful of meat poised before his mouth. His bushy eyebrows shot up. "What? How's that? What say?"

"The goddam food's not going to jump up and run away,"

Gertrude said, still entirely too loudly, her hands shaking worse than ever.

Max had taken one quick look at her face and had not moved. The meat stayed poised before his open mouth. Only his eyebrows twitched. "You speaking to me, Gertrude?"

"I sure as hell was speaking to you," she said, her own breathing now making a whistling noise in her throat. "You can't eat like that at my table. I've had to put up with goddam men all my life, but now that's over. Stop eating like a goddam animal!"

"Mrs. Leemer," said Pete so softly that his voice barely carried over the table.

Mrs. Leemer's head jerked on her thin neck, tendons leaping in her throat, and she faced Pete. "Did you say something to me?" she demanded.

Pete only watched her quietly for a moment. And what came to him now was the knowledge that he was trying to calm down a badly hurt and frightened animal. Whatever Mrs. Leemer was doing, it was not because she wanted to do it but because she *had* to. Everything that was human and reasonable in her was gone, leaving only a twisted and tangled bundle of nerves totally out of control. She was nothing but teeth and talon now, capable of destroying anything, including herself.

"Answer me, goddammit!" she shrieked. "You're in *my* house, at *my* table, eating *my* food! And you *will* answer me!"

As quietly as he had spoken before, Pete said: "Have you been asleep at all today, Mrs. Leemer?"

"What has that got to do with anything?"

"You're frightening your daughter. You don't want to do that, do you? Is that what you want to do, scare Sarah?" He had thoughtfully dropped his voice, so that she was leaning now to hear him. "I don't want to see her hurt and crying."

Max Winekoff eased the forkful of meat into his mouth and chewed slowly, his eyes swinging from Pete to Mrs. Leemer and back again.

"What I asked was if you had been to sleep today," Pete said, his voice as gentle as he could make it. "Did you get any rest at all?"

Mrs. Leemer's eyes blinked rapidly and she glanced down at the plate of food in front of her as if she did not know what it was. Across the table, tears had broken from Sarah's eyes and ran down her cheeks now.

"Look at Sarah, Mrs. Leemer. Those are tears on her face. She's crying."

Mrs. Leemer looked at Sarah. "Why are you crying, honey?"

"She's crying for you. She's crying for everything that has happened. She's crying for her mother. And her father. She's crying because of the way you're acting now. She doesn't understand. I don't understand."

Max Winekoff continued to eat slowly, watching them as if lost in a bloodless television mystery.

"Don't cry, honey," Gertrude Leemer said. "The time for crying is over. It's time to put it all back together and go on with it."

"But Daddy's gone and here we set with all this food and . . ." Sarah trailed off.

"Well," said her mother, "Henry's gone and he's not gone. Henry sent me for what all we got on this table." She looked from Pete to Sarah to Max. Only Max was eating, still chewing methodically, as though lost in thought, or maybe just waiting for the rest of a story he had only heard part of.

"Mama, Daddy is dead, dead and burned up." Sarah spoke slowly, as if trying to explain something to a mentally defective child.

"He wouldn't have had it any other way," said Gertrude, and her hard, grim face slowly softened into a beatific smile. She looked now at the food covering the table, her eyes, caught in a net of red veins, drifting from dish to dish. "Just like all this food." She was silent a moment. "Where did it all come from, this food?"

"You told me to go get it, Mama, to call a cab and go get it."

"Oh, well, yes. The cab," Gertrude said. "Henry told me to do it, to go and do it in a cab."

"In a cab . . . ?"

"In a cab."

Across the table, Max forked another piece of beef into his mouth, his slow, careful chewing never missing a beat.

"Daddy told you," said Sarah, glancing briefly at Pete, ". . . today?"

Gertrude Leemer's beatific smile went softer still. It was now she who spoke as if explaining to a mentally defective child. "Henry didn't tell me to do it *today.* He told me to do it on the day after he was dead. *And* changed."

"Changed?" said Max, looking up at Gertrude through his thick, twisted eyebrows from where he was hunkered over his place, his mouth open to receive another chunk of ragged beef.

"Burned," said Gertrude.

"Oh, yes," said Max. And then peevishly: "Somehow I got left behind on that trip." He chewed and rolled his eyes, giving a long sigh of satisfaction. "But *burned*—now that does change a man."

"He planned all this?" Sarah's voice was soft and unbelieving. "Daddy planned all this?"

"He planned more than you know," said her mother. "A man that's scared plans the day *and* night away. And him not able to do a thing about it, broke like he was. Until he died, that is. Him and that damn insurance. Started before you was even born. Before you was born, Henry already known he'd be able to do any damn thing he wanted to do after he was dead." She looked at all the food spread out and cooling before her. "He said load up the table, so I went to see the lawyer and get the ball rolling. That's how I come to send you in a cab with something to load up the table."

"Lawyer?" Max said. "Now that right there could be a mistake."

"Hush, Max," said Sarah. "You don't know a thing about this." Then to her mother: "Which lawyer would that be you were talking about, Mama?"

"Your daddy's lawyer," Gertrude explained. "He, the lawyer I mean, get his money right off the top of the insurance. No need to worry though. It's plenty to go around. Henry figured, without a lawyer, we'd be forever touching a penny of that money. He worried that out too. He worried everthing out."

"A lawyer that's got to get yours before he gets his," Max said. "Now a lawyer like that might be all right."

"I told you to hush, Max," Sarah said. "Mama, I don't understand about a lawyer. Nobody ever told me about a lawyer. I'm a grown woman and nobody ever told me."

"It's a lot nobody ever told you," her mother said, "and you can thank God for that."

"I still don't see why a lawyer," Sarah insisted.

"I may be from Bacon County, Georgia," said Pete, "but even I know you can't blow your nose in this country without a lawyer. One of the things I was thinking about when we went over there and stole Henry. He told me about that insurance of his, told me more than once. But it's a little matter of a death certificate. You ain't got a birth certificate, you were never born. No death certificate, you never died. That's the way they got it figured out. Ever sumbitch we elect to Washington's a lawyer. Lawyers make the laws and then they feed off them. So there's a problem right there."

Gertrude gave a little snort. "No problem atall. Already took care of. Lawyer seen to it, before he given me the advance."

"Advance?" said Sarah.

Gertrude waved her hand at the food going cold on the table. "You don't think this is insurance money, do you? Takes some longer'n one day to git it. But Henry had already worried that out too. He worried everthing out for forty years and more."

"Don't believe I've seen you eat a bit, Mrs. Leemer," said Pete. "You don't want none of this, do you?"

"What?" she said.

"Eat. You don't want to eat?"

"Ever bone in my body is tired and hurting. I got it on the table because that's what he wanted. But no, son, I can't eat nothing right now. And maybe you ought to call me Gertrude. Don't you think it's about time for that?"

"I do, Gertrude, and I think it's about time you got back there to your bed and went to sleep." Pete pushed back from the table and stood up. "Come on, Sarah, let's get your mother back to her room."

"I can't be any help," said Max, "so I'll just have me another little taste of the meat."

"You do that," said Pete.

"I believe I could eat every bite of it," Max said.

"I never doubted it," Pete told him.

When Sarah and Pete went through the door to her mother's room, Pete saw Sarah, her face pale, her lips pulled into a tight grim line, look up at the bedpost where they had last seen her father's skull. She stopped and stood in the open doorway while Pete, holding her mother's elbow, guided her to the bed, where she sat down.

"Where?" said Sarah.

"Sarah, come pull the covers down for your mother," said Pete. "Get her shoes off." He did not want to hear about the skull. He did not want Sarah to hear about the skull or even think about it. "Come on. Gertrude needs to rest."

But Sarah had not moved from the door. She was looking about the room, her eyes startled and darting. "Where *is* it?" she demanded.

"That's all over with," said Pete. "We're through with that."

"Oh, you mean Henry?" said Gertrude. "Linga's got him. She put him in a box and made George take him with them."

Sarah, her eyes closed, put out a hand to lean against the doorframe and did not move.

Well, thought Pete, maybe that's not all over with. Maybe we're not through with that after all.

15

The next morning Pete, dressing quietly and leaving Sarah asleep, went downstairs to make coffee. But before he ever got to the kitchen, he smelled fresh coffee, and he found Gertrude sitting at the table with a cup and a tablet of paper. He didn't know what time it was—around five, he thought—but it was still not light outside. He stopped in the doorway to the kitchen, not knowing quite what to say or how he was going to find her this morning. He hoped she would not start on skulls and ceremonies and what might or might not be Henry sitting in a mason jar on the mantelshelf. He was wondering how well she had slept or if she had slept at all. But when she glanced up from the tablet paper, which he could see was covered with columns of figures, her face was swollen, and although she sat quietly, her eyes had the wild look of somebody who has just come upon a grizzly bear in the deep woods, and her makeup looked as though it had been put on by a child. There was as much lipstick off her lips as on them, painted in such a fashion as to give her mouth a permanent snarl. Pete had never seen any mascara in the house, certainly not on Sarah and never on Gertrude, but the old lady was wearing it today. And it had done to her eyes—eyes that were little more than very red slits in her swollen lids—what the lipstick had done to her mouth. She did not so much wear the mascara as peep through the heavy, crooked layers of it. Her fire-singed hair looked as if it had not been touched since she got out of bed, if in fact she had been in bed at all. He suspected she had not. Pete had never seen the robe she had on, but it was stained badly, wearing the unidentifiable spots of countless past meals.

Pete's first thought was to go back upstairs and get Sarah because this looked like more than he could handle alone. And he was just about to do that when Gertrude spoke.

She kept her face down, looking at the figures, as she said: "It's coffee on the stove. Git a cup and set down. We need to talk."

If her appearance had startled him—maybe even frightened him a little—her voice so dumbfounded him that he felt his jaw unhinge. She had spoken in a smooth, pleasant voice that was totally at odds with her face.

"If you're going to stand there and stare and not move we'll be here all day," she said, still not looking up from the paper she was filling with columns of numbers.

He got the coffee and sat down. It was strong and bitter and black. There had always been sugar and cream on the table, but this morning there was none. Could she have been sitting here drinking this stuff most of the night? Because the coffee in his cup was thick and left a sharp, old bitterness on his tongue.

"Morning, Gertrude," he said with a heartiness he did not feel. "Did you sleep all right?"

"I think," she said, "we ought just skip all the chitchat this morning and git right down to business. It's a lot to take care of. Sarah still asleep, I guess?"

"Was when I left the room."

"That's all right, she ain't needed yet awhile."

"She's had plenty of rest. I could get her down here in—"

"Never mind," she said, waving him off with the blunted pencil she was working with. "Not important. The important thing is that we tighten up."

"Tighten up?" he said. The phrase seemed inappropriate here in the dark of the morning with her husband barely cold in his jar, and Pete was prepared for something nutty to follow it.

"We've got to run a tight ship if we're to make money," she said.

"Tight ship? Money?"

She put her pencil down and raised her eyes to meet his, and her eyes reminded him of a banker's eyes, calm, deliberate, and a little cold—the coldness that comes with the talk of business. She sighed and said: "Drink that cup of coffee, son. You're not awake yet."

"I'm awake."

"Drink it anyway."

He raised it to his lips and took a sip. "Too hot to drink right down."

She smiled, and he thought of his mother's smile before he had pushed her over the edge by destroying her youngest son. Pete could never remember Gertrude with a smile like that on her face before.

"I've got time to wait," she said. "If you'll pour me another cup I'll drink one with you."

Pete got up from the table and poured her another cup.

"Thank you," Gertrude said.

He sat back down and took a sip of the wretched stuff. It was still too hot to drink but he didn't mean to drink the goddam burnt shit anyhow. Her calm, normal behavior intimidated him. He realized that he would have felt better if she had been acting about half crazy. And that thought made him think he might be about half crazy himself. Jesus, he didn't like the feel of any of this at all. And with that came the thought: If you don't like the feel of this, you young fuck, what would you like the feel of? Would you rather have found her squatting in the middle of the kitchen table, frothing at the mouth? He didn't have an answer to that, and it quieted his heart, which he realized for the first time had been racing. He lifted the cup to his mouth again.

"That better?" she said. "You awake now?"

"I was awake before," he said.

"I didn't ask about before. I asked about now."

Jesus.

"Yes mam, I'm wide awake as I'm apt to get all day."

"That way of talking don't suit you."

"No mam, if you say so."

"I say so. You need another cup of coffee?"

"Another cup for what?"

"To talk."

"I might get me some more coffee in a bit, but I don't need it to talk."

"Do you need it to talk with a civil tongue?"

"What?"

"It's too early to be a wise-ass is what I was driving at."

"I didn't realize I was being a wise-ass."

"You weren't awake."

"Right," he said. "All right."

"Just because you got your eyes open doesn't mean you wide awake."

"I guess not."

"Fully on the track is what I mean."

"I think I'm on the track now, Gertrude." He was just going with it now, already convinced as he was that they were in a quagmire of craziness and sliding deeper. But it didn't piss him off. Not at all. She had a right. Everybody had a right this morning, after what happened last night.

"I think you are too," she said, "so we can talk money."

"Money?"

"Business."

"Business?"

"We ain't gone git very far if you keep saying everything I say."

"Sorry."

"I'm not interested in sorry, I'm interested in time."

"Well, I don't imagine it could be much more than six o'clock now, Gertrude."

"I don't mean that kind of time," she said. And then, snorting through her nose: "Damn!"

What other kind of time was there? But he only took imaginary sips at his nearly empty cup.

"The whole shootin match time," she said. "The whole enchilada."

"The whole what?"

"I don't know. I heard some kid say it on the street. It means all of it. All of anything. In this case, time."

Pete wanted to quietly get up from the table and climb the stairs and get back in bed. This was beginning to seem and sound like a bad dream.

Gertrude placed her left palm flat on her chest. "If this shit don't come back in five years, I might live."

"Five years," he said.

"Or I might not," she said. "It might come back in seven or ten or one or it might come back tomorrow. That's *time.* That's the whole enchilada. So whatever I'm gone do, I got to get on it and do it."

"I got you now," Pete said. "I think we on the same track."

"Maybe, maybe not. You know how much money Henry, that sorry, worrying, worthless bastard, left?"

"No, how much?"

"None of your business."

"Sorry, didn't mean to say that. Forgot myself."

"But I don't mean to set on that money. We going into business. I mean to leave Sarah set. Not have to pinch pennies the way I did. When the two of you getting married?"

"Hadn't really had time to think about it, Gertrude."

"Make the time."

"I will."

"But marrying'll wait. I was talking business."

"I think it's a fine thing you've got something you want to do and the money to do it with. But Gertrude, if you want a businessman you ought to go hire you one. The only thing I've got to sell is sweat."

"If that's all you had you think I'd let you be upstairs with my daughter? You got a good head on your shoulders. Besides, Linga and I pretty much got it worked out. What we're doing and how we're doing it."

"Linga and you?" Pete said, pausing a moment. And then: "Or you and Linga?"

"What?"

"I'd be careful with people who wanted to help me spend my money."

"You giving me advice?"

"No mam."

"Cause I don't remember asking for any."

"You got it right. You didn't."

"But if I need it I'll ask."

"I wouldn't be much help."

"I hate people who sell themself short. That was what Henry did his whole life, sell hisself short, take hisself cheap."

"Maybe he knew something you didn't know."

"Never. No, not once. Even when he did know it, he didn't know it."

Pete recognized that for what it was. He'd heard just such lines out of his own mama's mouth. His daddy never answered them or tried to. Pete didn't either.

"What do you think about sawmills?" she asked. "Get me another cup of that coffee." He got the coffee, but as he did, he thought the old lady had drunk too much already. He set it in front of her. "Well?" she demanded.

"Don't know a thing about sawmills."

"Not what I asked you. You got to learn to concentrate better. Or get a hearing aid. You need a hearing aid?"

"No mam."

"Hell, be a tax write-off if you did. You work for me now."

"I do?"

"If you want it."

"Doing what?"

"Sawmill."

"Never worked in a sawmill in my life."

"You'll work, but you're not going to be sawing boards, for God's sake. We've got all the labor we need, free labor."

"Free labor."

"Linga's Rastas."

"Gertrude, working people and not paying them is called slavery."

"You don't understand."

"I have to say you're right."

"Don't get too smart."

"I didn't mean it to be smart. But I meant it."

"They're getting paid. There's pay and there's pay. They're getting paid the way they want to get paid."

"And how's that?"

"You ask too many questions."

"Maybe, but I've been worked all my life for less than I was worth. I *do* happen to know something about that. Man's got work and you need it you work for whatever he's paying. But it doesn't make it right."

"Jesus, now we're into right and wrong."

"Seems to be pretty much where all of us are most of the time."

"You got a quick tongue."

"I've been told that, too."

"But it's me doing the telling this time. And I got something you want, don't I?"

"I hope you ain't gone say what I think you're gone say."

"Sarah."

Pete said: "You don't want to talk that way. It makes everything cheap, even Sarah. You ever say anything like that again and I'll leave and she'll go with me. Believe it."

"I didn't mean it that way, son," Gertrude said. "Go in the bedroom and git me a Kool. I feel a cough coming on. Kool's only thing that stops it."

"Ever think of what started it?"

"Just git it for me, son. Hell, I'm trying to quit."

"I shouldn't have said that. My daddy smoked unfiltered Camels since he was nine years old, or so he said. If that Sunoco truck hadn't got him, Camels probably would."

He got up from the table and brought her a Kool from the bedroom. She was already coughing before he got back. He lit it for her and she took a few long pulls and quieted down. "Now," she said. "We was talking about sawmills."

"I think you can pretty much count me out of that, but just out of curiosity, why—of all things—sawmills?"

"You know how much land Linga owns in Cedar Creek?"

"No, but it's nothing but a swamp anyhow."

"How far you been back in there?"

"Far enough."

"No you haven't, or you would a seen the stand of cypress back in there. We talking about two hundred acres or more of virgin cypress. It ain't never had a ax in it. Enough to stop you heart. Did mine anyway when I found out how much it sells for a board foot."

"How long's Linga known you and Henry and about Henry's heart and his insurance?"

"You on shaky ground, you know that? Henry's dead. And his insurance ain't insurance anymore, it's money. And the money's mine."

"Just thought I'd ask."

"Less you ask the better off we'll be."

"You know how much a cypress tree grows a year?"

"Questions, I told you—"

"Do you?"

"You know what it sells for a board foot?"

"Answer my question first."

"No, how much does it grow a year?"

"A cypress tree grows an inch a year. One . . . inch."

"Probably why it costs so damn much."

"Probably."

"What do you make in that boxcar?"

"Nothing. Lost the job."

"How much did you make?"

"One dollar an hour."

"And you want to support Sarah and her basketball team on that?"

"Damn, news sure does get around in this house."

"You didn't answer me."

"Henry supported you and his daughter with a bow saw, a mallet, and an ax."

"And worry. Don't forget worry."

"And worry."

Gertrude took a last drag on her cigarette, smoking mostly filter now, Pete noticed, and dropped it in her coffee cup. "Well, you in or you out? I didn't think I'd have to fight you to put a gold mine in your lap."

"This sawmill business, seems a little sudden."

"Nothing sudden about it. Been in the works a long time. We're setting dead on ready. Got it all planned. All we needed was the money to move."

"Just needed Henry to—"

"Shut up! Don't ever mention that again! He's dead. And I didn't kill him, goddammit!"

Maybe you did and maybe you didn't, Pete thought. But he said: "I'll talk to Sarah."

"Sarah knows."

"She knows?"

"She just don't know how fast."

"Fast?"

"She didn't know how fast we'd crank up. We're gonna make it happen."

Pete heard Sarah's light footfall on the stairs and when he looked up, she was standing there, smiling, her lean and beautiful face still a little puffy with sleep. Pete got up to go to the stove to get her a cup of coffee, but she pushed him back and stood staring at her mama.

"Good Lord, Mama, was you looking in a mirror when you put that makeup on this morning?"

"I'm too old and too busy to worry about makeup," Gertrude said angrily.

"And that thing you're wearing! Where in God's name did you get it?"

"I put on the first thing that come to hand. Anything that'll cover nakedness is good enough for me."

"Well, it's not good enough for me, and you must have had your hand in the dirty clothes hamper when you picked that up." She lifted her chin slightly and sniffed the air. Then she turned and took the lid off the huge coffeepot on the stove. "I hope you're not drinking this, cause you could use it to take the paint off a wall. It stinks."

"Young lady, you interrupting important talk me and Pete was having, and I'm still your mama, in case you forgot it, which it seems like you have," said Gertrude, her voice hard-edged enough to give Pete a little jolt of fear.

But it didn't seem to bother Sarah at all. She went around the table and took her mother's arm. "You coming with me. It won't take but a minute for you to look decent. It's one thing you and Daddy taught me it was to be decent."

Gertrude got up grumbling but her old voice went softer as she said: "You daddy's dead in case it slipped you mind."

"But *I'm* not," said Sarah firmly. "You come with me. Pete, don't just stand gawking. Make a decent pot of coffee and get some sugar and cream on the table." Without another word or a glance in Pete's direction, she led the old woman back into her room.

Pete smiled and shook his head. By God, he was going to have to walk easy around that woman.

By the time he had the coffee bubbling, Sarah was back with her mother. The old lady's face had been scrubbed clean of makeup, leaving it corpse white except for the dark circles under her eyes, and she was wearing a freshly washed robe.

Gertrude took her chair at the table and lit a Kool. Pete poured them all coffee.

"With your permission, Miss Know-it-all, we'll go on with what we were doing."

"Go right ahead, Mama. You look fine now." She turned to Pete. "Has she been being mean to my Pete-Pete this morning?"

"Pete-Pete. Is that what you said?"

"I think it's cute. I like it and I think it's what I'm going to call you."

He started to protest but thought better of it, looking at her. He knew in his heart she could call him anything she wanted to. She took a sip of her coffee and stifled another yawn.

"Damn, darling," Pete said. "I don't think you quite got your nap out."

Gertrude smiled and winked at Pete. "You'd let her sleep at night she'd do better in the morning."

It occurred to Pete that this was a Gertrude he had never seen before, smiling, winking, joking. Maybe getting cleaned up had improved her spirits. He knew well enough what she meant, but he decided to let the old woman go on with it. "Sarah sleeps like a log all night long."

"Son," she said, "it's nothing wrong with my ears. Matter of fact, I'm going to have to get a new pair of springs up there if I plan on getting any sleep myself."

"Mother!"

"Godamighty, girl, you're blushing," said her mother.

They all turned toward the sound of a car pulling up in the drive under the oak.

"That'd be George," Gertrude said.

"Well, thank God," Sarah said. "Maybe it'll get you off the subject of bedsprings."

"It's nothing wrong with a good heavy workout on a pair of bedsprings in the middle of the night. Time to worry is when the springs stop squeaking."

"I'm not even going to answer that," Sarah said, the blush spreading to her throat.

"Didn't think you would."

"What's George doing here this time of day?" Pete asked.

"Working," Gertrude said. "He's on the payroll."

"Payroll? Which payroll?"

"Mine. Quit the boxcar business this morning and come to work for me. Well, Linga and me both. She's got product but she's undercapitalized."

Pete didn't know where, but he'd heard the phrase "undercapitalized." And you didn't have to be very bright to understand what it meant. "Linga gave him twenty dollars a week out of his paycheck at the warehouse. How much you think she'll give him out of this one?"

"That's between the two of them, but more, I'd expect," said Gertrude. "He's on my payroll now."

"What difference would that make?"

"Roughly about fifteen dollars an hour."

"My God!" said Pete. "How much?"

"You heard well enough. Whose payroll *you* on?"

"Not on yours. Not for that. I'm not worth fifteen dollars an hour and neither is George. Fifteen dollars an hour is journeyman's wages. And neither George or me, either one, are journeyman workers at any craft known to man. He ain't got a damn thing to sell but his back and his sweat. Same with me. Taking fifteen dollars an hour of your money would be robbery."

"George didn't seem to have any trouble with it," said Gertrude.

"Linga tells George what to do. Nobody tells me. That's a trouble I don't have."

"Yet," said Sarah, laughing.

Pete only turned to smile at her.

"I known from the start I'd have trouble with you," Gertrude said. "But I sure never expected it'd be you turning down good money."

"I'm not turning down good money. I'm not *stealing* good money is what I'm doing."

Gertrude stared into her cup for a moment. "Well, tell me this. Will you go out there and look things over good, get back there in them cypress and see what I've been talking about, and then come on back here and talk with me about it? You all I got. Too old and broke down to do it myself. I'd be glad to pay you a good day's wages for it."

Pete waved her off with his hand. "I'll be glad to go and do the best I can with what you're asking for. But you won't owe me a dime for it." He smiled. "I'm part of the family now. It's only right that I go see what you trying to get yourself into."

"A gold mine is what I'm trying to get myself into," Gertrude said.

"We'll see," said Pete.

A car door slammed and Pete saw George, huge, blue-black in the morning sun, and smiling like the end of the world. He was wearing a new tie-dyed shirt and trousers that Pete had never seen before and he was stretching, his great arms outspread, his heavy mane of coiled hair falling across his shoulders as his head was thrown back and rolled on his thickly muscled neck—stretching there in the dappled shade beside his gold and gleaming Hudson Hornet.

"From the rate he's moving," Pete said, "he'll make fifty dollars before he gets to the house."

Gertrude was up from her chair and leaning out the screen door as the last word came out of Pete's mouth.

"I thought your mama was ailing," he said to Sarah.

"Does she look like she's ailing?"

Before Pete could answer, Gertrude was screaming, *screaming,* out the door: "HEY, YOU WORKING FOR ME?"

George's answer was instant: "Yuh, missy."

"Then why the hell ain't you sweating?"

She came back to the table and fired up a Kool. "Pour me a coffee, Pete."

"Yes, missy," Pete said.

"Nobody likes a smart mouth. And you've got to get right on top from the get-go if you running things."

George came through the door and stood by the table but made no move to sit.

"Well, no question who's running things. You are," Pete said.

"Wrong again—*you* are," said Gertrude.

"We'll see about that, but in the meantime—George, quit standing there like the house nigger and sit down. This old lady don't make a bad cup of coffee for a cripple."

"Your mama!" said Gertrude.

Now where the hell had Gertrude heard that? But he instantly knew he did not want to know. Pete put the coffeepot back on the stove.

Lighting another Kool, Gertrude squinted at George. "You haven't been smoking this morning, have you?"

"No, missy. No ganja."

"Good. That's good. Call me Gertrude. But if you git too uppity, it'll be Miz Leemer. We straight?"

George didn't answer, so Pete answered for him. "Straight as a plumb line. While we on this, you did tell me to call you Gertrude?"

"I don't know. Now that I think about it, I think Mother Gertrude might be nice," she said.

Pete would not have been more surprised if she had asked him to call her the devil.

"That is," she added, "if you intend to marry my daughter."

"We already married," said Pete. "Did it ourselves."

"Thought you might have," Gertrude said. "But you do plan to go to the courthouse and git a piece of paper to make it right in the eyes of the law."

"We are," Pete said. "We are going to do that."

"Good. Far as I know, it's been no bastards in the family, not yet anyhow."

Sarah said, "The first thing we're doing is seeing about cleaning up our way of talking around this house."

"No," said Gertrude, "the first thing is for George to take Pete out to the property. Do what needs to be done."

"Tell me again what it is you want me to do."

"Can't tell you any more than I already have. Do what needs to be done. Open your eyes. I'll come to you. We've got equipment moving out there today. Look at the—"

"You've got equipment moving already?"

"Don't interrupt. Look at the timber. Think about roads to get into it. Think about whatever needs thinking about. Linga's people are everything from engineers to carpenters to cooks to, well . . . bums, of course. But everybody pulls his goddam load."

"Or what?" said Pete.

"We'll figure that out later. Sarah and I and Linga have work to do today. We may not be back here before way after dark."

"Just so I'll know, when I'm looking at whatever's out there—when did you think to start cutting?"

"Oh, hell, nobody knows that. You have to have a permit to take a shit in this country. I found—"

"Mother!"

"I found that out anyway. But we got a good lawyer on it. You git on out there. Look at everything as best you can and then come back and talk to me. Well, don't just stand there looking at me. *Move.* You've already pissed away the best part of the morning."

"Mother, you got to quit this goddam cussing," Sarah said heatedly enough that she didn't realize what she'd said until her mother smiled and pointed a bony finger at her.

"You daddy never liked it, but it looks like it runs in the family. It was just under cover . . . until *he* went under cover."

16

"Linga missed her real calling in life," said Pete. "She should have been a captain in a line company in the Marine Corps."

George looked across the seat of the car, steering with only the heel of his right hand. They had both windows down. It had rained off and on all day and the rain had left the night air cool. There was very little traffic but George one-handed the car through the streets slowly. He had stopped at every stop sign and had not run a single red light.

Pete watched his face in the dim light of the dash and the light of the streetlamps popping by. George seemed worried. For the last several hours he'd said almost nothing. And his great braying laugh had been missing all day. Maybe he was just tired. Pete sure as hell was.

"You understand what I said about Linga?"

George looked straight ahead and nodded. "Warrior," he said.

Pete shifted in the seat, his wet trousers sticking to the backs of his legs. "Yeah," he said, "warrior is close enough. That'll do."

When Pete and George left the camp, the sun had been nearly down, but every living soul was still working the way they had been working when Pete and George got there at daylight. There was no one to drive them, apparently nobody in charge, because Linga was not in camp. Linga and Sarah and Gertrude had gone somewhere that day, so the working Rastas did not have Linga to worry about. How the three women were going and where they were going and what they were going to do after they got there, Pete had no idea. But that was all right, because Sarah was along to look after her mother. And Linga? She could go to hell as far as Pete was concerned. But these young men and women had bought outright whatever Linga was selling. Well, so be it, thought Pete, better them than me. He was only there to check out what he already knew in his heart had to be a scam. Linga was after money or power or both—probably both. And Pete had no quarrel with that either as long as none of the money was Gertrude's or Sarah's and Linga had no power over them.

When Pete had arrived that morning with George, dump trucks filled with crushed oystershell were lined up to drop their loads, and what looked like junked machinery of some sort was being frantically taken off flatbed eighteen-wheelers and, as soon as it hit the ground, splashed with red primer. The entire camp was in motion, working at one thing or another. Nobody gawked or talked.

Pete ignored them. And, strangely, so did George. The whole place could have been empty for all he said or did. One or two of the Rastas passed close enough for them to reach out and touch, but George spoke to none of them.

"Ya wan ta walk back an see de place dese Rastas built ta lib in?"

"No interest at all," said Pete.

"Dat some more good."

"All I want to see are the trees, how far out they are, and what kind of water is between there and here."

"Dat easy, mon."

"That's the way I like it—easy."

So Pete and George spent much of the day five miles deep in the swamp, having to pole most of the way in a flat-bottomed johnboat over the shallow water. But Christ, what a forest of cypress was back there. A hundred yards into the trees, their leafy canopies very nearly blotted out the sky. And these were not young cypress. They were old and tall and straight and thick-trunked. Prime, absolutely prime sawmill timber. The problem was getting to them and getting them out. From time to time, as they poled through the miles of saw grass, Pete had used the long pole to test the bottom. Putting the entire length of the twenty-foot pole down into the bottom, he never hit anything solid. Mud, slime—slick and malleable as owl's shit. Same with the forest of cypress. It was growing in generations of muck. If a channel was dredged from the cypress to the camp, the soft walls of the channel would cave in and the channel would be filled over and smooth again in minutes.

"Maybe we can float the damn things," said Pete, who had been around swamps all his life and knew there was no fucking way to float *these* trees in *this* water.

George had said not a single word since they got in the johnboat, which—to Pete's great surprise—George handled with the skill of somebody who had grown up in one.

Finally Pete looked back to where George was poling the boat. "So you going to just stand there looking good, styling and profiling, or you got anything to say about what we do with these fucking trees?"

"Linga," George said.

Pete waited. "So, is that it—Linga? Linga's all you got to say?"

"Mon," said George. "Linga do it. Jus nuh trus her, Pete-Pete. Ya nuh tell her again. But . . ." And here in the deep fastness of the swamp, he actually whispered. *"Obeah."* And for the first time, Pete knew that George was truly terrified of her. Looking at his friend's face, Pete wanted to go kill the bitch. Fucking scar-faced cunt. But he knew he was not going to do that, and he also knew that the only way he could help George, whom he'd come to think of as a brother, was to give him whatever comfort and support he could.

"O.K., George," he said. "If you say it I believe it. Fuck the water, fuck the distance and the size of the goddam trees, fuck the moccasins. Obeah. Linga and Obeah."

"You nuh poke de fun at Rasta Obeah, little white mon," said George. He was not smiling.

Pete dropped onto his haunches in the boat, wanting to laugh but thinking better of it. "Little white man? Little fucking white man? Where did that come from?"

George poled on, never missing a stroke, his eyes fixed on the green canopy above him. "Ain't nuh but you an me in dis boat. It nuh come from you, it mus come from me, *little white mon.*"

Pete was instantly on his feet. "Stop with that shit! It ain't but two of us out here. Maybe you can kill me but you can't eat me, as we say where I come from. I could take this maybe if I hated you, but I thought you were my brother, man. I won't take that shit from a brother."

"Ya nuh brudder," said George. "Nuh kin be de brudder to me. Ebber."

"Well, goddam. Fucking thanks, man."

"Ya nuh Rasta. Linga talk shit. She know she talk shit. She Obeah. Obeah know all in all de worlds. Only black mon be Rasta." Again his voice dropped to nearly a whisper. "She bad Obeah. Nuh fock wit Linga, Pete-Pete."

"Well, at least you got my name back. I don't think I much care for 'little white man.' For starters, I ain't little—strikes you that way because you so fucking big."

Pete expected George to smile. It was only good-natured kidding between two friends, but George was not in a kidding mood. All right. Serious he wanted, serious he could have.

"How the hell did Linga manage to get this timber? I wouldn't even know how to guess how much it's worth. You can't work it out by day labor, that's for dead solid certain."

"Nuh, nuh possible."

"Then how?"

"Better ya nuh fine out."

"Oh, good. Fucking great. Now you can't tell me what she paid for the stuff. You're beginning to piss me off, George, you know that?"

"Nuh pay."

"What?"

"Linga nuh pay money. She give a mon a gif."

"Must a been some gift."

"De gif o death."

Pete didn't sit down. He lost his feet and fell very nearly out of the boat. He lay very still. "You mean she killed the guy that owned it?"

"Nuh."

"Then what?"

"He wanted a mon dead. She let him die."

"Oh, well, fuck, that explains everything."

"Knowin nuh help."

"Dig it, brother, I don't want to know."

"Dat good."

"You damn right that's good."

Pete looked out the window of the car as it sped on toward his house. "You understand, I don't believe hardly a word you've told me today. But I think I've heard about as much as I want to. That business of her letting a man die so another man would give her what's probably a million dollars or more of prime cypress timber tops anything you've said yet."

George looked straight ahead. "Ya beleeb, ya nuh beleeb. It make nuh different ta me. De mon still dead. Linga still got de lan, still got de wood."

"She's some bitch, I'll give her that."

"Nuh call Obeah woman bitch."

"Didn't mean to piss you off, just popped out."

"Don piss me off. Linga make ya dead mon."

Pete thought about that. He had no doubt that Linga was dangerous, maybe—probably even—about three-quarters nuts. As they were pulling away from camp, quite by chance Pete had seen the Indian with the braided ponytail coming out of Linga's trailer. On his cheeks, where before he had had three blue parallel scars, there were three more parallel lines cut into the flesh under each of his eyes and dyed a bright green. The wounds had to have been cut with a straight-edge razor for them to be so completely straight. Blood leaked out of them and trailed down across his chin. His face and eyes clearly showed the heavy use of ganja. All the young Rastas who saw him leave the trailer stopped whatever they were doing and formed two lines shoulder to shoulder and facing each other—a gauntlet that he walked through—and as he passed each Rasta in the line on either side of him, a hand reached out and touched him. The Indian might have been sleepwalking, so steady and unnatural was his pace, and he looked neither left nor right, nor did he acknowledge the hands that touched him, the blood falling drop by drop off the point of his chin. The young men and women in the two lines were quiet as a church, their eyes staring straight ahead, not turning to follow him as he walked away.

Pete had his window rolled down and they drove out of a totally quiet camp. Not even a bird sang.

"What was going on back there, George? When we left camp," Pete said, realizing suddenly that sweat was running on his face.

"Ya see de Indian boy? Ya see him blood?"

"Yeah, and I asked what the fuck was happening."

"Ya wan ya some cuts? Ya wan de blood?"

"Hell no. To do that to me, you'd need strong rope and strong men."

"We got de strong rope and de strong men."

"Jesus, forget I asked. Just drive."

"Dat I doin, mon," George said. "Dat I doin."

When they pulled up and stopped under the oak tree beside the woodlot, Pete turned to George and said, "Want to come in for a cup of coffee?"

"Nuh time, mon, tanks. I be up half de night cleanin dis Hudson o mine."

Both men were wet and muddy from the swamp, and the inside

of the car no longer smelled new. It smelled of swamp, and the floorboards and seats were covered with drying mud. The dashboard and steering wheel and even the headliner were marked with dark streaks of mud.

"I didn't even think of that, George. Why don't we clean it up right here? I'll get a light run out and give you a hand. Two of us working won't take long."

"Tanks, Pete-Pete, but I nuh keep Linga waitin."

"Waiting? How long can it take? Hell, we haven't seen her all day. What's the hurry?"

When he turned his face to Pete, George looked genuinely happy for the first time that day. "Dis mak one mo year wit Linga. We be ten togedder on dis night."

Pete had already put out his hand to shake and was about to wish him a happy anniversary, when he thought of the huge horseshoe burns on George's shoulders and back. "Oh, fuck, man," said Pete. "You're not . . ."

"Sho now, mon," George said. "On dis night I burn. Linga—"

Pete had the door open and was out of the car looking back in through the open window before George could finish. "Don't tell me," Pete said, his voice angry. He couldn't help it. "And drive safe, you crazy bastard."

What the fuck else could happen? He wanted a shower and his bed and Sarah. And he wanted to rethink this whole thing. The young Indian's cheeks dripping blood and the sudden news that George was about to go back home to be branded yet again had made the scorching boxcar he used to work in look pretty damn good about now.

He was almost to the back door leading into the kitchen, when he noticed for the first time that every light in the house seemed to be on. Given the hour, that seemed odd but not odd enough for him to give it much thought. He was bone tired and it had only just occurred to him that probably the reason he felt so weak was that he had not eaten anything all day.

He walked slowly up the steps, opened the door, and stepped into the kitchen, expecting to see food on the table, maybe covered to keep it warm, and Sarah and her mother, or at least Sarah, waiting for him. What he saw was unmistakably his brother, seven years old now, twin purple indentations on his forehead above his nose, sitting on the floor against the far wall, his legs outstretched and spread, with a football helmet between them. There was a skull in the helmet with the chin strap buckled.

Pete stopped, his entire body turning cold, and whispered, "Jon? Jonathan?"

The child looked up from the skull, whose eye sockets he had been examining with great concentration, and smiled, which caused a long ropy string of slobber to slip out of his loose mouth and into what had been Henry Leemer's mouth.

With the agility of a young girl Gertrude leapt out into the kitchen from the door leading to her room, her wide, brown-toothed mouth stretching in a smile, her lipstick cracked and garish as a Halloween mask. Jonathan gave a shriek and began banging his head against the wall.

"Surprise!" screamed Gertrude.

Sarah came right behind her and went to Jonathan and soothed him, petting his head gently in a way that reminded Pete of someone petting a dog. Jonathan calmed down immediately and Sarah gave him a big kiss, and then she looked up at Pete, a string of Jonathan's slobber hanging from her chin. Pete had not moved. He had not even blinked. "Is this little thing a sweetheart or is he a sweetheart?" Sarah said.

Pete's throat had closed in a spasm, threatening his breathing, and he could not speak.

"Well, don't you want to hug you little brother?" yelled Gertrude, who seemed to be unable to speak in anything other than a scream.

It was, in fact, the last thing in the world Pete wanted to do. He felt his throat release, and even though he was not a Catholic, he did something that he had seen some of his buddies in the Marine Corps do. He crossed himself and whispered: "God help us all, now and at the hour of our death."

"What?" screamed Gertrude.

Sarah came to him, the little string of slobber swinging from her chin, and put her hands on his shoulders. "I know it's a shock, sweetheart." And then she pressed her mouth against his.

Pete took an involuntary step backward and wiped his mouth. He saw the look on Sarah's face and deliberately made his voice hard. "You ought to get something and wipe that off your chin."

"Is that all you've got to say? That I ought to wipe my mouth?"

"Not exactly. Where did you get him?"

"We got him from where he was at," said Gertrude, her voice a bit calmer.

"And how did you do that? *I* didn't even know where he was. My uncles and brother had him put . . ."

"Away," said Sarah.

"Right. Away."

"My lawyer found him," Gertrude said. "All you've got to do is throw money at a lawyer and he can find anything. Took him a while, but he found him. Got him out too."

"You and your goddam lawyer," Pete said. "I'm tired of hearing about your lawyer. How the hell did you get him turned loose? None of you are kin to him."

"Son, I think they would of give him to anybody. They had way too many just like him to give a shit who got him. Long as you had the right papers."

"He doesn't even know where he is," Pete said.

"But we do," said Sarah. "He's home."

"And he doesn't know who he is."

"But we do," said Gertrude. "He's blood. Don't you care about blood?"

"Yes, as a matter of fact, I do. But he doesn't even know what happened to him."

"But we do!" screamed Gertrude.

And Sarah added softly: "And you do, Pete."

"Don't you think it's a little warped for him to be playing with that?"

Jonathan had the skull out of the football helmet now and was batting it about on the floor in front of him.

"He just thinks it's a play pretty, a toy," said Gertrude.

"But we *know* what it is."

"Henry," Gertrude said, "wouldn't mind."

"Oh, Jesus. Do you think we could put him and the skull away and let me get something to eat? I've been hip deep in swamp water all day—swamp water and a lot of other things I didn't like."

"My God," said Sarah. "We've brought your lost baby brother home to you and all you can do is stand there talking about eating and the fact that you been wading around in swamp water all day. I don't understand. Could you explain to me what's going on?"

He looked at her and said nothing. No, he could not explain it to her. Or to himself. He had never imagined this moment because he never expected it to happen. And he was scared to death. Terrified. His worst dream—his terror—had come true. The wound he had carried all these years, the full horror of what he had inflicted, was sitting over there against the wall babbling and drooling—totally beyond his or anybody else's help—and they expected him to go over and pick it up and hug it and love it. Oh, Jesus, help me, he prayed, and was startled that he was praying. But he had to get the strength from somewhere. Because he really didn't know if he could do this or not. But he *had* to, and he *wanted* to. Yes, he desperately wanted to. But he was still scared. He felt his hands start to tremble and he jammed them into his pockets. His heart was tripping and fluttering as though it meant to explode.

"Was them trees everthing I said they'd be?" asked Gertrude.

Pete had only half heard her and understood her not at all. "What was that you said?"

"I asked what you thought about them trees."

"And we can leave them blessed trees alone too," said Sarah, nearly in tears. "We got a youngun here. Pete's baby brother. And you're asking about trees. I can't believe it."

Thank God for the trees, thought Pete. That would give him a minute or two to pull himself back together and deal with this. Because he had resolved in his heart to deal with it, deal with it all. No matter the pain. He took a deep breath and looked at Gertrude.

"The cypress were as fine and beautiful as they ever get, but we'll have to talk about them later." He had meant to talk to Sarah about them first. Gertrude was crazy and ripe to be robbed. And it was up to him to stop it. But first things first, and the first thing was his brother. He told himself to take one thing at a time and gut on through it. Jonathan had been given back to him and he did not mean to lose him again. "I'm too tired to talk about trees right now."

"I suppose you're too tired for this little boy that's your brother too?" said Sarah.

There was nothing to do but try to tell her the truth. He went to her and took her face in his hands and looked into her eyes, where tiny silvery tears were starting to build. "Darling, I love that little boy over there more than I love myself. But I never expected to see him again. He was dead to me. At least I thought he was. And when I walked in here, I thought my heart would stop. For a minute I thought I couldn't stand it. But I can. I've *got* to stand it."

She put her arms around him and drew him to her. "He's not lost to you. He's not dead. He's *home*. You're home. And I'm here to stand with you no matter what happens."

He pushed her gently away from him and smiled down into her face. "You've got yourself full of swamp mud from hugging me, is what you've done."

"It was cheap at the price," she said, tears on her cheeks now. "I've had mud on me before. It'll wash off. I'll set you a plate and feed you good. You go on over there and pick up your brother. He's not as heavy as he looks."

Pete said: "I thought you said Linga had Henry's . . ."

"Skull," said Gertrude. "It's called a skull."

". . . skull," said Pete.

"She did, but when she come over to go with us to get the youngun, she brought it with her. Had it in a shoe box is what she had it in."

"And why did she do that?"

"It'll help her cure the youngun. You remember, you know, about the skull being the final wound and your little brother is the final—"

Pete held up his hand to stop her. "That's enough, Gertrude. That's all I need to hear." He went over and took the skull out of the child's lap and set it on top of a china cabinet.

"Now how come you to do that?" said Gertrude with a tinge of hurt anger in her voice.

"Jonathan is not to touch that thing again. Ever."

"But Linga needs it to cure—"

Again he stopped her. "Linga is to have nothing to do with my brother. She won't cure him because he can't be cured. But never mind that—I don't want her even talking to Jonathan."

"I don't know how come you to be this way about Linga," said Gertrude, her voice now a phlegm-filled growl. She cut her eyes to the skull on the cabinet. "Or why you took Henry's—"

"Gertrude," said Pete, cutting her off. He went over to where she was sitting and knelt beside her. "Gertrude, I'm in your house, and I love your daughter. I have no other mother in the world if you are not my mother. But I am responsible for Jonathan. In a way—since Henry died so suddenly the way he did—I feel like I'm responsible for all of us. But there are things that I will allow with Jonathan and there are things that I will not allow. That's the way it has to be." He turned to look up at the skull. "You keep Henry wherever you think best. As for Linga, we'll talk—deal with her—later. Henry told me more than once there was a right time and a wrong time for everything. And this is the wrong time to talk about Linga. If I wasn't so dirty I'd give you a hug. Because I want to be a son to you and take care of you. I love you, Gertrude, and I'll do the best I can."

The old woman's face relaxed, and she raised a bone-thin hand to touch his cheek. In a voice so soft it was almost a whisper, she said, "But them trees *was* pretty?"

"They were beautiful, Gertrude. Really fine timber."

Pete got up and went over to stand in front of Jonathan. The child looked as if he didn't have a bone in his body. He was very pale and his entire body hung in rolls of fat. He smiled his loose, out-of-control smile at Pete and held out his arms to him.

Pete still could not bring himself to touch the child. His terror had only grown. He tried to think of something to say that was normal, something that would help him through this.

"He eat yet?" said Pete.

"Sure did," Sarah said. "He can feed himself and everything." She touched Pete gently on the shoulder. "And for God's sake, pick your little brother up." And then very softly: "He wants his big brother to pick him up."

And with his heart pounding as though it would tear out of his chest, Pete bent and lifted his brother into his arms. The little boy made a sound that might have been a word but it was not a word. Pete kissed him on his damp cheek. It was like kissing an open wound. The hunger that had been tearing at his stomach was suddenly gone. Jonathan put his baby-soft hands on either side of Pete's head, and Pete buried his face in the child's neck and hugged him and wept.

Sarah put her hand on Pete's back between his shoulder blades and moved it in a slow circle. Pete could not stop crying. Jonathan made a sound like laughter and Pete felt warm drool slipping down his neck.

"Yes, darling," said Sarah. "Oh, my poor darling. I'm so sorry. I'm so terribly sorry."

Pete, still crying, moved his face from the child's neck and kissed him soft and long on the twin purple scars on his forehead. The scars were like the lips of a mouth and he cried because they were not like scars at all but tender and dimpled and he felt as if he could—*would*—disappear into them, and the longer he had his lips on them the more he could remember the day and the hammer and the sound of metal striking flesh and the loss of his mother and father and the loss of his brother's love and his own intolerable loneliness in the world and he could not stop crying, and Sarah had moved to hug both him and the child, her arms around them, and then Gertrude's arms were around them too and she was crying now and Sarah was crying and Pete was choking on his own tears, unable to stop, unable to do anything but hug his brother, who in the midst of all the crying and wailing was crooning and gurgling as though this was just the happiest moment in the world.

"Don't," Sarah said finally. "It's over. He's back where he belongs and it's over."

"No," Pete said. "It's not over. It won't ever be over."

"Come and eat your supper, son." Gertrude was still crying and could hardly make herself understood. "You eat and you'll feel better."

Pete, his lips still on the scar, said, "I'm not hungry."

"Then come have coffee," Sarah said. "Jonathan'll sit with you."

Pete had been holding the little boy with his right arm under his baby-soft bottom. He leaned back to look into the child's eyes for the first time. He had avoided looking into Jonathan's eyes since he came into the room, and he did not know why. They were startlingly blue and clear, with an intelligence that the child seemed to be keeping as his own personal secret.

"Will you sit with me, Jon?" said Pete.

Jon's loose mouth made a long wet sound that could have meant anything or nothing.

"See," said Sarah. "I told you." Pete looked at her, puzzled. "Jonathan just said he'd love to come have supper with his big brother."

Pete smiled and set his brother down. The child was surprisingly steady on his feet. "Let me wash my hands anyway," Pete said.

"Your face, too, darling," said Sarah. "It looks like you've been working in a coal mine."

"That bad, is it?" He walked over to the sink and looked into the little mirror hanging there. "Yep," he said. "That bad." It was only then he noticed that his brother had followed him over to the sink. Under his arm he had the football helmet. "You want to wash up with your brother? Good enough, but let's put this thing up here on the shelf." He took the helmet and set it on a shelf on the wall. The child's blue gaze had watched him intently as he took the helmet, and his eyes never left it where it sat on the shelf. A shadow seemed to pass over his face. He stretched his arms over his head, reaching for the helmet. Pete had soaped his face and his hands and arms to the elbow before he saw Jonathan reaching, staring, tears beginning to form in his eyes and his loose mouth starting to twist.

"You're going to make him cry if you don't give it back," Gertrude said.

"He can have the helmet," Pete said.

"It's Henry he really wants."

"He can't have that. I'll get him a football or something."

"We tried that. Sarah tried a lot of things. All he did was bang his head and scream. He misses Henry."

"I don't want to sound hard or ugly, but he'll get over it. We'll all get over it. He'll just have to bang and scream. I can stand it if he can. I don't know how much discipline he can learn, but whatever it is, I intend to teach it to him. Knowing what he can do and what he can't do might even help him. It sure as hell won't hurt him."

"And it won't hurt you to stop that cussing either," said Sarah.

Pete smiled at her. "You know some men would call that nagging."

"You can call it what you want to, but I'm going to keep right on doing it until you stop."

"Well," he said, still smiling, "I told you it wouldn't be overnight."

"And I told you that was fine with me. But a few reminders might make it happen faster."

"It might at that."

Pete was dumbfounded when Jonathan suddenly took him by the finger and led him around to the table, turned his finger loose, and pulled his chair out for him. But his eyes were still on the shelf holding the helmet more than they were on him.

"Jesus," said Pete, "what else can he do?"

"He can scream like a banshee, claw your eyes, butt and bang his head against anything handy for six solid hours without stopping," said Sarah, dipping food from the stove. "And strong? That youngun is strong as a horse. Don't let that baby fat fool you."

"Somehow," said Pete, "I don't think anything much is going to surprise me anytime soon."

Jonathan had taken a chair beside Pete and made a long ugly noise that ended with about three inches of his tongue out of his mouth.

At the stove, Sarah only smiled. "He wants a plate of his own."

"Sarah," said Pete, "you're going to make a wonderful mother."

"I *am* making a wonderful mother," she said.

Sarah set Pete's food in front of him, along with a glass of iced tea. She put cutlery and an empty plate and glass in front of Jonathan.

Pete looked at the empty plate and glass. "What's this?" he asked.

"You'll see," said Sarah. "He's a very neat eater at the table. But he likes to copy people too. I guess it's a kind of game for him, like wanting to wash his hands and face when you did just now."

"I don't get it," said Pete.

"You will. Just eat your food."

Pete forked some green peas into his mouth, and almost simultaneously Jonathan lifted his empty fork from his empty plate and put it into his mouth. His chubby little fist holding the fork went back to his plate while he chewed. Pete stopped chewing and watched his brother. Jonathan stopped chewing and watched Pete. Pete put his fork down and had a long drink of tea. Jonathan put his fork down, in the identical way his brother had—in the middle of his plate, tines up—and had a long drink from his empty glass.

Pete was amazed and, at the same time, a little proud. "You sure he's not hungry?"

"Goodness no," said Gertrude. "He's already eat enough for two people."

Pete watched him. "We'll have to put him on a diet."

"We'll do no such thing," Sarah said. "He's a growing boy."

"He's a *very fat* growing boy," said Pete.

"I think it was his diet at the home he was in," she said. "We got there at lunch, and when we found him in the cafeteria, there wasn't a thing on his plate but starch."

"Damn."

"I bought him a burger on the way home and he didn't know what to do with it. I had to go back and buy myself one so we could eat it together. The child's no trouble at all as long as he can do what you're doing. He can even tie his own shoes if you're tying yours too."

"Great," said Pete, "that's just great."

"He's your brother, Pete," she said. "It's no use in being sarcastic. You'll get used to it in time."

"I guess that *was* sarcastic. But I didn't mean it that way. And I didn't thank you for finding him, but I'm grateful."

Gertrude had sat down at the table with a cup of coffee and a Kool, which she smoked relentlessly. "Linga thinks she can cure him."

Pete stopped chewing and looked at her. "Cure him of what?"

"Of himself."

"Even if you are going into business with her, I don't like that woman and I don't want her messing with my brother."

"I'm not going into business with her. I *am* in business. But I think you ought to know that it was her that got that helmet off his head. Me and Sarah tried but he'd just bang his head against anything he got close to. You ought to see the bruises on my ribs."

"I think I'll pass on that."

"Then you can look at Sarah's. But when she walked into this room, it was all the difference in the world. She took him over in the corner, set him down, and talked and petted him for only a few minutes. I don't know what she said, but when she took that helmet off, he was cool as a cucumber. He hasn't had it on since."

"Between the helmet and Linga," said Pete, "I think I'll take the helmet."

"I don't know what the woman's ever done to you for you to talk like that about her."

"Just say it's a feeling I've got about her. I don't trust her, not for a minute."

"Have any kind of feeling you want to, but if Linga can help this child get better she's going to be given the chance to try."

"No she won't, Gertrude. He's my brother, and I don't want her anywhere near him."

She smiled a gentle smile. "And you are my son."

Pete had no answer for that and he was too tired to argue. He mopped up the vegetable juice from his plate and watched as Jonathan mopped up his empty plate with an imaginary biscuit caught in his chubby little fist.

"How did things go out there today?" asked Gertrude.

"None of them are lazy, I give them that. Oystershell and rock are being hauled in and a road is being put down. George and I spent most of the day in the biggest stand of cypress I ever saw. And that's the real problem right there. I don't see any way of getting them out. I thought of floating them out, but the water's too shallow."

"Where there's money, there's a way," Gertrude said.

"We'll talk about it later," said Pete. "I'm too tired to make sense now."

Pete picked up his plate and glass and carried them to the sink. Jonathan was right behind him with his plate and glass, with his knife, fork, and spoon stuffed in the front pocket of his overalls.

Pete looked down at him, ruffled his hair, and said: "Thanks, pard."

The boy responded by pointing to the helmet and then to the skull on the cabinet.

"You're going to have to trust me on this, Jon. The helmet you can have. That other thing is a no-no. You understand? The other thing is a definite no-no."

"That other thing is definitely my father," said Sarah. "I'm even glad Mama did what she did, bringing him home with us. It seems kind of nice having him around the house."

"You're beginning to sound like Max."

"What if I am? Being different doesn't make Max bad."

"I didn't say he was bad. He's got his ways. I've got mine. And the more I see of his the less I like him. Max is a fool."

"You don't know a thing about Max except he's old and walks a lot."

"He lives in a world he makes up himself. Makes up as he goes along. He can't see a thing when it's looking him dead in the eye. Worse than a damn child."

"What would you know about that?" said Sarah.

"Yaks."

"Yaks? Is that what you said?"

"That's what I said. Everything he said about them is a lie. They look like milk cows that's being slowly starved to death. They ought to be killed."

"That's not what you said."

"I lied too."

"Are you saying you lied to me?"

"I didn't want you to be disappointed. That's no excuse, but yeah, I lied to you."

"How could I be disappointed? I'd never seen them before. You made me walk nearly two miles and nearly get the stroke to see something that looked like a dying milk cow? I wouldn't have done that to you."

"I wouldn't do it to you *now*. But now is now and then was then. You had me pissed off—I mean angry."

"You still shouldn't have done that."

"I know," said Pete. "You don't think I feel good about it, do you?"

"I don't know what you feel or think," said Sarah.

"Here comes the first argument," Gertrude said, firing up a Kool to stop a coughing fit that had started. She tried to laugh but her cough wouldn't let her.

"It's not the first one," said Sarah.

"Could we save it for another time, Sarah?" Pete asked. "I'm tired, really beat, and I need to get some sleep. Where's Jonathan sleeping tonight?"

"With us," said Sarah.

"There's hardly enough room on that bed for the two of us already."

"He's still sleeping with us. It's his first night away from that horrid place he was kept. He's liable to have nightmares and not know where he is."

"Happens to me all the time. It won't hurt him."

"If it's going to cause an argument—which both of you been right on the edge of since Pete come home—he can sleep with me," Gertrude told them. "It's plenty of room in my bed."

"He's my son now and he's sleeping where I say he sleeps." Sarah reached over and stroked his hair. "Poor little thing's been throwed away most of his life, but he's home now."

"*Your* son?" said Pete.

"That's what I said."

"How'd he come to be your son?"

"The same way you came to be my husband."

For the first time it occurred to Pete what a strong woman he had joined himself to. And strangely, it pleased him. Damn woman had fire in her blood. He liked that. His mother had been the same way. When it got too bad for everybody else, it was getting just right for her. A woman like that would keep a man steady in the world.

"If that's the way you want it," he said.

"That's the way I want it. You go take a shower and get the stink of that swamp off you. I'll take him up and get him ready for bed."

"He's too heavy for you to be toting up them stairs." He stood up. "Let me do it."

For an answer Sarah bent and effortlessly lifted the sleeping child. His head lolled back across her shoulder and a wet spot immediately appeared on her dress, but he didn't make a sound as she turned for the stairs.

Gertrude dropped the butt of a Kool in her coffee cup. "Either she's stronger than you thought or he's lighter than you thought."

Pete shook his head. "She surprises me every day I live with her."

"That Sarah's a lot of woman. If I don't miss my guess you'll learn to walk easier around her."

"Maybe, maybe not," he said. But he knew damn well he would. And more than that, he'd be glad to do it. She *was* some woman, Sarah was, and it surprised him that he was only just beginning to find it out.

He started out of the room, stopped, and looked back at Gertrude. "You're a pretty damn strong woman yourself."

"And don't you ever goddam forget it, son."

He smiled. "You better watch that cussing."

"You're just her fucking husband. I'm her fucking mother. I'll talk any way I please."

"I think, by God, you probably will."

"Bet on it."

"You have a good night."

She winked. "Better'n yours probably. Won't be much going on in that bed, I wouldn't imagine, with that youngun jammed in there."

"My daddy always said where there's a will, there's a way."

"That's the kind of men I like, the hard ones—the harder the better."

"I think I better leave that one alone and go on to bed."

"Don't get a move on she'll be asleep."

Now it was Pete's turn to wink. "I can always wake her up."

"Be easy."

"I'm always easy."

"A woman don't want her man to *always* be easy."

"Damn," said Pete, shaking his head as he left the kitchen.

He wedged himself into the tiny bathroom at the head of the stairs, stripped, and left his clothes in one corner, before stepping into the stall and turning on the water as hot as he could stand it.

When he went into their bedroom, wrapped in a towel, there in the middle of his bed was his little brother on his back, fast asleep, with his football helmet held with both hands on top of his chest. He was wearing pajamas with a pattern of rosebuds on them.

"Pajamas?" said Pete.

"I got'm for him today."

"Nobody in my family ever wore pajamas, not to my knowledge anyway. Long johns in the winter, but the rest of the time it was naked."

She came to him and put her arms around his neck. Her long, lean body with the unexpected curving and firm flesh pressed into him. "You're not in *your* family anymore, my precious husband, you are in *our* family, the one we're making together."

"Is it my imagination, or has something changed in your voice since I last heard it downstairs?"

"It's not your imagination," she said, and her tongue, sharp-tipped and wet and incredibly long, traced the length of his mouth quicker than it took to think.

"What about the child?" he said.

"You can quit calling him 'the child' or 'it' or anything else that comes to mind. He's your brother. Call him Jonathan. Actually," she said, tilting her pelvis deeper into his, "I kind of like 'Jon.' "

The cheeks of her ass cupped firmly in his hands now, he whispered hoarsely: "What about Jon?"

"There's a quilt on the other side of the bed on the floor. I think I'd like it on the floor with you. The floor'll hold it right where you put it."

"He still might wake up."

"I'll just have to try to be quieter when you get me off," she said. The towel he was wearing rose between them. "Now look what I've done."

"Oh, Jesus." The sound he made could have been pain. He reached for the switch on the wall.

She let the light robe she was wearing slip from her shoulders. "Leave it on," she said.

She led him to the quilt and drew him down after her. He felt totally at one with himself and the world—he had his woman and he had his brother—and then gradually and happily he watched her face as he took her round the bend.

Later, when they were on the bed with Jon between them and

the light out, he whispered, "Can't we do something about this goddam helmet?"

"We can do something about the way you talk," she said, but her voice was soft and relaxed and full of love, and although he could not see her, he knew she was smiling.

"Right," he said. "But if nothing worse happens to us than the way I talk we'll probably be all right."

"Maybe." She sighed, and he could tell from her breathing that she was instantly asleep.

But something worse did happen later in the night. He woke suddenly, as though startled awake, and there on his chest sat the dark-socketed skull of Henry Leemer. The streetlight falling through the window showed it in stark and brilliant detail. He lifted his hand and stroked it softly, and softly again. It was smooth and cool under his warm palm. This was the first time he had ever touched it. He could feel himself smiling, and could feel too his own skull grinning in death just there behind his smile. With the warm palm of his hand on the crown of what had been Henry's head he felt himself falling back into a peaceful deep sleep.

17

Pete awoke hearing his name called. The first thing he thought of was the skull. And the second thing he thought of was how comforting it had been: Had he dreamed it? He must have.

"Pete, you better get up, hon," called Sarah from downstairs, "because I'm about to make your breakfast."

He looked all around the bed, then on both sides of it, and finally, dropping half his body over the side, he looked under it. No skull. No helmet. It must have been a dream.

He got up and went to the bathroom, washed his face, and brushed his teeth. Back in his room, he put on fresh jeans and a shirt and his good pair of low-cut shoes. There would be no mud or swamp water today.

Sarah appeared in the doorway, smiling, fresh-faced, looking as beautiful as he'd ever seen her. "Good," she said. "You're dressed. I've got you a great omelet whipped up in a bowl. All I've got to do is pour it in the pan. Did you sleep O.K.?"

"I slept fine," he said. That skull dream. Sooner or later he'd ditch that fucking thing. He coughed. "You sleep O.K. with Jon in the bed with us?"

"Never better. You know what that little rascal did this morning?"

He looked up at her from tying his shoes where he sat on the side of the bed, but he did not answer. He hoped it had been a dream, but in this house anything was possible.

"You want to guess what that little rascal did?"

"Sarah, I just woke up, for Christ's sake."

"Try to leave Christ out of this, Pete."

He shook his head. This would all have to come to a head sooner or later. He was not going to stop every time he had something to say and see if it might or might not suit her. But this was the wrong time. He had other fish to fry.

"You want to guess?"

"No, Sarah, I don't want to guess."

"He went potty."

"Potty?" He was still half asleep with a skull on his mind and it took him a moment to figure out what she was talking about.

"Sure did," she said. "Of course, I had to wipe him."

"You think this could wait until I've had my breakfast?"

"Pete, he's your brother."

"And you're my wife. But I don't much like to think about you taking a shit."

She turned abruptly and in a quick-tempered little voice said over her shoulder: "I'm making your breakfast. You want it, eat it. Don't, I'll throw it out."

He was off the bed and between her and the door almost before she could finish.

"Get out of my way, Pete."

"Forgive me. Can you forgive me? Me and my god—doggone ugly mouth has got me into more trouble than both of us could name. But can you forgive me and come sit down a minute? We've got to talk. And we've got to do it now."

"But your breakfast is—"

"This is more important than my breakfast. But first, say you forgive me for talking like that. I really am sorry."

"I forgive you, Pete. For goodness sake, did you think I was going to leave you over something you said when you was barely out of bed in the morning?"

He said: "It's been some who've left over less than that."

"I'm not one of them, though. I mean to stay for the whole trip. The only way you're getting me off this bus is to throw me off."

Pete smiled. "I might throw you on your back, but not off the bus."

Now he had her smiling. Good. That was good.

"Do we really have to talk," she said, "or do you just want to fool around?"

For the briefest moment he watched the beautiful little flecks of gold in her eyes. "Unfortunately, we got to talk. We in some . . . well, trouble. Linga's going to rob your mama blind if we don't keep her from doing it. It's got to be us because I just don't think your mama is up to the job right now."

Sarah turned her head to look out the window briefly. "You can go ahead and say it. I'd have to be deaf and dumb not to know that Mama is . . . well, that sometimes she don't think right. I'm around her more than you and I've seen her do and say things that don't make good sense." Her face went hard and her eyes seemed to go lightless with anger. "Starting with how she treated poor old Daddy after he died. A jar of dirt from a burned-up spot in the middle of an ugly swamp sitting on the mantelshelf! That's his last resting place!" She slapped her forehead with the flat of her hand. "I can't believe I let that happen. I won't ever forgive myself until that's changed. Even then, I don't know if I can ever stop hating myself for just standing around watching and doing nothing."

"I was there too," Pete said.

"But he was my *daddy,* God help me."

Her shoulders were starting to shake and he knew that if she started crying there'd be no talk. He'd not find out what he needed to know. He gripped her shoulders and made his voice hard when he spoke. "That was *then,* this is *now.* No way to get the past back, undo it, and do it up another way." He guided her over to the bed and sat her on the edge and then sat beside her. "We've got to go from *here, now!* Now"—he took a deep breath—"I wasn't raised to talk about other people's money, how much they got or how much they don't. It's more than just bad manners—where I come from, it can be a killing offense. But there's some things I've got to know, and the only way I can know is ask, bad manners or not. Even if Linga owned that cypress out there—and I'll believe it when I see a survey and a deed—it still wouldn't make sense to try to cut it. But even if it could be cut, and maybe there's a way to do it, Linga would be the last person in the world I'd want to see your mama go into business with."

"Mama's not going into business with Linga," Sarah said matter-of-factly.

"Sarah, Gertrude *is* in business with her. I'd bet my last cup of blood that Linga didn't pay for any of that junk they're hauling up out there, your mama paid for it. And I'd bet the same cup of blood that there's no contract between your mama and Linga. Linga's going to walk away with every penny your daddy ever worked for and left in that insurance unless something's done."

Pete could not understand why Sarah was not more upset, but she sat there as tranquil as if they were discussing a recipe for corn bread. "I haven't been out there to see what they've done, but that's where the first five thousand dollars went. But Linga will never see another penny of Mama's money. Like you say, the past is over and done, but from here on I'll know where every nickel of Daddy's money goes or it won't go anywhere. Maybe I can make up for a little of the wrong I've done him by taking care of Mama and what he left us."

"You've done him no wrong, darling," Pete said, stroking her hair. "Death and grief gets everybody a little out of their heads. I feel like hell asking, because it's none of my business, but what makes you so sure Linga won't touch your mama's money again? I sometimes think she could talk Gertrude into anything."

"Oh, I don't doubt what she might be able to talk Mama into believing, but the money Daddy left is safe. Daddy saw more than we thought he saw. Just two days before he died, he went down and had a codicil put on the will."

"Codicil?" said Pete. "Don't think I ever heard the word."

"I hadn't either until the lawyer called me yesterday and explained it all to me. It's just a piece of paper that is written up and put on the will. The lawyer himself wanted to speak to me and not to Mama because Daddy told him—the lawyer, that is—that Mama wasn't just right in her thinking and he wanted the will changed. That's what the lawyer did. Make a codicil and changed the will. Mama doesn't even know about it. That will Mama keeps waving around is not even the will, leastwise it don't have the codicil that says when the money comes, both of us has to sign for a check before the money can be taken out of any bank we put it in. And I don't care how mad it makes Mama, I'll never sign for money for that ugly, strange-looking Linga. The will'll be read tomorrow and we'll get the money. I know Mama'll raise a ruckus when she hears I got to have my name on any check we write after we put the money in the bank. But she'll get over it. She has to. And I'm not giving Daddy's money to anybody that looks, talks, or smells like Linga."

"From what's going on out at her camp," said Pete, "she's got money from somewhere."

"We got beat there." Sarah sighed. "The money that paid for what's going on out there come from the same place as the money I used to call a cab and go get that London broil we had. I didn't know anything about it until the lawyer explained that Daddy had arranged to put five thousand dollars in Mama's hand so we could live until the insurance come through. There was no strings on that money. Either Daddy forgot or he just wanted her to have the money whether she was thinking right or not. His life's savings is lying out there at Linga's circus."

"You think she gave it all to her?"

"Every nickel. I know because Mama told me she did. I hope Linga enjoys it because there won't be another nickel. This house is rotting down around our ears and Mama is already talking about buying the biggest and finest car she can find when the will is read. She's not going to do that. I'm not going to stand for it. And *that's that.* There'll be some serious thinking going on before we spend any more of Daddy's money."

"I'm glad it's you that's got to deal with her and not me."

"Oh, I don't mind or dread it at all. It'll be like taking care of a spoiled child. But I can handle it. Believe it."

"I do believe it, darling," said Pete. "If I believe nothing else I believe that."

And he did. Sarah was no longer the terrified, confused young girl she had been when he first met her. She was a woman now. A woman to be reckoned with. And God, was he grateful, as grateful as he could remember being for anything that had ever come into his life.

"Thank you," he said. "Thank you for taking some of this onto your own shoulders. The load had started being too heavy for me to carry by myself."

She turned on the bed where she was sitting and drew him into a tight embrace. "Don't thank me, love me," she whispered, her face buried in his shoulder. "Besides, that's what a wife does, help her man. And strange to say, I learned it all from Mama. She wasn't always that old, breastless, half-addled woman sitting downstairs. She was always right with Daddy, step for step." She paused and finished with a choking voice. "Until things started going bad for her."

"I never doubted the woman she was," Pete said, pulling back to smile at her. "She had you, didn't she?"

"We got her to thank for having Jonathan," Sarah said. "God forgive me for saying so, but I don't think putting in to find that child was the work of a woman that's completely together. She went to the hospital four days after you moved in next door and told Max the story of your life through a bottle of whiskey. I reckon it's some good in everything on God's earth. Because it was the next day he come over and told us all about you, along with about a hundred other things. God, that old man can talk. But to get right to the point, when I told her that I thought I'd found my man and you was him, nothing would do her but for Daddy to put that lawyer to trying to find out where he was. The lawyer knew about the will—same one that made it—and knew about Daddy's heart, so he said he'd find Jonathan on his own money at eighteen percent interest, and that he could be paid later."

"Don't take this wrong, darling, but it seems like everybody and his brother was standing around waiting for your daddy to drop dead."

"No reason to take it wrong," she said. "That is just exactly the way it was. Daddy never told me so, but I know he knew it too. He had to know that about a half a dozen people was just standing around waiting for him to die. I sometimes think it's what hurried him to the grave."

"But that's over and done and there's not a thing we can do about it. Over, finished."

"The strange thing is," she said, "that somehow gives me comfort."

"I can understand that."

"All this will work out the way it works out." She sat up straight and took a deep breath. "We'll do what we can, and what we can't do we'll leave alone. I'm some tired of thinking of what might have been."

"I believe I can eat my breakfast on that," Pete said. "Myself, I'm tired of fighting and fussing. Let's get on with being alive."

Sarah leaned over and kissed his cheek and walked out of the room without another word. He followed her downstairs, where Gertrude was sitting at the table in front of a cup of coffee, a cloud of Kool smoke hanging about her head. Her face was made up and her hair had been arranged a new way, this time with little spit curls over her forehead. She looked ghastly.

Jon was sitting on the floor spinning his football helmet round and round, but when he saw Pete, he let out a long wet sound and came running toward his brother. Pete put his hands under the boy's arms and lifted him high into the air and then hugged him, saying: "You speak a strange language, little brother."

Sarah already had a mug of coffee on the table for him and was at the stove working on his omelet. She looked back over her shoulder and said, "Get used to that sound, Pete. He just called your name."

"That was my name?"

"That was your name."

"How do you know that?"

"I just know, that's how I know."

"That youngun's not the dummy some people might think he is," said Gertrude, lighting another Kool. "He's a right smart little boy."

"You're looking good this morning, Gertrude," said Pete. It was just as cheap to tell a lie as to tell the truth, especially if it made this sick old woman here at the tag end of her life feel any better. Hell, he'd tell her she was beautiful on her deathbed. "And I'm glad you think my brother's not completely hopeless."

Gertrude gave a little snort of twin columns of smoke through her nose, coughed, and said, "Ain't much in this world that's completely hopeless." She watched Sarah put Pete's eggs in front of him and an empty plate in front of Jonathan so he could copy his brother's every move. "Take them trees out yonder at Linga's that we ain't talked about. You *did* say they were beautiful. Ain't that what you said last night?"

"Exactly what I said." Pete looked directly at her, chewing his eggs slowly and thinking about the argument he was not going to get into. "Never seen a finer stand of cypress."

"Then how do you feel about the sawmill business me and Linga's setting up?"

Pete didn't miss a beat with his eggs or his answer. "Completely hopeless," he said. There were lies and there were lies and Pete saw no way to hedge here.

"Bullshit!" said Gertrude in a strangled, phlegmy voice.

"Please, Mama. Not at the table with the child."

Gertrude's eyes were suddenly caught in a web of veins. "*Bullshit! Bullshit! Bullshit!* There, how's that, Miss Priss?"

Sarah smiled and quietly said, "I never heard anybody do it better."

Pete put his fork down, and beside him, Jonathan put his own fork down. "Look, Gertrude," said Pete. "Mine's just one man's opinion. I looked at everything out there and decided it was a job of work you would never turn a profit on. But don't take my word for it. Find some real sawmill men and ask them how that cypress got to be as old as it is, and as fine as it is, without somebody putting an ax in there on them."

"You can bet your last nickel I'll do just that."

Sarah, who was putting dishes into the sink, said in a deadly calm voice: "It doesn't matter what anybody says, not another nickel of Daddy's money is going into anything that Linga's got a hand in."

Gertrude's entire face seemed to swell as blood blushed up her thin neck to turn it flame red. Finally she was able to speak. "It's about time you and me got a few things straight. We due for a goddam talk!"

Without turning from the sink, Sarah said, "Long overdue."

Gertrude had barely half a word out of her mouth, when Pete raised his hand and said, "Excuse me."

She swallowed whatever word she was strangling on and turned her blazing eyes on him. "Can't you see we—"

Pete was already standing up. "Yes mam, I can see and I just wanted to tell you that me and Jonathan's calling a time-out."

"A time what?" demanded Gertrude.

"Out. We're pulling the chain on today. Flushing it, so to speak. I don't believe we can do much good here, so we're going to see if we can find us a store that sells baseballs and gloves and then I think we'll look for a park where we can play a little catch." He looked at Sarah. "How's that sound for two brothers that just decided it was time to be lazy and just not give a damn for a day?"

"Just great, Pete-Pete," she said. "But what do you want me to tell George if he comes by?"

Jonathan had taken Pete's finger and they were halfway through the door, when Pete looked back at Sarah and said: "Somehow I got a feeling you won't see George today. But if you do, tell him to keep on painting that Hudson Hornet and . . ." He paused and looked out at the bright blue sky for a moment. "And then tell him I love him."

"That you love him?"

"Yeah, tell'm that."

Jonathan led him out into the yard where a crosscut saw was

half embedded in an oak log. As they passed the woodyard, Pete heard Gertrude's voice screaming, "Now who's crazy? Did you hear what that sumbitch said?"

"Yes, Mama, I did."

Walking beside him, Jonathan made the long wet sound that was Pete's name. Pete only smiled and kept walking.